PENGUIN BOOKS
The Old-Girl Network

'Her books are supremely readable, witty and moving in
equal measure and she has a brilliantly sharp ear for dialogue'
Daily Mail

'Possibly my favourite writer' Marian Keyes

'An addictive cocktail of wit, frivolity and madcap romance'
Time Out

'Sensitive, funny and wonderfully well written'
Wendy Holden, *Daily Express*

'Another charming tale of heartbreak from this wonderfully
warm and witty author' *Woman*

'A poignant but charming journey of self-discovery.
A bittersweet and captivating novel' *Closer*

'We defy you not to get caught up in Alliott's life-changing
tale' *Heat*

'A fun, fast-paced page-turner' *OK!*

ABOUT THE AUTHOR

Catherine Alliott is the author of twelve bestselling novels including *One Day in May*, *The Secret Life of Evie Hamilton* and *A Crowded Marriage*. She lives with her family in Hertfordshire.

The Old-Girl Network

CATHERINE ALLIOTT

PENGUIN BOOKS

PENGUIN BOOKS

Published by the Penguin Group
Penguin Books Ltd, 80 Strand, London WC2R ORL, England
Penguin Group (USA) Inc., 375 Hudson Street, New York, New York 10014, USA
Penguin Group (Canada), 90 Eglinton Avenue East, Suite 700, Toronto, Ontario, Canada M4P 2Y3
(a division of Pearson Penguin Canada Inc.)
Penguin Ireland, 25 St Stephen's Green, Dublin 2, Ireland (a division of Penguin Books Ltd)
Penguin Group (Australia), 250 Camberwell Road,
Camberwell, Victoria 3124, Australia (a division of Pearson Australia Group Pty Ltd)
Penguin Books India Pvt Ltd, 11 Community Centre,
Panchsheel Park, New Delhi – 110 017, India
Penguin Group (NZ), 67 Apollo Drive, Rosedale, Auckland 0632, New Zealand
(a division of Pearson New Zealand Ltd)
Penguin Books (South Africa) (Pty) Ltd, Block D, Rosebank Office Park,
181 Jan Smuts Avenue, Parktown North, Gauteng 2193, South Africa

Penguin Books Ltd, Registered Offices: 80 Strand, London WC2R ORL, England

www.penguin.com

First published by Headline Publishing Group 1994
Published in Penguin Books 2012

001

Copyright © Catherine Alliott, 1994

Set in 12.5/14.75 pt Garamond MT
Typeset by Jouve (UK), Milton Keynes
Printed in England by Clays Ltd, St Ives plc

ISBN: 978-0-241-95830-8

Export edition ISBN: 978-0-241-96129-2

www.greenpenguin.co.uk

MIX
Paper from
responsible sources
FSC™ C018179
www.fsc.org

Penguin Books is committed to a sustainable
future for our business, our readers and our planet.
This book is made from Forest Stewardship
Council™ certified paper.

ALWAYS LEARNING   **PEARSON**

For George

Chapter One

I sat down and ran a practised eye over the ten people sitting opposite me. I saw at once that it wasn't a good day. In fact, it was a particularly bad day. Six women and only four men, and as if that wasn't bad enough, all four of the men looked as if they'd narrowly survived major car crashes. A singularly unpromising selection and I had to go to bed with one of them. Damn.

I sat back in my seat narrowing my rather myopic eyes and studied the four contenders: Too Fat, Too Young, Too Chinese and Too Ginger. Typical. Where was Too Handsome when I needed him most? Still, it was no good belly-aching about lack of talent; rules were rules, and one of these lucky guys was about to get even luckier. I gritted my teeth and appraised them individually, searching for hidden depths. I was going to have to dig pretty deep.

Number one was a fat slob masquerading as a businessman. The buttons of his blue nylon shirt were doing sterling work as they strained under the pressure of his ample bosom, and the waistband of his trousers was nowhere to be seen as his gut spilled out over the top of it. Lovely. Not only that, but he was bald too. Long flowing locks had been grown from somewhere beneath his left ear and swept carefully over the top *à la* Bobby Charlton, but that didn't fool anyone. Sensing early depression,

I dismissed him out of hand and moved smartly on to number two.

I suppressed a shudder. This callow youth was still grappling with something I'd got to grips with long ago and I didn't fancy going through it again. Puberty. As I cast a cold eye over his acne-festooned, hormone-infested face, his upper lip suddenly curled into a leer, a lazy eye winked at me, and a lolling hand scratched at the fly of his jeans. Good grief, the very idea! I tossed my head in disgust. Bloody nerve.

I swiftly turned my attention to number three. Ah. Now this was a tricky one. You see, I've nothing against Chinese men *per se*, in fact the one in my local takeaway couldn't be nicer, it's just that – well, on balance I prefer my men to be, er, you know – English. I'm quite sure the Chinese make wonderful lovers but, as I said, my personal preference is for something a little closer to home, like – well, like Harry, of course.

For one blissful moment I allowed a fleeting glimpse of the divine Harry Lloyd-Roberts to seep into my consciousness. Ah yes, there he was, with his mop of blond hair, his tanned, smiling face, his bright blue eyes, his long lean legs, his broad shoulders, his – I gave myself a little shake. Concentrate, Polly, Harry is not on the menu this morning, but this Oriental gentleman is and you'll have to do a little better than simply admitting to a preference for Englishmen.

I grudgingly appraised him again and realized, with joy, that he had a mighty peculiar set of teeth. I seized gratefully on his unusual dental arrangement. Oh no, I'm sorry, I simply have to have straight teeth; they must be regular and they must be white, I make a point of insisting on it. No, I wasn't being racist at all, I was just – yes, I was just being a little toothist, that was it!

As I rejected him I realized with a sinking heart that I was now left with only one contender and – oh, horrors, I was about to be gingerist too. I studied the red-headed gentleman before me and sighed. But not deeply. Because, hold on a minute, Polly McLaren, not so fast. On closer inspection this one wasn't so bad. Ginger, certainly, but not flaming carrots or nasty nasturtium red, more of a – well, more of an autumnal russet really. And was I seeing things, or weren't those features remarkably regular? And wasn't that face rather attractively tanned? And didn't we have here a particularly piercing pair of blue eyes? We did! Complete with crinkle-cut laughter lines at each corner! That very nearly did it, I'm a sucker for crinkle cuts, but I had the good sense to run an eye over the rest of the goods before I clinched the deal. Shoulders broad, legs long, no sign of a paunch, good.

He was wearing a pale blue Brooks Brothers shirt topped with an expensive navy jacket, a good quality leather belt and heavy cotton trousers – not too baggy, not too tight – and, more to the point (and how foolish of me not to have spotted it before), he was sporting a signet-ring on the little finger of his left hand. I leaned back in my seat, heady with relief. I had myself a winner.

There was no true competition, but I gave the opposition another cursory glance just to ensure fair play. Too Chinese and Too Young had never got off their starting blocks, Too Fat was definitely Too Bald and, let's face it, a girl has to have something to run her fingers through, even if it is red, so Ginger – I charitably omitted the 'Too' – it was. He'd run an easy race and won by an absence of baldness, hormones and buck teeth. What a lucky guy!

I stood up, flushed with success and pleased with my prize. So pleased, in fact, that I did something unforgivable. I smiled at the victor. It slipped out before I had a chance to retract it or even to turn it into something like a nasty little twitch. There it was, all turned up at the corners, wide and welcoming, teeth flashing away like beacons. Ginger looked up in surprise and returned the smile, blue eyes crinkling as predicted.

Horrified with myself, I wrapped my scarf around my flushing neck and made for the sliding doors, just as – thank God – the tube pulled into South Kensington station. There was a nasty moment when the doors stuck for a second, but a minute later I was off and running – well, walking fast – in the direction of the escalator.

How ghastly! He must have thought I was sizing him up for real, propositioning him even! I glanced nervously over my shoulder as I joined the moronic trudge for the exit, but thankfully there was no sign of his russet locks hovering hopefully behind me.

But that was a lucky escape, Polly, I told myself sternly; don't do it again, for God's sake – who knows what sort of trouble it could get you into? It's bad enough that you stare at them every morning, without giving them the come-on too.

I grinned sheepishly as I thought of the way I amused myself on the way to work. Blind date without the blindfold, and without, of course, the actual date. Harmless fun, but these days increasingly depressing. Take yesterday, for example. I shuddered as I recalled. Yesterday, due to an unprecedented number of women commuters, I'd been forced to climb between the imaginary sheets with a slack-jawed octogenarian with bubbles on his lower lip. There'd been a moment back there when I could have become a lesbian, but no, I played the game. After all, it was my game, and I couldn't cheat on myself, could I?

As I jostled for position in the line up to the escalator, I spotted the leering Too Young ahead of me in the queue. Oh dear, he really didn't know the ropes did he? There he was, pushing his way through, and committing the unpardonable sin of standing firmly on the left which, as every urbane traveller knows, is for climbers only. I had the satisfaction of seeing him being bundled over to the right by a hoard of embattled commuters amidst a sea of shaking heads and tutting tongues. 'You stand on the right,' someone muttered by way of explanation – only muttered, you understand, no one who did this on a regular basis would be so gauche as to talk. I joined in the 'glare past' on the way up to complete the ritual humiliation. To my surprise, he had the balls to leer back at me.

Oh well, I thought, as I trudged on up the moving staircase, it's always nice to be ogled, even if it is by a spotty fourteen-year-old: I must be looking quite good today.

We reached the top and I geared myself up to catch a glimpse of my reflection in the photo-booth mirror that everyone looks in and pretends not to. Christ, I thought as I caught my millisecond's worth, he must be desperate. Bad hair, bad make-up (too hurried) and a very bad jacket covered in dog hairs. Lottie's fault for buying a bloody Yorkshire Terrier. I brushed myself down, cursing my impulsive flatmate. At least it was all superficial. The hair could be washed, the jacket changed, and the make-up carefully reapplied in time for tonight's little excursion with the divine Harry. Please God, let there be an excursion! Please God, let him ring!

I allowed myself a moment's luxury as I considered the joys of going out with the utterly mouth-wateringly delicious Mr Harry Lloyd-Roberts. My heart pranced around in its usual foolish manner, but after an initial burst of skippy enthusiasm, sank a little too. I sighed. If only he wasn't so elusive. If only every date wasn't such a trumpet-blowing-red-carpeted-big-deal because they were so few and far between. If only – oh well. Don't bang on, Polly.

And that was another thing, I thought bitterly as I barged and elbowed my way towards the ticket barrier, it was all so time-consuming. I really didn't want to be the sort of girl who only thought about boys, but until I'd well and truly ensnared this one, I honestly didn't think I could get my mind around anything else. Of course it went without saying that once he was as besotted with me as I was with him I'd spend a lot more time thinking about – oh well, you know – Shakespeare, art, starving orphans, charity work, that kind of thing; but until that glorious, glorious day came, I'm afraid I just didn't have the time.

As I approached the barrier, I dug into my pocket for some change. The diminutive ticket collector already had his hand out, palm upward. It was a tacit agreement we had. He knew I was a lazy slut who couldn't be bothered to buy a ticket at the right station, and I knew he was a thieving bastard who pocketed my sixty pence. We smiled sweetly at one another, both happy with the arrangement, and London Transport was none the wiser.

As I walked up the few remaining steps to the main road, I felt as if I was walking into a Persil advert. South Kensington was awash with bright, primary colours bathed in sunshine. Tall white houses soared up into a bright blue sky, and the little patches of green grass at their feet played host to the very first signs of spring as snowdrops, crocuses and a few lonely daffodils bobbed around in the sunshine. It was a beautiful day, and my spirits rose.

They rose even higher as I turned the corner into Cresswell Gardens, for this was where I'd met Harry and it never failed to please. Number twenty-four, to be precise – yes, this was the one. I paused outside, allowing myself a moment of sentimental nostalgia.

If I say so myself, I'd looked pretty damn sexy that night; seductively clad in a black Alaia dress which clung to every curve – of which I have a few; some would say too many – and with a liberal sprinkling of Butler and Wilson's finest baubles at my ears and around my neck, my long, wavy blonde hair freshly highlighted, and the remains of a tan still glowing . . : I hadn't looked bad.

The occasion had been a birthday drinks party, but to this day I can't remember being invited, although I do remember the hostess's look of surprise as I kissed her warmly on both cheeks. I'd obviously crashed it, probably with Lottie, who knows everyone. It had been a small, select gathering, and the venue had been the drawing room of this majestic townhouse. It was chock-a-block with original oil paintings, tasteful antiques, and other expensive and eminently breakable family heirlooms, and in fact the atmosphere had been so rarefied that people were talking in whispers. They didn't stray from their own little groups of two or three, and it seemed to me that everyone was in danger of turning to stone and joining the rest of the precious treasures dotted around the room.

Thankfully, as the evening limped along, the hostess was suddenly alive to this possibility, and hastily poured a two-litre bottle of brandy into the insipid punch. A rather horsy girl standing next to me said she thought it was the stupidest thing she'd ever seen. I thought it was inspired. Within twenty minutes the party was revving up like nobody's business, and I delved deep to summon up all the Dutch courage I possessed to chat up the most attractive man in the room.

He was standing by the window wearing a pair of ageing beige cords, a blue shirt and a bright red skiing jumper. An unruly mop of floppy blond hair was constantly falling into the bluest eyes I'd ever seen. He was such a cliché it was untrue. He was calmly eating pistachio nuts and staring out of the window to the street below, pretending he didn't know how divine he looked and what a commotion he was causing.

No less than three knock-out-looking girls were prowling and circling around him, tossing back metres of silky hair and adjusting their hemlines up or down, according to whether they had good or bad legs. I decided to skip these formalities and move in for the kill. Buoyed up by too much bevvy and my revealing little black dress, I took a deep breath and dived in.

Somehow, and to this day I know not how, I managed

to monopolize him totally for the rest of the evening, engaging him with my witty repartee whilst at the same time staving off the competition. The circling harpies evidently decided I'd scored and limped away to nurse their egos and, within the hour, I'd secured myself a seat opposite him in a restaurant of my choice somewhere on the Fulham Road. Before you could say your place or mine, it was back to his for Rémy and rumpy-pumpy – and the rest, as they say, is history. Unfortunately I was under the distinct impression that, unless I could recapture some of that original wit and vitality, I was in danger of becoming history too. I bit my lip miserably. Why was love such bloody hard work? Perhaps I should have a few sun-beds.

I turned the corner into Egerton Street where the houses are even taller, even whiter and even lovelier. My second pause on the walk to work was just coming up, right . . . here. I stopped in front of one of the tallest and whitest and gazed up at it, for this was where Harry and I were going to live when we were married. I'd picked it out ages ago as being the perfect house. I could almost hear my Manolo Blahnik heels tip-tapping around the highly polished wooden floors as I checked on my beautiful blond children asleep in their bedrooms and adjusted my Chanel suit in the enormous hall mirror before skipping off to join my husband for dinner or the theatre – or both.

Before I went I would dispense a few last-minute instructions to the Swedish nanny – did I say Swedish? Lord, no, I meant Romanian or, um . . . yes, Mongolian. Or did Mongolians have those rather attractive high cheekbones? I was rattled. Well then, we wouldn't have one at all, why bother? Baby-sitters were just as good, and cheaper. But younger. I sighed. Even I could see the poverty of my situation, when even in my fantasies Harry was incapable of keeping his hands to himself.

With these weighty problems still preying on my mind, I climbed the steps to my workplace, Penhalligan and Waters, number thirty-three. I pressed the buzzer urgently, as if I'd been waiting there for some time and wasn't late at all.

''S me!' I yelled into the metal squawk box, and another buzzer obligingly let me in.

The only delay I was now likely to encounter was Bob. I looked nervously around the marble hallway. Bob was a large black labrador who belonged to Maurice, the aged and grumpy commissionaire who fielded visitors and clients up to the various offices in the building. They say a dog resembles his owner, but these two really couldn't have been more different.

Maurice was a Yorkshireman; dour, miserable, grizzled and past it. Bob, on the other hand, was well-bred, bouncy, friendly, in peak condition and well up to it. He greeted most people simply with enthusiasm and affection, which was fine as long as his paws were clean and you weren't wearing white, but I was a different matter. Bob adored me. Let's face it, Bob had the hots for me. The mere smell of me would make his nose twitch with delight, and the sight of me would have him yelping with joy. Within seconds, his front paws would be up on my shoulders, his tongue frantically licking every scrap of make-up off my face. If I pushed him away, he'd think it was all part of the foreplay. He'd goose me in the crutch, whimpering with delight, and it wasn't funny because Bob was a big dog.

There I'd be, pinned to the Regency staircase or the Georgian hall-table, with Bob on top of me, pleading with him, or Maurice, or both, to give me a break.

'Wants to play, by the look of things,' Maurice would observe at length from the safety of his chair.

'Yes – yes, he does, doesn't he?' I'd pant as Bob's big black head would give me another excruciating buck in the groin. 'Ooof! Geddof, Bob! But the thing is, Maurice, I'm just a teensy bit late, could you possibly – you know, call him off? Aarrhh!'

'Humph,' Maurice would grunt in an offended fashion. 'He's only being friendly like, better than being all aggressive like one of them Rottweilers, i'n't it?'

'Oh yes, yes, absolutely, much better,' I'd gasp, nodding furiously. 'It's just that – well, you know, I do have to get to work and I am rather late . . .'

'C'mon then, Bob,' Maurice would growl grudgingly, jerking his head. 'She don't want your attentions. Save them for them that do.'

Luckily Bob was remarkably obedient to Maurice's commands – probably terrified of him like the rest of us – and he'd respond immediately, slinking back to his basket. Muttering my thanks to Maurice, I'd then back gratefully up the stairs, flapping my skirt in a vain attempt to get the air to it and dry the nasty wet patch where he'd slobbered before I got upstairs.

This morning, thank goodness, there was no sign of the amorous Bob. Maurice appeared to be asleep behind his desk, so I tiptoed past, hoping Bob was also kipping deadly in his basket beside him or, even better, at home with a bad case of doggy flu.

I looked at my watch and leaped up the stairs two at a time – Christ! I hadn't realized I was that late. I flew down one of the many corridors in the grand old house, which at one time would have been full of oil paintings and family portraits. Now that the second floor housed an advertising agency, the walls were lined with stills from cat-food commercials and Tampax ads. I barged through reception shouting, 'Morning!' to Josie the receptionist, then, out of breath and panting heavily, shouldered open the nearest door and fell into the pit I share with Pippa.

Even by my standards it was a mess. It was a small office, dominated by two enormous desks which were almost totally obscured by magazines, newspapers, TV scripts, show reels, voice-over tapes, commercials, and the odd word processor or two. The walls were plastered with Polaroid photos which appeared to chart the progress of a particularly debauched office party – a veritable collage of tongues, silly hats, bare bottoms, gin bottles and sus-pender belts. The windowsill, the filing cabinet, and any other spare surface area, spewed over with rampant Busy Lizzie plants and their offspring; cuttings of cuttings of cuttings had taken over in triffid-like proportions. The floor was covered with yet more magazines; in piles, in bundles, in general disarray. In the midst of this chaos, a young girl in a blue coat was slumped in a heap at her desk.

Pippa had obviously died at her typewriter. She was sit-ting with her head cradled in her arms, her face pressed nose-down on to her blotter. She was one of those girls who had an amazing capacity to look ravishingly attractive one day and hideously atrocious the next. Today it was obviously the latter. Her insatiable appetite for night clubs, late nights, gin and tonics and men – not necessarily in that order – was also instrumental in determining how she looked in the morning. My best friend, soul-mate and partner in grime at Penhalligan and Waters raised a pale green face from the blotter and peered at me through severely bloodshot eyes. 'Don't talk to me,' she whispered.

'Chocolate milk and bacon sandwich?' I ventured sympathetically.

'Please, if you're going.'

It was all she could manage. Her head dropped back on to her desk like a stone. I dumped my bag and moved a few papers around on my own desk to make it look as if I'd been in for hours.

'If Nick gets back from his meeting, say I've been in for ages and I've just popped out to the bank,' I commanded.

Pippa moaned in agreement and I galloped downstairs, this time escaping through the back entrance, thereby avoiding Maurice and Bob.

I exchanged the usual pleasantries with the friendly Italians in the sandwich bar, in pidgin Italian on my part and in pidgin English on theirs, and with '*Arrivederci, Bella!*' still ringing in my ears, sped back to the patient, hangover cure in hand.

As I deposited it on her desk, I decided she'd improved, but only marginally. She was still wrapped up in her navy blue winter coat, even though it was a warm spring day, but her head was off the desk and she was at least indulging in some sort of activity. She was smoking her one, two, three – fourth cigarette of the morning, judging by the ashtray. If Pippa were having a frontal lobotomy, she'd find time to light a fag.

'Was he worth it?' I asked smugly, from my frightfully healthy position at the opposite desk.

'Oh, very definitely,' whispered Pippa, fumbling to open the chocolate milk and quietly ramming home the fact that I might be the picture of health, but I'd earned it by spending a mind-bendingly boring evening in front of the television, working my way through two chocolate oranges and a box of Maltesers. I'd suffered the added indignity of dog-sitting for Lottie whilst she too pursued life in the fast lane. Between them, Pippa and Lottie went to more clubs and parties than I'd had hot dates. What was the point of having a boyfriend if I never went out with him? I didn't voice this last complaint to Pippa, as I already knew her jaundiced views on the subject of Harry.

'And you?' It was a supreme effort on Pippa's part, but she managed to form the two short syllables. After all, the morning ritual of, 'What did you do last night?' had to be gone through, come hell, high water or hangover.

'Oh, you know, just a quiet evening in. Quite nice for a change,' I lied. I hoped she wasn't going to ask, 'With Harry?' but she was opening her mouth ominously, so I cut in quickly, 'No, not with Harry. Something came up.'

Pippa sighed. 'Probably his dinner.'

'What do you mean?' I pounced quickly, realizing she had classified information.

'He was in the same restaurant as me last night, absolutely plastered.' It was still an effort to speak, but our code of honour meant this horrendous piece of news had to be transmitted as soon as possible. I felt cold as I waited for the inevitable bombshell.

'No, don't worry, he wasn't with anybody, just a whole crowd of hoorays having a bun fight.'

I breathed a sigh of relief and my heart slipped out of my mouth, down my throat, and back to a more normal position. So it hadn't been a candlelit tête-à-tête but, even so, why hadn't I been there? I like restaurants, I don't mind hoorays, and I'm game-on for a bun fight. I quizzed Pippa mercilessly, ignoring her frail condition, but she either didn't know much or was being very kind. Her answers were suspiciously diplomatic.

'. . . About ten of them, mostly men.'

'. . . No, he didn't see me.'

'. . . Um, a blondish girl on one side and a man on the other.'

'. . . No, not very pretty, more mousy than blonde actually.'

'. . . Oh, a blue dress, very Topshop.'

'. . . Um, about twelve-thirty, I think, in a taxi.'

'. . . No, not with Topshop, on his own – Polly, please don't bully me any more, you know he's a dead loss, what more can I tell you?'

Her body slumped forward again and her head dropped back into position. The interview was over. I sighed and lit what was for me a very premature cigarette. She was right, of course, he was a dead loss. Always out, but never with me. I decided for the millionth time to end what passed as our relationship the next time I saw him. For sure. Yes, definitely. The very next time. He simply wasn't worth it. Having made that little porky-pie of a resolution I felt better, and even had the appetite to tuck into my own daily fix of egg mayonnaise on brown and the *Daily Mail*.

Nick, my boss, and in fact *the* boss, was still in a client meeting, and when Nick was away the rest of the agency played. We lounged around on desks, sofas and – after a heavy lunch – floors. We draped ourselves decoratively around the reception area watching the television, exchanged dirty jokes, made calls to Australia, drank the 'strictly client meetings only' drinks cupboard dry, threw up in loos (new boys only), and generally behaved like any other normal advertising agency. When Nick was around, we did exactly the same but made sure he didn't notice.

Which brings me to another sore point. Another bitter blow to add to my long and doleful list of disappointments. Nick Penhalligan.

When I switched from the overworked and underpaid world of publishing to the sexy and glamorous world of advertising six months ago, I had very definite ideas about what life at Penhalligan and Waters was going to be like. OK, it was a small agency, only fifteen people, but small agencies were by all accounts great fun. I was also going to be working for the chairman, which of course guaranteed me an enormous slice of the action.

I daydreamed about being an indispensable girl Friday to a wild and wacky ad-man full of crazy impulsive ideas like, 'Let's get out of the agency today and go and bounce a few ideas around in the wine bar.' I imagined a snappy sartorial dresser with a fine line in enormous red-framed spectacles and swivelling bow-ties who lived in a creative dreamworld and needed a sensible, reliable girl by his side to guide him through his hectic day.

I foresaw long boozy lunches in dimly lit Soho restaurants, where he'd confide in me and tell me all his marital problems, after which we'd pile into a taxi together and charge off to a shoot. As we swept into the studio, the crew would mutter, 'That's Nick Penhalligan: he's brilliant, but of course he can't *move* without Polly, she's his right arm; in fact I don't know where he'd be without her.' To illustrate this point, Nick would then discover he'd lost the script for the commercial and would rummage frantically through his briefcase as everyone waited.

'It's not here!' he'd cry, 'but I'm sure I put it in!'

There'd be an awkward silence, then I'd smile indulgently and produce a wad of paper from my handbag. 'Don't worry, Nick,' I'd say soothingly, 'I've got a copy.'

Everyone would heave great sighs of relief and say things like, 'Gosh, thank goodness for Polly,' and I'd spend the rest of the afternoon being chatted up by the director, the producer and Nigel Havers who happened to be starring in the commercial, before being whisked away to the Zanzibar for several large gin and tonics by my grateful boss. As you can see, I have quite a stranglehold on reality.

The real Nick Penhalligan turned out to be about as wacky as a filing cabinet, and the nearest I got to a shoot was nearly being fired on my first day.

I had arrived on day one of my employment dressed in what I imagined people in the ad-racket probably wore. Short leather mini-skirt, white Katherine Hamnett T-shirt complete with anti-establishment slogan, black biker's jacket, Doc Marten-type shoes and an extraordinary pair of dangly white earrings which Pippa later told me she'd thought were tampons. Dead trendy, or so I believed.

Pippa's eyes were out on stalks when she collected me in reception in her navy blue Puffa, Liberty print skirt and velvet hairband. She eyed what passed for my skirt in disbelief and mumbled something incoherent like 'shit', before leading me into Nick's office.

Nick didn't recognise me. Hardly surprising really, since the girl he'd interviewed for the job had been buttoned up to the eyeballs in Laura Ashley and bore no resemblance whatsoever to the apparition sitting in front of him now. He gaped at me for a long time, opening and closing his mouth a lot, and then very slowly the penny started to drop.

'Ah, yes, you're um . . . you must be Polly, is that right?'

Ah yes, just as I'd thought: short memory; mind on higher, more creative things. Any minute now I'd be producing the forgotten script from my bag.

'That's right.' I smiled and helped him out as one would help a small child. I leaned forward and spoke very slowly. 'You interviewed me last week, remember?' I smiled encouragingly and nodded.

'Yes, yes, of course I did. It's just that last week you looked, um, different . . . more sort of businesslike.' Nick coughed and adjusted his extremely businesslike navy blue tie which I could tell was never going to swivel.

Now, I'm sensitive to atmosphere, and the one we had here was not good. In fact it dawned on me that I'd cocked up. I surreptitiously slid the bubble-gum from my mouth to my hand and pulled the leather skirt down from around my knicker-line, trying to make it look less like a belt.

Nick was shifting around in his chair looking uncomfortable. 'I suppose I'd better make it clear right now that we have quite a lot of important clients coming in and out of here, and whilst some of them I'm sure are very broad-minded, they're probably not used to seeing quite such, um, unusual clothing in an office. I don't want to appear dogmatic or old-fashioned, but I was wondering if in future you could, um, well – tone it down a little?'

'Oh, it's OK,' I said quickly, 'I can explain. I know exactly what you mean about the clothes, but you see I stayed at my sister's place last night and had to borrow some of her things. She's only sixteen and going through a rather rebellious stage, hence the – well, hence the rather avant-garde style! Not me at all!'

'Oh, I see.' He wasn't totally convinced.

'Yes,' I hurried on, 'she's such a worry to my parents: thinks life is just one big party, you know; sex, drugs, rock and roll.'

'Drugs?' he looked alarmed.

'Oh well, not strong ones, no,' I laughed nervously. 'Just, you know . . . recreational.' Was that the word? Nick's eyebrows shot into his hairline. Obviously not.

'No, no, not recreational, I don't mean that, just aspirin really, oh, and the odd paracetamol or two,' I nodded sagely, 'nothing to worry about really.'

'Ah.' Thankfully his eyebrows were coming down from orbit and it seemed his alarm had turned to mere surprise.

I was desperate to change the subject and get away from my fictitious junkie sister. I slapped my thigh in true jolly-hockey-stick style. 'But don't you worry, I'll be back in my own wardrobe tomorrow.'

'Ah good, so tomorrow we can expect to see something a little more, er, restrained?'

'Back to the tweeds and the brogues!' I grinned. And so, I seem to remember, did he, which must have been a first and only.

It wasn't that I didn't like Nick, it was just that he was so bloody difficult to get to know. He was always so incredibly busy, and when I did manage to speak to him, he was invariably abrupt, off-hand, and sometimes downright rude. He would nod his thank-yous and bark out his orders.

A normal opening gambit of a Monday morning would be, 'There's a meeting in half an hour, I'd like tea, coffee and an agenda,' not, 'Good morning, Polly, how was your weekend? If you've got a moment could you possibly find time to make some coffee and then maybe type a little agenda if it's not too much trouble,' to which I would have smiled sweetly and acquiesced. As it was, I barged around in the kitchen slamming cups on to saucers and invariably breaking something.

He was still pretty young to be in his position – about thirty-three or thirty-four – and I had to admit quite good-looking, if you liked that sort of thing. Of course, I didn't. He was tall and slim but with broad shoulders, very dark hair and dark bushy eyebrows. His eyes were dark brown and deep-set and he had very striking angular features, including a rather hooked nose which somehow suited his face. Unfortunately he spoiled the effect by looking continually tired and harassed which he probably was since he was the only one in the agency who appeared to do any work.

As far as sharing conspiratorial lunches in groovy restaurants was concerned, the only thing I'd ever seen him eat was a hastily grabbed sandwich at his desk in between meetings. By all accounts he was screamingly intelligent, or so Pippa – whose brother had been up at Cambridge with him – told me, so he naturally despised the rest of us who survived on one brain cell between us.

As I inanely filled in the D of Dempster with Tipp-Ex and yawned with boredom, in he swept with a face like reinforced concrete. His old tweed coat streamed out behind him like Batman as he flew past at speed, his black eyebrows knitted together in fury.

'Good presentation?' I ventured, closing the paper and trying to look intelligent.

'Bloody client didn't pitch up!' he bawled as he charged into his office slamming the door behind him.

'Oh dear,' I said lamely.

'Happy days,' murmured Pippa, grimacing.

I was just about to grab my notebook and take his messages in, when the door opened again and he poked his head round. 'By the way, Polly, there's a chap downstairs waiting to see you.'

'A chap?' I said in surprise. 'Downstairs?'

It's a bit of a habit of mine to repeat what people say, especially when I'm nonplussed. It obviously irritated the hell out of Nick. He ground his teeth together and shut the door without replying.

Who on earth could it be? No one ever came to see me at work. Suddenly my heart leaped into my oesophagus. Of course! Harry! Harry had come to see me. He knew Pippa had spotted him last night and he'd come to explain himself, to ask my forgiveness and implore me to go out with him tonight, that was it! But why hadn't he telephoned? Why had he come all the way from his computer screen in the City just to see me? Love? Impulse? Even I was clued-up enough to realize he didn't know the meaning of either word. All the same, I jumped up from my chair with joy in my heart and a kiss ready and waiting on my lips. Just in case.

'How extraordinary, Pippa, a man downstairs to see me! Who on earth d'you think it could be?' I babbled excitedly as I brushed my hair and scrabbled around in my drawer for my lipstick.

'I don't know. But I'll tell you one thing, it's not who you think it is,' she said caustically, eyeing my preparations with suspicion.

'Oh God, you're such a killjoy, how do you know?'

'Take it from me. I just know.'

I sighed. Why couldn't any of my friends share my enthusiasm for the man I loved? Never mind. Wouldn't it just show her if it were Harry? I snapped my make-up mirror shut and bounced off down the corridor.

I leaned over the banisters and peered down to the marble hallway below. Whoever it was was sitting on the sofa, most of which was obscured from my view by the stairwell, so all I could make out was a pair of long slim male legs clad in beige trousers with a pair of Docksiders at the end of them. Not Harry's, definitely not Harry's; his Docksiders were brown, not blue; but funnily enough I thought I recognized them. I craned my neck, but couldn't see any more of the body without doing myself a serious injury.

I shrugged. Oh well, it wasn't Harry, but the legs didn't look too bad, so I bounced down the stairs in what I hoped was an attractive, skippy manner, with my blonde hair bobbing around behind me.

'Can I help you?' I inquired in my most imperious, up-market, I-just-bash-a-word-processor-for-a-lark, I-don't-need-the-money, voice.

At that moment the beige trousers uncrossed, the Docksiders hit the deck, and the legs straightened. As he stood up and turned to face me, I realized why the trousers had looked familiar. I'd seen them less than half an hour ago; sat opposite them, in fact. I gasped and my hand shot to my mouth. Good God, it was Ginger!

Chapter Two

I gasped in amazement and gripped the banister rail. Oh Christ, he'd followed me. He'd seen me giving him the glad-eye on the tube and got completely the wrong idea. Now he was going to force himself on me right here on the cold marble stairs and I was too frightened to scream. I looked around desperately. Where was Maurice? Where was Bob? Even a sex-crazed dog was preferable to this. I wasn't even carrying the rape alarm that Mummy had given me for Christmas. Ginger walked towards me. I moaned softly and backed upstairs.

'Hi,' he said.

'What do you want?' I whispered in a very small, unimperious voice.

He took another menacing giant stride in my direction and placed a large freckled hand on the banister rail. I whimpered in terror and jumped back up another step. He smiled in an extremely unthreatening way and the blue eyes crinkled.

'Hey, I'm sorry, I'm not trying to frighten you or anything, I just want to talk to you.'

Pure Ivy League. I'm very hot on accents, especially American ones. I was somewhat relieved, but keen to be totally relieved.

'But you followed me,' I squeaked. 'You followed me from the station, I saw you on the tube.'

'You're right, I did follow you, but hey' – he laughed – 'there's a perfectly innocent reason. I'm not a mad rapist or anything; I'm certainly not after your body, if that's what you're thinking!'

'Oh.'

He made the very idea sound so absurd I was rather miffed. I drew myself up to my full five feet three inches and adopted a second-position ballet stance, which I've been told gives one poise. Dignity and composure were slowly beginning to course through my veins again.

'So what exactly do you want? Only I'm rather busy. I was in a meeting,' I said haughtily.

I had to admit he didn't look like the mad axe-man and, anyway, now I'd got my breath back, I was sure I could scream the place down if I felt like it.

'Actually, I need your help,' he said. 'Look, I'm sorry I followed you, but I couldn't help noticing your scarf.'

'My scarf?' I clutched my neck. I wasn't wearing a scarf. Sometimes I wear a silk scarf under my shirt, but today I definitely wasn't. He *was* mad. A madman with a scarf fetish. Perhaps he wanted to strangle me. 'I'm not wearing a scarf!'

'Your woollen scarf,' he said patiently. 'You were wearing it on the tube this morning.'

'Oh, that one!'

'Yes, that one.'

'What about it?' Was this guy for real? He liked my old school scarf? OK, it was about the only decent legacy I'd got from St Gertrude's, a rather dashing college-style affair with bright red and green stripes, but even so, come *on*. 'It's just my old school scarf, St Gertrude's.'

'Yes I know, I recognized it, that's why I followed you.' Suddenly he reached inside the front of his jacket and went for his gun. Christ! I ducked down on the stairs, hands on head, Miami Vice-style. He pulled a wallet out of his breast pocket.

'Hey, calm down, I just want to show you something.'

He produced a rather crumpled photograph and put it under my nose as I straightened myself out with the help of the banisters. Feeling more than a tad foolish, I took the photo. It was a girl of about my age, maybe younger, with wavy fair hair and quite a sweet face. Pretty-ish, but nothing special.

'Do you know her?' He looked at me intently.

'No . . . I don't think so.' I shook my head.

'Her name's Rachel Marsden, she was at school with you,' he said with some urgency.

'Really? At St Gertrude's?' I had another look. 'Can't say I do, I'm afraid. How old is she?'

'Twenty.'

'Ah well, that's a little bit younger than me, and if she wasn't in my house, which I don't think she was, I wouldn't know her from Eve.'

'I'm pretty sure her house was called something like Finch or Fich –'

'Finches. No, well in that case she definitely wasn't in my house. Well, there you go, sorry. Can't help you, I'm afraid.' I handed back the picture.

He looked crestfallen. 'Are you absolutely sure?'

'Absolutely.'

'Perhaps you'd remember some of her friends?'

'Who were they?'

'Well, that's the problem, she was a bit of a loner really. I'm finding it pretty hard to locate anybody.'

He put the photo back in his wallet and ran his hands through his hair. He really was rather good-looking. Especially when he did that. I was intrigued.

'So um, you're looking for her, is that it?'

He sighed. 'Yeh, that's it.'

'Why, has she done something wrong?' What was he, Special Branch, MI5?

He laughed hollowly. 'No, she hasn't done anything wrong, she's my . . .' He hesitated '. . . My fiancée.'

'Your fiancée!' I was flabbergasted. Some mousy nobody probably a year or so below me at school who I didn't even remember had got herself engaged to this yummy American hunk, done a bunk, and left him moving heaven and earth to find her? And how in God's name do you lose a fiancé? I know if I had one I'd have him locked in a little cage in my bedroom with a heavy padlock on the door.

'Well, if she's a missing person, why don't you go to the police?'

He sat down on the bottom step and shook his head. He looked all in. He was also getting cuter by the minute. I quickly sat down next to him and looked sympathetic, sweeping my hair back from my forehead so he could see my profile, and opening my eyes wide.

'Well, she's not a missing person exactly,' he said. 'Her father knows where she is, but he won't let me see her.' He gave a wry smile and scuffed the toe of his Docksider on the marble. 'He doesn't exactly approve.'

'Oh! Why ever not, you don't look like too much of a reprobate to me.'

He laughed. 'I'm not, he just doesn't . . . Well, let's just say we don't see eye to eye.'

I looked at him warily. Perhaps he had done something terrible after all. Walked off with the family silver, seduced the parlourmaid, made a pass at the dog – it would have to have been something in that line for my own parents to disapprove. Mummy practically tripped men like this up in the street for me, so desperate was she to shorten my shelf-life and climb into her mother-of-the-bride outfit.

'Why on earth doesn't he like you?' I asked nosily.

He hesitated and I thought he was about to tell me, but he obviously thought better of it. 'Oh, it's a long story.'

I took the hint and got to my feet briskly. 'Well, I'm sorry I can't be more helpful, but I honestly don't remember er, whatsername, Rachel Thingamy.'

He stood up immediately and held out his hand. I shook it. What charming manners.

'That's OK,' he said, 'thanks a lot for trying, anyway. I really appreciate it.'

'Not at all.' I almost said, Do come again.

'Well goodbye, and thanks.' He turned to go and was walking towards the door when he suddenly swung around and stared at me intently. He looked desperate.

'Look, if you see anyone from school who remembers her or who might have seen her recently, would you please let me know? I'd be really grateful. You see, I've got nothing to go on at the moment, and to be honest I'm really at the end of my rope, I just don't know what the hell's happened to her. I mean, maybe if you rang a few people up? You know, old schoolfriends? I don't want to be a nuisance but I just . . . I just don't know what to do next. I'm staying at the Savoy till the end of the week, so you could get me there if you come up with anything. My name's Adam Buchanan, by the way. Shall I write that down?'

'No, it's OK.' Adam Buchanan. Somehow I thought I'd remember. Savoy, eh? I smiled. 'I promise I'll ring you if I hear anything.'

'Thanks. It would mean so much, really. Well, goodbye, it was good to meet you.'

'Um, you too. Bye,' I smiled.

This time he went, closing the door softly behind him. Well! I stood on the stairs for a moment, inwardly digesting. Then I walked slowly back upstairs. Poor chap, what a shame, and how horrid Rachel Thingamy's father must be not to like him. Fancy searching London for his girlfriend; he must be crazy about her. I couldn't see Harry looking under the bed if I went missing.

'Well?' asked Pippa eagerly as I wandered into the pit, chewing my thumbnail thoughtfully. 'Was it him?'

'Who?'

'Harry, you goon.'

'Oh, Harry, no, but it was quite interesting . . .' I explained at length, embellishing the story a bit here and there for her benefit. She was suitably horrified at the potential rape situation, clapping her hands over her mouth and rolling her eyes in terror, and then was almost moved to tears, as I knew she would be, by the futility of the lover's quest.

'Oh Polly, how awful! You mean he's an innocent abroad, combing the streets of London and grilling complete strangers in an effort to find her,' she said dramatically. 'God, he must have been desperate to follow you.'

'Thanks a bunch,' I said drily, but I knew what she meant.

'Well, ring up some old schoolfriends and see if they remember her!' she said eagerly.

'Oh, come on, Pippa,' I said, eyeing the enormous pile of typing Nick had obviously just deposited on my desk, 'I have enough trouble sorting out my own life, let alone someone else's.'

'But you could really help him, Polly, someone might have seen her. Just ring a couple of people, please,' she impassioned.

'I will later, if I have time,' I lied. 'Just let me get through some of this first.'

I went on to auto-pilot and started bashing out the first contact report of the day. One of only two million, I was sure. Pippa always made me feel like such a heel. She'd help every lame dog she came across and positively went looking for them. There was an old tramp at South Ken station who should have been wearing designer labels saying, 'Clothes by Pippa Harvey', she threw so much money at him. I bashed away, taking my lack of humanity out on the typewriter. Suddenly my hands froze in mid-air. How had he known my name? How on earth had he known who to ask for, for God's sake? Bloody hell, there was something fishy going on here! I pushed back my chair and charged into Nick's office without bothering to knock.

'Who did he ask for, Nick? Did he know my name?' I gasped.

Nick was behind his desk, and sitting opposite him was

Mr Hutchinson, probably our most important client. He could have been the Queen for all I cared.

'Did he say Polly? Or Polly McLaren, or what?' I urged.

They both stared at me. Mr Hutchinson was on the edge of his seat: he liked a bit of drama because he led such a dull life. He was a little rat of a man with thin grey hair, a pale waxy face, and thick pebble glasses through which he blinked a great deal. On rare occasions he gave a tight little smile, but mostly his expression was similar to that of an undertaker's. His front teeth protruded slightly, just like a rat's, and he did a lot of slurping and sucking in an effort to cover them with his upper lip. He was a great one for giving Pippa and me the vicar's handshake, a two-handed ever-so-sincere jobby, and we decided that was probably the closest he ever got to sex. A hell of a nasty thought. We always washed afterwards. He was blinking away at me now like a Belisha beacon, but the tight little smile had yet to surface.

Nick looked at me coldly, keeping his own eyelids well under control. They didn't bat once. 'If you mean the gentleman downstairs,' he said evenly, 'he simply asked for Miss McLaren. I've no idea how he knew your name.'

'But that's so spooky, isn't it, don't you see?' I was raving now. 'I mean, he must have been on to me for days, he probably knows where I *live*, for God's sake, and there I was falling for his story and even trying to *help* him when all the time –'

'*Polly!*' Nick cut in furiously and with volume. It did the trick. I'd never heard him raise his voice and I ground to a halt. He glared at me. 'I've no idea how he knew your name, nor, come to that, what the hell you are talking about. Now let's sort this out later, shall we?' It was said with about six inches of solid steel blade running through the middle of it.

My P45 fluttered briefly through my fuddled brain and I saw his point. I retreated, closing the door quietly.

Pippa looked at me with horror as I came out. 'Mr Hutchinson's in there!' she hissed.

'I know,' I whispered, 'but how did he know my name?'

'Who, Hutchinson?'

'No, idiot, scarf-spotter downstairs.'

'Oh! Did he?'

'Yes! He asked for Miss McLaren!'

'Oh!' Pippa looked almost as shaken as I did for a moment, then she suddenly swung round and grabbed my scarf from the hat stand.

'You said it yourself, he's a scarf spotter! It's got your name on it, sec?' she said, waving it under my nose. 'Here, look!'

And of course there it was. P. E. McLaren, red letters on a little strip of white tape, sewn on by my ever-loving mother, years before I embarked on my career as a job-wrecker.

'He'll sack me!' I wailed. 'I was like a loony in there!'

'No he won't,' said Pippa doubtfully. 'He'll just be furious.'

And so he was. Bloody furious. When Mr Hutchinson had gone he asked me, murderously, to come into his office. 'Now, please!'

I slunk in meekly and sat down opposite him at his vast, leather-topped desk. I decided to get my story in quickly before he had a chance to ask, thereby deflecting the shit from the fan.

32

'Look, Nick, I'm terribly sorry about bursting in on you and Mr Hutchinson, but the guy downstairs followed me from the tube, can you believe it? I mean, OK, I was staring at him first, but only as a joke – you know it's this game I play every morning, which man would you fancy going to – er, well anyway – I thought he'd got the wrong idea, and that was why I was so alarmed, but in fact he's lost his fiancée and was following me because he recognized my old school scarf and the reason he knew my name is that –'

'Stop!' Nick had his hand up like a policeman stopping traffic. His eyes were tightly shut. 'Just stop!'

I stopped. He opened his eyes. Except they didn't look like eyes, more like bits of flint. I had a feeling the shit was making a detour my way. He leaned forward and folded his arms on his desk. His face was about a foot from mine. A muscle was going in his cheek and he looked deadly.

'Listen to me, Polly,' he said quietly. I listened. 'This is not a large agency: in fact it's extremely small. We have a few minor clients who provide us with a smattering of income, but we have one major client who happens to bill a great deal of money with us, namely Mr Hutchinson. He is, as you know, a total jerk but, be that as it may, he has us by the short and curlies. Because if he decides, for whatever reason, to take his revolting instant coffee away to another agency, we're sunk. Snookered. Finished. Washed up. Bankrupt. Am I making myself clear?'

'Yes,' I whispered, feeling about twelve.

'Our image is extremely important. Like it or loathe it, it sells us. It is therefore absolutely imperative that we create a good impression in front of clients. You come charging into my office, ranting and raving like a banshee, and we look like a Mickey Mouse agency. D'you get my drift?'

'Yes,' I whispered again, squirming in my seat. What did he think I was, a moron?

Nick leaned back in his seat and surveyed me, tapping the desk with a pencil. 'And another thing, Polly. If you ask me, your private life is intruding too much on your work. You just haven't got your mind on the job, have you? If you're not sitting at your desk filing your nails, you're mooning around thinking about your boyfriend and waiting for the telephone to ring. Well, that's harmless enough as long as you've done all your typing, but now I find you're picking up men on trains, bringing them into the agency, and chatting them up downstairs. I'm afraid that's just not on. I don't give a damn if you behave like that in your spare time, although frankly I'm surprised, but for God's sake don't bring these guys into the agency.'

Steam was pouring from my ears now, and I opened my mouth to speak, but the policeman's hand flew up again.

'Let me finish! It's quite simple, Polly, and we don't need to discuss it any further. I simply ask that you don't bring your men friends into the office, and that you don't burst into important client meetings raving like a lunatic. Is that clear?' The telephone rang, he picked it up instantly. 'Yes, hello? Oh, Mr Rawlings, yes, I was going to get back to you . . .'

My mouth was wide with indignation, which I was bloody well going to voice in no uncertain terms, but Nick waved me out of the office. I ignored him and sat tight. He was not getting away with this. He carried on talking, saw me still sitting there, and frowned, waving me off again. Still I sat there, determined to have my two penny-worth.

Suddenly he put his hand over the mouthpiece. 'Polly, if you don't get out of my office this minute and let me talk to Mr Rawlings, I will really lose my temper!' he hissed.

I ran. But by golly was I livid. Exactly who did he think he was talking to? Mooning about my boyfriend! Picking up men! Filing my nails! I don't even have a nail-file – come to that, I don't even have any nails! He'd just thrown that in to make me sound like a Sharon, the bastard.

Pippa tried to placate me with numerous cups of strong, sweet tea, but the steam was gushing out of every orifice now, and I gnashed my teeth in fury, waiting for my chance to set Mr Penhalligan straight.

Unfortunately, Nick shut himself away for the rest of the day to work on a presentation, giving the strict instruction that under no circumstances was he to be disturbed. I don't have that much of a death wish, so I left him alone and finally went home on the dot of five-thirty, seething with rage and plotting my revenge.

Chapter Three

I marched up the steps to our front door in Tregunter Road, slammed it behind me, and stomped up the innumerable stairs to the garret flat I share with Lottie. I was still steaming. *No one*, I repeated to myself, *no one* has *ever* spoken to me like that. *No one*. I viciously shouldered open the flat door which always sticks, flung my bag on the floor and collapsed on the sofa in a deep depression. Fine Young Cannibals assaulted my eardrums at full volume. The flat was in the most disgusting mess: dirty glasses, wine bottles and overflowing ashtrays covered every conceivable surface area, a line of bras and knickers in varying shades of sock-grey were drying on the radiator, bits of chocolate digestive had been trodden into the rug, there were dog hairs everywhere, and penicillin was sprouting from the various coffee mugs that were littered around. Why doesn't anyone ever tidy *up*? I thought savagely.

'Harry rang!' shouted Lottie from the bathroom.

I sprang to my feet, eyes shining. Suddenly the flat seemed beautifully cosy and lived in and – oh, just charmingly Bohemian, and the music was joyous and uplifting. I ran to the bathroom where Lottie was brushing her teeth in her underwear. A bath was running, bad sign, I'd have to have her water.

'When! What did he say? Is he ringing back?'

Lottie paused, her mouth full of froth. 'Ten minutes

ago, he's coming over in an hour to take you out to supper and no, he's not ringing back.'

She gargled, making sure she didn't swallow any toothpaste – we'd read somewhere that it was full of calories – and then went back for some more vigorous brushing, her D-cupped boobs bouncing up and down under the strain and her long dark hair dripping in the basin.

'Oh joy! Oh joy! Oh thank you God!' I did an ecstatic little dance and wrapped the shower curtain around me in a dramatic Grecian sweep.

Lottie put her toothbrush down and looked at me accusingly. 'So you're going,' she said grimly.

'Well of course I'm going.' I dropped the curtain in disbelief. 'I've been waiting for this phone call for six days now!'

'Exactly.' Lottie rinsed her mouth. 'If you were really cool you'd ring back and say you were busy. Look at the way he just assumes you're free!'

'Oh I know.' I felt deflated. 'But don't make me do it, Lottie. I can't, I'm mad about him,' I wailed.

She sighed. 'I know. And the worst thing is he knows it too. Rung up for his weekly bonk, I suppose.'

She peered in the mirror, looking apprehensively at potential blackhead areas. I watched her reflection as I perched on the side of the bath. Her round sweet face was framed with long dark silky hair and she had beautiful huge dark eyes that looked at me critically now. Oh dear, I was in trouble.

Lottie was my only truly sensible friend. She ran her life in an orderly, no-nonsense fashion, and boy did she get results. I once analysed the secret of Lottie's success and

37

realized it was mind-blowingly simple. During the day, she focused her mind on the job in hand, which in her case was that of being a solicitor in a large city practice. That was what she was there to do and that was what she did. She didn't loll all over her desk nursing a hangover, eating chocolate and dreaming about men. She didn't block the office phone-lines gossiping endlessly to girlfriends, neither did she go shopping in office hours searching for that elusive little black number. No, no. Lottie did something that was anathema to me. She worked. Consequently she was well respected, well liked and well paid. A simple formula, you might think, but one that had yet to filter down to my neck of the woods.

Then there was Lottie's love life to consider. OK, she was experiencing a temporary lull at the moment, but purely at her own instigation. A particularly sweet (but rather short) antique dealer was probably at this very moment throwing himself off Blackfriars Bridge because Lottie had gently but firmly eased him out of her life. Lottie finished with men. They did not finish with her. Lottie was pursued into cupboards, behind sofas, into expensive restaurants: you name it, she'd been there.

Now admittedly she's a good-looking girl. But if I say so myself, and she would say it too, I'm not bad looking either. Granted, I'm prone to pushing the scales over nine stone, but who isn't? And I have nice blue eyes, a good complexion, a pair of rather stylish cheekbones (a rare commodity these days, I've noticed), longish, blondish hair, a thankfully unremarkable nose and pretty remarkable legs, so how do I manage to get it so wrong?

Do I have an unattractive personality? Am I perhaps

lacking in humour, or a sartorial sense of style? My friends tell me no. As far as humour's concerned I like nothing better than a good laugh and, as for style, if they handed out O-levels in how to accessorize, I'm sure I'd have a shed-full.

Ah, so perhaps it's something more sinister, I hear you whisper. Perhaps there's a personal hygiene problem lurking nastily under the armpits. Again, the answer, I assure you, is no. I happen to be a rigorous pit sniffer – just my own – and I'm also an avid, and noisy, mouthwash gargler. So what exactly is my problem?

Simple, says Lottie, I aim too high. Way, way too high. Apparently I should be aiming lower – much, much lower; underground preferably, somewhere around pit level, amongst the slugs and the worms. Lottie is actually the greatest exponent of her theory, her maxim at a party being, 'Go ugly early.' Why waste valuable time, she says, lining up behind all the other prospective female candidates to chat up the best-looking man in the room, when you know you're going to end up with that short, balding insurance broker in the corner?

All this, of course, makes huge sense, but sense and I have never made very good bedfellows. The one and only time I took Lottie's advice, sense did indeed turn out to be huge, about six feet nine inches, in fact; more of a giraffe than a human being. And hard though I tried to keep his 'good personality' to the forefront of my mind, I couldn't help being distracted by his colossal nostrils (of which I had an excellent view from my low vantage point), and his enormous expanse of smooth white forehead which seemed to go back and back in an uninterrupted fashion almost to the nape of his neck. Needless to say he had to go and, as he went, my feet went dancing off to the sunny side of the street again, where the beautiful people live.

Of course, this side of the street is harder work. Back on the sensible side I'm way up in the pecking order, but over here with the stunners, I'm only fair to middling. I had to fight my corner, and fight I did, until one day I went home with the prize. Harry. Now this should have been my moment of glory. I should have been able to dangle his delectable personage in front of Lottie's sensible nose crying, 'You see! You see! I hooked one in the end!' But no. The more I dangled, the more Lottie was able to shake her head at me and sigh. Like now. Oh-oh.

Lottie set aside her toothbrush and sat on the linen basket facing me. She folded her arms in an ominously businesslike manner. 'Polly, let me ask you something. Do you honestly enjoy your dates with Harry?'

'Enjoy them? Of course I do! What a question! Enjoy them? I positively live for them!'

'Yes, I know that, I know you spend every waking hour dreaming about them and listening for the phone, but when you actually go out, do you relax? Is he good company? Does he make you laugh? Does he – I don't know – look after you, see that you're having a good time?'

'Lottie, don't be absurd; we never stop laughing, he's marvellous company!'

'But do you feel relaxed? I mean really? Or d'you feel that you're constantly making an effort with him? It's just that whenever I see you with him it all seems such a strain, so sort of – artificial really. I mean, you never just get a video out and curl up on the sofa with him, do you? You never just have a quiet evening in. It's always night clubs and parties and restaurants; and you always have to look marvellous, and it's not as if you've just met him, you've been going out with him for ages now, and I shouldn't think he's even seen you without lipstick, let alone no make-up at all.'

'Oh Lottie, what's make-up got to do with it? You know I wear a lot anyway.'

'Not around the flat, you don't, and not when you go to your parents.'

'Oh well, that's different –'

'But why? Why aren't you more natural with him? Let him see what you're really like instead of, I don't know, always being perfect. I'm not trying to spoil things, and I know you're excited because he's phoned, but honestly Polly, it's been about nine months now and I sometimes wonder if you really know this guy at all!'

I sighed and picked my nails, feeling hemmed in. 'I know what you mean, Lotts, but honestly, everything's fine. Harry just likes me to be like that, you know, made up and dressed up and –'

'Exactly! That's exactly what I mean!'

'I know, I know, but, well, if Harry likes it, well then I like it too . . .' I trailed off lamely. I could see from Lottie's face how pathetic that sounded, but my argumentative powers were fading fast. I rallied myself.

'The thing is, I can't explain why, but I enjoy it all. The preparation and – and the excitement, the build up. I don't want us to be mundane and boring – living on takeaways and watching telly and taking each other for granted.'

'No, but surely there's a happy medium. I mean –'

'Please, Lottie. I know what you're saying, but seriously, I reckon I've nearly cracked it with Harry. A couple more weeks and he'll be eating out of my hand! In fact, I'm pretty sure he's mad about me already,' I lied.

Lottie looked totally unconvinced. I took a shifty look at my watch. Christ, quarter-past six already.

'Look, I promise, everything's fine, I couldn't be happier! And honestly, I'd love to talk about it more with you, but the thing is he'll be here in about an hour and I desperately need a bath,' I said, eyeing her water enviously. 'I couldn't possibly . . .?'

'Yes, yes, go on, have it,' she said, caving in dramatically, 'I'll have it after you. I'm only going to the cinema with Sophie, I'm sure she won't mind if I'm covered in scum and leg shavings.'

I hugged her, grateful for the water and for her submission. 'Thanks, you're an absolute star, and I promise I'll think about what you've said.'

'Promise?' she said, knowing I wouldn't.

'Promise,' I said, knowing she knew that I wouldn't.

When she'd gone, I quickly poured half a bottle of my most expensive bubble-bath into the water, hoping it would overpower her Radox, and leaped in. Only an hour! Even less, in fact! I didn't have much time and there was so much to do! I scrubbed and shaved and plucked and washed and rinsed and sloshed around a bit, then jumped out and ran dripping to the bedroom where I emptied the entire contents of my wardrobe on to the bed.

I looked at the mountain of clothes and groaned. 'Oh God, I've got nothing to wear!' I wailed. 'Lottie, can I borrow your suede trousers?'

'They're at the cleaners,' she yelled back.

'Oh no! What else have you got?'

I ran into Lottie's bedroom where she obligingly emptied her own wardrobe on to the bed. I wriggled in and out of things like a maniac, but eventually ran back to my own mountain and settled on a short black skirt and a silky red jumper with a slashed neckline which slipped seductively off one shoulder. I clinched it all in with a black suede belt. The shoulder looked a bit anaemic, so I rubbed on some fake tan with tiny pieces of make-up sponge which Wellington, Lottie's Yorkie, had thoughtfully chewed into little bits. I ran into the sitting room where Lottie was ironing a shirt.

'What d'you think?' I said, balancing on the sofa and peering into our only decent mirror above the fireplace. I'd coaxed my hair into mad gypsy curls of the blonde variety, and completed the look with some enormous gold hoop earrings which had eaten up most of last month's salary and were so heavy that they almost made me walk with my head bowed.

'Wow!' Lottie was genuinely impressed. 'That should knock him for six.'

'Really?' I was pleased, Lottie was a tough critic. 'Not too tarty?'

'Oh well, it's tarty all right, but you can't have it both ways.'

I hoiked the jumper up a bit to cover the shoulder. 'Better?'

'Well, it'll come off later anyway, so what does it matter? I take it you're playing away tonight?'

I ignored Lottie's disapproving tone, and jumped

around on the sofa with excitement. 'I expect so! Don't double-lock, but don't expect me either – and stop looking at me like an old fishwife with a rolling pin. Haven't you ever been wild and irresponsible?'

Lottie sighed and said truthfully, 'Just give me half a chance. Seriously though, Polly, don't hang on to his every monosyllable, and don't race him back to his flat when he suggests coffee, and don't iron every single shirt he possesses, and don't –'

The doorbell rang in the middle of the lecture. I leaped off the sofa, then leaped back on again, yelping with panic.

'He's early! You go, Lottie.'

'Oh sure, then he'd really think it was his lucky night.' Lottie was still in her underwear. 'A flat full of push-overs.'

She went off to dress and I buzzed Harry in, my heart beating as loud as the thump-thump-thump of his feet coming up the stairs.

I knew I'd settle down eventually, but for the first half an hour with him you'd think I was on drugs. I'd leap around like a maniac, talking in a strange high-pitched voice, breathing heavily, offering him cigarettes when he didn't smoke, and pouring him large gins when he drank whisky. Anyone else, said Lottie, would get terribly insecure and think there was a chain-smoking, gin-swilling hunk knocking around the rest of the week, but not Harry.

He came bounding into the flat like a golden retriever puppy, all long-legged and blond and floppy-haired. He looked, as usual, divine. He was tanned from a long weekend skiing, and his hair was blonder and streakier than ever from the sun. I could feel my much touched-up roots sizzling with jealousy.

'Polyester!' he yelled as he came charging through the door, rugby tackling me on to the sofa. 'How the devil are you? Hang on, we're off!'

I shrieked with laughter as the sofa got under way and we slid across the room on the coasters. Lottie wandered in wearing her dressing gown and munching a jaffa cake. She sidestepped the cruising sofa with weary indifference. She'd seen it all before.

Harry looked up as we came to a standstill next to her. 'Hi, Lottie, how's your sex life?' he said, pulling her dressing gown cord undone.

'Not as complicated as yours, I suspect,' said Lottie drily, tying the cord up again.

Harry laughed nervously. He wasn't sure about Lottie, she was a bit too smart for him. He swept his hair back in a practised gesture. 'I see it's nice and tidy in here as usual,' he said, taking in the debris-strewn flat. 'That ironing board seems to be a permanent fixture! Modern art, is it? Ha-ha!'

'No, we're looking back in anger,' Lottie quipped, but it was lost on Harry.

He turned his cornflower-blue gaze on to me. God, he was attractive. I bit my hand to stop myself from giving him the first kiss. Wait for it, Polly, wait for it . . . Ah, here it comes. He leaned down and kissed me briefly on the mouth. He always started with a little one, a teaser, then bent his head down again for the big clinch. I responded enthusiastically, considering Lottie was still in the room.

When I eventually let him go, his lazy, sexy grin spread over his face and his blue eyes roamed all over me as we lay on the sofa. He took my chin in his hand. I smiled, overwhelmed with love.

'So, young Polly,' he murmured, 'what have you been up to all this time? I haven't seen you for absolutely ages. Been a good girl?'

He made it sound as if I'd been deliberately avoiding him instead of staring at the phone willing it to ring.

'Oh, I've been out and about,' I said as casually as I could. Harry liked independent girls. 'A couple of drinks parties, out to supper once or twice.'

'Terrific, that's what I like to hear. Got to keep your finger on the pulse.'

My own pulse was going like a bongo drum as he ran his fingers through my hair. He was making slow progress, and I leaped up as I realized he was wading through half a ton of mousse and gel. 'Must have a ciggy,' I said quickly.

He sat up and watched me as I lit a cigarette. I knew I was being appraised, so I lit it slowly, then stood with my back to the fireplace – chest out, tummy in – reclining against the marble shelf. Quite uncomfortable really, but it worked. He looked me up and down approvingly.

'You're looking extremely tasty tonight, Poll. Where shall we go to eat before I ravage you? Or shall we skip the meal and I'll ravage you here, much easier!'

'Easier on your wallet,' muttered Lottie.

Harry missed it, but I caught it and said bravely, more for sisterhood than for myself, 'Actually, I'm quite hungry.'

'Of course you are, my little pumpkin, I was only joking. Where d'you want to go?'

'Oh, I don't know. How about Giovanni's?'

'Right, Giovanni's it is. Let's go then.' He drained his glass and stood up, ready for a change of scene.

I was always staggered by his low boredom threshold. He was like a small child, constantly needing to be amused by new toys.

I jumped up too, hurriedly stubbed out my cigarette, and knocked back my drink, throwing most of it down my jumper and choking on the rest. Lottie shook her head in disbelief.

'Steady darling!' Harry patted me on the back, laughing. 'Don't choke on it! Right, we'll be off then. Packed a bag?'

'Er, no, not yet.'

I hadn't, because the last time I'd packed one he'd dropped me back at my flat at ten-thirty saying he was going on to a dance – hadn't he mentioned it? He hadn't, and I'd felt like a complete berk trudging up the stairs to the flat, overnight bag in hand.

'Won't be a minute!' I said, grabbing a pair of knickers from the radiator and stuffing them in my handbag. 'There.'

Harry raised his eyebrows. 'That's it?'

Yes, that was it, or did that look slutty?

'Er, well no, not quite, hang on a sec . . .' I ran into my bedroom.

'No rush, no rush!' he called after me, but I was too wound up to slow down now.

Nothing seemed to be clean, so I rummaged through my dirty linen basket and recycled a navy blue shirt that didn't show the dirt, and grabbed my cleanser, moisturizer and toothbrush, although I always liked to use his. I rummaged under the bed, found an old carrier bag, and shoved everything in.

When I got back to the sitting room he was standing by the door, jangling his keys and looking impatient.

'Sorry,' I panted, 'couldn't find a shirt.'

'No worries. All set now?'

'Yes – bye Lottie!'

I gave her a backward wave, not having the nerve to meet her judgemental eyes; and anyway, I had to run, because Harry seemed to be half-way down the stairs already. I pounded down the stairs after him. Funny how he's always one step ahead, I mused, as I jumped the last few and ran out on to the pavement. He was already revving up the car. I ran around to the passenger door and limbo-danced my way into his low-slung crumpet-catcher. With a good deal of throttle we set off for the restaurant.

And that's another thing, I thought as I settled back into the impossibly-difficult-to-get-out-of bucket seat, how come I never rip him off? How come I never have the nerve to say, 'Well actually, I thought we'd go to Le Gavroche tonight'?

On the other hand, I reflected, as he pulled up outside the extremely reasonable little Italian I'd picked, this was where he'd fallen for me on that first magical night, and I always hoped he'd remember and fall for me all over again.

As we ploughed our way through the only edible food on the menu – avocado, mozzarella and tomato followed by veal marsala – I had him rolling in the aisles as I recounted various anecdotes, apocryphal or otherwise, that I'd saved up and made up during the week. My efforts were rewarded handsomely.

He leaned back in his chair wiping his eyes at one of my more outrageous witticisms. 'Polly, that's hysterical. I don't know where you get these stories from!' he cried.

From my imagination, of course, was the answer to this, but why tell the boring truth when you can tell a good lie? Flushed with success, I helped myself to another glass of wine by way of celebration, although I couldn't help thinking that things were slightly arse about tit here. Wasn't he supposed to be laughing me into bed? And how come I was pouring the wine? Lottie's wise words came briefly to mind, but I banished them hastily. Utter rubbish, I was having a marvellous time.

Oh God, he was off and I hadn't been listening. I rearranged my face so that it took on an absorbed expression as we had our weekly bulletin of Stockbroking News.

I didn't understand stockbroking, but since Harry had explained it twice already, the second time in a painstaking, stockbroking-for-morons tone of voice, I didn't feel I could ask again. I just smiled knowingly and nodded a lot, and when there was a gap in the monologue, made what I thought were appropriate remarks like:

'Really, as much as that?'

'Forty-two per cent, my goodness.'

'No, of course not, that would be insider dealing.'

'Isn't that what they call a bear market?'

It was all pretty hit or miss stuff, but he never seemed to suss me. Once he'd got into his stride he was unstoppable, and he didn't really notice what I said anyway. It suited me because it gave me a chance to catch my breath and think of some more outrageous lies to amuse him with later.

'Polly?'

Harry was wiping his mouth with his napkin and looking none too pleased. Oh God, he'd come to the end of his story which I now remembered he'd prefixed with the words, 'I think you'll find this rather amusing', and I couldn't for the life of me remember what he'd been talking about. Too late for a belly laugh? Definitely. I shook my head and twisted my mouth into what I hoped was a wry little smile.

'How funny, but when you come to think about it, sad too, don't you think?'

Harry looked rather taken aback. 'Er . . . well, I suppose so, for his wife maybe. You can bet your bottom dollar the bra wasn't hers.'

It was my turn to look mystified, but before he'd had time to rearrange his brain cells, I charged off on a completely different tack and told him about my encounter with Adam Buchanan. Of course I hammed it up like mad, and had the distraught man practically crying on my shoulder, begging me to help him find his girlfriend. I naturally expected Harry to laugh like a drain and sneer at such love-struck, unmanly behaviour, but not for the first time in my checkered career with him, I was wrong. Harry was on the edge of his seat; in fact, Harry was leaning forward, keen to hear more. Now this was a first. Harry always leaned back. I was the one who leaned forward. I once tried leaning back in the hope that he'd come in, but we just ended up yelling at each other across the table in an effort to make ourselves heard. But here he was now, eager for details, gripped, engrossed and, wait for it, sympathetic.

'How extraordinary. You say they're engaged?'

'Apparently.'

'And now she's just vanished?'

'That's what he says.'

'And the father thinks he's a bad influence. You can bet your life Daddy's hiding her somewhere, the bastard. And presumably this American guy doesn't know where to start looking for her; he probably doesn't know anyone in London, does he?'

'No, he doesn't, that's why he followed me, you see, because of the school scarf.'

'So what are you going to do?'

'Do?'

'Yes, to help. Didn't you say you'd try and help?'

I fidgeted a bit. 'Well, no, I didn't really.'

'Why not?'

'Well, for a start I didn't even know the girl at school; and secondly, well secondly, what on earth can I do?'

'More than he can in a strange country, that's for sure. I don't know, use your imagination!'

This stung. I smiled sweetly. 'Yes, but it's none of my business really, is it?'

'Except that he's made it your business by following you to work and asking you to help. God, Polly, aren't you intrigued? I mean, how amazing to fall in love and find the person you feel you can spend the rest of your life with, but then have her vanish into thin air! Pretty irritating, don't you think?'

I snorted with derision. 'Hardly thin air, Harry. She's probably shacked up with some hunk in Bayswater. I mean, who knows if this guy's telling the truth? Who knows what's going on?'

'Not you, obviously,' said Harry, helping himself to more wine.

I took a sharp intake of breath and reached for my wine glass. My God, he was pissed off. Pissed off because I couldn't end the story, couldn't give him the punchline. Harry's new toy had been taken away from him just when he was enjoying it. Well gosh, I'm sorry.

But my indignation was misdirected and I knew it. What had really knocked me sideways was that all-revealing sentence of his: 'to find the person you feel you can spend the rest of your life with'. Had he really said that? Harry, the happy hunter, who couldn't even commit himself to a quick drink in the pub, let alone the rest of his life with a wife? Harry, who I'd naturally assumed was an emotional cripple because he'd never come up trumps in the love and slush department?

I'd convinced myself that it all stemmed from his childhood. In fact I'd spent many happy hours fantasizing about a strict and puritanical upbringing at the hands of uncompromising and no doubt brutal parents – too many smacks as a child, not enough chocolate, not enough telly – comparing it to my own cuddly, chocolatey, telly-viewing childhood. I was sure that this had soured his outlook, but that with a little patience I could show him the way, lead him up the Mills and Boon path of true romance, teach him what love was all about. But he knew! He knew about it, and what's more – and this was where I nearly gagged on my courgettes – he thought it was 'wonderful'! Harry, like the rest of the human race, was on the prowl for that elusive love match, and all along I'd put his compulsive prowling down to an insatiable desire to stick his hand up girls' skirts.

I struggled womanfully with the courgettes, pushing them firmly down my throat and trying desperately to remember what had brought about this earth-shattering revelation. Oh yes, Rachel Whatsername.

'Anyway,' I said, swallowing hard, 'I don't suppose I could have helped. I mean, I didn't know the girl at school. I only know what she looks like from that photo he showed me.'

'That's it,' said Harry snidely, 'put your head in the sand as usual.'

I was furious. 'How dare you! What do you expect me to do, ring up all the old girls I can find in the phone book and quiz them rigid?'

'Wouldn't hurt,' he said. 'Give you something to do at work for a change.'

Harry was enjoying himself now. I'd worked myself up into a nice little state, and he was steadily winding me up.

Like a moron I took the bait. 'Well for your information,' I said furiously, 'I said I'd look into it for him!'

Harry threw back his head and roared with laughter. 'Oh, really? Inspector McLaren's looking into it, is she? Off to sniff the pavements, eh? Well I shall look forward to hearing how you solve the case!'

The waiter arrived to take our order for pudding. I fumed and tore my napkin into a million pieces. We sat in stony silence as Harry demolished a delicious-looking crême-brûlée which I'd petulantly refused. Just you wait, I thought. It'll take me exactly two minutes to find that girl. Just you wait. I downed the rest of my glass in one gulp, which seemed to have a calming effect. Get a grip, Polly old girl. This is ridiculous. This is no way to end the evening.

Harry was obviously thinking along the same lines. After all, it's not much fun going to bed with a grumpy girlie. He crowbarred his way back into my good books. 'So, how are your parents?' he asked with a glittering smile.

I smiled back reluctantly. I was potty about my family and, given half a chance, could bore for England about my wonderful parents and my gorgeous older brothers.

'They're really well, thanks.'

'Still living in the country?' he grinned maliciously.

He had to spoil it, didn't he? When I'd first met Harry, I'd told him I was going home to the country one weekend. He'd roared with laughter when he discovered we lived in Esher.

'Esher's not country, Polly! You might as well live in Surbiton!'

I'd blushed hotly; I'd always rather liked Esher. Harry's parents lived in Derbyshire, in 'proper country', where his father was a farmer, a gentleman farmer, of course, none of that ploughing the fields and scattering lark for him: he employed people to do that. No, Harry's father strolled around his thousands of acres doing important things like ordering fences to be put here and ditches to be dug there, shooting the odd recalcitrant pheasant; or peasant probably, if he felt like it.

My father wasn't nearly so grand, he was just a consultant at the local hospital. A humble doctor who did little more than save lives every day and bring people back from the dead, that sort of thing. His work was very mundane: a brain tumour one day, a heart attack the next; run-of-the-mill stuff. I'd always been terribly proud of Daddy, but Harry had shown me the error of my ways.

'Very middle-class, Polly, like all the professions.'

He'd once introduced me to some smart friends of his as 'the doctor's daughter from Esher', and laughed. Why? No matter, I was keen to learn. Luckily I'd learned enough already to know that one house just wasn't enough. It was with this in mind that I answered his question.

'Yes, they are in Esher at the moment,' I replied. 'Just back from our place in London, actually.'

'Oh really?' Harry looked surprised. 'I didn't know your parents had a house in London.'

Neither did I, but apparently I'd just invented one.

'Oh yes,' I lied, 'we've always kept a little place up here. So useful.'

'Ah,' he grinned, 'a little place. What is it, a flat?'

'No, it's not actually. I say "a little place" out of habit, but it's quite a big house.'

'Really?' He looked startled. 'How big?'

'Oh I don't know, about six or seven storeys, the usual sort of townhouse.'

'Six or seven storeys!' He was incredibly impressed. I'd obviously overdone it. 'Whereabouts?'

'Oh, um, Knightsbridge.'

'Really? Whereabouts in Knightsbridge?'

Whereabouts again? We'd just done that one, hadn't we? Wasn't he being just a touch nosy? I began to panic. Think of a street, any street, but make sure it's in Knightsbridge.

'Montpelier Street.'

'No! Montpelier Street? My aunt lives in Montpelier Street. What number?'

What number? Christ! Pick a number, any number, just don't let it be Auntie's. I hesitated, this was like Russian Roulette.

'Don't you know?' asked Harry.

'Yes, of course I know, it's number twenty-three? . . . four!'

'Twenty-four! But that's right next door. Aunt Rose lives at number twenty-six! How extraordinary!'

'Well, not really. I mean someone has to live next door, why not Aunt Rose?'

'But she must know your parents. I'm seeing her on Sunday, I'll ask her, she's bound to!'

'No! I mean, um, I wouldn't ask her, because she won't necessarily know them. You see the thing is – the thing is, it's rented! It's rented on a sort of permanent basis to other people.'

'Rented? But I thought you said your parents had just come back from there?'

Ah yes, Polly, you did, you did.

'Oh! Oh yes, well, they were there for a few days last week, that's true, but that's because, um, that's because they know the people it's rented to. Old family friends, you see, known them for years, so they let my parents stay whenever they're in London.'

'What are they called?'

'My parents?'

'No, idiot, the friends, who are they? Aunt Rose will probably know them.'

Yes, Polly, who are they? These very old trusty family friends, practically your godparents, who exactly are they?

'Well, I er, I don't exactly know them myself, they're friends of my father's really. Daddy's the one who's known them for years, they're colleagues of his, you know, doctors.'

'Ah.' Harry looked more than a little confused, and who can blame him. 'So you never actually use the house yourself?'

'No, oh no, never.' It was such a relief to say something truthful that I said it with a vengeance, with gusto even. I shook my head vehemently. 'Never ever, in fact.'

'Oh. Seems a bit odd really.' God he *would* go on. Couldn't we talk about something else? His ego perhaps? Or his sex appeal? 'I mean, to have a house in London that you can't use ...' He looked thoughtful, then he sneered. 'I suppose your parents need the money.'

I bristled furiously. 'Certainly not! Need the money? Good gracious, no. In fact these people don't even pay the rent, they just borrow it.'

'Oh!'

Oh indeed. So what do we have here now, Polly? A massively philanthropic gesture, is that it? On behalf of some poor impoverished doctors who have been close to your family for many years but whose names escape you? A nice, rent-free, six-, nay, seven-storey house in the middle of Knightsbridge for which they pay not a sausage? What are your parents anyway, missionaries? Born-again Christians?

Happily, in the nick of time, the waiter arrived with a bottle of wine which, according to Harry, was corked. This took Harry's mind off things as he sent the waiter scurrying back and forth with new bottles. I blessed the hapless waiter from the bottom of my heart. But I also realized I'd done irreparable damage. It was quite obvious that Harry could never meet my parents now. I imagined him settling down to a quiet chat with Daddy after Sunday lunch in Esher. 'Polly tells me you have a house in Montpelier Street, Mr McLaren.' Oh no, that would never do. They must never meet. Oh dear, so I couldn't marry him! Or if I did, my parents wouldn't be able to come to the wedding! It was too horrrific.

I'd talk to Mummy, she'd understand, if a little vaguely. I'd catch her while she was gardening; I could see her pausing for a moment as she pruned the roses. 'Yes, of course I'll pretend, darling, but I don't understand why you said we had a house in London in the first place. Whatever made you imagine we had? We haven't, have we?'

Daddy would be a different matter, glaring at me over his glasses in the study, stern and unamused. 'No, Polly, I'm sorry. If you're ashamed of our house here, that's too bad, but I will *not* become a millionaire overnight just to please your playboy friends.'

I sighed as Harry tasted the new bottle. Oh well, something would come up. Perhaps we could sell it. Yes, that was it, we'd sell it! Get rid of the sodding house once and for all. I brightened considerably. It would be sold tomorrow – but quietly. So Aunt bleeding-nosy-parker Rose didn't get to hear about it.

The new wine had obviously been deemed drinkable and was apparently on the house, so Harry was agreeable now and wanting me to be agreeable too.

'And how is that dreadful boss of yours? Still bullying you and Pippa and throwing his weight around?' he asked.

I smiled. This at least was a subject we both agreed on. As far as Harry was concerned, any man who spent his working days west of the City and certainly west of Fleet Street was either a shirt-lifter or an estate agent. Failing that, he had to be an ad-man, which was the lowest of the low. If he felt like it, Harry could put on a high moral tone and pontificate for hours about the immorality of off-loading unwanted products on to an unsuspecting, gullible public through the medium of advertising. Then he'd put the boot into spineless individuals like Nick who, failing to get a proper job, had gone into advertising to propagate this corruption and earn enormous salaries.

Of course, he'd concede, it was all right for girlies. Girlies had to work in the West End to be near the shops and to have lunch with each other and discuss their boyfriends in the City. But for a man, advertising was the pits.

I told Harry how Nick had shouted at me today when I had simply knocked on his door and very politely interrupted his meeting to ask a pertinent question.

Harry leaned across the table and took my hand. He stroked it sympathetically. 'But he's an ad-man, poppet, that's what you have to remember, he's not like the rest of us. He wouldn't have the first idea how to talk to a lady. He probably didn't even go to public school.'

Nick had gone to Harrow, but I let that pass. I liked the hand-stroking bit and I also liked the bit about the lady. Harry ordered me a Cointreau without even asking, and I sipped it while he signed the Access slip, feeling decidedly perkier.

I even kept my cool when a drop-dead blonde in a spray-on black Lycra dress walked passed us and Harry nearly knocked the table over, so desperate was he to spring to his feet and kiss her very enthusiastically on both cheeks.

'See you tomorrow at Ransome's,' he called after her swaying bottom as it undulated off to the loo like a metronome, mesmerizing most of the men in the room.

I tried not to but I couldn't help it. 'What's happening at Ransome's?'

'Oh, it's just a little party. A guy I've known for donkey's years is having a birthday dinner there. He's paying for the whole bash so it's invitation only, of course. Sorry, my sweet, I'd love you to come, but there it is. Actually, it'll probably be rather boring, but I've got to go.' He drained his glass. 'Ready, darling?' He stood up and held my coat out for me.

Again, I was taken by surprise, but I obediently knocked back the Cointreau and stood up. 'Ready.'

And with that I slipped into my coat, slipped into the front seat of his car, slipped into his flat, slipped down a Rémy and slipped into bed.

Well, that's how it always was with Harry, I reflected as I lay there waiting for him to brush his teeth. I felt like a well-trained poodle jumping through the hoops as he skilfully manoeuvred me round the course. From restaurant, to car, to flat, to bed. You know the rules, Polly. Not that I was complaining, of course. Perish the thought.

Harry appeared in the doorway looking like a toothpaste commercial – tall, blond, brown, and with a whiter-than-white smile. I giggled because I knew what was coming next. Harry had pinched a child's diving board from his parent's swimming pool and screwed it into the floorboards at the end of his bed. He would bounce up and down on it before launching himself, with a blood-curdling scream, on to his victim. It always reduced me to fits of giggles, but when I'd told Lottie about it she'd looked at me with horror, her eyes like saucers, as if I'd said he dressed up as the fairy queen and cried, 'Beat me, beat me!'

The dive from the board very much set the tone for the rest of the evening, because what always ensued can only be described as a romp. Our particular form of rumpy-pumpy was punctuated with great gales of laughter from him and screams and giggles from me. Pillow fights would occur on a regular basis and even, on one memorable occasion, a water fight with squeezy bottles. Anything, basically, to stop Harry from getting bored. It was certainly fun, and I reckon I lost pounds in the process – one had to be reasonably confident figure-wise, as there was never any question of the light going off – but it was never, by any stretch of the imagination, romantic.

It would have been quite out of place, for example, for me to murmur anything more romantic than, 'Oh no, not on the chest-of-drawers again!' or, 'Come and get me!' from the top of the wardrobe.

I did once, in an extremely drunken and foolhardy moment and after a particularly passionate bout of love-making half-way out of the window, venture, 'Oh Harry, I do love you,' but it was met with such a look of mock horror and surprise that I never tried it again.

This evening was no exception. The squire and his

wench, for wenchy was how I always felt, romped and rolled and screeched and chortled until oh, two-thirty in the morning.

And that was when Harry sat up in bed and gave me a strange and questioning look. 'What would you like to do now, Polly?' he asked.

What would I like to do? Well, sleep was pretty high on my list of priorities. After all, it was two-thirty a.m. and I had to go to work in a few hours. I also felt we'd pretty much run the gamut as far as re-enacting the raunchiest of *The Canterbury Tales* was concerned but, not wishing to be a party-pooper, I opened my eyes wide and let an inquiring little smile play around my lips.

'I don't know, Harry, what would you like to do?'

'Well, how about a little shave?' he asked, innocently enough.

A shave? I sat up and stared at him. What on earth did he mean? I thought I had shaved. I felt my legs . . . fine. One or two bristles, but that was only to be expected considering the time I'd been given to get ready. I frowned. Under-arms! I gasped in alarm, had I forgotten? Was I sitting in Harry's bed like an Italian shot-putter, unmanageable pits flowing on to his whiter-than-white Conran bed linen? My hands shot under my arms. No, false alarm, smooth as a baby's bottom. So what did he mean, a shave? I looked at him quizzically, keen to learn.

'Down there Polly.' He pointed downwards.

I followed his finger and almost gagged on my tonsils. Down there? A shave down there? What, off? All of them? Surely not! He couldn't be serious. I looked up at him again, wary of falling for a practical joke which would later be relayed to a group of friends in the pub. 'Polly thought I wanted to shave her! Can you believe it?' I studied his face. I'd better believe it. A huge grin was spreading slowly from one ear to the other. Harry had thought of a new game. It was called disfiguring Polly. I gulped.

'So what d'you think?' he asked.

Yes, what d'you think, Polly, eh? Baldy? Eh? What do you think? I stalled and played for time.

'Well, I'm not really sure. I mean won't it be a bit, um, prickly, you know, afterwards? For both of us really?' I didn't want to appear selfish.

'Well, a bit maybe, but it won't take long to grow.'

'Really?'

Stupid, very stupid. Harry instantly took this mad impulsive 'Really?' as a sign of accord; in fact he obviously regarded it as being tantamount to a 'Yes please!' He jumped out of bed with alacrity.

'Great!' he cried, joyfully making for the bathroom.

With trepidation I listened to him clattering around in there; taps were running, blades were being changed, probably sharpened too. Oh Lord. I peeped under the bedclothes and gave myself a last lingering look. In a trice he was back, stark naked, armed with a large bowl of steaming water, a fluffy white towel, a razor and a mad, Jack Nicholson grin. He arranged his equipment on the bed in an unnervingly practised fashion. I half expected him to pull a pair of rubber gloves out from under the bed.

'Now hold still, Polly, there's a good girl.'

'I've changed my mind!' I squeaked.

'Don't be silly, you won't feel a thing.'

Won't I, I thought, feeling a lot of hot soapy water sloshing around my nether regions? All of a sudden I knew I'd gone past that point. The one you can return from. Harry was humming a merry tune as he went about his business, 'Tum-ti tum-ti tum-ti tum.' I dared not move. I lay there as if I'd been turned to stone, not moving a muscle, not even lifting my head from the pillow to view the operation because *what if he slipped*! Yes, dear God, what if his hand slipped a millimetre? It just didn't bear thinking about.

'More soap!' cried Harry joyfully, and I looked up to see him trotting off to the bathroom for supplies, whistling away, happy in his work.

I took a sneaky look down. Great Scott! I was receding rapidly; in fact I was half bald. I looked about eight years old on one side and twenty-two on the other. Maybe, I thought desperately, maybe if he stopped now I'd still be in with a chance. Maybe I could sweep one side across to hide the bald patch, yes, that's it! That would do the trick!

Too late. The demonic barber was back again, a razor shining in his hand and madness glinting in his eye. I thought long and hard of England as he deftly completed his task before giving me a wash and . . . no, no brush up this time.

'There you go!' he said, busily putting away his equip-ment. 'All finished!'

I sat up and gazed down at the alien territory below my tummy. Was that me? And if so where were my knickers – quick, it was obscene! Ah, there they were on the diving board. I grabbed them and whipped them on inside out.

'Polly, don't . . .' He pulled at them; I pulled back. I won.

I sat there in my knickers, forcing a smile.

'So what do you think?' he grinned. 'Something for the weekend, madam?'

'How about a toupee?' I said with forced jollity, rallying a brave smile.

'So you like it?'

'Oh yes, it's great, yes, thanks a lot!'

Should I tip him? I thought wildly. I mean, what does he expect? He deprives me of my womanhood with one quick flick of the wrist and wants to know what I think. I think I'm going to cry, that's what. Tears were welling. One even escaped down my cheek. Harry spotted it.

'Oh Polly, what's wrong? Don't you like it? You should have said!' He put his arm around me. 'You are an old silly!'

Yes, I am, aren't I? But then I'm in love, and love makes us do crazy things. I snuffled a bit and nuzzled into his shoulder.

'Look, don't worry. If you don't like it, it'll grow soon!' he said cheerfully.

Now where had I heard those words before? They sounded very familiar. Ah yes, that was it, about twice a year at my hairdresser's. Of course, it was all just a bad dream and in fact Harry was just Raymond in disguise, taking two inches off my split ends before I left, as usual, in tears.

'Yes, of course it will grow,' I smiled bravely. And it'll hurt like hell too, I thought grimly.

When I woke up the next morning I realized he'd made a pretty awful job of it too. I already had the makings of designer stubble. George Michael, I thought, would be proud of that. Harry wasn't.

'Oh sorry Polly, I've made a bit of a mess of that, haven't I? Tell you what, I'll have another go.'

I stood my ground very firmly this time and clutched my George Michael possessively. 'No bloody fear.'

I pulled the bedclothes around me. Harry looked slightly miffed. 'Polly, really . . .'

Don't upset him. 'I mean, no thanks. Thanks awfully, jolly kind of you to offer, but no more, thanks all the same.'

He accepted this, albeit sulkily and reluctantly, but he accepted it, and anyway he was late for work.

'Oh well, if you must go around looking like a diseased hedgehog,' he said as he jumped out of bed.

Yes, I must, I thought. It's all your fault, but I must, if I want to stand any chance of looking like a normal twenty-two-year-old again, that is. Thank God I wasn't in a rugby team or something. At least I wouldn't have to suffer the indignity of communal showers.

Harry bathed quickly, then raced around the bedroom throwing his clothes on while I dragged myself out of bed and into the bathroom. I peered blearily into the mirror and lanced a spot before it even had time to surface. Splat. Harry appeared just as I was cleaning it off the mirror.

'Must dash, darling – doing a spot of housework? Thanks so much, the washing-up needs doing if you've got a moment. See you in a day or two.' He kissed me noisily, goosing me at the same time. 'Bye Polyester!'

'Bye!' I called down the stairs after him, wishing for the millionth time I'd never told him that the 'E' in my initials stood for Esther. It had been a practical joke of my father's way back in the swinging sixties when I'd been born. A friend of his had given his daughter the singularly groovy name of Silk, so Daddy, for a laugh, had called me Polly Esther. What a wag. Stupidly I'd told Harry, who'd laughed like a drain and couldn't leave it alone. Ah well, my fault again, I suppose.

I dragged myself away from the mirror and looked at my watch. God, eight forty-five already, I didn't have much time. I had a quick shower, jumped into my clothes, and set about my weekly task of looking for 'signs'.

These 'signs' were unspecified in appearance, but could take the form of jewellery – perhaps a pair of earrings or a necklace; scent bottles; clothing – especially underwear, anything of that nature; all of which would have sent me completely ballistic. Thus far I'd never found anything, but one could never be too careful and I always had to look.

It wasn't a long job, because Harry had such a trendy minimalist flat with very few searchable places. A couple of cupboards, one or two drawers, no shelves. His walls were full of urgent white space with just one or two obscure pictures hanging in strange places, like near the skirting boards or above a window. The floor was polished and wooden and bits of twisted chrome or knotted leather were dotted about here and there making statements, about what I don't know. Occasionally you'd come across something made of both chrome and leather which could be a chair or a sofa, but was certainly uncomfortable. It wasn't my sort of flat at all but, because it was Harry's, I bullied myself into thinking it was beautiful.

Consequently, the search for 'signs' was really confined to the bedroom and the bathroom. I went through both with a fine-tooth comb, terrified of what I might find but totally unable to stop myself.

There was the usual dried-up lip gloss in the bathroom cabinet and the tarnished silver bracelet in the second drawer down in the bedside table, but they both pre-dated me, so that was OK. No letters, no earrings, no scent bottles; in fact no sign at all of any other female visitor. Good.

Feeling much perkier, I threw a cup of tea down my throat, made the bed roughly, almost washed up but just managed to stop myself, grabbed my handbag and charged off to work, putting my lipstick on as I ran downstairs.

Chapter Four

Pippa was rolling her eyes and gesticulating madly when I arrived panting like a dog at nine forty-five a.m.

'He's been waiting for you since nine-thirty!' she hissed, jabbing her finger in the direction of Nick's office.

'Oh Christ!' I wriggled out of my coat, leaving it where it fell on the floor, and dashed into his room, grabbing my shorthand book on the way.

'Sorry, Nick,' I gasped as I flopped down on his leather sofa. 'I had a bit of trouble with the tubes.'

'For someone who lives two tube stops away you seem to spend a hell of a lot of time commuting,' he said sardonically. 'Anyway, let's get on, I've got a lot to do today. Letter to Dick Appleby. Dear Mr Appleby, Further to our conversation yesterday . . .' and he was off.

He paced around the room, talking to the walls, the window, the carpet, his shoes, dictating like a steam train while I scribbled away like mad, trying to keep up.

'Slow down!' I screeched in desperation when I was at least a paragraph behind. I was fast, but I wasn't that fast.

He stopped pacing and turned, surprised. Then he grinned sheepishly. 'Sorry – getting a bit carried away.'

'Can't imagine that ever happening,' I said without thinking, and then blushed, instantly wishing I hadn't said it.

Nick raised his eyebrows. He looked at me inquiringly,

a slight smile playing on his lips. 'Oh really? It's something you've thought about then, is it?'

'No, of course not.' My blush deepened and spread to my neck. I squirmed around uncomfortably on the sofa. Well really, this was most unlike Nick. Indulging in friendly banter and sexual innuendo first thing in the morning, or for that matter at any time of day. Whatever was the matter with him? I glared studiously at my notebook and let my hair fall over my flushing face.

He grinned. 'Right! Well, I'll try to go a bit slower then.'

He set off again at a slightly more sedate pace, and then the telephone rang. It was our media buyer. I doodled on my pad as I waited, and drew a rather unflattering picture of him. It just showed, though, I thought, as I added a large and rather phallic nose to my portrait; when he loosened up a bit he could be almost human. I drew a pair of bushy eyebrows, Dennis Healey-style, and studied him as he sat in his big leather chair, sideways-on to the window. His profile jutted out against the skyline of tower blocks behind. It had to be said that his nose was definitely on the large side, but then again his jaw was very square, which seemed to balance it. The eyes were deep set and slightly slanted, and his hair was thick, straight and very dark. Somehow it all worked rather well if you liked a lot of angles on your man. Personally I was much more into soft, boyish good looks with melting baby-blue eyes and honey-gold hair. Funny that.

Nick was issuing instructions down the phone in a quiet, authoritative way, his voice deep and thoughtful. A lock of dark hair flopped into his eyes and he pushed it back impatiently. Suddenly he swivelled round in his chair to consult his diary and caught me staring at him. He smiled. He smiled! I mean, for God's sake, whatever next? And not just a little twitch, a dazzlingly broad grin. Good grief, perhaps he was flesh and blood after all, and not just a collection of old memo pads and documents held together with paper clips. That smile had definitely been directed at me, hadn't it? I had a quick look over my shoulder just to make sure – no, there was definitely no one else here.

Well well. Could it be that he was finally coming round to the discreet and subtle charms of one Polly McLaren? Had a beam of sunlight darted through the window and lingered becomingly on my blonde curls for a moment, making them shine like spun gold and reminding him of a cornfield in summer perhaps? Had he at last noticed my finely chiselled features, my sparkling eyes, and that attractive dusting of freckles over my pert little nose? Odd that he'd never noticed all this before, but no matter. He'd got there in the end. And if it was going to make him all smiley and agreeable, I would obviously have to draw more attention to my assets, thereby ensuring myself an easier, happier, and hopefully bollock-free working environment.

First a smile, heavens, whatever next? Intrigued, I carefully arranged myself in what I believed to be a seductive manner. I rested my elbow on the back of the sofa and balanced my chin on my hand. Then I curled my legs up beneath me in a kittenish style, failing to notice that I'd also curled some papers up with my feet. Once in position I sucked my cheeks in and stared moodily out of the window, pouting slightly as I sucked the end of my pencil.

I made sure I could still see him out of the corner of my eye in order to clock his reaction and – good grief! He was doing something with his hand, flapping it around from side to side, could it be – yes, he was, he was *waving* at me. How odd! Gosh, he was really letting himself go now. Well there was nothing else for it, was there? Rude not to. I raised my hand and fluttered back, eyes wide, smiling encouragingly. Was that OK, I wondered? This waving lark was a new one on me. Winking yes, smouldering looks, fine, I could cope with all that, but waving? He barked a final order down the phone, making me jump slightly, and slammed the receiver down.

'For goodness sake, Polly, stop lolling around over those papers. I've got to sign them later.'

He flapped his hand again, gesturing for me to move. Oh Christ!

'And sit up properly, please, you're not at home now.'

Bastard! I flushed furiously and sat bolt upright. Who did he think he was, my father?

The telephone call had obviously put him in a filthy mood. His brows were knitted together now and a thundercloud settled in its usual position on his face.

'Right, let's go again. Dear Mr Hutchinson, Please find enclosed a pre-production schedule . . .'

Once again we raced off at breakneck speed, and this time I didn't have the nerve to slow him down. Luckily, I was saved by the bell again, and I scribbled away, making up lost ground as he answered the phone.

'Yes?' he shouted impatiently. God, he was charming. 'Oh it's you, sorry, darling.'

Darling? I felt like Dr Spock as my ears sprang into

action. It was obviously the bird, Serena. I kept my head well down, pretending I was still writing.

'I know I said I would,' he was saying wearily, 'but honestly, I'm so snowed under here I'll probably be working till about midnight.'

I carefully studied the spiral binding in my notepad. A low profile was all-important if I was to go unnoticed.

'Well, can't you go on your own, or get Hugh to take you?' He was irritated now, and so was she, judging by the long silence at this end as he listened to the monologue. The Hugh suggestion had obviously gone down like a cup of cold sick.

'Look, I said I'd try, I can do no more. I'll ring you as soon as I know how long I'll be, but don't bank on it because I think it's highly unlikely. For one thing –' He broke off suddenly, remembering I was still in the room. He put his hand over the mouthpiece.

'Polly, if you don't mind, we'll carry on with this later.'

I nodded, smiled sweetly, and went back to my desk, closing his door softly behind me.

'Serena saved my bacon,' I said to Pippa, who was buried in *Harpers & Queen*. 'He was going for the world shorthand speed record in there.'

'Mmmmm . . .' she murmured as she stared longingly at London's twenty most eligible men, salivating slightly as she digested the profusion of titles, bank balances and good looks assembled before her.

'I can't imagine him with a girlfriend,' I said, flicking through a pile of TV scripts that had been put on my desk for typing. 'I wonder what she's like.'

'A bit of a handful, by all accounts,' said Pippa, licking

her lips greedily as she dissected one particularly affluent viscount. 'Keeps him on his toes.'

'Really? Well he certainly wasn't giving an inch on the phone. I wonder if she lives with him.'

Pippa didn't answer. She was miles away – in Dorset, in fact – walking slowly up the aisle of a private chapel on her father's arm. Resplendent in an ivory silk wedding dress, a flurry of little bridesmaids behind her in matching ivory with apricot sashes, she smiled shyly at her guests from beneath her veil. As she neared the altar, the organist reached his crescendo and her viscount turned to watch her, bursting with pride at her beauty. She smiled at him serenely . . .

'I wonder what she looks like,' I mused.

But Pippa was still walking, her head held high to Purcell's 'Trumpet Voluntary'.

'I shouldn't think she's much of a beauty,' I went on. 'Blue-stockinged I expect, with buck teeth and a smattering of acne.' I giggled.

Pippa stuck her finger firmly in the viscount's bank balance, determined to keep her place. 'You know what she looks like,' she said, tearing herself away from her future husband for a second.

'I don't. I've never met her.'

'No, but you know what she *looks* like.'

'What d'you mean?'

'Serena Montgomery, you've seen her in films, haven't you?'

'Serena Montgomery! Nick Penhalligan is going out with Serena Montgomery! I don't believe you!' I shrieked.

'Shh, he'll hear you. He's been going out with her for ages.'

'Good grief! How did he meet her? What does she see in him? Are you sure, Pippa?'

But Pippa was already in her receiving line, a countess now, standing next to her husband and graciously greeting all her friends – particularly those friends who thought themselves rather grand and who, at one stage or another, had snubbed her, left her off their drinks party lists, or failed to send a Christmas card, and who, at a later date, would no doubt be grovelling to be guests at her balls and shooting parties. She smiled at them benignly, tiara twinkling.

I left her to her dreams as I picked my jaw up from somewhere around bra level, digesting this bombshell. Serena Montgomery, no less! Miss Montgomery was a startlingly beautiful English actress who had up and come at the tender age of about twenty-five. She only appeared in frightfully tasteful arty films, usually English or continental, and had achieved her fame without getting her hands dirty with any gratuitous smut or violence. She was extremely successful and extremely sought-after, and Nick Penhalligan, my boss and cross to bear on a daily basis, was going out with her! My mind was boggling so much I thought it would boggle out of my earholes.

I simply had to drag Pippa away from her wedding reception. 'But what on earth does she see in him?' I repeated.

'Well, you know, he isn't bad looking, Polly, and he's probably totally different out of the agency. I mean, you work for him, so you're bound to be jaundiced.' She looked thoughtful. 'I think he's rather cute, actually, and, you never know, he might be a demon lover.'

'Demon lover! That lump of rock-solid granite in there. He hasn't an ounce of sensibility! Are you mad?'

I shook my head in disbelief and began to bash away at my scripts. As I waded through coffee plantations in Kenya, where the highly optimistic creative team had set their commercials in the hope of wangling a trip abroad, my thoughts oscillated between Nick and Serena and, just for a change, Harry. I went over our little débâcle in the restaurant. I hadn't forgotten. I was determined to find Rachel Thingamy, just to show him. Just to show him what, I wasn't sure, but just to show him something.

Every so often I caught a glimpse of Nick through his glass door, scribbling away. I tried to imagine him in a clinch with Serena Montgomery. Hidden depths, all right. I was jolted out of my daydreams by the telephone. It was Lottie.

'Polly? It's me. Listen, I completely forgot, Caro's coming round for supper tonight and I haven't got any food. You couldn't be an angel and get something on the way home, could you? I'm up to my eyeballs here.'

'Sure, I'll go to Safeway's.'

'Great, get a lasagne and some salad stuff. How was last night?'

'Brilliant,' I lied. 'We went to –'

'Tell me later, I can't talk now.' Lottie couldn't rabbit on for hours like the rest of us.

'OK, oh Lottie' – I suddenly remembered – 'very quickly, d'you remember someone at school called Rachel Marsden?'

'No, why?'

'Curly fair hair, bit mousy looking, a year or so below us. Have a quick think.'

'Can't say I do, but Caro might, ask her tonight. Polly, I must go. Bye.'

I put the phone down. Of course, Caro might know. She was Lottie's younger sister and would probably have been in the same year as Rachel. Caro made occasional visits to our flat, principally to view the latest collections in our wardrobes and walk off with most of them. I'd ask her.

I left the agency, as is my wont, at five-thirty on the dot – I don't believe in unpaid overtime – and made my way to Safeway. Wednesday night is late-night shopping and, being in the middle of the King's Road, it takes on the atmosphere of a drinks party rather than a supermarket. I reapplied my lipstick at the door and grabbed a basket. True to form, the aisles were already throbbing with bright young things snapping up dinner party fodder.

A shriek of delight rang out as someone rounded a corner and bashed trolleys over the dog food with a neighbour they hadn't seen for at least a day. There was lots of noisy kissing and, 'Darling! How lovely to see you!' as they compared trolley loads, exchanged gossip and threw in the Lapsang Souchong.

There were always plenty of single men sniffing around, advertising their availability with a solitary cod steak and a packet of frozen peas. Predictable chat-up lines would pop out over the freezers as lone males exclaimed, 'Oh, I see you've got Chicken Kiev. Is that good?' or some such other notable opening gambit, whereupon the lone female would reply, 'Oh, frightfully, haven't you tried it?' to which the response would come, 'Well, I'm not very good with ovens . . .' hoping that the offer of a practical demonstration would come his way.

I always reckoned you could tell a lot by what a man had in his basket – his wire basket, of course. Fillet steak and peas were fine, and a bottle of Sancerre wouldn't go amiss, but it was always a good idea to steer well clear of the Pot Noodles, Carlsberg Special and extra-strength deodorant brigade.

I threaded my way through the usual merry throng, throwing necessities into my basket along the way: avocado pears, gravadlax and quails' eggs, as well as one or two frivolous little luxuries like oven cleaner and washing powder.

Having located the lasagne and salad, I made a detour to a less fashionable part of the shop to chuck in some loo paper, which should have been a necessity but in our forgetful household was often a luxury. It always made a nice change from the *Evening Standard* or Lottie's dressmaking patterns. Maddeningly, they always put the loo paper high up on a shelf above a freezer, so that midgets like me had to stand on tiptoe and pretend to be a tree to reach it.

I was just stretching up and trying vainly to flick a couple of rolls off the shelf, when suddenly I teetered wildly, completely lost my balance and fell, with a mighty shriek, head first into the freezer. I lay there, pole-axed with shock, my nose pressed up against the Arctic Roll, my legs sticking straight up in the air behind me. The freezer was deep and relatively empty and I'd landed at a pretty acute angle; so acute, in fact, that I couldn't move. Jesus Christ,

I couldn't move! And apart from anything else it was bloody cold and my jumper was sticking to the ice.

'Help! Could somebody help me?' I wailed feebly as I eyeballed the Arctic Roll. I waited a second, but didn't detect the sound of pounding feet running towards me, and no helpful hands appeared to be winging their way down, so I desperately tried to rock backwards and heave myself out. I spread my hands on the floor of the freezer and pushed hard. 'Huurmphhh!' Alas! Too much of my vast weight was freezer-bound and, strong and meaty though my thighs are, they didn't have the muscle to lever me out. It was no good, I would have to climb in, turn around, and then climb out again.

I set about this task with a vengeance, curling my legs round and down into the frozen wastes – my skirt at this stage was somewhere up around my earrings. I scrambled to my feet and from here began the tricky ascent up the south face of the freezer.

By now I was aware that, far from being alone as I'd assumed, a small army of shoppers had broken off from selecting their mid-week groceries and were collecting in a gawping, open-mouthed semi-circle around me.

'What's happening?' someone at the back asked.

'There's a girl in the freezer,' came the muttered response from the front.

'Oh, thanks very much, don't help, will you!' I spat furiously at no one in particular, glimpsing out of the corner of my ice-packed, bloodshot eye, an extremely attractive girl who looked terribly familiar. She was laughing her head off.

Puce with shame, I brushed my wet hair out of my eyes, swung a leg over the side, and began to clamber out.

Unfortunately, in my haste, I was unlucky enough to catch the heel of my shoe in a wire basket full of oven chips.

'Bugger!' I shook my foot furiously, straddled, as I now was, over the side of the freezer, but I couldn't for the life of me shake the basket free. Finally, in desperation, I leaned down and wrenched it off, pulling the heel of my shoe off with it. No matter, at least I was liberated. I swung my leg over, knickers no doubt flashing wildly, and landed, pretty unsteadily, on the other side. With shaking hands I straightened out my skirt, pulled down my jumper – which had ridden up to bra level and was covered with little bobbles of ice – and, with my head held high, I turned on my broken heel and marched, or rather hobbled, through the gawping crowd, shopping basket in one hand, broken heel in the other.

By the time I'd arrived at the check-out desk my teeth were chattering like a monkey's, my hair was dripping wet and the ice bobbles on my jumper were beginning to melt.

I slammed my groceries down on the conveyer belt, muttering oaths and obscenities under my breath. The gum-chewing check-out girl raised her eyebrows in surprise as she took in my dishevelled, damp condition. Of all the snooty, stuck-up people – what did they think I was doing in there? Stealing fish fingers? Stuffing frozen peas up my jumper? Jesus, it was unbelievable. I could have died of frostbite and no one so much as raised a finger to help!

Safely back in the flat half an hour later, I wrapped myself in a blanket, poured myself a large gin and tonic, and lit a rather shaky cigarette. When I'd consumed about half of each, I recounted my miserable expedition to Lottie and Caro.

Lottie cried with laughter. 'At least you didn't knock yourself out: you could still be there now, lying unconscious in the raspberry ripple. Imagine someone reaching in for some ice-cream and grabbing hold of your nose or something.' She wiped her eyes with her shirt. 'Oh God, Polly, you are an idiot!'

Caro smiled politely, staring at me with naked incredulity. She was so self-possessed and perfect, she'd be incapable of tripping over a rucked-up piece of carpet, let alone falling into a freezer.

Caro and Lottie were obviously sisters, with their long dark hair, hazel eyes, pale skins and sooty lashes and eyebrows, but Caro was very definitely the beauty. Lottie's eyes were big and round, but Caro's were almond-shaped with long sweeping lashes. Her mouth was a perfect little rosebud and, whereas Lottie was prone to plumpness and had a round, sweet face, Caro was reed-slim with a little heart-shaped face. She had the sort of dark silky hair that looks so good spread out on pillows, and she wouldn't know a split end if it ran her over.

Like her sister, she had an enormous bust, which I didn't envy her for; but, unlike her sister who tried to disguise it with baggy T-shirts and sloppy jumpers, young Caro positively flaunted hers. Most of her tops were snug-fitting clingy numbers, and she was very fond of stretching up and locking her arms behind her head, or lying with her back on the floor, propping herself up with her elbows, chest to the fore.

She didn't have a line on her face, principally because she betrayed very little emotion. When she smiled it was a controlled, tight little smile, like the one she was giving me now. She wouldn't dream of rocking around like Lottie, who was clutching her stomach and roaring with laughter. I am quite sure that Caro has never, ever farted.

Lottie doted on her little sister and spoilt her rotten. Their mother was dead and Lottie had always felt responsible for Caro. Caro took everything Lottie had to offer and, as far as I could see, gave very little in return. Let's just say she wasn't my favourite person.

This evening, as usual, Caro had her eyes firmly on our wardrobes. 'Can I see what you've bought recently, Lottie?' she said, making a bee-line for Lottie's bedroom. I stuck to her like glue. As usual, half my wardrobe was in Lottie's room and vice versa. I didn't want her to get her thieving hands on anything precious.

'Yes, but tell me what you're borrowing,' shouted Lottie, who was glued to an old *Dallas* repeat.

Caro was already riffling through her sister's drawers. I sat on the bed and lit a cigarette.

'Ooh, this is nice, I'll have this,' she said, pulling out the only cashmere jumper I'm ever likely to possess.

I snatched it out of her hot little hands and smiled sweetly. 'Sorry, Caro, that's mine.'

Caro pouted sulkily. 'You obviously lent it to Lottie, it was in her drawer.'

'Yes, but then I know that Lottie won't come home doused in red wine and aftershave.'

'Oh, all right.' She threw it back in the drawer and added cattily, 'Black's a bit old for me anyway.'

I smiled, suddenly remembering that I needed her help. 'I have got a lovely red polo neck you could borrow, though.'

'Oh?' Caro was interested. She tried it on and looked infuriatingly stunning. I stood next to her as she admired herself in the mirror, and then stepped hastily away again to avoid the comparison. My tatty old candlewick dressing gown with make-up stains down the front and holes in the bottom where Wellington had chewed it didn't really stand up against her slimming black ski pants and the red jumper stretched tight across her ample bosom. Neither, I thought, looking at her clean silky hair, did my rather dirty blonde curls, streaked with grease rather than high-lights.

'Yes, I'll take this,' she said, as if she were in a shop. I gritted my teeth, thinking that a please or a thank-you wouldn't be out of place, but since I needed to pick what passed as her brain, I wisely held my tongue.

'Listen, Caro, d'you remember someone at school called Rachel Marsden?'

'Mmmm, vaguely,' said Caro, picking up a skirt of mine and holding it up against herself in the mirror.

'What was she like?'

'Very quiet, brainy, musical, not my type at all.'

That figures, I thought.

'D'you know what she's doing now?'

'Haven't the foggiest,' said Caro, slipping off her skirt and stepping into mine. I prayed it wouldn't fit. 'Why?'

'Oh, someone I know was asking after her. Who were her friends at school, can you remember?'

'She didn't really have many, she was a bit of a loner, but I suppose Sally Lomax was her closest friend. She lives in Paris now.'

'Do you know where?'

'No, but her parents live in Godalming, you could ring them and find out, I suppose.'

Well, that at least was a start. Adam could get in touch with Sally if I got her number for him, but Paris seemed awfully remote.

'Anything else? What about her family?'

Caro took off my skirt which was miles too big for her – a mixed blessing – and sighed. She was getting a bit bored by this inquisition.

'Well, her father is ghastly, I know that. He's a judge, and a pretty Victorian one at that. He doesn't agree with girls having too much education – thought needlework and a few French lessons was good enough for Rachel, can you believe it? Anyway, he dragged her out of school before her A-level year saying she didn't need to pass exams. There was a terrible row, because of course she was so bright. I remember he came up to the school and they were all locked in Miss Harper's study for ages with Rachel crying her eyes out. Anyway, he got his way and Rachel left. Whose is this?' she said, holding up a yellow shirt.

'Mine,' I said wearily. 'Yes, I suppose so, Caro.' She folded it and put it on top of the little pile she was collecting.

Well, this was getting more interesting. And now I came to think about it I vaguely remembered someone's father storming up to school and dragging his daughter out before A-level year. There was quite a row about it. Old man Marsden sounded like a complete nightmare. Not only didn't he approve of very passable boyfriends, but education too. I had one last shot.

'What about the teachers, did she get on with any of them particularly well?'

'Well, she was brilliant at music, played the piano and one of those fluty things, so you might try Mr Saunders. Oh, and she was good at maths too, so that would be Mrs Compton . . . Polly, why are you so interested in Rachel Marsden? She was bloody boring, you know.'

Caro had obviously had enough, so I left it at that and started smearing on a mud face-pack.

'Oh, no reason really, thanks, Caro; oh, and can I have my red jumper back in a couple of weeks, please?' I said without much hope of success.

'Sure.' She gathered all my clothes together and went into the sitting room to catch the end of *Dallas*. Just then the doorbell rang.

'I'll get it,' yelled Lottie.

I padded into the kitchen in my cosy old slippers, trying to keep my face still as the mud-pack began to set like a rock. I was dying to wash it off, but the packet had said ten minutes. I mulled over the information Caro had given me. Quite good for starters; at least I could give Adam a few snippets, I thought, as I shoved the frozen lasagne in the oven.

I lit a cigarette with difficulty, then spotted a rather scrummy-looking chocolate cake sitting on the side. Caro had obviously brought it. I cut a large piece and couldn't decide whether to eat that first or finish my cigarette, so I did both, trying to keep mouth movement to a minimum on account of the concrete on my face. I paddled off down the corridor back to the telly. My slippers were flopping around like boats and I had to clutch my dressing gown like a bag lady because it had long since lost its cord. As I shuffled through the sitting-room door, cake in one hand, dressing gown in the other, cigarette therefore in my rather muddy mouth, I suddenly stopped dead in my tracks. For bounding through the front door, in his own inimitable, puppy-dog style, was Harry.

Chapter Five

Understandably, Harry didn't recognize me at first, but then slowly the penny started to drop. If I hadn't been the freak show, it would have been pretty to watch. His eyes glazed over, his forehead puckered thoughtfully, his jaw fell. Then it dawned. He bent double, clutched himself with his arms, his eyes bulged, his mouth got wider and wider, and he ultimately let rip with an enormous bellow of what I supposed was laughter. So enormous, in fact, was the animal-like bellow he'd summoned up, that poor Harry had to hold on to his stomach to stop it from falling apart at the seams. As he clutched his aching belly with one hand, he grabbed the door frame for support with the other, obviously in imminent danger of losing control of his legs. Was he going to have a hernia?

'Oh God, Polly, you look like – you look like you've just stepped out of a horror movie or something! What's that muck all over your face?' he gasped between convulsions.

I felt like running into my bedroom and sobbing uncontrollably into my pillow, but I kept as cool as I could with my face burning away beneath the mud. Any minute now the bloody thing would melt with the heat. I couldn't actually speak properly but, depositing cake and cigarette in a nearby ashtray, I flashed my brave old eyes, wiggled my hands about Al Jolson style and, old pro that I am, threw myself into a spirited rendition of the opening bars of 'Maa-amie – Maa-amie!' Then I gave him a quick flash of George Michael, just for good measure. When in doubt, play it for laughs. This had him rolling in the aisles.

'Oh God, you look such a sight!' he gasped. 'What is it?'

'It's a face-pack, you berk, haven't you ever seen one before?' I mumbled in my ventriloquist's voice.

'And there was I thinking it was all natural,' he spluttered. 'I didn't realize you had a face-lift every other night, and what an incredibly sexy négligée that is!'

Once again he dissolved into a helpless heap as he took my ten-year-old candlewick on board. I did a catwalk twirl in response and he roared even louder. He was easily pleased. I turned to my flatmate.

'Perhaps you'd get Harry a drink, Lottie?' I said with as much dignity as I could muster under the circumstances. 'Meanwhile, I shall get changed into something less hysterical.'

Lottie, who'd been horror-struck when she first saw me, was now beside herself with giggles. She ran around getting ice and whisky, glad of something to do.

Right on cue, Caro sauntered in with freshly applied make-up, looking as if she'd just walked out of *Vogue*. She was still wearing my red jumper – and good grief! Weren't they my new black leggings?

Harry had collapsed in a heap on the sofa where he was still convulsing but, as she sauntered in, the bellowing ceased, and he looked up in wonder. There was a rather too meaningful silence. His eyes lit up like a pinball machine as they took in one attraction after another. The face – those eyes – that mouth – that figure – those – those boobs! Bloody hellfire, those enormous, gigantic, socking great boobs! The poor fellow tried desperately to tear himself away from the upper torso to smile at the face. Who was this divine creature?

'Caro Hamilton, Harry Lloyd-Roberts,' I said by way of explanation, flipping my hand from one to the other and trying to keep the misery from my voice.

Caro, realizing she'd made something of an entrance, milked it for all it was worth. The saunter became a swagger, a slow, bottom-wiggling, undulating stroll, which finally came to rest in *my* favourite position, propped up against the mantelpiece, back to the fire, chest out, tummy in, etc., etc. She got out a cigarette, lit it slowly and, raising her chin and pursing her rosebud lips, blew the smoke seductively into the air. It was more than I could bear. She did it so much better than I did. With a strangled little yelp which I turned into a cough, I ran for the safety of the bathroom.

I slammed the door and yelped for real, adding one or two muffled wails for good measure. Oh, why had he come? I couldn't have looked more repulsive if I'd tried! I scrubbed away at the face-pack, which wasn't going to relinquish its position easily. I looked around wildly, desperate for a hammer and chisel, and hit upon a nail-file which would do just as well. I chipped and scrubbed and chipped and scrubbed until finally something vaguely resembling a face was revealed, albeit a pretty blotchy one. Oh God, I looked diseased! I frantically slapped on a bit of Polyfilla foundation, added a shaky black line under each eye, and applied the only lipstick I could find – which was Lottie's and too red for me. I whimpered in dismay at my by now trollopy little reflection, and ran a comb through my hair.

Lottie poked her head round the door. 'You'd better get in there quick,' she hissed. 'They're getting on like a bloody mansion on fire!'

'But I look so disgusting!' I wailed.

'No you don't,' said Lottie doubtfully. 'A bit of make-up might help, though.'

'I'm covered in make-up!'

'Oh. Oh well, never mind, just hurry up! You've been in here for ages, he'll know you're upset.'

She was right. I ran into my bedroom, shed the hateful dressing gown, and pulled on a pair of jeans and a jumper.

When I eventually returned, it was quite obvious that Harry wouldn't have noticed if I'd sprung another head, let alone been a little upset. He was reclining in the corner of the sofa with his arm resting along the back, his hand within about an inch of Caro's hair. For Caro had relinquished her position by the fireplace in favour of an altogether more cosy one. She'd curled herself up into a cute little ball, not at the other end of the sofa where most newly acquainted people would sit, but in the middle, right next to Harry. So close – without actually touching, and so snug – without actually snuggling, that she was in danger of disappearing up his armpit. I was in danger of throwing up.

I fought back the bile as it rose in my throat, and forced a bright little smile on to my unwilling face. I sat down on the sofa opposite the happy couple, next to Lottie who, appalled at her sister's antics, was looking decidedly grim. We faced them across the coffee table and watched, spellbound, as the show unfolded before us. A bag of popcorn might have come in handy, but I settled instead for a lungful of nicotine.

Meanwhile, on the Harry and Caro show, the protagonists were busy unearthing mounds of mutual friends as a front for their outrageous flirtation.

'Oh the Watson-*Smiths*!' Caro was saying with lots of Sloaney random emphasis. 'Yes of *course* I know them, they're *really* good friends of mine – I simply *adore* Hugo and Amanda. Gosh, so you're a *cousin*! I'm surprised I haven't met you *before*!'

'They must have been keeping you from me,' murmured Harry, devouring her with his baby blues.

'I quite often go there for the weekend, actually, they have the *most* beautiful house, don't they?' Caro gushed on. 'I must ask them all about you!'

'Don't believe a word they say,' he flashed her his most winning smile. 'It's all lies, every word of it!'

'Ah-ha! Got a bit of a reputation, have we?' She prodded his chest playfully. 'Bit of a playboy, eh?'

I ground my teeth, still smiling broadly.

'Oh well,' he feigned modesty. 'I wouldn't say that . . .'

'I think I'm going to puke,' muttered Lottie *sotto voce* on my right.

Caro giggled. 'Well, I've certainly heard a lot about you from Polly!'

'Oh, really?' Harry grinned. 'Such as?'

'Oh well, I know for instance that you're a stockbroker, and you live in Flood Street, and you've got a beautiful flat, all sort of minimalist and trendy, and you drive a Porsche – oh, and a motorbike, and – oh gosh, all sorts of things!'

'Well, well,' drawled Harry, 'I had no idea I was such a topic of conversation!'

I flared my nostrils most becomingly and made a sort of strangled chicken noise. Thanks, Caro. No, really, thanks a lot. I made a mental note that the red jumper was leaving this flat over my dead body. I pushed the corners of my mouth up again and tested my voice for cracks with what I thought was a surreptitious little hum.

'Hrmmm . . . so what brings you so far from Chelsea, Harry?' I sounded like Kermit the frog. 'Slightly off the beaten track for you, isn't it? I trust you've brought your barley sugars for the journey home?'

Harry pulled a little yellow pill packet out of his trouser pocket and waved it in the air. He grinned. 'Well, talking of sweeties, darling, you forgot your Smarties.'

I flushed unattractively. 'I've got plenty more where those came from, thank you!' I snatched them out of his hand.

'Well we don't want any, ha-ha, cock-ups, do we? I thought it best to be on the safe side.'

Caro giggled.

Typical, I thought, seething: the only thing that gets Harry over to my flat in a flaming hurry is a paranoiac fear of becoming a father. I composed myself with difficulty.

'Well, I'm sure I can rely on you to face up to your responsibilities should the situation ever arise, God forbid; but in the meantime I dare say you'll be wanting to get off to the dinner party at Ransome's – it is tonight, isn't it?' I said sweetly.

Harry had returned his lust-glazed eyes to my jumper, the one I wasn't wearing, but he managed to tear them away for a second. He looked at me in surprise.

'Oh yes, that.' He'd forgotten. 'Yes, I suppose I'd better

go at some stage – don't suppose they'll miss me for a bit, though.'

His eyes seemed to be on a piece of elastic which was inexorably twanging them back to the red cable-stitch. And who could blame the poor boy? For the red cable-stitch was being stretched to within an inch of its life. Caro was uncurling herself languidly from her little ball, yawning widely and str-e-tching her arms up, way, way up in the air, arching her back and sticking her ample bosom out further and further – gracious, there was so much of it, it was almost obscene! She reached the climax of her stretch, gave a little moan, then relaxed her elbows and rubbed the back of her neck, thereby still keeping her assets well to the fore. It was one helluva routine.

'Ooooh, I'm so stiff!' she groaned.

'Really? Perhaps you should have a massage,' murmured Harry.

'Mmmm? . . . I suppose I should really, it's sitting at a typewriter all day that does it. Oooh? . . . gosh, I've got quite a crick in my neck.'

She unfurled her legs, splayed them out in front of her, pointing her bare little toes, then brought them in again to sit cross-legged on the sofa, back ramrod straight now, hands on her knees. Now what? She shut her eyes and dropped her head forward, then she rolled it around rhythmically on her swan-like neck. Round and around it went.

'Mmmm . . .' She sighed in what can only be described as an orgasmic fashion. 'That's better . . .'

By now we were all totally mesmerized. Even Lottie and I had our mouths open. Any minute now she'd slip into the lotus position, or even, I thought in wonder, that one with the ankles behind the ears. Saliva was positively dripping from Harry's mouth, and he was making no effort to hide it.

'Better?' he murmured salaciously, as his boggling eyes roamed around her gyrating figure, savouring the swaying bosom, the tiny waist, the firm thighs spread akimbo on the sofa . . .

'Mmmm? . . . Much . . . a little bit of yoga works wonders, you know. You should try it, it's so relaxing and really easy.'

'Really?' He leaned in, keen to receive his tuition right now if she had a moment. 'D'you, er, practise a lot?'

'Quite a lot. Keeps me supple.'

'I should say . . .' Harry drooled.

'Um, Harry, I thought you were supposed to be going out to dinner?' Lottie burst in desperately, eyeing her sister's contortions with horror.

Caro took a break from the head-rolling routine and opened her eyes wide. 'Oh, I always think dinner parties are so boring. All that talking and not enough action.'

'Well, I suppose some people might find them a little taxing if they're not used to exercising the brain!' I spat in what remained of my voice as I ground my teeth to powder.

'And there's nothing worse than turning up late, it's so incredibly rude, don't you think?' said dear Lottie, jumping up quickly. 'I'll get your jacket, Harry.'

She rushed off and returned in a flash, brandishing the jacket like a matador shaping up to a young bull. Harry drained his glass unwillingly and allowed himself to be helped into his jacket, eyes still glued to Caro. He pecked me perfunctorily on the cheek and patted my bottom.

'Bye Polyester,' he grinned. 'Keep taking the pills.' He kissed Lottie. 'Look after your little sister, Lottie, or someone else will!' He winked at Caro who squirmed and giggled; I tried to ignore the electric current that seemed to be zig-zagging between them. 'Goodbye, Miss Hamilton, it was a great pleasure to have made your acquaintance.'

Caro giggled and simpered, fluttering her hand in a dinky little wave. 'Bye, Harry!'

As soon as he was out of the front door, Lottie rounded on her sister furiously. 'Why didn't you take all your clothes off and wriggle around on the floor? You might just as well have done!'

But Caro was unmoved. 'Don't be silly, Lottie,' she said yawning widely, 'I was just doing a bit of yoga. He is rather cute, though, I'm not surprised you keep him to yourself, Polly. What's happened to your face, by the way? It looks a bit blotchy.'

I didn't trust myself to speak. I stared at her perfect face, the corners of the rosebud mouth turned up in a mocking little grin, and a wave of pure hatred swept over me. I wondered for a moment if I was perhaps about to commit murder. How interesting, I'd never killed anyone before. I looked around for a handy implement, but by the time I'd decided that the heavy china fruit bowl, hurled forcefully and accurately, was just the thing to bash her brains out with, the wave of hatred dissipated and was replaced by one of misery. Why take it out on Caro? I was the one who'd made a comprehensive laughing stock of myself. Why not just kill myself? Ah, so it was suicide, was it? Again, interesting, but not so much fun, I hazarded. Just me, a large tub of paracetamol, and then a wafty little float through the stratosphere in a white nightie. Hang on a minute, a large tub of . . . Suddenly a think bubble appeared over my head – of course! I knew exactly what I was going to do. It was less messy, less drastic, and ultimately more satisfying than either murder or suicide could ever be.

I leaped up and strode purposefully into the kitchen, making straight for the fridge. There was something inside shouting to be let out. Lottie was after me in a trice, five years at school and two in the flat had left an impression. She raced ahead and flattened herself possessively against the fridge door, arms spread out defiantly, shielding it from the imminent onslaught. It was a spirited defence, but doomed to failure from the outset. My hand was already firmly on the handle.

'Out of my way, Lottie,' I said between clenched teeth. 'I don't want to have to hurt you.'

Lottie suppressed a giggle. 'Don't do it, Polly,' she implored, 'he's not worth it!'

'OUT OF MY WAY, LOTTIE!' She stood her ground for a moment, but only a moment. There was a dangerous glint in my eye and Lottie wasn't very brave. She hesitated, then stood aside. I flung the door open dramatically and made for the ice-box. Ahhh? . . . There was my prize, nestling innocently between the frozen peas and the ice-cubes. A family-sized tub of Häagen-Dazs chocolate ice-cream, ready and waiting for just such an emergency. I removed it carefully using both hands, slid a knife around the outside of the precious confection and up-ended it ceremoniously on to a large plate – plop! What a divinely decadent noise. I stood back, arms in the air as if I'd just produced a rabbit from a hat. It got a ripple of applause from Lottie and more giggles. I felt better already.

'There,' I said triumphantly, and then, in case anyone was in any doubt, 'and it's all mine!'

'Not the family-sized, Polly,' wailed Lottie, wringing her hands in mock despair. 'Look,' she delved into the ice-box and pulled out a meagre little choc bar, waving it around in front of my nose like a carrot. 'What about one of these nice big choc ices: that'll do the trick, won't it?'

I brushed it aside scornfully. 'Don't be ridiculous, I'm feeding a crisis, not a minor incident. Now for the topping, ooh look!'

A large slab of cooking chocolate had found its way like magic from the back of the fridge to the palm of my hand. I tore open the wrapper like a five-year-old on Christmas morning, and broke it savagely into little pieces, sprinkling them with greedy abandon over the ice-cream.

'Now, what next?' I murmured thoughtfully. 'Ah yes, the cream.'

I strode purposefully back to the fridge, enjoying myself hugely, and seized a carton. I was just about to pour it all over the top when – oh-oh, not so fast, Polly old girl, take a look at the label. My suspicions were confirmed, it was only single. I sniggered. Lucky I spotted that before it was too late, I thought, as I replaced it and returned with the double. Lottie was eyeing the proceedings with deep concern.

'He's not worth it, Poll!' she cried as I poured the cream

from a dramatic height, making nice big swirly dollops over my feast.

'Now for the nuts!' I cried, ignoring her pleas. I tore open a large packet of roasted peanuts – I could almost see the monosodium glutamate crawling all over them as I threw them on top. I rubbed my hands with glee: that should do it! I went to sit down. But wait a minute now – I paused in mid-sit – had I got enough calories here? I eyed my plateful with suspicion. I had to have at least two thousand five hundred, it was no good going off half cocked.

I got up again and prowled slowly around the kitchen, looking for inspiration, searching for hidden carbohydrates. There was definitely something missing, an elusive little *je ne sais quoi*. I scratched my head, what could it be? Of course! The maple syrup! I rounded on my hapless flatmate.

'Have we got any maple syrup, Lottie?'

'I . . . I . . . I'm not sure, no, I don't think –' So we *had*!

I ran to the cupboard she was so obviously shielding, threw it open, and spied a tin, glinting in the fluorescent strip-lighting. Only about a third of a tin, but no matter. I scooped away, scraping it to within an inch of its life. A little metal poisoning wouldn't go amiss either. I sat down with a spoon poised over the top of the mound. Did I need a tablespoon? I dithered.

Lottie saw my hesitation and misread it. She was beside me in an instant. 'You don't really want to do it, do you, Polly?'

I grinned demoniacally. Did I!

'A moment on the lips, a lifetime on the hips?' she

ventured. I gave her a withering look. 'You'll have to do better than that.'

She tried harder. 'Remember Monica Stewart?'

I remembered, and wavered for an instant, but only an instant. Monica Stewart was far and away the largest girl we had ever known. She'd been in our year at school and we used to fight to sit next to her at lunch so as to marvel at what she put away. Half a steak-and-kidney pudding, mounds of mashed potato, saucepans full of seemingly inedible cabbage, jugs of custard, bowl after bowl full of wobbly pink blancmange: nothing was too much trouble for Monica. And as she ate one could almost see it visibly adding to her enormous bulk. A little more padding on the thighs, one more ripple on the tummy, another chin, perhaps. She, and she alone, could lay claim to the epithet, 'A legend in her own lunch-hour'.

'That was glandular,' I muttered. My spoon was dangerously close and getting closer by the moment.

'OK, OK, your new tartan trousers from Kenzo.' The spoon wobbled like a jelly. 'The ones that cost over a hundred and fifty pounds,' she went on ruthlessly.

Oh that was cruel, very cruel. I'd hardly been able to squeeze into them in the fitting room, but I'd bought them anyway in the hope that a week or two of concentrated dieting would do the trick. I racked my brains for a way out of this one. Of course! The summer was coming, tartan trousers would be much too hot, they'd been a big mistake.

Nothing could stop me now, the green light was on as far as I was concerned. I dug in and scooped up a spoonful of mammoth proportions. Lottie put her hand on my arm as it made its way to my mouth. Good grief, what now? A last-ditch attempt? She stuck her face in front of mine and stared deep into my eyes. 'Think,' she said slowly and carefully, 'think of Caro's long . . . slim . . . legs . . .'

It was done with all the best intentions, but it was the biggest mistake she could have made. I gave a sort of blood-curdling, *Last of the Mohicans* shriek, pushed her hand away, and ladled about two hundred and fifty calories into my mouth. If anything was going to make me eat this, it was the thought of Caro's legs which, coincidentally, were at that very moment strolling nonchalantly through the kitchen door. I eyed them speculatively as they passed by, almost tempted to take a chunk out of one of them with my teeth, but I thought better of it. Not meaty enough.

I tucked in with relish as Caro sat down at the table with us. She looked at the mountain of food with disbelief, and then stared at me in horror as I shovelled it into my willing mouth by the spadeful. She turned to Lottie with eyes like saucepan lids.

'What's she doing?' she asked.

Lottie grimaced. 'Getting her own back.'

'I don't understand . . .' said Caro.

'You wouldn't,' I said, looking at her twenty-two-inch waist.

'It's called comfort food, Caro,' said Lottie.

'But I thought we were having lasagne . . .'

I paused between spoonfuls, ice-cream and chocolate dripping from my chops. 'Change of plan,' I said, spraying her with cream and nuts. 'Not fattening enough.'

Lottie giggled and got a couple of spoons from the

drawer. She handed one to Caro and then got stuck in herself. 'If you can't beat 'em, join 'em!' she cried joyfully, tucking in with a vengeance.

'Atta-girl!' I cried back, crunching on the nuts and imagining for a moment that they were Harry's – only for a moment, mind.

Caro got up from the table in disgust. 'Honestly, this is just too silly,' she said pompously. 'I don't think I can bear to watch such a dreadful display of pigging out. That is what you're doing, isn't it? I mean, what's it all in aid of?'

'You,' I said under my breath, but she'd already left the room for the safety of *Dallas*, where she could identify with the skinny-hipped, lettuce-eating glamour pusses at her leisure.

Lottie and I ploughed on, but I'm happy to say were defeated by at least half of my calorific concoction. We chucked it in the bin then sat back in our chairs, giggling and holding our stomachs. Totally replete. Or were we?

'Lasagne?' suggested Lottie mischievously.

'Clever girl!' I replied admiringly.

She went to the oven and brought it out, a little burnt and frayed at the edges, but still eminently edible.

'Caro, supper's ready!' I called.

She appeared at the door. 'You didn't really eat all that, did you?' she said in amazement.

'Certainly we did,' I replied. 'Just a little starter, and now it's time for the main course.'

She sat down, thoroughly bemused, and we ploughed womanfully through the lasagne, which defeated us none too soon. I staggered back to the viewing room again and sank into a sofa, feeling a million times better for my binge, but knowing I'd regret it later. As I heaved my colossal legs up on to the sofa, I suddenly remembered something. Of course! There was just one other thing I needed to do to get even with Harry. I grabbed the mobile phone and took it into my bedroom.

'Who are you ringing?' asked Lottie to my disappearing back.

'I'll tell you when I've done it,' I said mysteriously.

I gathered together a glass of wine, a packet of cigarettes and an ashtray, and shut the bedroom door behind me. Then I sat cross-legged on the bed and lit a cigarette. Should I ring him? I practised a few smoke rings, which I've never been able to do, and still couldn't. I took a large gulp of wine and rang the number quickly before I could change my mind. At this stage I didn't really have much to lose, did I?

After only a couple of rings a girl answered. 'Savoy Hotel.'

'Hello, could I speak to Mr Adam Buchanan, please?'

I licked my lips nervously as I heard the telephone ringing in his room.

'Hello?'

'Mr Buchanan?' I decided to keep it formal and business-like. 'It's Polly McLaren here. You asked me to volunteer my services yesterday.' Oh God! My attempts at formality had led me to sound like a prostitute. 'I mean, um, you asked me to help – you know, find Rachel and that sort of thing.'

From prostitute to blithering idiot. Get a grip, Poll. I took a gulp of wine.

'Hey, yes, of course!' He sounded keen and excited. 'Did you find anything?'

Ah-ha! I had him dangling on the end of my line all right. I paused, enjoying my brief moment of one-upmanship. I have so few, but I was too soft-hearted to tease him for long.

'Well, I've been speaking to a girl who was in the same year as Rachel at school and she told me a couple of things, but the thing is –' and this had only just occurred to me – 'I thought maybe I should hear the whole story from you before I – you know, divulge anything.'

What if she didn't want to be found? What if she hated his guts and was avoiding him like the plague? He saw what I was getting at immediately.

'Of course,' he said quickly, 'I totally understand. Why don't we meet and I'll tell you all about it – tell you what, have dinner with me tomorrow night.'

Tomorrow night? Dinner? I was rather thrown by this suggestion, but not displeased.

'Er, well – tomorrow might be a bit difficult.' One couldn't be too readily available, and tomorrow was Friday, rather an uncool night to be free. 'How about next week, Thursday perhaps?'

'Thursday would be fine. Why don't we eat here? The Grill Room's very good, shall I book a table?'

Things were looking up: the Grill Room, no less.

'Why not?' I said in an off-hand way, as if I lived in the Grill Room.

'About eight-thirty?'

'Perfect.'

'OK, I'll look forward to seeing you then. Bye now.'

As I put the phone down I felt breathless and strangely elated. It's not every day I meet strange American men for dinner at the Savoy. I leaped off the bed and ran into the kitchen to tell Lottie. She was scraping burnt lasagne into Wellington's bowl who, not surprisingly, was turning his nose up at it.

'He's a Yorkshireman, Lottie, not a bloody Italian.'

'More's the pity,' said Lottie, putting some Pedigree Chum on top to fool him. 'We could do with some hot-blooded continental talent around here.'

'How about a bit of Yankee talent?' I told her about my date on Tuesday.

'Wow!' Lottie was impressed. 'So he's employed you as his private detective, has he? Paying you in kind with a slap-up meal at the Savoy.'

'Why not? I mean, if Harry's out on the tiles every night, why shouldn't I be out with a hunky rich American?'

'Why not indeed?' Lottie narrowed her eyes specula-tively. 'How hunky? How rich?'

I laughed. 'If we don't find Rachel, I'll point him in your direction. He's a redhead, not my type, but quite cute, you might like him.'

'Carrots?' she said warily.

'No . . . more, more russety really, like a red setter.'

'Mmmm . . . bring him home in a doggy bag.' We both giggled as Caro drifted in.

'I think I might go home now. I've left your clothes on your bed, Polly. I thought, you know, you might need them.' She avoided my eyes. 'Anyway, they look better on you.'

Good grief, was this her conscience talking? I met her half-way.

'Have them if you like, Caro, I won't miss them for a week or two.'

'Thanks, but it's OK, I think I'll leave them. Bye Polly, bye Lottie.'

She kissed us both, looking rather ashamed of herself. Lottie went to the front door with her. I think they had a little talk. She came back, biting her thumbnail and looking thoughtful.

'Sorry about Caro,' she said gruffly. 'She asked me to apologise. She's a bit, um, insecure at the moment.'

''S alright,' I said. 'It's not your fault your sister's a tart.'

We giggled and spent the rest of the evening polishing off the wine.

When I went to bed that night, I was surprised to find that for the first time in ages my thoughts didn't revolve around Harry. Instead, my mind was full of Thursday night's *tête-à-tête* with Adam Buchanan.

Chapter Six

The rest of the week passed uneventfully, which was pretty much par for the course in my life, and then eventually Thursday evening arrived. A taxi dropped me off in the Strand exactly ten minutes late, and in my nervous state I overtipped wildly. I ran my hand down the back of my black dress as I got out of the cab, smoothing out the wrinkles and hoping it hadn't creased too disastrously. Linen was always a nightmare. It was also a bit tight and I probably should have taken my pants off to avoid a knicker line, but Lottie had been horrified when I'd suggested it.

'Suppose he notices!'

'He's hardly likely to, unless he crawls under the table and looks up my skirt.'

'Take it from me, Polly,' she'd said, giving me her wise old sage look. 'Some men can just tell.'

That was enough for me: the knickers stayed put. I fingered my pearls as I walked to the Savoy entrance. Should I take them off? Wasn't a little black dress and pearls just a trifle unimaginative? Probably, but they gave me something to fiddle with when I wasn't smoking. They stayed put too.

First stop was the loo. I nipped in and had a quick look in the mirror. Not too bad at all, considering. My skin was surprisingly clear and my eyes looked almost blue in this light. I put my head down and shook it around to jazz up my curls, then threw it back and gave it a blast of hair-spray. I considered the effect. Hey. This could almost be called glamorous. Almost.

Feeling faintly giggly, which might have had something to do with the bottle of wine I'd shared with Lottie for Dutch courage, I pushed through the glass double doors on which 'Grill Room' was written in discreet little gold letters. I remembered the last and only time I'd been here. It was for a sixteenth birthday treat with my parents and two older brothers. I'd been wildly over-excited on that occasion too, and had my first legitimate taste of champagne, my illegitimate tastes being the dregs left behind in the glasses after my parents' drinks parties which I used to quaff with a vengeance. My expensive tastes developed at a tender age.

I strolled in, trying to look nonchalant and hoping to God he was here before me. I had a quick look round, but couldn't see him; mind you, I'm pretty myopic at the best of times. The *maître-d'* cruised up beside me in an instant.

'Can I help you, madam?' he murmured.

'Yes, I'm dining with Mr Buchanan, perhaps you'd show me to his table?' I murmured back, as if I had a bit part in a 1940s film and this was my big line.

Not one eyelid batted. This was obviously the way most people spoke in here. He ran a finger swiftly down a list. 'Ah yes, follow me, please.'

I followed the ramrod-straight, dinner-jacketed back through a sea of tables as we wove our way across the elegant dining room. With its panelled walls, brass fittings and green velvet seats, it could almost be a gentleman's club.

Out of the corner of my eye I spotted Roger Moore having supper with his wife and children. I resisted the temptation to stare, and, anyway, I'd spotted Adam.

He was wearing a beautifully cut charcoal-grey suit with a pale blue shirt and navy spotted tie, all of which did wonders for toning down the red of his hair and bringing out the delphinium blue in his eyes. Things were looking up. He was sitting in the far corner of the room over by the window, and he instantly stood up as I was led to the table. This was a tricky little manoeuvre, as the table had banquette seating so he couldn't push his chair back and he had to maintain a rather uncomfortable skiing position as we shook hands. I sat down quickly to ease the discomfort and he sank back, relieved.

'Hi. It's good to see you, Miss McLaren.'

Oh God, the forties movie was rolling on apace: my fault, no doubt, for being so pompous on the telephone.

'Polly's fine, really,' I said, smiling.

He visibly relaxed and smiled back, eyes crinkling. 'Good. Polly it is. Champagne?'

He gestured towards a bottle cooling in a bucket by our table and, as if by magic, an obsequious little waiter appeared to pour me a glass. I lit a cigarette, the first of many. Christ, this place was so understated it was in danger of not existing at all. A little different from the South Ken wine bars I frequented, where you had to rugby tackle your way to the bar, limbo dance your way to a seat at a table, and have a voice like Pavarotti to stand any chance of being heard. I hoped I wasn't going to get loud and raucous.

Adam was obviously a professional mind-reader. He

grinned. 'I know, it is a bit subdued in here, but I thought it would be easier to talk. I guess you're more used to Langan's or something?'

'Er, yes, something like that' – but cheaper, I thought – 'but this is, um, charming.' Oh stop it, Polly, when have you ever, ever, said anything was charming? I must be nervous. I hid my face in the enormous menu and guzzled the champagne greedily.

'Any idea what you're going to have?' asked Adam. 'The Dover sole's pretty good, but feel free to have anything you like.'

'Oh no, I'll have the sole,' I said, relieved that at least one major decision had been made for me. 'I love fish.'

Fish? Was that really the way to describe Dover sole meunière? We're talking bank-breaking seafood here, Polly, not cod and chips wrapped in newspaper. Oh dear. I sank into the champagne refuge again.

'Two Dover soles it is then,' he said, snapping the menu shut.

The waiter seemed to sense a decision and reappeared out of thin air. Adam ordered for us both with the assurance of a man who'd ordered more meals than I'd had hot dinners. That done, he turned to face me. He put his elbows squarely on the table and fixed me with his steely blues.

'Look, I was thinking, instead of making polite conversation and skirting round the subject for hours, why don't I just tell you all about me and Rachel and get it out of the way? Then we can just forget about it and enjoy the meal, how does that sound?'

I nodded enthusiastically. 'Sounds good to me.' I was

all for enjoying myself, whenever, wherever and with whomever – in the nicest possible way, of course.

He sat back, folded his napkin into a neat little square and took a deep breath. 'OK. Well, I could start with how I met her, but I'm going to go back a bit, so bear with me, it'll make sense in the end, you'll see.'

'OK, fire away.'

He leaned forward again. 'Rachel, as you know, was at the same school as you – St Gertrude's, right?'

I nodded. 'Right, poor thing.'

He shrugged. 'Well, funnily enough she rather enjoyed it. Her home life was pretty non-existent, so I think she was glad to be away at boarding school, that's probably why she did so well. She buried herself in her books in the holidays too, as far as I can gather. I guess there was nothing else to do.'

'Ah well, that's obviously why I did so badly at school. My home life was far too happy by half. Too many treats, parties, outings, ponies, friends – all my parents' fault, of course. I have them and them alone to thank for my lack of O-levels.'

Adam laughed and stopped folding his napkin into squares. Good. I may not be the brightest pixie in the forest, but I can perk up an atmosphere at the drop of a joke or two and I wanted to keep this as jolly and light-hearted as possible. His eyes looked a lot less steely.

'At least it sounds as if you had a good time. Unlike Rachel. She just swotted away at school and, consequently I guess, got straight As in all her subjects. By all accounts she was brilliant at music and maths and all set to glide through her A-levels and then go on to music school. But uh, uh, no such luck.'

I grimaced. 'Enter the wicked father.'

Adam looked surprised. 'You know about this?'

I could have bitten my tongue out. I wanted his version, not mine. 'Oh, I heard vague rumblings from someone in her year, but go on.'

'Well, as you say, enter the father. Wicked is probably a little strong, but reactionary, Victorian and bloody-minded will do just as well. Anyway, right out of the blue he arrives at the school and, bold as brass, insists that she packs the whole thing in and comes home with him. Can you believe it?'

'I can't really, I mean why? It's not as if he couldn't afford the fees or something, just to drag her out for no reason seems crazy.'

'He is crazy. In fact I think he's certifiable. Apparently he had some archaic idea about her turning her hand to a little flower-arranging or needlework – crap like that, something feminine and undemanding. Said he didn't want her turning into a hardened career woman and that educating girls was a waste of time anyway because all they did in the end was get married and have babies.'

'Good grief, he's positively Dickensian.'

'Totally. Well, anyway, Rachel may be a bit timid and shy in other respects, but she's pretty passionate about her music and she wasn't going to take this lying down. By all accounts she put up a hell of a fight, as did your headmistress incidently: she was pretty horrified too.'

'I can imagine. It's not as if she had many star pupils,'

I said, licking my lips as the most enormous Dover sole I've ever seen was put in front of me.

He paused for a second as silver dishes full of juicy little new potatoes and gleaming, *al dente* broccoli florets were flourished around. Adam seemed oblivious to the food. He pushed it dreamily around his plate, then started fiddling with his napkin again. I covered the fish's eyes with a piece of lettuce so he couldn't eyeball me, and tucked in with relish while Adam talked.

'Of course, there was no contest really. Old man Marsden was, after all, holding the purse strings, and Rachel's pleadings were like water off a duck's back as far as he was concerned. Let's face it, he's used to dealing with the criminal classes on a daily basis, so a schoolgirl was no match for him. He'd made up his mind and that was that.'

He picked up his fork again and toyed idly with his sole. I wondered if it would be terribly gauche to offer to eat what he didn't want, and decided on balance it would.

'Was she terribly upset?'

'Devastated. Cried and cried for ages, which rather disconcerted her father. I think he thought she'd sulk for a bit and then toe the line; but she shut herself in her room for days on end, refusing even to speak to him.'

'Good for her.' I was attacking bare fish bones now, and he hadn't even started. I played with my broccoli, trying to make it last a bit longer. The champagne was slipping down nicely, thank you very much, and I was beginning to feel rather lightheaded. Thus far, of course, I knew the storyline. It was the next bit I wanted to hear.

'I guess she decided that all she really wanted was to get away from him, so she asked if she could go abroad for a bit. It was the first time she'd said two words to him for days, and he was so nonplussed he just agreed on the spot, on the condition that she didn't just travel around, bumming and rucksacking, but went to stay with my family in Boston.' Adam reached for the bottle and topped up my glass.

'What's the connection?'

'Marsden and Dad were at Oxford together, they go way back and they've always kept in touch. According to Dad, he wasn't such a bad guy in those days, although it's hard to imagine him being anything other than a complete bastard.' He abandoned his sole and lit a cigarette. I watched longingly as a waiter whipped his plate away.

'So that's how you met her?' I lit one myself to keep him company.

'Right. I was staying with my folks at the time, and they asked me to pick her up at the airport.'

'You'd never met her before?'

'Never. It was her first time in America, and I'd never bothered to look her up when I'd been in England. So anyway, off I went to the airport with "Miss Rachel Marsden" written on a little placard, thinking this was all a bit of a bore and I could be getting on with some work or having a drink with the guys or something . . .'

He paused and slowly blew a long line of smoke over my head. His hand was caressing his wine glass. He seemed to be miles away. 'I'll never forget my first glimpse of her . . .' he said softly.

I smiled wryly. Now come along, Mr Buchanan, I thought, you're not going to tell me you were dazzled by her beauty or something, are you? I mean, judging by that photo you showed me she's OK looking, but she's not going to stop the traffic. Do you, perchance, carry a white stick?

If he did, his telepathic powers made up for his bad eyesight. He smiled ruefully. 'OK, OK, I know what you're thinking and you're right, she's no great beauty, but Polly' – he leaned in earnestly – 'you should have seen her that day. Not beautiful, I grant you, but still pretty enough and so young and innocent-looking as she came through the gate with her baggage. She looked – I don't know, it sounds so corny – lost and wide-eyed, her pale, worried little face searching for a friendly face: she just looked so vulnerable. I knew it was her without even having to hold up my sign. She was wearing her school coat . . .'

I nose-dived into my champagne glass at this – Christ, her school coat? That dreadful old green thing? Did this girl have no sense of style whatsoever? Next he'd be telling me she wasn't wearing any make-up.

'. . . and that ridiculous scarf you all seem to wear. Sounds crazy, I know, but I reckon I fell for her almost immediately.'

'How romantic,' I murmured. I was totally unconvinced, but none the less made a mental note to dig out my old school coat and try out the vulnerable look. I couldn't help thinking it would need a good six inches off the hemline and not a lot of clothing underneath to make it anywhere near alluring, though. I was enjoying myself hugely now, lapping up the champagne and the dialogue with a vengeance.

'So you whisked her off her feet there and then?'

'Well, not exactly, but I had some time on my hands so

I spent the next week or so showing her round Boston, going to concerts and museums and taking her to my folks' country place by the sea.'

Ah-ha! My ears pricked up. I know all about those empty little cottages in the country. I had the feeling we were coming to a sexy bit.

'Well, one thing led to another, I suppose . . .' He paused, was that all he was going to say? He looked miles away, he wasn't going to go all misty eyed and withdrawn on me, was he?

'And?' I said, breathlessly and shamelessly.

'. . . and . . . within only a couple of days, we were . . . well, we were lovers.'

'A couple of days!' I squeaked. 'What, of her arriving in Boston? Gosh, you didn't waste much time!'

Adam looked alarmed. 'Hey, look, I didn't push her into it or anything, if that's what you're thinking. She was pretty willing, I assure you.'

Ah-ha. So Rachel was the instigator was she? Fast work, kid, and all achieved with a pale face, mousy hair, and an old school coat. I had to hand it to her.

Adam sighed. 'Look. I know it sounds ridiculously soft and unbelievable considering how long I'd known her, but honestly, Polly, I was already in love with her.' He was desperate for me to believe him and I did. I liked the way he said my name, too. Paully.

'Hell, no, it don't sound soft at all.' Why was I speaking with an American accent all of a sudden? And a deeply southern one at that. I cleared my throat and reverted to Queen's English. 'I think it's wonderful, actually. I only wish that sort of thing happened to me,' I added truthfully.

He grinned. 'Well, it had certainly never happened to me before.'

'So you just stayed there? I mean at the cottage? In a romantic little huddle?'

'For a while; then we went home to Boston and I talked to my mom about it. I'm pretty close to her, and she was great about the whole thing, if a little alarmed at first because Rachel was so young.'

'She can't have been more than seventeen!'

'Eighteen, actually, but I agree, still very young, and re-member her father had entrusted her into my parents' care.'

'Serve him bloody well right!' I said, waving my cham-pagne glass around. I was more than a trifle pissed. 'You didn't tell him, did you?'

He grimaced. 'Well, given his rather manic disposition, we decided to keep quiet for a while. I didn't particularly want him arriving at Boston airport bearing a meat cleaver with my name on it. Rachel wrote saying what a terrific time she was having –'

' – but not *who* she was having!' I interjected drunkenly, roaring with laughter at my own pucrile wit.

He smiled. 'Quite.'

It was rather a polite little 'quite'. Simmer down, Polly old girl, I thought. Lay off the juice for a sec or you'll never get to the end of the story. I laid off for precisely one sec before hoovering up again.

'Anyway, the old boy seemed to soften slightly and wrote back saying she could stay on for a bit. Maybe he was feeling guilty about wrecking her academic career, I don't know. Meanwhile we moved back into the house by the sea in Marblehead. He was none the wiser because my parents sent her mail on.'

'Did they mind?'

'A bit, I suppose, but they knew we wanted to be together and they knew he'd come and get her if he ever found out. Mom and Dad are pretty laid back. Rachel couldn't believe them. D'you know she'd never even been allowed to have a date with a boy, even a boy of her own age. Don't you think that's weird? Maybe that's the English way, but Jeez, in the States the kids are dating at about fifteen!'

'Well, I think that's a little early, but even so . . .' I thought of my own relaxed parents who had generally let me do what I liked at that age, providing they met the boys in question and providing I came in at a reasonable hour. I couldn't begin to count the number of times I'd crept up the stairs after a late party, shoes in hand, always to be greeted by my mother's sleepy voice as I got to the landing, 'That you, darling?'

'Yes,' I'd whisper, 'go back to sleep.'

In the morning she'd come and sit on my bed and quiz me mercilessly, wanting to share it all. Who had been there? What had the girls been wearing? Had I met anyone nice? It was all part of the fun of the night before, and I couldn't imagine it any other way. I'd never had to go behind her back – although I have to say, Daddy would have gone into orbit at the thought of me shacking up with some older guy in America. I drained my glass rather conspicuously and it was instantly refilled.

'Sho you lived together?' I was dimly aware that I was slurring my words slightly.

'Yep.'

'How long for?'

'About a year or so, I guess, and then I asked her to marry me. She said yes and . . .'

'Congratulations!' I cried, swinging my champagne glass towards his own unsuspecting vessel and ricocheting off it with a loud clink. I swayed backwards into my seat rather unsteadily. 'Here's to the bride and groom! The happy couple!' I was flying now, and one or two people on the next table were turning round to look. They smiled, probably thinking we'd just got engaged.

Adam laughed, if a little nervously. 'Er, thanks – shall I go on?'

'Pleash continue!' I slurred, making a magnanimous sweeping gesture with my glass and indicating that the floor was all his.

'Well, we talked about the wedding, where it should be – in England or America, how many people we should have, bridesmaids, flowers, etc., and the more we talked, the more we realized there was no getting away from it. We'd have to tell Rachel's father eventually, so we might as well tell him straight away. We could have gone behind his back and just got married, but Rachel didn't want that, and I agreed. I was also quite prepared to wait a year or so if he thought she was too young.'

Even in my inebriated condition, I could see that Adam was looking pretty miserable now. He hadn't even touched his summer pudding, which was a dead giveaway, and he was busy picking the table decoration of rosebuds to pieces.

'So . . . I put her on a plane to England about two weeks ago. That was the last time I saw her.'

He scattered the petals over the tablecloth, rested his

elbows on the table and ran his hands through his hair. I sat quietly, sensing no smart-arse remarks would be welcome.

He sighed and lifted his head. 'I thought she'd ring after a day or so and give me the low-down, and when she didn't I rang her father's place. He just put the phone down on me. I tried again and again, same response each time. I wrote a letter and got no reply. I telegraphed – still nothing. After about a week of this I got on a plane and came over. I was terrified he'd dragged her off to Australia or something.'

He leant back wearily in his seat and still, miraculously, I managed to hold my tongue. I looked down and tried to focus on my hands which, rather alarmingly, seemed to have reproduced. If I wasn't very much mistaken there were about twenty fingers on that tablecloth. I started counting them, to myself you understand, but moving my mouth a lot so I didn't lose count. One, two, three . . .

'I went to his house and he slammed the door on me. I shouted through the letter-box, threw pebbles at the windows, camped outside the house in a hired car. I even' – and here he looked rather abashed – 'I even tried to break in one night, but the place is wired up like Fort Knox. But that's how worried I was about her.'

He was worried, I thought, staring at my hands; what about my bloody fingers? How would he like to have twenty-two of the bloody things, or was it twenty-three? They seemed to be fluctuating all the time as they moved in and out of focus. Better have a recount just to be on the safe side. I'd got up to eighteen when the coffee arrived. I took a large gulp. It had a surprisingly dramatic effect. Hot, black and strong, it surged through my furred-up veins and made a quick dash to my brain where, miraculously, it brought a brief moment of lucidity. I took another slug. Yes, this was definitely doing the trick; lo and behold, a few bruised and battered little grey cells were surging into action and making a dramatic comeback. Now what were we talking about? Ah yes, of course, Rachel; we were looking for Rachel.

'But she could be anywhere!' I managed to articulate and, flushed with success, roared on to form yet another sentence. 'She could be, well – in the country, abroad' – I gestured wildly round the room – 'in here even!' Should we look under the tables, I wondered thoughtfully? Might that not be a start?'

'She's not abroad and she's not in the country,' said Adam decisively. 'She's here in London.'

'She is? How d'you know?'

'Because I've seen her.'

This shock tactic worked better than any black coffee could.

'You've seen her! Where?'

'In a taxi. She was with her father in the back of a taxi in Piccadilly. I was stuck in a jam going in the other direction, so there was nothing I could do – but it was her all right.'

'Did she see you?'

'No, she was looking straight ahead. I just remember how pale and sad she looked.'

'Oh!'

God what a mess. What a complete bastard her father must be. I drank a whole cup of coffee down in one and suddenly felt tolerably sober. I looked at my hands. Ten. What a relief: the offspring had flown.

'So where else have you looked, now you know she's in London?'

'Well, apart from laying siege to their house in London, I've waited outside court to try to speak to her father; but that's impossible, he goes everywhere by chauffeur-driven car, which whisks him away before I can get to him. He never walks anywhere, so there's no chance of tripping him up in the street.'

He rubbed his eyes. He looked tired. 'Two days ago I flew to Paris.'

'To see Sally Lomax?'

'You know her?'

'I don't remember her, but I asked around and found out she was Rachel's best friend.'

'Her only friend really. I was desperate and I thought Rachel might have managed to get a message to her. She hadn't, but she'd written Sally a letter on the plane going over to London, obviously posting it at the airport. Sally gave it to me.' He smiled ruefully. 'She said it was more mine than hers anyway.'

Adam took his wallet out of his breast pocket and produced a thin sheet of paper that had obviously been smoothed out, read and re-read over and over again. I spread it out on the table and concentrated like mad. I seemed to be focusing reasonably well. It was written in a round, schoolgirlish hand.

Dear Sally,

If my writing's terrible it's because I'm scribbling this on a rather bumpy plane journey to England, so bear with me. Fabulous news, you'll never guess — Adam's asked me to marry him! I'm so thrilled I can hardly believe it. I've been mad about him from the

moment I saw him – when he picked me up at the airport, in
fact – and now I'm going to be Mrs Buchanan. Isn't it fantastic?
He's so divine, Sally, I know you'll adore him. He loves the same
sort of music as me, a real bonus, added to which he's incredibly
good looking (well, I think so, but then I'm biased!).

I couldn't help looking up at this point. He caught my eye
and grinned sheepishly. I grinned back and read on.

I can't wait for you to meet him; we're actually thinking of coming
to Paris for our honeymoon, but before that I want you to come to
London and be my bridesmaid. Please say you will. I'll let you
know when, but it'll probably be around the end of September.
   The only dark cloud on the horizon is the one waiting for me at
Heathrow. I'm flying home to ask Daddy for his permission, and
you know what he can be like – help! We'll go ahead and get
married whatever he says, but it would be so much nicer to have
his blessing. Anyway, I'll let you know how it goes. Must dash, the
inedible plastic lunch is on its way round. Write soon,

Masses of love, Rachel.

I folded it in half and handed it back to him. 'Well, that's
one of the leads I had for you blown. I should have realized you'd know who her best friend was. The only other
thing I discovered was that she got on very well with a
couple of teachers at school. I could ring them up and see
if either of them has heard from her, if you like?'
   'If you think it might help, I'd be grateful.'
   He paused and looked at me steadily for a good ten
seconds. I instinctively put my hand to my face. What?

Had my make-up slipped? Did I have eyeshadow on my nose? Lipstick on my teeth? A bogey? What? He leaned forward and kept those steely blues boring into my shifty greens. What! I thought desperately, what is it?

'Polly, would you do something for me?'

'How can I possibly refuse?' I burbled, relieved that he'd finally spoken and feeling decidedly giggly.

'Would you go and see her father for me?'

'What! Me!' I nearly ate my coffee cup. 'Why?'

'Because he might talk to you. You can say you're an old schoolfriend, which is half true, and ask him if he knows where she is. Say you're organizing an old girls' reunion or something. He'll never suspect you're anything to do with me.'

He had a point there, but did I really want to get that involved? Up to now it had been a bit of a laugh, but I wasn't sure I wanted to do battle with a crusty old judge with a meat hook.

I hesitated and tried not to look at Adam's eyes, which were pleading with me to say yes. Damn. I looked at them. 'OK,' I said weakly, 'I'll have a go.'

His whole face creased delightedly and his mouth grinned so hugely it almost split his face in half. He gave me such a hearty slap on the back I thought my Dover sole was going to reappear on the plate in front of me.

'You're a hell of a girl, Polly!' he boomed joyfully. 'A hell of a girl!'

Well, aren't I just? He seemed so overwhelmed by my agreement that it occurred to me he probably hadn't reckoned he had a snowball's chance in hell of getting me to do it. Ah yes, but then he'd reckoned without the sucker of all suckers, Miss Polly McLaren. No job too small, no fee too low, all assignments considered. Need a secretary you can really wipe the floor with? I'm your girl. Looking for a girlfriend you can park inside your front door with 'please wipe your boots' printed on her back? Look no further. Got a little problem with an axe-man of a judge? You've come to the right place. Polly McLaren's the name and gullibility's the game.

'This is where he lives,' Adam was saying, eagerly scribbling the scene of my death on a piece of paper. 'You'll obviously stand more chance of finding him in at the weekend or in the evenings . . .' When it's nice and dark, I thought, and when my blood won't show up quite as much on the carpets. 'Just keep your head' – no chance, it'll be rolling around on the floor, severed inexorably from my neck – 'and I know you'll be fantastic. I can't tell you how grateful I am . . . Tell you what, let's celebrate. More champagne!'

God, I had made him happy, hadn't I?

'Oh no, I couldn't possibly.'

''Course you could!'

'No no, really, I'm sobering up nicely on this black coffee.'

'Just a couple of glasses.'

'Oh well . . .'

'Waiter!'

The deed was done. He obviously thought I doth protest too much and he was absolutely right. All that making other people happy lark had given me one hell of a thirst. The bottle arrived. The one that would pour the glass too far. The one that would send me tumbling over the edge.

We both relaxed considerably as we quaffed the champagne. He was now doing his damnedest to keep up with me, but I could tell he was an amateur and, anyway, I had a two-bottle start on him. I started to tell him about Harry — trying to make him sound like the best thing since filtered cigarettes, but somehow he ended up sounding like a bit of a jerk. Surely I wasn't experiencing a touch of *in vino veritas*?

'Sounds like a bit of a jerk to me,' said Adam, echoing my thoughts, which I must say I thought was a bit strong considering he was talking about the father of my unborn children.

'What about the guy you work for,' he said, 'the guy I met on the stairs. He seemed nice enough, and isn't he what you girls would call a hunk?'

'Ah, now you really *are* talking jerks.' I warmed to my favourite subject and gave Adam a thumbnail sketch of Nick, pitching it somewhere between Paul Daniels and Saddam Hussein.

'And he's the boss, is he?' asked Adam.

'Yes, he set the place up about five years ago with a chap called Hugh Waters, but Waters doesn't have much say, he's just a sleeping partner. Apparently we're doing really well, as small agencies go. Nick's pretty bright, but he will spoil it by charging around barking out orders and instructions as if he owned the bloody place.'

'I thought you said he did.'

'Oh. Yes I did, but he doesn't have to show off about it, does he?'

I fumbled for my cigarettes. My fingers had once more gone forth and multiplied, and it was hard to remember which were the ones I usually used to pick things up with.

Adam laughed. 'You English really crack me up. It's considered bad form for anyone to make money and be a success, isn't it? What accounts do you have?'

We took an appropriate commercial break here as I seemed to be hell-bent on massacring cigarettes as they came out of the packet, but third time lucky I managed to extract an unbroken one. Hand-to-mouth coordination was becoming a real problem now, as someone appeared to have moved my mouth. It certainly wasn't in its normal position. Luckily Adam came to the rescue, turning my cigarette the right way round so I didn't light the filter, sticking it in my mouth and lighting it for me. It occurred to me that he could have gone the whole way and smoked it for me too, but I guess that was asking too much. I inhaled deeply. Now what had that last Brain of Britain question been about? Our accounts? Really? At this time of night? God, he really knew how to tax a girl: was he trying to kill me with a mixture of alcohol and Mensa?

I opened my mouth, hoping the words would just come out of their own accord: these accounts were tongue-twisters at the best of times. Nothing happened, so I decided to go the whole hog and recite them in Swedish, or was it Russian?

'Well, wev got Sujuper Roztie Cwoffee, um Lemonjina Sjoft Drinkz, um . . .'

Adam magnanimously let me off the hook. 'OK, OK,' he laughed, 'some other time perhaps. Somehow I think it's time to make a move.'

'You're going to make a move?' I looked alarmed, this guy was indeed a fast worker, and a fickle one at that.

'Home, Polly,' he explained patiently. 'I think it's time we were going.'

Ah yes, going. This was the moment I'd been having mixed feelings about. What remained of my brain definitely knew it was time to leave, but I wasn't sure how my legs were going to take it or, more particularly, my knees. The table was pulled out for us, and I tested them gingerly as Adam instructed the waiter to add the bill to his room tab. The knees weren't too bad, but the top half of my body seemed to have been caught up in a hurricane: it swayed dangerously from side to side. Had someone left a window open in here? I looked around suspiciously. Adam caught me as a particularly strong gust blew me sharply to the left, nearly knocking me over. I clung on to his arm and, slowly, we began the tricky little exercise of navigating our way out of the restaurant. Some bastard had thoughtfully placed an obstacle course in my way, but I rose to the challenge and meandered through a sea of tables, chairs and fellow diners with surprising agility, although I must say Adam's arm was necessary as well as decorative.

This time I couldn't resist cocking an eyebrow at Roger Moore, who didn't cock one back, which I thought was pretty unsporting. I stuck my tongue out at him. Yeh, I can be rude too, you know, I thought.

Just as we were lurching past the penultimate table, I spotted a very familiar figure in black tie walking into the restaurant. I knew him well but couldn't quite place him; nonetheless I greeted him like the old friend he undoubtedly was.

'Hi there!' I shouted, much to my fellow diners' amusement. I waved cheerily.

'Don't tell me, no – don't tell me, it's on the tip of my tongue?' I went on, bashing my forehead for inspiration. 'You're um . . .'

'He's the *maître-d*',' Adam hissed in my ear.

'May Tradee? May Tradee?' I said loudly. 'No, that's not it, I'd have remembered a sissy name like that. How many men are called May, for God's sake? Don't be ridiculous, Adam.'

'He showed you to the table,' said Adam, forsaking the whisper – what was the point? The whole dining room had laid down their knives and forks with amusement and were damned if they were going to miss anything.

'He showed me a table?' I thought hard. Ah, yes, obviously an assistant from Peter Jones. I was in there so often. 'Adam tells me you once showed me a table!' I cried as I was propelled past him at speed. 'Well, I think that was very sweet of you! Adam wait, I want to thank him, I –'

Somehow I found myself approaching the front entrance. An east wind was whipping around my kidneys as I was escorted from the premises and out on to the street by this burly American. Ah-ha, this was obviously the same wind that had tried to knock me over in the restaurant. Where was it from: Siberia? Were the Russians buggering around with our weather again? Bastards. I wrapped my pearls a little more tightly round my neck for warmth and shivered. A taxi purred up alongside us and Adam swiftly poured me in the back.

'Where do you live, Polly?' he asked.

'Chunder Road.'

He looked taken aback. 'Chunder Road? Are you sure?'
I tried again. 'Chegunder Road.'

'It's all right, mate,' said the taxi driver through his partition. 'That's pissed for Tregunter Road. I'll see she gets home safely.'

Adam grinned and waved me off. I turned round to wave back as the taxi rolled away, and wished I hadn't. The cab lurched round the corner into the Strand and so did my tummy. I clutched the handrail with one hand and my mouth with another. A friend of mine had once thrown up in the back of a taxi after just such an evening, and been forced to sit watching her dinner roll from side to side in the back as the cab lurched round corners with the driver screaming blue murder at her at the top of his voice. I tried not to think about that, nor my brother's joke about a man hailing a taxi and asking the driver if he had room for eight pints of lager and a takeaway curry before throwing up in it. Oh no. I kept my lips tightly pursed as we trundled down the Fulham Road, up Hollywood Road, and finally came to rest in Tregunter Road.

I tumbled out and handed the driver my purse, trusting him not to rob me of all my worldly goods. I certainly couldn't trust myself to try and open the damn thing. He handed it back to me with a grin.

'It's OK, luv, your boyfriend paid.'

Harry? Good Lord, how extraordinary. The taxi driver waved a cheery goodbye before disappearing over the horizon, leaving me to chew on this dramatic turn of events. Harry? Where on earth had he sprung from, and how uncharacteristically generous. I shook my head in awe and wonder as I staggered up the front steps.

Before long, however, I had an even bigger conundrum to consider. Like how to get the key in the front door. How bizarre. The keyhole was much too small for my key and it also refused to keep still, leaping around all over the place whenever I tried to stab it. Stab stab stab. Move move move. Well, this was a bit of a blow to morale. I thought hard. Ah yes, Lottie had obviously changed the locks while I was out. Too many men had been laying siege again, pestering us for dates. I'd have to break in.

I failed, but made so much noise attempting it that the door flew open and Lottie appeared in her nightie brandishing a tennis racket.

'Lottie! Couldn't get in, bloody lock, bloody key . . .' I mumbled, swaying violently. 'Been playing tennis? Little late, isn't it?'

'Get in!' she yelled, dragging me forcibly by the arm. 'I thought you were a bloody burglar! I was just about to bash you over the head!'

She pulled me in, swearing like a trooper and promising all kinds of vile deaths as she pushed me up the stairs, frogmarched me through the sitting room, and propelled me into my bedroom. She deposited me unceremoniously on my bed, where I lay until morning in a deep and blissful coma, boots still firmly on my feet like all good cowboys.

Chapter Seven

When the fire alarm went off the next morning I realized, with a start, that I was dead. More than dead in fact, reincarnated. Because this sure as hell wasn't my body I was lying in. Whoever I'd come back as had got the most enormous tongue: large and furry and much too big for her mouth. At least, I hoped it was a her. All sorts of problems loomed if it wasn't, most of which were either sexual or lavatorial and didn't bear thinking about in my present condition; or, should I say, this body's present condition.

And what a head this person had: full of throbbing, hammering noises which caused the eyes to ricochet around in their sockets quite unnecessarily. I'd have to sort that out when I knew who I was: no doubt there was a little man in Harley Street who could soon put a stop to all this funny business. As for the throat, how could anyone bear to have that amount of sandpaper stuffed down their neck? Or was it birdseed? Whatever it was, it would have to go. This reincarnation lark was a real eye-opener, a real revelation as to how the other half live. The bloody fire alarm was still ringing. The body swung out a hand and knocked it on the head.

An hour later the alarm went off again. Ten past nine, said the clock through blurred vision. My blurred vision. Oh God, I was still alive!

'Jesus!'

I leaped out of bed and instantly regretted it. I groaned and clutched the head that so manifestly belonged to me and sank back down on the bed again. Any form of movement was agony, but move I would have to, unless I was planning on forsaking my present job and swelling the ranks of the unemployed.

I fumbled through to the kitchen, feeling my way along the walls and hanging on to door frames for support. I drank a pint of water, instantly regretted it, and sat down, weak with exhaustion after so much activity, and feeling sure that any second now I was going to be sharing my water with Wellington, who was sitting at my feet looking up at me quizzically, his head on one side. Perhaps he didn't recognize me in my present condition. Let's face it, I'd only just made the connection. God, my head hurt, I must have been drinking for England last night.

I made my way shakily to the bathroom, pausing en route to poke my head into Lottie's room. It looked like the *Marie Celeste*. There was no sign of life but all the lights were on, the radio was blaring, and her curling tongs, I noticed, were just about to burn a hole in the carpet. I switched everything off. She must have left in an almighty hurry; probably overslept after her disturbed night, it occurred to me guiltily.

Ah yes, Lottie. She hadn't been happy, had she? Evonne Goolagong in a winceyette. I giggled. What was it she was going to do to me? Forcibly extract the larger of my intestines – I remember she'd been most precise – string it between two trees and use it as a washing line: a variation on the guts for garters theme, no doubt.

I made it to the bathroom and ran a bath. It was all

coming back to me now. Or was it? There were still some pretty huge gaps, whopping great big chasms, in fact, like what happened between seven o'clock and midnight. I remembered a large Dover sole had been involved somewhere along the line – I clutched my mouth, don't even think about Dover sole – and I vaguely remembered promising to see a judge about a daughter, but I could easily extricate myself from that one. I also remembered making very free with Mr Buchanan's champagne bottle, but had I disgraced myself in the process? I racked my addled brain trying to recall any moments of debauchery, indiscretion or indecent exposure, none of which, I hasten to add, usually feature in my repertoire – well, not all at once. I thought hard. Nah. Not a sausage. I lowered myself gingerly into the bath. I'd obviously behaved impeccably, bringing not one iota of shame upon either myself or *mein* host. What a relief.

The warm Radoxy waters were behaving almost as they'd promised in the advertisement, refreshing the parts I didn't even know I had, or could reach – or was that called mixing my commercials? Anyway, after a brief soak I climbed out, feeling reasonably human and strong enough to face up to clothes and make-up. I pottered into the bedroom.

But not so fast. On closer inspection every single pair of tights I possessed had a ladder in them, and both pairs of trousers were at the cleaners (I didn't count the leopard-skin ones with the chains hanging from them, as I didn't think Nick would find them as amusing as I did). It would have to be jeans. I retrieved them from the bottom of the heap on the floor, pulled them on quickly, and added a black silk shirt that wasn't too disgustingly creased. This clothing lark had taken longer than I'd envisaged. No time for make-up now: it would have to be the natural look.

I grabbed my coat and bag, but as I was running like stink down the passageway to the front door, I was unlucky enough to catch a glimpse of myself in the hall mirror *en passant*. I dug my heels in and skidded to a halt, almost singeing a hole in the carpet. Backtracking slowly, I reaffirmed my suspicions with another peek. Oh-oh, just as I'd thought. So natural that no one would recognize me; in fact I might even frighten some timid soul.

I hastily applied some muck to my face, but no sooner had I put it on than it was sucked down into the parched and arid depths as my poor dehydrated skin acted like a demented sponge. No matter, it would have to do: I was seriously late now.

On the shelf next to the mirror sat the telephone, and for one crazy moment my hand hovered over the receiver. Should I pick it up and call in sick, or dead, or dead-grannyed, or something? I dithered, then happily thought better of it. Four times in three weeks might well be construed as taking the piss, and since I'd already killed off most of the geriatric members of my family, I'd have to start on the more immediate members, which I couldn't quite bring myself to do.

Instead, like a brave little soldier, I tottered stoically off to Earls Court tube, feeling incredibly virtuous and quite forgetting my delicate condition was entirely self-induced. Once there, I found the nearest pillar and hugged it gratefully. I couldn't even summon up the strength to buy the

Daily Mail. I just snuggled up to my pillar, breathing heavily and feeling slightly dazed.

As I stood there, basking in the gloomy April drizzle, I felt something soft and warm nestling against my foot. It wasn't an altogether unpleasant sensation, in fact it was rather comforting, but I thought I'd better take a look down in case it was a furry little rat that had decided to curl up and die on my foot. I was close. Because there, poking out of the end of my jeans and about to fall on to the platform, were my knickers.

They were instantly recognizable as mine because of the crumbling elastic and the uniform grey colour that all my knickers go when they've been lucky enough to join in with the sock wash. Blushing furiously, I grabbed them and stuffed them quickly into my handbag.

Thus deposited, I kept my face well down, concentrating like mad on my shoes as I felt my blush spreading to my fingers, toes, buttocks: you name it, it spread there. Still staring platformwards, I vowed furiously that never again would I take my jeans and knickers off in one fell swoop, thereby leaving myself open to just this sort of embarrassing predicament whereby I not only take them off together but put them on again together too. Furthermore, I vowed that I would eliminate all forms of sluttish and disgusting behaviour from my life once and for all. Thus resolved, I deemed it safe to look up.

I peered under my fringe. OK left, no one seemed to have noticed. Good. I rather over-confidently swivelled my eyes to the right, only to encounter a sadistic little pin-striped chappie grinning at me from behind his *Financial*

Times. Mortified, I instantly turned my back and was about to walk away when the tube came in.

I managed at least to get into a different carriage, but as I stepped on I looked down the platform and saw him winking at me. Bastard. It could have been worse, though. It could have happened at work with Nick there to witness it. I shuddered. At least I'd been lucky enough to have a premature ejaculation at Earls Court tube.

Pippa, of course, was the picture of sobriety, good health and secretarial efficiency when I finally arrived at the agency. She was in the middle of greeting a telephone caller in the correct manner – 'Good morning, Penhalligan and Waters, how can I help you?' – when I lurched in clutching the furniture. Her highly polished shoes, nails and telephone manner were almost too much to bear; but, bless her, she had the decency to put the phone down on the prospective client as she caught sight of my miserable condition.

'Coffee?' she asked anxiously, sensing my distress.

'Please,' I bleated feebly, lowering myself thankfully into position. As I did so, a mound of correspondence rose up to greet me from my in-tray. I rested my head thankfully on this thoughtfully placed, snowy-white, A4 pillow.

'Polly, can I give you a list of things I'd like done this morning, please?'

My head shot up from its resting place and I opened my eyes wide, smiling in a bright and alert manner. God it hurt.

Nick was towering above me in his coat. I'd obviously beaten him by seconds, although it was a pretty pyrrhic victory as my last venue had been bed whereas his had been a client meeting on the other side of London. With any luck he wouldn't realize I'd only just arrived.

'Have you just arrived?' he demanded.

'Er, no, I've been here ages,' I lied.

He put his hands on my desk and bent down to have a look at me. He frowned. 'Are you all right?'

'Yes, why?' I said between a smile and clenched teeth, not wanting to breathe on him.

'You look a bit sort of . . . odd, that's all.'

'Oh, do I?' He was getting closer now, peering at me under my fringe; and what's more, he looked concerned.

'Are you cold?'

'No, why?'

'Well you've still got your coat on.'

'Have I? Oh, how extraordinary. I was so busy I didn't notice.' I wriggled out of it.

'And your eyes look like something out of an Ordnance Survey map.'

'Thanks very much,' I muttered, dropping the bright and alert look. 'I've probably been overdoing it a bit lately.'

'Oh I see, it's like that, is it?' He in turn dropped the concerned look. 'Burning the midnight oil while you brush up on your shorthand, I expect,' he said drily.

'Something like that,' I said, gritting my teeth. What the hell did it have to do with him how I spent my evenings?

'Right, well since there's obviously nothing wrong with you apart from a touch of alcohol poisoning, let's get on with some work, shall we?' he snapped. 'I'd like this document copied eight times and then bound, neatly please. All this correspondence needs typing, as you're probably aware, although I fail to see that you've made any inroads into it so far, and I'd like these two big call reports corrected. If Jason thinks that that's the budget the client agreed to, he and I were clearly in completely different meetings. Although I must confess,' he added wearily, 'sometimes I think he's just on a completely different planet.'

I giggled. Poor Jason was a young account exec, terrifically keen but very green and nervous. He couldn't even pour the coffee in meetings without scalding a couple of clients along the way.

'So change the budget from two million to two thousand, and could I have tea and coffee for six in my meeting at eleven, please? Yes?' This last bark was directed at a caller who'd been put through to him on my telephone. It was the hapless Jason phoning from a meeting at a production company, obviously completely out of his depth. As Nick patiently explained the difference between a double head and a rough cut to the poor boy, I took the opportunity to examine this man-mountain in front of me. From my low-vantage point, I had to admit he was a pretty impressive sight.

Beneath the shock of dark hair his rugged features jutted out at some pretty acute, and even cute, angles, and what a gigantic scale it was on. Imagine throwing the rope around that Roman nose and scaling the rolling chest before perching on the dizzy heights of those broad shoulders. It must be quite a view from up there. I giggled. Good grief, that champagne must have been quite something to give me a hallucinogenic hangover: I'd be seeing him in psychedelic Technicolor next.

Unfortunately, whilst I'd been tripping merrily, Nick had replaced the receiver and was busy issuing yet another instruction which I appeared to have missed. He hissed through his teeth as he repeated it, ending with the ominous threat, 'And if I were you I'd get this done as soon as possible. You're on thin ice, Polly, thin ice.'

With that he swept off into his office in search of something better to do than torment me, and I rattled away at the word processor feeling decidedly rough.

As soon as he'd gone, Joss and Ron, our only creative team – art director and copywriter respectively – emerged from their office. They sat on my desk to inspect my hangover, for they were, after all, the experts.

'Undercooked fried egg sandwich, Polly?' suggested Ron.

'Nice glass of dog piss?' ventured Joss.

Ron put his hand on my thigh, supposedly to test my reactions. I swept it away, giggling.

'Hmmm? . . . A little slower than usual, darling,' he reflected.

Joss and Ron were a pair of ageing hippies who couldn't quite believe that the sixties had really gone for ever. They were forty-three going on twenty-three, and both had long greying hair which curled over their collars, and even shoulders in Ron's case. They'd met many years ago at college in Scotland, come down to the smoke together, and twenty years on still behaved like a couple of likely lads who'd just discovered Carnaby Street. Their life-support system consisted of a series of free lunches, one-night stands and piss-ups, and they didn't give a toss about anything. Luckily, the ad racket provided them with all the ingredients they needed to live a debauched and happy life, but they led a precarious existence, treading a fine line between taking four-hour lunch breaks and doing just enough layouts, scripts and headlines to avoid a P45. If they stepped over the line once too often, which, let's face it, wasn't hard, and failed to return from lunch more than, say, ten times in a month, they were invariably fired from whichever agency they happened to be freeloading on at the time.

Once unemployed, a period of austere sobriety would ensue. The boys (for that is what they were at heart) would stay sober for at least a week, carefully comb their greying locks, rearrange their portfolios, adding their latest commercials — and pinching one or two along the way — before sallying forth to seek re-employment. After a few false starts they would invariably land on their feet through an endearing mixture of charm, experience (these boys were drinking in Charlotte Street while Charles and Maurice were still barmitzvahing) and, it has to be said, talent. Once their designer trainers were firmly planted under new desks, they'd rattle off a couple of ads before, worn out and thirsty, they'd be off to check out the nearest hostelry, feeling they'd earned their money for that month.

Every so often, nervous young account executives like Jason would dare to enter their office. Pale, trembling, sweaty with fear and clutching long-overdue briefs in their hot little hands, they would approach the sleeping/drinking/hungover couple only to be told, like Oliver Twist: '*More*! You want *more* work? Fock me, laddie, it'll have to be Kettner's first!'

A table would be duly booked and Jason would have sleepless nights wondering how to explain yet another expense-account lunch to Nick. Once ensconced in their favourite watering hole, the boys would ignore Jason and greet all their creative friends – of which there were many, for, remember, these boys had been around – who were also being wined and dined by anxious, timid souls in suits. Towards the end of lunch (about five p.m.) Ron and Joss, who were not unkind, would take pity on young Jason and languidly scribble a couple of layouts on the paper tablecloths so thoughtfully provided by Kettner's, which they would then rip off and hand to the young boy.

'There you go, lad. Now run along and don't lose it. That's an award-winner there if ever I saw one!' they would declare, beaming graciously at him.

Jason, flushing scarlet with relief and clutching the precious paper to his chest as if it were a signed Picasso, would thank them profusely before rushing to the loo to have a long, relaxing, well overdue pee.

Work completed, the boys would sidle off and steadily work their way through the bars of Soho in hot pursuit of chicks, as they still called them. They were childishly obvious in their methods. Joss thought nothing of accidentally spilling beer on a blouse in order to rub it off again, and Ron was forever dropping coins to look up skirts. It landed them in all sorts of trouble, and once back at the agency they were constantly ducking phone calls from irate wives/mistresses/chicks/ships-in-the-night, all of whom were demanding to know what the hell was going on. It would be at this point, when they were well and truly hemmed in, backs against the wall, chips down, that they'd look at each other, shake their old grey heads and declare, sadly, that there was no such thing as a free bonk.

Of course, once a mixture of cajoling and downright lying had been used to extricate themselves from a potentially hazardous situation, the larks would continue apace, but it was all so bad and so obvious you simply couldn't take offence. Everyone in the agency adored them, including Nick, who, although he refused to be twisted round their little fingers, recognized a creative talent he couldn't begin to imitate.

On this particular morning, Ron and Joss, having completed a series of headlines and layouts the week before, were going through one of their resting periods. I typed away, trying to ignore them. This was hard, as Ron was stroking my cheek and Joss was staring deep into my eyes.

'What colour are they, darling?' he asked thoughtfully.

'Blue.'

'Really? Blue knickers? How nice.'

I giggled, it was all so predictable. Then I paused for a moment and told them about the knickers-on-the-station episode, knowing it was right up their alley. They cried with laughter.

'Oh God, Polly,' said Joss, wiping away a tear, 'I always thought you were the sort of girl who'd drop 'em at a moment's notice.'

Just then Ron's phone rang. He pressed the requisite number and picked it up at my desk. It was the wife. Her indoors. His back went rigid and he held up his hand for complete silence. We all obeyed, listening in with bated breath. Unlike Joss, who was on wife number four, Ron was still married to his first wife, but only by the skin of his teeth. She was a teacher, and apparently he was terrified of her.

'Yes, my sweet? . . . No, no, never too busy . . . Oh, a

PTA meeting? What a shame . . . you quite forgot. Well, not to worry . . . No, no, I'll get my own supper . . . Sausages will be fine . . . and baked beans yes . . . Apple pie in the fridge, I'll find it . . . Yes, my sweet . . . No, my sweet? . . . No no, don't rush, I'll be fine . . . Have a good meeting then . . . bye bye.'

He put the phone down and looked at Joss, eyes shining with excitement. He rubbed his hands together gleefully. 'Oh joy! Joy! A PTA meeting! Ron, my boy, there'll be bevy and rooty-tooty for us tonight!'

Joss shook him warmly by the hand, and there was much back slapping and jubilation, at which point Nick's head appeared round his door as if it were on a stick. He cast his eye around the room, taking in this happy, unprofessional scene.

Pippa had her feet up on her desk, mine was occupied by Joss and Ron, and Jason, who was back from his meeting, was sitting on top of a filing cabinet, giggling away at the big boys showing off. Nick's face darkened. Jason disappeared behind the filing cabinet and Joss and Ron slipped off my desk in a trice. They tiptoed into their office and closed the door quietly. They could spot a harassed, overworked boss at fifty paces.

Nick turned to me wearily. 'Polly, if you're not too busy' – was that sarcastic or what? – 'could you get me something to eat, please?'

'Sure, what d'you want?' I was dying to ring Adam to thank him for last night and apologize for any outrageous behaviour. At this rate I wasn't going to have a moment.

'Oh, just a couple of sandwiches, tuna and um, peanut butter will do.'

I ambled off to the sandwich bar, wondering if Harry would ring today. He sometimes did midweek if only to tell me what a fantastic weekend he was about to have and how sorry he was not to be seeing me.

At Giovanni's takeaway café I had my usual first-form Italian lesson with my friends the proprietors – '*Ciao, bella. Come stai?*' on their part and, '*Sì sì bene!*' on mine – before sauntering back to the agency.

Nick was scribbling away at his desk when I delivered his lunch. 'Thanks, poppet,' he mumbled, miles away no doubt, as I put them down. You could have knocked me down with an iron girder.

He looked up and came back to reality. This was no poppet, this was the woman whose effigy he stuck pins into every night. He looked flustered. 'Oh, er, Polly, sorry, thanks a lot, what do I owe you?' He unwrapped his sandwich.

'Oh, about one-eighty, but have it on me, you can buy me one next time.' I was still staggered by the endearment, and I always throw my money around when people are nice to me.

He smiled and looked surprised. 'Thanks, I'll do that.'

Suddenly he made a face like he was going to throw up. Perhaps he was. I looked around desperately for the wastepaper bin. He stared at the sandwich in disbelief. 'What's this?'

'What you asked for, tuna and peanut butter.'

He groaned. 'Not together, Polly,' and then he went on in the voice he reserved for morons and retards. 'You see, they don't really *go* together.'

'Oh! Oh gosh, sorry, I wasn't thinking, I'll get you some more.'

He waved me out of his sight. 'No, never mind, never mind,' he said wearily, chucking the disgusting concoction in the bin. 'Just go and finish that pile of typing. I'll get something later.'

I walked out miserably. Why did I have to cock it up, just when we were making progress? Pippa was going out so she offered to get some more sandwiches. I decided to ring Adam. I needed to talk to a man who could bear the sight of me. The switchboard at the Savoy put me through in a second, and all at once I was being soothed by his dulcet, laid-back, North American tones.

'Hi, Polly, how's it going?'

'Badly. I've just been balled out by my pig of a boss.'

Nick's back stiffened behind his glass door. Christ! How much could he hear in there?

'Listen,' I went on, 'I wanted to thank you for last night. It was brilliant.'

'My pleasure, I had a ball!'

'Really? I thought I might have been a bit, you know, tipsy?'

'Hell, Polly, you were flying!'

I laughed. 'Oh dear, I'm afraid that doesn't come as too much of a surprise. Look, Adam, about this judge business . . .' I wondered how I was going to get out of this. I should have thought it through before I picked up the phone.

'The judge? Will you see him tonight?'

'Um, well no, perhaps not tonight, you see I was wondering –'

'Oh sure, sure, tomorrow will do, don't you worry.'

'Oh, well . . .'

'Yeh, yeh that's fine, it'll keep a day or two, but be sure and ring me the moment you get back to tell me how it went. I'm counting on you, OK?'

'Er, yes but –'

'Great. Listen, I gotta go, I'm meeting some guy from back home downstairs in the bar. I'll hear from you soon though, OK? And listen – look after that hangover. Hair of the dog's what you need! Bye now.' He put down the phone.

You berk. You complete and utter moron. You completely cocked it up. Now you'll just bloody well have to go, won't you?

As I sat there feeling sorry for myself, Pippa arrived back with the sandwiches, closely followed by a stunning-looking girl in the most beautiful Armani jacket. I'd clocked it in their window last week, but it was beyond even my wildest overdraft.

She had the sort of cropped, blond, boyish hair that you can only get away with if you're very young or very beautiful. She was both. She was as slim as a piece of macaroni, had perfect, regular features, and her slanting green eyes did parallel lines with her cheekbones. Aside from the covetable Armani jacket, she was wearing – just – a tiny black Lycra skirt which showed off her incredibly long slim legs, clad as they were in dark opaque tights, black suede pumps and a silky yellow polo shirt. The effect was breathtaking. She was beautiful, but also somewhat familiar.

'Can I help you?' I asked in awe.

'Yes, I've come to see Nick – don't I know you?' It dawned on us both at more or less the same time.

'Of course!' she cried. 'You're the girl in the freezer!' and off she went into peals of tinkly laughter.

Ah yes, and you, I thought grimly, are the girl who stood watching me. Famous film star, raving beauty, and Nick's girlfriend all rolled into one. Serena Montgomery. The incessant tinkling was getting on my nerves.

'That's right,' I said breezily, 'I was doing a spot of research for one of our clients with a frozen food product. He wanted to find out what temperature the freezers are kept at. It's to do with shelf life, that kind of thing, but I don't suppose that would mean much to you.' I smiled, but with my mouth only. 'I like to throw myself into my job, you see.'

'Yes, you certainly do, don't you!' she chortled, and went tinkling off into peals of laughter again, obviously under the mistaken impression that she'd made the pun.

Out of the corner of my eye I saw two faces squashed against a glass door. Joss and Ron had heard a mating cry and were instantly alerted, tails up, sniffing around.

I raised my eyebrows efficiently. 'Is Nick expecting you?' I asked, as if he were the chairman of ICI.

'Er, no, but I just thought I'd drop by and take him out to lunch. I just can't tell you how funny you looked in that freezer. You –'

'Then please don't try,' I interrupted smoothly. 'If you'll just wait here, please, I'll see if Nick's available. And you are?'

'Sorry?'

'Who exactly are you?' I asked, giving her a sickly smile as I walked towards Nick's door.

'Serena Montgomery,' she snapped.

'Thank you so much,' I purred. 'I won't keep you a moment.'

I went into Nick's office and leaned against the door. Bitch. But why should I hate her? I probably had looked pretty ridiculous. I sighed, feeling rather tired of life.

Nick looked up expectantly. 'Did you want me?'

'Serena's here to see you.'

He looked alarmed. 'Here?'

'Yes, she's outside, she wants to take you to lunch. Just as well you didn't have a sandwich after all.'

He put down his pen wearily. 'Ask her to come in, would you?'

I opened the door and purred in my best Miss Moneypenny voice, 'Miss Montgomery? Mr Penhalligan will see you now.'

Nick looked at me in amazement and I detected the ghost of a smile on his lips as Serena marched past, glaring at me. I smiled sweetly and shut the door.

A few minutes later she was out again, looking extremely sulky as Nick steered her gently across the room towards the stairs.

'I do think you're being a bore, Nick. I've booked a table at Bibendum, and Justin's waiting for us,' she said.

'Well, I'm sorry,' we heard him say as they clattered downstairs, 'really I am, but I'm absolutely rushed off my feet. I've got a million things to do today. Give Justin my regards and apologize but –'

The rest was out of earshot, but Pippa, Joss, Ron and I rushed to the window and looked down in time to see him guide her around a Mercedes convertible and deposit her in the driving seat with a peck on the cheek. She pouted but looked slightly mollified.

'Wow. He's quite a coolie, isn't he?' breathed Pippa, steaming up the window. 'Not many men would turn down Serena Montgomery, Bibendum and a Mercedes convertible all in one lunch hour.'

'Mmmm . . . Ice coolie,' I agreed reluctantly.

Joss and Ron were speechless with admiration and incredulity. 'The mon's a fockin' nutcase,' Joss managed eventually, shaking his head.

Ron just looked shattered, and they retired hurt to their office, lost in wonder at a fellow man's totally inexplicable behaviour.

Suddenly I realized that Serena would undoubtedly spill the beans on the freezer episode to Nick, probably later tonight, in bed or something. I saw the two heads, one dark and one blonde, sharing a pillow, and I could imagine him roaring with laughter saying, 'But that's just so typical of Polly. She's a complete head-case!'

Footsteps could be heard on the stairs, and Pippa and I jumped back into our seats just as Nick came marching through the room.

'Polly, Pippa, I'm going to write a presentation now, so no telephone calls and no more interruptions, OK?'

'OK, Nick!' we said in unison, grinning from ear to ear like a couple of schoolgirls.

He grinned back and shut himself in his room.

'*Very* sexy when he smiles,' whispered Pippa.

'Oh, Pippa. Anything in trousers.' But I had to agree, the odd flashes of humanity in Nick were quite agreeable.

My hangover seemed to get worse and worse as the day wore on, and once or twice I reached such a low ebb that I was tempted to ring Harry.

Pippa talked me out of it. 'Once he starts treating you like a girlfriend and less like a rabid dog, I'll let you ring him.'

'But I miss him,' I wailed feebly.

'Tough,' she retorted.

I sighed. She was right, and I knew the rules. I eventually went home and crawled straight into bed with *Tatler*, a Big Mac and a hot water bottle. To be quite honest, I really don't think I could have raised the necessary energy even if Harry had crawled in next to me, added to which, George Michael was becoming unbearably prickly, and I'm not at all sure that he, or should I say she, would have thanked me for submitting to any funny business.

Chapter Eight

The next morning I got up early and rang the school. It was a Saturday, so there wouldn't be many people around, but as far as I could remember, Mrs Compton took a tutorial on a Saturday morning. Miss Arnold, the school secretary, answered, and for a moment I could have been fifteen years old again, with a too-short skirt and ten Number Six hidden in my pocket. I automatically twiddled a strand of hair around my finger, a nervous adolescent habit I'd almost grown out of, but as her belligerent, argumentative voice came resounding down the line, I instantly regressed.

'Yes? St Gertrude's school,' she barked. 'Yes? Speak up, I can't hear you!'

I hadn't said a word. 'Hello, may I speak to Mrs Compton, please?'

'MRS COMPTON!' she bellowed incredulously, as if I'd said Archangel Gabriel. 'Mrs Compton is taking a TUTORIAL, she can't POSSIBLY be disturbed.'

'Oh, I see, well, could I leave a message for her, please? Perhaps you'd be kind enough to ask her to ring Polly McLaren? My number is 723–1982, I'm an old girl, she'll remember me.'

'Don't bank on it!' she snorted – the charm-school department of St Gertrude's had really rubbed off on her – 'We can't be expected to remember all the gels that pass through these gates, you know, especially those who didn't exactly distinguish themselves, eh?'

I smiled. She remembered me all right.

'Thank you so much, Miss Arnold and please remember me to your charming sister.'

'Humrph!'

She put the phone down. Her sister had been the matron, an equally nasty piece of work. One icy glance from her had been enough to cut off the blood supply to your heart. She didn't believe in illness. You had to be dying from cholera before she'd grudgingly admit you to the san, and even then you'd rather just die quietly at your desk, thank you very much.

I was quietly burning some toast, mulling over old school days and wondering what one wore when one made house calls to judges, when the telephone rang. It was Mrs Compton.

Now Mrs Compton was a rare breed amongst the teachers at St Gertrude's. Not only was she a wife and a mother, but she was also totally devoid of warts, bunions, hairy legs, varicose veins, bad breath or BO. She was relatively young, most certainly pretty and God knows what she was doing there.

'Hello, Polly, I gather you rang. Don't tell me you've decided to brush up on your algebra at this late stage?'

'Not likely, I can still count to twenty with a packet of cigarettes to help me; that's enough, isn't it?'

She laughed. 'Obviously. OK, so what can I do for you?'

'Well, I was wondering if you'd heard anything from Rachel Marsden. I tried to look her up the other day but she seems to have vanished.'

'Rachel? Hardly the lipstick and disco brigade, was she?'

I laughed. 'No, I suppose not, it's just that a few of us thought we'd get together and somebody suggested Rachel . . .' I trailed off lamely.

'Well, the last I saw of her was when her father took her out of school. Shame, such a clever girl, but no, I haven't heard a dicky bird from her since.'

'What about Mr Saunders. He taught her too, didn't he?'

'Oh, yes, they got on very well, because of course she was a brilliant musician, but he moved to another school in Sussex quite a while ago. I don't suppose he's spoken to her since, but I could give you his number if you like?'

'No, don't worry, I'm sure I'll find her through some of the other old girls. Thanks very much, anyway.'

'Not at all, give her my love when you find her, won't you? And take care of yourself, Polly, try to keep out of mischief. I seem to remember you had rather a penchant for it!'

I laughed. 'I'll try. It was nice to talk to you.' I put the receiver down.

Well, that had proved to be a dead end, as I'd rather suspected it would. There was nothing else for it. I'd have to go and face Judge Marsden. Once again the eternal question loomed large. What on earth was I going to wear?

I abandoned my toast and ransacked my drawers, hoping for a solution. Quite by chance I found one nestling in the bottom drawer. A kilt. I shook it out and held it up for inspection. How eminently suitable; I'd forgotten I even possessed one. OK, it was a bit short, and the tartan was Fiorucci rather than Black Watch, but what the hell? I put it on, adding navy blue tights and lace-up shoes, which was perhaps taking things a little too far, but I do like to look the part. I wrapped my school scarf around my neck, and tied my hair up in a pony tail. All I need now is a satchel and an apple for the judge, I thought, as I bounced down the passageway into the kitchen, singing the school song at the top of my voice.

Lottie was huddled at the kitchen table in her dressing gown, her nose oscillating between her cornflakes and the *Daily Mail.* She looked up in disbelief. 'Don't tell me. Harry's into schoolgirls and you're going off for a good caning. He gets to wear the gown and mortar board.'

'Wrong, it's all for the judge. I'm supposed to be an old buddy of Rachel's, remember? And she is a few years younger than me. What d'you think?' I asked, giving her a twirl.

'Oh yes, very Lolita. I hope you've got your navy blue knickers on, he's bound to check.'

I laughed and ran out of the flat feeling unaccountably excited. It was obviously the underhand nature of my mission that was appealing to me and prompting all this adrenalin to whoosh around. Perhaps I should have been a spy.

Adrenalin abounded in the garden too. It was a beautiful early spring morning and the bulbs in the tiny patch at the front of the house were responding eagerly to the call. It was as if they sensed that spring had come rather late this year, and were now doing their damnedest to catch up. A dozen or so slim green tongues were pointing straight up to the sky, like a row of little green soldiers standing to attention, straining to make themselves as tall as possible on the parade ground. Up in the sky a gentle breeze was playfully buffeting a few clouds around, but other than that it was a clear, bright blue morning.

I jumped into my old Renault Five – previously known affectionately as 'Rusty' owing to his chronic problem around the wheel arches, but now just plain old 'car' since Harry had told me that giving a car a name was about the twee-est thing imaginable. And I'd had no idea! You see, I was learning all the time. Going out with Harry was really quite an education.

I jammed on my seatbelt, turned the key in the ignition, and shut my eyes as I prayed fervently to God, Allah and Buddha, thus wildly hedging my bets. Miraculously it started first time. I kissed the battered old steering wheel passionately and hurtled off to Kensington, still singing the old school song at the top of my voice.

The Honourable Mr Justice Marsden lived in just the sort of house you'd imagine a man in his position would inhabit. A tall, inscrutable white number with an elegant little square of garden at the front. It was just the sort of garden I wanted to mess up, actually. I had a violent urge to rush around emptying packets of seeds all over it, planting lots of bright vulgar flowers like marigolds and nasturtiums just to break up the tedious tastefulness of it all. A few off-white daffodils were nodding their discreet little heads in the breeze, and even the carefully pruned magnolia tree placed, just so, in the centre of the lawn seemed on the brink of budding. Odd how rich people's flowers even seem to come out first. Do they have the monopoly on sunshine, do you suppose?

I stared up at the house for a moment. Naturally I was

looking for clues, like any good private detective worth her free meal at the Savoy would. Ah-ha. Up on the third floor, an Austrian blind in a dotty pink Laura Ashley fabric suggested a young girl's bedroom. Was she there? And if so, was it any of my business?

I could feel my courage running off down the street, and I wanted to run after it. The school song seemed to be stuck in my throat; I warbled middle C just to keep my pecker up. What on earth was I doing here? Did I have a death wish or something?

I tiptoed up the front path, hoping my shoes weren't making too much of a mess on the immaculate gravel, and stopped at the bottom of the marble steps which led, inexorably, up to the front door. They looked about as steep and uninviting as the ones going up the pyramids in Egypt, and at the top was a large, forbidding, black front door. There was still time to turn and run, but for some crazy reason I didn't. I climbed those steps – although how I managed it without a few crampons and a length of heavy-duty rope, I'll never know. The air was decidedly thin at the top, but I took a deep breath, pressed the brass bell, and then feverishly rubbed off the dirty fingerprint with my sleeve.

I cleared my throat and murmured, 'Good morning' to myself a few times to see if my voice still worked. After a while, I heard the steady click-click of heels on a polished wooden floor. They came to a halt at the door, and there was a pause as someone obviously had a look through the spy-hole. I tossed my pony tail in the breeze and struck an attitude of frozen gaiety. The door opened a crack but the safety chain was still firmly in place.

'Yes?' inquired a woman's voice.

'Oh, hello,' I said brightly, 'I was wondering if Rachel could come out to pl – was at home, if she was at home.' Christ, get a grip, Polly.

'Who are you?'

'Oh, I'm just an old school chum of hers.' I resisted the temptation to verify this by doing a merry jig on the step, and wondered briefly how this 'chum' word had mysteriously entered my vocabulary.

I had a quick peek around the two-inch gap and caught a glimpse of the owner of the voice: a middle-aged woman with steely-grey hair drawn tightly back from her face in a no-nonsense bun. She had a pointy little face and a pointy little red nose which almost certainly had a dew drop hanging from it. She was wearing a white housecoat, which obviously placed her firmly in the lower orders. Ah yes, this would be Mrs Danvers, the loyal but insane housekeeper.

'Just a moment,' she said.

I grinned in a 'Bunty has fun in the Lower Fourth' sort of way, and she shut the door in my face. Charming. A moment later the door flew wide open and I stepped back in surprise, a sure sign of guilt, I thought later.

I was confronted by a very tall man, at least six foot four, thin as a reed and with a shock of thick white hair swept back from his forehead. His head was slightly bowed, and he reminded me somewhat of one of his daffodils in the garden. He was elderly without being ancient, and was wearing a patched old cardigan over a checked Vyella shirt, tatty old corduroys, and a pair of carpet slippers. He was not an intimidating sight. In fact the only thing that made him look vaguely judicial were the half-moon spectacles perched on his nose. He smiled and peered over them benignly.

'My housekeeper tells me you're looking for Rachel.'

'Yes, I am actually,' I said rather breathlessly.

'Won't you come in?'

'In?'

'Yes, do, come in.'

'Oh!' I nervously crossed the threshold. Even in my most pessimistic moments I'd imagined that when I was being bludgeoned to death with the blunt instrument I'd still be outside on the doorstep. It never occurred to me I'd have to go inside. I made a mental note to put my fees up and hold out for dinner at Annabel's next time.

I followed the carpet slippers into a beautiful pale yellow drawing room full of books and pictures and dominated by a baby grand piano. A roaring fire was crackling away in the grate and the mantel above it was stiff with invitations. Well, he was obviously popular. Shafts of light were streaming in from the large bay window at one end of the room and the open French doors at the other. One or two sunbeams lay across a pile of legal-looking papers and textbooks on a desk in the corner. The wages of sin, I thought grimly. An ancient golden retriever lay stretched out in front of the fire. He watched my progress across the room and thumped his heavy tail on the floor, apologizing for being too old to get up and greet me properly. There were lots of silver-framed photographs dotted around and quite a few of Rachel. Any minute now, I thought, she'll walk in and I'll just yell, 'Adam's at the Savoy!' and run for my life through the French windows.

Mr Marsden motioned for me to sit down in a blue

Colefax armchair. I perched nervously on the edge. He sank down in a comfortable old chair opposite me with his back to the window.

'And you are?' he asked, getting a pipe out of his cardigan pocket and stuffing it with tobacco. Hardly a murderous gesture.

'Oh, my name's Polly McLaren, I'm an old schoolfriend of Rachel's.'

'Oh really?' he smiled, patting his cardigan pockets for his matches. 'You were one of the St Gertrude gang, were you?' His eyes were friendly and encouraging; in fact I'd go so far as to say they twinkled.

I relaxed. 'That's right,' I said, gaily throwing one end of the scarf around my neck as if I never took it off, even in bed. 'Gosh, we had such fun there!'

He smiled and lit the pipe. 'Well, you know what they say: best years of your life, supposedly, although I was never totally convinced myself. All I remember from my school days are cold showers, fagging, and a great deal of unpleasant food.'

'Ah, yes. Well, the food hasn't changed much, they still put putty in the custard, but you'll be pleased to hear that warming up the loo seat for the prefects has gone out of fashion.' Perhaps a little risqué, Polly? You only introduced yourself a second ago, and already you're getting lavatorial.

Luckily he threw his head back and laughed, obviously appreciating my fine line in scatological humour. Plenty more where that came from, your honour, I thought, warming to his merry eyes.

'Well, I'm very glad to hear it,' he said. 'Would you like a cup of coffee? I was just going to have one.'

'I won't, thanks awfully, I can't stay long.'

'Ah. Oh well, never mind.' He looked disappointed. Poor old boy, perhaps he didn't get many visitors. After all, it probably wasn't every day he got to reminisce about his schooldays and engage in witty repartee with a pretty young gel like me. I was so relaxed now, I felt I could almost put my feet up on the table and turn the telly on.

'I drink too much coffee anyway,' he was saying, as he puffed away at his pipe. 'Keeps me awake at night.'

The dog ambled over for a pat and he stroked his head. I eyed the impressive array of spirits and bottles on the Georgian cabinet in the corner and wondered idly what time the judiciary limbered up to Bloody Mary's of a Saturday morning. It was getting on for midday. He caught my eye, and my drift.

'What about a glass of sherry, then?' he ventured eagerly, raising his eyebrows and sensing a kindred spirit. He consulted his watch. 'I think we could declare an early drinks time, don't you?' he added naughtily.

'Oh, I don't see why not! As my father always says, it's got to be twelve o'clock somewhere in the world!' I bandied back, resisting the temptation to wink. The old rogue, that was quite a sparkle he had in his watery old eye.

He rubbed his hands together like a mischievous little boy and jumped up with alacrity. He was over to the drinks cupboard in a moment, busily picking out beautiful crystal glasses, holding them up to the light, checking for smears, etc. He turned and peered over his specs. 'Sherry all right, or would you prefer something else?'

'No no, sherry would be lovely.'

There was a satisfying glug-glug-glug noise as the

golden liquid left the decanter. It wasn't strictly my tipple, but I could certainly rise to the occasion. He handed me an extremely large drink.

'Thanks, gosh, I'll have to get the bus home!' I quipped.

He laughed. 'Leave it if it's too much: I'm told I'm rather heavy-handed when it comes to pouring sherry.' He sat down in his armchair again. 'Were you a special friend of Rachel's?' he asked in a distracted way as he wiped the rim of his glass with a rather dirty-looking spotted hanky. He held the glass up to the light, peering critically at it.

'Oh well, perhaps not special, I don't suppose she'd have mentioned me, but then she had so many friends.'

He looked surprised. Well done, Polly, first boob of the morning.

'You were in the same year?'

'Er, no, not quite. I was a couple of years above her.'

'Same house?'

'Er, no . . . but we both um' – my eyes roved wildly round the room and lit on the baby grand – 'we both played the piano, you see,' I said, sitting firmly on my stubby, highly unmusical hands.

'Ah, another musician.' He smiled and looked at the piano. Christ, there was no way he could ask me to rattle off a little sonata to prove it was there?

'Er, yes, but I'm not in Rachel's league at all,' I said quickly.

'Oh come now, I'm sure you're very accomplished. It's just a question of practice really, isn't it? At least, that's what Rachel tells me. Can't play a note myself, I'm all fingers and thumbs. Anyway, I'm rambling on and you're probably very busy. You'd like to get in touch with her, is that it?'

'That's right,' I said brightly. 'Thought it was time we got together again, maybe play a few symphonies together or something.'

He looked surprised. 'Symphonies? You play with an orchestra?'

'Er no, not symphonies, I mean – well, you know, duets, that kind of thing. Anyway, I just thought it would be nice to see her again really,' I gabbled, desperate to get away from all this musicality.

'Ah.' He nodded, sucking hard on his pipe which had clearly gone out. He tutted with annoyance and started the pocket-patting routine again.

'Your matches are on the little table,' I said kindly. This old buffer was more like a benign and scatty professor than Hanging Judge Jeffreys.

'Ah! Thank you. Damn thing goes out all the time. Terrible habit, you know. Can't seem to give it up, though.'

'Oh, I know, I'm the same with cigarettes,' I said soothingly.

'Any particular reason?'

'Oh, just something to do with my hands, I suppose. Mind you, I'm pretty addicted to nicotine now. I gather there's a nicotine chewing gum you can buy that's supposed to make you give up, but I thought I might just buy some to chew when I'm not smoking. I rather like the idea of constant nicot –'

'No, no,' he broke in. 'Sorry, I meant any particular reason why you want to see her again?'

'Oh!' I was rather taken aback. 'Oh well yes, actually. You see, I'm organizing an old girl's reunion.'

'Really?' He smiled encouragingly, but the next question came zooming out of nowhere like a ballistic missile. 'Whereabouts?'

'Er, well, I'm not quite sure yet, um . . . my flat maybe, or, or, a restaurant.'

'I see, and when is it likely to be?'

'When?' I was beginning to feel a little hemmed in here as I dodged these quickfire questions. 'Well, quite soon really. Er, probably within the next couple of weeks if I can get everyone together by then.'

'Everyone? Sounds like quite a big gathering. Who have you got lined up so far?' He crossed his legs, rested his head back, and puffed away at his pipe, but it seemed to me he also fixed me with a pair of rather steely-grey eyes over some equally steely-grey bifocals.

I could feel my fringe begin to curl as it always does when it gets wet. My forehead must be getting sweaty. It was awfully hot in here, too hot for a fire. I thought hard of people Rachel might know.

'Well let me see, there's Sophie Steward-Jones, and er, Caro Hamilton and um . . . oh yes!' I cried, suddenly inspired, 'Sally Lomax is coming!'

'Sally Lomax? From Paris?'

'Yes, from Paris!' I smiled happily. What a triumph!

'Really? Good Lord.'

Mr Marsden stood up and walked slowly towards his desk, then he paused, drumming his fingers thoughtfully on the blotter. He picked up a heavy leather-bound legal tome and blew some dust off the spine. He opened it and flicked through a few pages, occasionally running his finger down the margin. Evidently he'd just thought of some vital piece of law which was pertinent to his next case. Well fine, don't mind me, I thought, taking a slug of sherry from my basin.

Then he started to hum. The book was still open but, good Lord, he wasn't reading at all, he was staring into space. What on earth was he doing? I studied his profile, he seemed to have almost forgotten that I was in the room. Of course! Yes, of course, he was about to take me into his confidence, and he was wondering how to go about it. Yes, that was it. My playing the Sally Lomax card had worked a treat. He was about to tell me exactly where his daughter was: locked in the basement, living on a Kibbutz in Katmandu, dancing with the Tiller Girls – I couldn't have cared less; what mattered was that he was working himself up to tell me. Obviously he was agonizing over how he should go about asking me to keep it to myself. How could he explain that it was a deadly secret and that on no account should I divulge her whereabouts to any living soul? I gripped my sherry tightly, intent on his response.

Suddenly he turned to me and smiled. 'How nice,' he murmured softly, 'I'm very fond of Sally, I had no idea she was coming over. She must of course stay here, Rachel will insist.'

'Oh well, er, yes, I expect she'd love to.'

'Unless of course she's staying with you?'

'No, no, not to my knowledge – I mean, no, she isn't.'

'Good. Then we're agreed that she stays with us.'

'Sure, no problem.' I said, nodding in agreement. I

couldn't really care less about Sally's sleeping arrangements, and I was rather unsure where all this was getting us. It was getting us rather neatly over to an address book and a telephone.

'I may as well ring her now and let her know there's a bed for her here. Don't want her doing anything foolish like booking a hotel. In a couple of weeks, you say?'

The crafty old bugger. He flipped through a large flowery address book written in a feminine hand, and his wise old finger came to rest in the 'L' department. My forehead was dripping now and my fringe was frizzing with activity. He found the requisite number and reached for the telephone. He began to dial.

'No!' I jumped up in alarm and started towards him.

Slowly he replaced the receiver. Then he turned to face me. 'No? Why ever not, Polly?' This sudden, rather menacing use of my Christian name chilled me to the marrow. I tightened my grip around my bowl of sherry and stared up at him. The sweet, kindly old man had vanished for ever, and in his place was a wicked, bitter, twisted old judge with murder on his mind. He didn't take his eyes off me.

'Why ever not?' he said again.

'Well, because, um because – you were right after all, you see, she is staying with me. I'd just forgotten! Momentarily forgotten!' I jabbered.

I abandoned my drink to a little tripod table and took a couple of steps backwards in the direction of the door. I had my eyes firmly on the judge, so I very nearly tripped over the dog who yelped and hid under the sofa. I yelped too and considered joining him.

'Miss McLaren, if that is indeed your name,' said the judge quietly, in the voice he no doubt usually reserved for terrorists and serial killers, 'I'm afraid to say that I think you've come into my house under false pretences. In fact, I would go so far as to say that I believe you to be a liar and a fraud. Now what do you have to say to that?'

'I—I say, I say, I say,' I bleated shrilly in true joke-telling music-hall style, only this wasn't funny. Oh God, no. This was bloody frightening. I didn't know what to say.

'I don't believe you know my daughter at all. Neither do I believe you went to school with her. You certainly don't have her best interests at heart. You thought you could trick me, didn't you? You thought all you needed to do was wrap a borrowed scarf around your neck, adopt a silly schoolgirl manner, reel off the names of a few old girls and I'd lead you straight to Rachel. That's what you thought, isn't it?'

The judge was advancing towards me slowly. Where were my twelve men good and true? Where was my defending counsel? This wasn't the English legal system I'd come to know and respect, was it? I kept going backwards in the direction of the front door and the free world.

The judge had finished his summing up and was about to pass sentence. 'You are an evil woman, Miss McLaren' – Christ! Bit strong wasn't it? – 'and you're obviously in cahoots with a certain American gentleman who, as I've made perfectly clear, will simply NOT BE TOLER-ATED!'

This was bellowed at about twenty million decibels.

The dog yelped again and tried to dig a hole in the floor-boards.

I stammered something incoherent like, please don't kill me, and backed even further away, scared out of my few remaining wits. He was still bearing down on me as I backed round the drawing-room door and down the hallway, the once friendly, kindly eyes flashing angrily now. How could I ever have thought he was as mild and reassuring? He was about as mild and reassuring as a Rott-weiler. All this over an unsuitable boyfriend? The man was absolutely barking.

'I want you out of my house,' he said softly but danger-ously. I was whimpering like a demented kitten now, and my hair had gone completely Afro as a result of the down-pour erupting from my forehead.

'I'm going, don't worry, I'm going,' I whispered, as I backed up in terror, trapping myself like a fool against the front door. I felt behind me, desperate for the door han-dle, frantic to twist a friendly little knob. It was at that moment that he raised his hand to deal the death blow.

'Please don't hurt me!' I screamed, covering my head with my hands and sinking to my knees like the lily-livered coward I am.

His raised hand reached beyond my cowering head and found the door knob. As he swung the door open he almost knocked me flying, and I actually had to advance towards him in order to creep out around the door. Once out, I ran like hell. I took off down those marble steps, half expecting a carpet slipper in my backside as I went, but I was spared that indignity.

'And don't come back!' he yelled after me, at which point a million neighbouring curtains, or drapes as they were probably called in this area, seemed to twitch in unison as a whimpering Afro-haired, overgrown schoolgirl hurled herself down a mountain of steps.

I scrambled to my feet at the bottom and ran down the path, leaping the garden wall and charging across the road to my car. I can run when I feel like it, and I really felt like it.

I wrenched the door open and flung myself into the driving seat, then with a desperately shaky hand turned the key in the ignition. Nothing.

'Oh come on, come on!' I shrieked. 'Don't desert me now, Rusty!'

In my despair I reverted to his pet name, but there was zilch reaction. Not a sausage. My temperamental little car was having a siesta, and nothing in the world would stir him, except, for I know my car of old, a wait of say ten or fifteen minutes.

I bashed my head on the steering wheel two or three times. Oh God, I wanted to get out of this place so badly! I wanted to get away from that axe-man of a judge who was no doubt sharpening his weapon as I sat here trapped like a rat in a rust-heap.

'Help!' I shrieked, and looked frantically up at the house, expecting the door to fly open at any second. There was no sign of him. And he didn't even seem to be watching from the window. But he'd be out here in a minute, wouldn't he? Out here, axe in hand, demanding to know why I was still sitting in his road, practically outside his house. I wondered if I should rig up a sign or something, write a message in lipstick on my windscreen perhaps.

'I'd really love to be going, I hate you as much as you hate me, but unfortunately, my car's broken down.'

I looked at my hands. I was shaking, really shaking. As far as I was aware, this had never happened to me before, and I sat watching my trembling fingers with a morbid fascination. It reminded me of an accident I'd seen when I was young. A man had been knocked over by a car in the middle of the road and was shaking so much that somebody had covered him with a blanket. My mother had propelled me past as the ambulance arrived.

'Why was he so cold?' I'd asked.

'He wasn't cold, he was in shock, darling, that's all,' she'd murmured as I stared wide-eyed.

I eyed my hands rather proudly. Oh yes, I was definitely in shock, no doubt about it. So where was my blanket? Or my mummy, for that matter?

Experience dictated that I had to wait a bit longer before I could try the car again, so I lit a shaky cigarette which seemed to have something of a blanket/mummy effect and calmed me down just enough to contemplate for a moment the awfulness of Judge Marsden.

I blew a stream of smoke at the windscreen. The man was certifiable, no doubt about it. I didn't fancy Adam's chances at all. In fact, if I were Adam I wouldn't fancy Rachel either. Who'd want to end up with a father-in-law like that? I'd have to tell Adam the whole story. There'd be no need to embellish it with additional graphic detail: it was graphic enough as it was. He wouldn't be too happy with the outcome, but after all, I'd done my best, hadn't I? I certainly wasn't bloody well doing any more, that was for sure.

The cigarette was helping enormously. I took nice long drags right down to my boots and looked at my watch. Another couple of minutes and this old heap of a wagon might just about start. I looked in my rear-view mirror. What a sight. Coils of frizzy hair stuck out like bedsprings from my pale little face. I found a lipstick on the dashboard and added shocking pink to my quivering blue lips, so that they ended up deep purple. Yuck. I rubbed it off. I looked at my watch again. One more minute and I'd try again. I bit the skin around my thumbnail and thought about Rachel. Poor, poor Rachel. Was she locked in the attic or something? Was she manacled in chains in the cellar with just a bowl of water and the rats for company?

I looked up at the house, half expecting to see a little white face at the third-floor window mouthing, 'Help me'. Instead I saw the front door opening. Jesus Christ, he was after me again! I fumbled for the key and turned it quickly. There was an initial splutter, then a rumble – it started! I looked up as I revved the engine and crunched the gears, half expecting to see him bearing down on the bonnet, but to my surprise I realized it wasn't the judge at all who was coming down the front steps, it was the housekeeper.

She was wearing an old tweed coat and a green felt hat and was half carrying, half dragging, a rather battered old suitcase. It was bulging fit to burst. Was she leaving? Had she handed in her notice in disgust after witnessing the most unpleasant scene imaginable between her bullying employer and a sweet, fresh-faced young girl?

Intrigued, I shunted back into neutral and sat and watched as she made her way slowly down the front steps. The case was small, but was obviously quite heavy, as she was clearly having problems lifting it. She dragged it along the gravel path, then bumped it down on to the pavement. All this activity was too much for the old case. It flew open and spewed its contents over the pavement. I seriously considered helping her, but was understandably wary of going anywhere near that house again, so I stayed put.

She huffed and puffed with growing irritation as she stooped to gather up her clothes, throwing them back in again and muttering away to herself. But hang on a moment. Black Levis? A leotard? Leggings? I looked at the old tweed coat and felt hat. Surely not? She reached for something that had fallen in the gutter. A Walkman? Good grief, was this woman a funky dude in disguise? Was she taking advantage of her day off to go and get on down? Or did all this groovy gear . . . belong to someone else? Of course it did. Of course. I felt a sense of excitement growing within me. It belonged to a young girl. It must belong to Rachel.

Chapter Nine

I kept my head well down as she bundled the suitcase back together again, forcing it to close and snapping it shut. She heaved it towards a battered old Mini parked right in front of the house and opened the boot. It was a strain, but she managed to haul it in. I slid right down in my seat and covered my face with my hands, peeping through my fingers as she walked around the car and got into the driver's seat. My heart was thumping with excitement. Her mission was obvious. To take a change of clothes to the prisoner. Make no mistake about it, this woman was Rachel-bound and I had to follow her.

By rights, of course, I shouldn't have witnessed this little scene. They obviously thought I was long gone, and so I would have been if it hadn't been for trusty old Rusty failing me so magnificently. I mentally patted his battered old bonnet affectionately, keeping my eyes firmly on the action on the opposite side of the road.

The aged Mini was objecting to being woken from its slumber under the trees, and there were one or two false starts before the engine grudgingly turned over and spluttered into action. Luckily my own vintage car was still quietly shuddering away, and as she pulled out in the direction of Church Street, I followed at a discreet distance.

As we trundled down the hill, I opened the glove compartment and fumbled around amongst the sweet wrappers until my hand closed upon my Ray Bans. I rammed them on my nose, pulled at my pony tail letting my hair fall over my face, and wrenched the school scarf from my neck. If she was anything like me, she wouldn't use her rear-view mirror too assiduously, but it was as well to make sure that, if she did, she didn't recognize me. To this end, as we slowly wound our way down Church Street, I had a quick look over my shoulder, surveying the back seat for further disguise. I always travel heavy, and there are usually quite a few props lying around amongst the cigarette packets, plastic bags and general debris that seems to collect there. Today most of it seemed to be seduction paraphernalia – high-heeled shoes, low-necked tops, etc. – but, nestling underneath a leather skirt and an empty beer can (not guilty, incidentally), was my father's old brown felt hat. I jammed it over the wayward curls and pulled the brim down over my eyes. I looked in the mirror: shady and incognito. I didn't even recognize myself, so she didn't stand a chance.

I gripped the steering wheel hard as buckets of adrenalin whooshed around my body. I'd already used up a tankful today, and I only hoped I'd kept enough in reserve for this little escapade. We turned left and motored off towards Kensington Gardens, my nose practically pressed against the windscreen due to chronic shortsightedness and the night-time driving conditions foisted upon me by my incredibly dark glasses.

On we cruised, up the hill and on past the immensely phallic Albert Memorial which usually brings a wry smile to my lips. Victoria must have reckoned he was a helluva guy to have had that enormous great thing erected in his memory, and bang in the middle of the park, if you please, for all the world to wonder at. You'd think she'd have parked it somewhere private, like outside her bedroom window or something. This morning, however, my mind was on even weightier things than Albert's member, and I didn't give it a second glance as we swept towards a surprisingly uncongested Knightsbridge.

As we cruised through two sets of green lights together, my hands became sweaty with excitement and the old heart hammered away somewhere in the region of my oesophagus. Where on earth were we going? I had a quick look at my petrol gauge and hoped to God we weren't setting off for a day in the country. I had about a gallon at the most. I cursed my false economy of only putting in a couple of pounds'-worth at a time.

We manoeuvred Hyde Park Corner, which proved to be quite a challenge as she caught the tail end of each set of lights and I had to jump a couple to stick with her. I have to say I was enjoying myself enormously now, and just wished she'd put her foot down a bit so I could really show off. We crawled along at a couple of miles an hour. This lady was no speed merchant, and I had trouble keeping down with her but I curbed my *Miami Vice*-like instincts and rounded every single corner in second, steadfastly resisting handbrake turns.

The Palace was crawling with tourists, and the traffic had come to a standstill as the massed bands of the Coldstream Guards strutted their stirring stuff in the middle of the road. Boom Boom Boom went the kettle drums, and Boom Boom Boom went my heart. Please God, don't let me lose her here, I thought as we waited: it wouldn't be difficult. The band played on as one guard left and another one took its place. Come on, boys, hurry it up, I murmured as the soldiers marched past. I couldn't help noticing that the officer in charge looked rather attractive, as far as one could tell under that bearskin. Oh well, not now, Polly. At last the guard was well and truly changed, and our little Mini and Renault convoy was waved through by a benevolent policeman. We crawled off towards Parliament Square.

By now I was almost lying on the floor. All this stopping and starting had provoked even me to look in my mirror once or twice, and I was praying she hadn't glanced behind once too often and wondered why a dirty blue Renault was sticking to her like chewing gum on a jumper.

As we turned left along the Embankment, a rather nasty feeling stirred in my waters. We were getting closer and closer to the river entrance of the Savoy. What was going on? Was this some kind of weird, elaborate joke? It was something of a relief when we sailed past the hotel towards the city and – oh God, yes, of course – the East End! Poor Rachel was obviously holed up in some dirty little attic room above a launderette or a chip shop, chained to a rusty iron bed, no doubt, with nothing to eat or drink. Never fear, fellow Old Gertrudian: help is on its way!

I wiped my by now damp hands on my skirt and felt a rousing mixture of guts, determination and the old Dunkirk spirit stirring in my soul. In my excitement I inadvertently gave the accelerator a bit of welly which almost blew my cover: I damn nearly went up the back of her as we turned left – left? What here? – through some enormous black iron gates that I didn't even know existed. And I thought I was a girl about town. Where the hell were we?

I followed blindly as we drove under an arch and then up a narrow lane with ancient stone buildings towering above it on either side. I nearly bumped my head on the car roof as we crunched over a couple of sleeping policemen and then turned sharp right under another arch and into a courtyard.

To the right of the courtyard was a beautiful garden surrounded by iron railings. An immaculate lawn was laid out like an enormous green tablecloth, and all around it were well-tended flower beds full of mature shrubs, rose bushes, lilac and crocuses. Opposite the garden was a large brick building that looked like a hall and – hang on a minute, this all looked vaguely familiar. Wasn't this where all those barrister chappies had their offices – or chambers? My suspicions were confirmed as a couple of young men rounded the corner and ambled past. They were dressed in their weekend mufti of cord trousers and tweed jackets, but under their arms they clutched bundles of papers tied up with pink ribbons and, if I wasn't very much mistaken, those papers were otherwise known as briefs. Ah-ha, nicely deduced, Polly.

I also had a vague and distant memory of a vague and distant cousin who, having bagged herself a particularly attractive young barrister, clinched the deal in a church not a million miles from here – Temple church, that was it. And of course, if this was the Temple, as I believed it was, Marsden would undoubtedly have chambers here. Things were looking up!

Far from being deserted as one might expect on a Saturday there were quite a few cars dotted around the car park. There were also one or two tourists who were wandering around, snapping their cameras at the Dickensian backdrop complete with old-fashioned gas lamps.

I hung well back and tucked myself in behind a Range Rover as the housekeeper parked her car in the bottom right-hand corner of the courtyard. I switched my engine off.

Mrs Danvers, as she'd become in my mind, got out of the Mini, walked round to the back of the car, opened up the boot and dragged the case out. She carried it with some effort and made her way to . . . now, let's see – yes, the very last doorway on that side. Number . . . forty-one? Was that it? Yes, forty-one! I kept my eyes fixed firmly on that doorway as she disappeared inside. My eyes were watering under the strain of staring wide-eyed for so long, but after what seemed like an hour but was probably more like two minutes, she appeared again, minus the case.

She got back into the Mini and started the engine. I slid right down on to the floor and peered over the dashboard as she performed an immaculate three-point turn and drove up towards me. She must have passed right by me, but by now my knees were in my ears and I was inspecting the brake pedal. I counted to sixty then crawled up on to the seat and looked around. All clear.

Tingling with excitement, I wondered how I should go about covering the ground between my car and number forty-one without anyone taking too much notice of me. Should I stroll casually down to the door as if I had nothing better to do than mooch around the Temple of a Saturday morning, or should I run like the blazes and get it over and done with? In the end I compromised and did the most conspicuous thing of all: an incredibly guilty running tiptoe incorporating a few deft little zig-zag turns – which I felt were important – as if I were under fire. All I needed was the Sundance Kid giving me cover from behind and I could really have drawn attention to myself.

I ran up the stone steps to the open doorway and peered inside. There was a small flagstone hallway with steps leading up to the next floor. On my right was a black door with a list of names printed on it: Mr Michael Nelson, Mr Charles Morgan-Browne, Mr Richard Solmes, and so on and so on. I gingerly turned the handle. Locked. These were obviously chambers. I ran upstairs and on the next landing found a similar black door with yet another list of names. I quickly ran through them. There was no mention of Marsden. I tried the handle – locked again. The staircase seemed to go on and on, so I followed it up to the next landing.

As I rounded the corner to the third floor, I was confronted by yet another black door, but instead of a list of names, there was just the one. Above the door in gold letters about four inches high was written: SIR EDWARD MARSDEN. If this had been a movie the gold letters would have flashed in and out of focus and the orchestral score would have risen to an almighty great crescendo. As it was, I had to clap my hand over my mouth to force my own crescendo down into my throat. Sir Edward Marsden! This was *it*! I'd *found* it! There was absolutely no doubt about it, Rachel Marsden was behind that door!

But what a door. I stood back and surveyed it. Unlike the ones I'd encountered downstairs which had glass panels and brass handles, this one was completely solid and seemed to be made from half a tree. It had no handle to speak of, and no less than three large keyholes: it was like something out of the Tower of London. I couldn't begin to get her out of there on my own. I needed help. I needed a man, or preferably men and – yes, of course, I needed Adam!

There was no doubt about it, I had to get Adam over here immediately. There was no point in trying to break that door down on my own, I'd just end up in hospital. I was just about to batter on the door, shout Rachel's name and tell her I was off to telephone for help, when I suddenly had a thought. What if she weren't alone? Suppose there was someone in there with her, a guard of some sort? Yes, suppose she was being watched over by a heavy? Suppose, as I bashed on the door, he came out and boffed me over the head? Tempted though I was to reveal myself as her rescuer, I decided that the mature thing to do would be to wait until I'd collected a little more muscle in the shape of Adam and perhaps even the police.

I charged down the staircase, bubbling over with excitement. I had to find a phone-box. As I ran, I imagined myself telling Adam and hearing first the disbelief, then the astonishment, and then the joy in his voice as I broke the news. I gave a yelp of delight as I jumped the last few steps and scampered out into the sunshine.

Of course, Rachel and Adam would feel indebted to me for ever, I thought, as I ran in the direction of an exit to the courtyard. Once we'd released her and they'd done their preliminary hugs and kisses, they'd clasp hands, look at me with dewy eyes, and say things like, 'Oh Polly, how can we ever repay you?' Then they'd try to shower me with all kinds of presents – jewellery, money, blank cheques, that kind of thing – but I'd be so magnanimous. I'd smile modestly and refuse everything, saying that all I really wanted was to see them happily married.

Ah yes, the wedding. Naturally, I would be the guest of honour, mentioned in the speeches – mentioned? Good grief, there'd be a whole speech devoted to me, delivered by Adam, of course. I'd blush prettily as a hushed audience listened to him recounting tales of my tenacity, my bravery, my undiluted courage – what was the name of that film about the resistance fighter? *Carve Her Name with Pride*, that was it; that would be a good theme for the speech, wouldn't it? I'd suggest it to him, discreetly, of course.

I dashed out into one of the little sidestreets that led from the Temple and encountered a row of tatty old warehouses, a few decidedly closed pubs and not a lot else. Somewhat lost now, I tried desperately hard to remember the A-Z, and hung a left in what I imagined was the direction of Fleet Street. It was a successful gamble, and I was rewarded by a glimpse of a red bus flashing past and what looked like a shopping parade.

As I hurried on, my mind scurried back to the wedding reception. People would be clamouring to meet me and pointing me out to each other. 'That's her,' they'd say, 'that's the girl who risked her life to bring them together. Isn't she wonderful?' They'd all want to hear the story and I'd repeat it over and over again – probably embellishing it very slightly to include me dodging a few blows to the head from the mad judge – oh, and of course I'd speed up the bit about me following the housekeeper, making that more of a life-threatening car chase. Everyone would be incredibly impressed and all the good-looking men would ask for my telephone number and Harry – God yes, Harry would have to be there, I wanted him to witness all this – yes, Harry would be looking on with pride, casting furious looks at all the predatory men and I'd overhear him saying things like: 'Yes, very proud ... oh I agree, terrifically brave.'

I spotted a phone-box in Fleet Street and fairly skipped into it. I never seem to carry any change, but today God had placed a whole ten pence piece in my purse. I dialled the Savoy's number which I knew off by heart now and rammed in my coin.

'Adam Buchanan please, room twenty-four.'

'One moment please,' said a man's voice.

I heard the telephone ring in his room. I heard it ring, and ring and ring. Oh God Adam, come on, come on.

'I'm sorry, Mr Buchanan doesn't appear to be in.'

'Could you try again?' I asked desperately. 'He might be in the bathroom or something.'

We tried again. 'I'm sorry, he's still not answering. Would you like to leave a message?'

Damn! Where the bloody hell was he? He knew I was due to see the judge today; he should have been sitting by the phone waiting for me to call. My heart sank deep into my lace-ups.

'Could you please just make sure he hasn't left a message for me? He really would have been expecting me to ring. My name's Polly McLaren.'

'Just a moment please, I'll look.'

I drummed my fingers impatiently on the receiver.

'Yes, madam, there is a message for you.' My heart

made a quick dash up to my blue-stockinged knees. 'It says he's just popped out for a quick lunch and will be back at about one-thirty.'

One-thirty! I looked at my watch, it was nearly one o'clock. That wasn't too bad.

'In that case, I'd like to leave him a message, and it's very important that he receives it the moment he comes in. Do you understand?'

'Yes, madam, I understand,' said a rather tight-lipped voice.

'Please could you say that I've found Rachel.'

'You've found Rachel.'

'Yes, she's at number forty-one, Queens Bench Walk in the Temple. Oh – and please could you direct him to the Temple and tell him I'll be there waiting for him? Could you read that back to me, please?'

'She's at forty-one, Queens Bench Walk in the Temple, and you'll meet him there.'

'You'll be sure he gets it?'

'Yes, madam.'

'The moment he comes in?'

'Madam, I'll make a point of personally tripping him up the second he steps through the door,' said the voice drily.

'Thank you so much.'

I put the receiver down and raced back to the scene of the crime. I wish I'd thought to mention that if Adam could lay his hands on an axe it would come in handy, but no doubt we'd improvise when he arrived.

I took the stone steps two at a time and arrived at the third floor panting and breathless. The big black door loomed up before me again. I looked at the name again. *Sir* Edward Marsden, no less and I'd called him Mister. Good job too. Suddenly all reserve and restraint failed me. That poor girl had been cooped up in there for weeks now, and the least I could do was let her know that help was on its way. If she was being guarded, which in retrospect I somewhat doubted, it would do the thug good to know that I was out here – probably put the wind up him a bit. Thus decided, I really let that door have it. I hammered with both fists making a terrific racket, shouting at the top of my voice:

'RACHEL! RACHEL! IT'S OK! WE'RE GOING TO YOU OUT OF THERE!' I paused for a second, then pounded some more, yelling even more loudly: 'RACHEL! RACHEL! WE'VE COME TO TAKE YOU AWAY, IT'S GOING TO BE ALL RIGHT! YOU WON'T HAVE TO STAY THERE MUCH LONGER, WE'RE GOING TO GET YOU OUT OF THERE!'

Just as I was working myself up into a nice little frenzy, the door swung open and Rachel stood there, staring at me in amazement. My fists were flailing around in mid-air and I damn nearly punched her in the eye.

She looked terribly pale and thin and her little heart-shaped face was drained of all colour, totally washed out. She was wearing an equally washed-out blue T-shirt over grey leggings which had gone baggy at the knees. Her mouse-blonde hair looked greasy and bedraggled: she obviously hadn't been able to wash it for weeks, poor thing. Her pale blue eyes blinked nervously, obviously unaccustomed to daylight.

I stepped back in surprise. 'Rachel!'

'Er, yes?' she said doubtfully.

'Thank God! I was so worried you might be dead or something – how did you manage to open the door? Did the housekeeper leave it unlocked by mistake or something, how extraordinary! How ironic, just think you could have *walked* out! You could have just opened the door and actually *walked out of here*!' I gabbled.

'Um . . . yes, I suppose I could.'

'Gosh, you look dreadful you poor thing, absolutely dreadful, so thin and pale, and those ghastly filthy clothes. I bet you don't even know what day it is, do you? Well, it's Satur-day.' I said it slowly in case she had trouble dealing with this, she'd probably been scratching little marks on the wall to keep abreast of the days and I hoped this coincided with her calculations. 'Did you know it was Saturday?' I asked anxiously.

Rachel's mouth was hanging open and her eyes were wide with wonder, 'I'm . . . I'm sorry, do I know you?'

'Oh!' I whipped off my hat and glasses. 'Of course, you wouldn't have recognized me, but you see I had to wear a heavy disguise just to be on the safe side. Good, isn't it?'

She blinked. 'Er, yes, very good, I'm sorry I still don't . . .'

'Polly McLaren, at your service, I was at school with you, remember? St Gertrude's?'

'Well . . . yes, vaguely.'

Vaguely? She vaguely remembered me – a bit of a schoolgirl legend if I say so myself – or she vaguely remembered St Gertrude's? Either way it was worrying. I peered at her anxiously, scanning her face for evidence of cuts or bruising, bumps on the head and suchlike. None were apparent, but she looked decidedly vacant. Drugged perhaps?

'Are you all right?' I asked anxiously.

'Yes, very well thanks, and you? Would you like to come in?'

Would I like to come in? Do you ask the Seventh Cavalry if they'd like to come in? Or the SAS? Or Bodie and Doyle? Very well thanks, and you? Is that what the Scarlet Pimpernel had to contend with when he flung open the cell doors for the French aristocracy? Oh, hi there, Pimpernel. Yes, very well thanks, and you? I admired her *sangfroid*, but really.

I shook my head in disbelief and followed her dumbly into the drawing room. The drawing room? Hang on a minute, this was supposed to be some sort of chambers, and yet here we were in a beautiful eau-de-nil room with large shuttered windows overlooking the courtyard. The neck-rickingly high ceiling sported an enormous chandelier and on Persian carpet level there were quite a few spindly-legged antiques dotted around, plus two enormous powder-blue sofas that looked as if they'd swallow you up whole if you so much as perched on the edge of them. Hardly what you might call cell-like. More what you might call lap of luxury-like.

'What's this?' I said, not bothering to close my mouth when I'd finished my utterance.

'What's what?' she asked politely.

'This place, I mean it looks like a flat or something.'

'It is,' she said patiently. 'It belongs to my father: quite a few judges have them.'

'Bet they don't keep their daughters locked up in them, though, eh? Boy, I bet you're glad to see me, aren't you!'

She didn't seem to know quite what to say to this, and instead of throwing herself on my bosom and sobbing out her heartfelt gratitude, she perched on the edge of a powder-blue sofa and narrowed her eyes at me in a confused manner. Then it came to me. Oh God, had they brainwashed her or something? Was that it?

'Rachel . . .' I knelt down in front of her and peered earnestly into her pale blue eyes. She looked even more confused at this; in fact she looked downright bloody bewildered, poor kid. I spoke very slowly and carefully. '. . . Rachel, can you hear me?'

'Er . . . yes.'

'Listen to me, Rachel, have they hurt you in any way? The housekeeper? Your father? Did they swing gold watches in front of your nose? Try to hypnotize you or anything? Can you remember?'

She frowned and looked annoyed. 'Now, look here –'

'All right, it's OK.' I took her hand and spoke soothingly. 'We don't have to talk about it now if you don't want to. Some other time. Have you had anything to eat at all?'

She wriggled her hand away from mine and moved nervously along the sofa. 'Yes, I've just had lunch, actually. Look here, what's this all about?'

'About? What's it about? I've come to get you out of here, of course!' Christ, talk about ingratitude, but then, I thought kindly, she's probably still in shock. I sat down next to her and put my arm around her, resting my hand reassuringly on her shoulder. She sat bolt upright and looked at the hand on her shoulder in disbelief, then she looked up at me, her eyes like saucers.

I gave her a bit of a squeeze. 'Rachel, I've been looking for you for a while now,' I said quietly.

'Christ!' She leaped off the sofa in alarm, holding her arm where I'd touched her as if I'd singed her with a cigarette. 'You have? But I don't even know you, why?' Her eyes were flying saucers now.

'Oh, not just me, of course!' OK, I thought, I'll sock it to her now; watch her face light up like a Belisha beacon. I licked my lips with anticipation. 'Your boyfriend's been looking for you too!'

'My boyfriend?' Her face, if anything, darkened.

'Yes, your boyfriend,' I said impatiently. I was getting rather tired of all this playing hard-to-get nonsense. I also had the distinct impression that, far from showering me with jewellery and presents, even a simple thank-you might be out of the question. 'Adam of course, Adam Buchanan.'

I waited for the hug, the tears, the emotion. Instead she backed away from me, her face ashen. Her hand leaped to her mouth. 'Adam? Adam's coming here?' she whispered.

'Yes, Adam's coming here.' Why did she have to repeat everything I said? It made conversation so long-winded, and she'd got me doing it now.

'Oh my God!' Her voice cracked. 'When?'

I consulted my watch. 'Oh, in about ten minutes I should think!' I said jauntily. 'You've just got time to put a spot of make-up on,' I added, eyeing her peaky little face. She wouldn't want him to see her looking like that. I rummaged in my handbag and produced a leaky mascara and my favourite hot pink lipstick. I wasn't entirely sure her face could take hot pink, but it was better than nothing.

'Here, borrow mine,' I said, offering them up generously.

'Oh God!' This came out as a sort of strangled cry, as if someone had got her by the throat, and she rushed out of the room, one hand still clasped to her mouth.

I sat on the sofa, still proffering my make-up and feeling more than a little confused. I frowned and put the lipstick away. Somehow this scenario wasn't going quite as I'd envisaged it would. I bit my lip and wondered where I'd gone wrong. Had it all been too much of a surprise for her? Too much of a shock? She did play the piano, after all, and they were terribly sensitive, these artistic types. Perhaps I should have broken the news a little more gently?

An awful lot of banging around was coming from a room down the hall. I cocked an ear in the direction of the noise and then got up, wondering what on earth I should do. There was certainly a lot of frenzied activity going on in that room. Was she doing some kind of happy-clappy dance to celebrate Adam's return? As I've said before, she was very musical.

I crept tentatively down the passageway and poked my head around the bedroom door. Rachel was opening drawers and cupboards, grabbing armfuls of clothes and throwing them on the bed. Ah-ha! Now this was a scene I recognized, this was straight out of Tregunter Road! Of course – she was wondering what on earth to wear for this momentous occasion. I stepped forward eagerly, wondering if I could be of assistance – convinced, in fact, that

I could: this was after all my specialized subject. I was just about to offer my services when I noticed that the clothes on the bed were now being stuffed into a red hold-all. I frowned. They were going to get awfully creased in there, and what was the point? Skirts and jumpers were flying in, vests, vests? So small? A teddy, another teddy – Good Lord, how many teddies did a girl need – and, heavens, what on earth was that dreadful wailing noise?

I followed the wail to the end of the bed and there, lying in a carry-cot and peeping out from beneath a pale blue blanket was a little ginger head. A baby! A real live baby.

Everything on my face was as open as it could be now: eyes, mouth, even my nostrils gaped.

'It's a baby!' I cried moronically.

Rachel carried on stuffing the bag as if I didn't exist. Still slack-jawed with disbelief, I watched as Rachel grabbed the carry-cot by the handles and barged past me into the kitchen. I followed blindly. She grabbed bottles from shelves and jars of baby food from cupboards and rammed them in the bag, hissing and snarling as she went. As she flung yet another lorry-load of bottles in, she swung around to face me. Her face was white with loathing and her mouth had curled up into a terrifying snarl.

'You stupid cow,' she hissed. 'You stupid, interfering cow!'

My jaw was still hanging from its hinges, and I tried to form a sentence or two, but could find neither wind nor words. One thing was becoming remarkably clear though. I'd made a major miscalculation somewhere along the line. Rachel was kind enough to fill me in on what it was.

'He wants the baby, you dickhead!' Her voice was rising to an hysterical level. 'Don't you understand? HE WANTS MY BABY!' She screamed straight into my face, her nose about two inches from mine.

In retrospect I'm glad she pitched it thus, because somehow the proximity of her distorted face and the volume at which this staggering piece of news was imparted did actually have the effect of passing through my thick skull and into my brain. I recoiled from her in shock. Adam wanted the baby. He didn't want the girl, he wanted the baby. I'd led him to the girl, therefore I'd led him to the baby. I felt sick.

'Oh my God!' Now it was my turn to rise to fever pitch. 'He'll be here any minute, you've got to hurry, *hurry*!'

I grabbed her bag but, not very surprisingly, she grabbed it back and pushed me forcibly back against the wall. Flattened against the eau-de-Nil, I watched in despair as she hauled the bag over her shoulder and picked up the carrycot which was equally heavy. Puffing and panting, she heaved her load out of the front door and began the tricky matter of descending the stone stairs with half a hundredweight of layette in her hands. It would take for ever. Ignoring her snarls and protests, I snatched the red bag from her and lugged it down the steps ahead of her.

'You've got to believe me!' I shrieked as I pulled the bag down on its bottom, my head swivelling back like a periscope as I pleaded with her, 'I had no idea! Absolutely no idea! He used me; he told me this long story about how you wanted to marry him and your father wouldn't let you. He said he was devastated, he said *you* were devastated, he never even *mentioned* a baby, I swear it. Honestly, Rachel, I had no idea. Please, *please* believe me!'

She staggered down behind me, tight-lipped and word-less, concentrating like mad on not tipping up the baby.

'I know I'm a stupid, interfering fool, I know I am, but I'll make it up to you, I swear I will. Honestly, I would never have got involved had I known, but – but he seemed so honest, so believable – well, you must know what he's like, how persuasive he can be, I just had no idea!'

She didn't look in the least convinced, but some of my hysterical ranting must have had some effect, because when we eventually arrived at the bottom, blinking and sweating in the sunlight, she looked one way, then the other, and then, in sheer desperation, at me.

'You absolutely swear it?' she hissed. 'You didn't know?'

Almost on my knees I swore on my life, my mother's life, my grandmother's grave, my dog – I thought desper-ately of other precious things – Harry, Harry's parents who I'd never met but who were obviously precious to him and therefore precious to me, Harry's dog – but she interrupted me.

'*Shut up, will you!*' I shut. 'Quick, where's your car?'

'Over here!'

We ran to the car, sharing the burden of the carry-cot. The little redhead looked up in surprise as we raced him over the cobblestones. Rachel's breath was coming in hys-terical sobs now as we flung the carry-cot on the back seat and leaped in the front. I fumbled with the keys, terrified that any minute now Adam's face would appear at the window and a large freckled hand would reach in and close firmly over mine. The car started first time and I made a mental note to treat it to a service one day as a mark of my eternal gratitude.

We shot out of that car park in true Hollywood style, and flew over the ramps in Middle Temple Lane like Free-bie and the Bean before coming to a screeching halt at the Embankment. The traffic was roaring in both directions, but at the merest hint of a gap I shut my eyes and put my foot down. A lorry swerved violently and slipped behind my tail, missing me by millimetres, honking his horn and shaking his fist. I swung into the stream of traffic on the other side of the road amidst more honking and fist-shaking and various allusions to my anatomy, but I cared not. We revved and roared and lane-hopped and light-jumped our way towards central London.

Neither of us spoke for a while. Out of the corner of my eye I noticed that Rachel's face was the same colour as her leggings and she was doing a great deal of blinking and lip-quivering out of the window.

I dug deep and found a very small voice. 'I'm so sorry, Rachel, I really am.'

Her chin began to tremble and a tear trickled down the side of her nose. She brushed it away furiously. 'Why couldn't you just mind your own bloody business?' she hissed savagely.

Yes, why couldn't I? I'd never felt so awful in my life. Apart from that time at junior school when I'd trodden on the school hamster in front of the whole class. By mistake, of course: he escaped and I went to catch him. Yes, quite dead. But this was all my fault, I'd screwed up quite comprehensively. I'd fallen for everything Adam had said without even considering Rachel's position. Off I'd shot like an unguided missile, tearing round to her father's house, who, I now realized, had simply been protecting his daughter and grandson, and then, not satisfied with upsetting him, I'd charged off again and exposed her quite brilliant hiding place. It had been brilliant, too. How many people would have the faintest idea that those flats existed? Not many Londoners, and certainly not an American.

I still couldn't quite get my mind round all this, though. Rachel had a baby. Adam had a baby. They both had a baby and they both wanted it. What they didn't want – yes, yes, I was getting there slowly – what they *didn't* want was each other. Brilliant, Polly. I would have liked to have known why, why they'd fallen out, what had gone wrong in the idyllic house by the sea in America, but I had a shrewd suspicion that now was not the time to ask.

I took another sideways glance and assessed the damage to her face. She seemed to be under control now. In a second or two we might have a bash at a conversation and try to determine the best place for her to go. But then of course she wouldn't have any idea, why should she? I'd only ousted her from her flat ten minutes ago, and she was hardly likely to have yet another brilliant hidey hole up her sleeve. I had to come up with something, and fast. I called upon my under-worked brain to perform some kind of miracle for me. Let me see, let me see, we couldn't go to her father's – God, what a nasty piece of work he must have thought me, I'd dwell on that later – and we couldn't go to my flat because Adam knew where I lived. Did she perhaps have any friends in London?

'Do you have any friends in London?' I ventured timidly.

She shook her head, and either this sad admission or the violence of the shake provoked another fresh trickle of tears down her nose. God I felt a heel. I plunged into my mental file of my two hundred closest friends and went straight to the top. There was really very little competition for this job. It was a position that had to be filled by someone with a big enough heart and a big enough flat to house a distressed girl and a baby. There was only one person who was unlucky enough to qualify, and that was Pippa. Big heart, even bigger house. Pippa it was.

By now, Rachel seemed to have abdicated all responsibility, and didn't even bat an eyelid as we did a U-turn in the middle of the road and headed off to Kensington. She did look up as we approached the bottom of Church Street though.

'Not to my father's,' she said in alarm, 'that's the first place he'll look!'

'I know, I know, don't worry. We're going to a friend's house.'

We dodgemed our way down Kensington High Street, turned left by the cinema and then right into Pippa's road. We came to an abrupt halt outside her house and my head dropped like a stone on to the steering wheel. Thank God that journey was over, I'd aged about a year in ten minutes. My hands, released from their position on the wheel, now began to shake like a couple of pink blancmanges. They'd been getting a lot of exercise in that respect today.

I raised my head and looked at Rachel squarely. It was an effort because her eyes were still understandably hostile, but I felt it was the least I could do.

'I'm so sorry, but believe me, you'll be all right. I promise I'm going to look after you and see that he doesn't find you. I absolutely promise.'

She nodded dumbly. What else could she do? She was in my extremely incapable hands. But I meant what I said. One way or another, I'd see this one through until she and the baby were safe, and well away from the clutches of Adam Buchanan. For once in my life, I, Polly McLaren, would not screw up.

Chapter Ten

When Pippa eventually answered the door it was obvious she wasn't alone. Her usually sleek blonde hair was some-what tousled, her face was flushed and her eyes were far too bright. She was wearing a short white towelling dress-ing gown and not a lot else. She pulled the dressing gown closer around her as she peered round the door at her visitors, brushing the hair out of her eyes. 'Polly! What a lovely surprise!'

It clearly wasn't, but I was desperate. 'Pippa, this is Rachel,' I said, pushing a wordless Rachel ahead of me into the house.

'Oh, hi Rachel, um, come in.'

She was in, I'd seen to that, and I was right behind her with the carry-cot. This didn't escape Pippa.

'You've got a baby!'

'He's Rachel's,' I replied, staggering in. God, what did she feed him on?

'Well, I'm glad to hear he's not yours. He's lovely though, isn't he?' she said, bending down to do a bit of cooing. 'How old is he?'

'Five months,' muttered Rachel.

'Oh, he's divine. Is he really yours? You lucky thing.' She straightened up and peered at Rachel. 'Oh gosh, hang on – you're not *the* Rachel, are you?'

'How d'you mean?'

Pippa turned to me. 'The Rachel you've been looking for? Adam's Rachel?'

'Er, yes, but you see the thing is, Pippa, she didn't actually want –'

'Oh! Oh, how exciting!' She turned to Rachel and gripped her arm enthusiastically. 'But that's brilliant, isn't it! She found you, the clever old thing found you! Aren't you thrilled? You must be! Gosh, you look worn out, you poor thing. Have you been hidden away for ages? Yes – yes, how silly of me, I can see that you have, you look simply ghastly. I expect you're dying to have a wash and get out of those filthy clothes, aren't you? I can lend you some things if –'

'I'm perfectly all right, thank you. I had a wash this morning, my clothes are quite clean and no, I'm not remotely thrilled she found me!' Rachel hissed, shaking her arm free. She grabbed the carry-cot and stalked into the drawing room.

Pippa looked bewildered. She raised her eyebrows at me. 'What did I say?' she whispered.

'I'll tell you in a minute. Oh, it's awful, Pippa, you've *got* to help us!' My voice cracked; I was on the verge of tears.

'Yes, but Polly, the thing is I've got –'

'In a minute, Pippa, I'll explain in a minute, come on.'

I grabbed her arm and pushed her into her own drawing room. For a moment I thought she'd been burgled. Every conceivable square inch of carpet was covered in debris, mostly of the clothing kind, but there was also quite a lot of pizza around. The coffee table was on its side, all the large sofa cushions were on the floor, and full ashtrays and empty bottles abounded. Even Pippa looked slightly nonplussed, she obviously hadn't ventured downstairs since the night before.

'Oh, er – sorry about the mess, we had a bit of a raucous evening last night.' She jerked her head meaningfully in the direction of the stairs and rolled her eyes dramatically. I got her drift but pretended I hadn't: I needed her much more than he did, whoever he was.

Rachel was picking her way across the room to a chair. She turned it the right way up, and with forefinger and thumb removed a rather dirty bra before sitting down with the baby in her arms. She turned away from us and stared out of the window into the garden as if she'd temporarily vacated her body.

'I was um, just about to make some coffee,' said Pippa. 'Would you like a cup?' Rachel didn't respond.

'I'd love some,' I said quickly, 'I'll help you make it.'

We escaped to the kitchen and she shut the door. 'What the hell's going on?' she said in a hoarse whisper. 'Is she demented or something? Few sandwiches short of a picnic? She doesn't look all there.' She wiggled her finger around on her temple.

'I'll explain in a minute, Pippa, but listen, promise you'll help us. We're in real trouble.'

'Polly, do you have any idea who I've got upstairs?' hissed Pippa as if she'd trapped a wild animal.

'Who?'

'Only Charles Stanley!'

'No! Charles Stanley? Really?' In spite of my predicament I gasped in admiration. I'd never met the man, but I'd heard him talked of in hushed and hallowed tones by Pippa and various other girlfriends of mine, and was clued up enough to know that in terms of finds he was something of a Holy Grail.

'Exactly, Charles Stanley. I've been after him for *months*, Polly, as you well know. You just can't *do* this to me, in fact you're not going to do this to me, so why don't you just quickly tell me what the bloody hell's going on so I can tell you to bog off and get back to him.'

I groaned. 'Oh no, Pippa, please don't do that, I really need you. Couldn't you just have a tiny word with him and say — say something earth-shatteringly important's come up and you'll see him very soon? Please do, please,' I begged.

Pippa gasped. 'Get rid of him? Now?'

'Oh, I'm sorry, I know I shouldn't ask you, but I'm desperate, really *desperate*!'

'Polly, you must be mad!'

I certainly must have looked it, because she stared at me for a few seconds then shrugged her shoulders in despair. She threw a few mugs on a tray and threw in the towel at the same time.

'All right. But it had better be good. Bloody good. You make the coffee and I'll go and have a word with Charles.' She rammed the Nescafé into my hand and made to go upstairs.

I fell on her arm with relief. 'Oh thank you, Pippa, thank you! Listen — you could meet him later, it's just we must talk to you now, and um — borrow a bit of your house.'

'Oh really?' Her eyebrows shot into her fringe. 'Oh yes, well, please feel free. Which bit would you like: my bedroom perhaps?'

I didn't laugh, in fact I was just about to cry. She sensed

it and gave my arm a squeeze. 'Look, don't panic, Polly. Just make the coffee and I'll go and square it with Charles. Tell me all about it in a moment, OK?'

'OK,' I whispered shakily as she ran off up the stairs, dressing gown flapping.

I wondered if my blancmange-like fingers were capable of getting boiling water from the kettle to mugs without giving myself third-degree burns. I just about managed it, and was on my way back to the drawing room with the tray when Pippa reappeared down the stairs followed by one of the most beautiful men I've ever seen. He was tall and long-legged with dark wavy hair which was currently attractively tousled, slanty green eyes, and a huge, lazy, sexy grin which I had the feeling was pretty permanent. He extended the grin even further towards his ears when he saw me.

'Hi, you must be the desperate friend,' he said, tucking his shirt into his jeans.

'I'm terribly sorry –' I began, but he'd already turned to Pippa, taken her in his arms, and was in the midst of giving her the most thorough kissing I've ever seen outside the cinema. I stood there like an usherette with my tray of coffee as he finished the scene.

'Bye, angel,' he whispered as he held her face in his hands. 'I'll see you later.' Pippa whispered something back and opened the door for him. I was impressed. I'd never seen Pippa in action before.

'Right! In here,' said Pippa in a businesslike manner when she'd shut the door. She shepherded me into the drawing room. I put the coffee down and flopped on to the sofa. The white-faced girl in the corner didn't appear to have moved an inch.

'Now, what's this all about?' said Pippa, looking at me. 'I am right, aren't I? This is the Rachel that chap Adam whatshisname was looking for? The guy who took you to the Savoy for din –'

'Yes, yes,' I said, interrupting her hurriedly. I didn't want my free meal at the Savoy to feature too heavily in my tale of courageous – albeit misguided – fortitude. 'This is Rachel, only – oh well . . .' I took a deep breath and dived in, gabbling away about judges, housekeepers, disguises and car chases, but trailing off miserably when I got to the bit about bursting into Rachel's sanctuary.

Pippa turned to Rachel. 'So that's how she found you?' Rachel didn't respond. Pippa turned to me. 'So that's how you found her? She was in the flat all the time?'

'Yes, but you see –'

'Well, so what's the problem then?' said Pippa staunchly. 'It seems to me you've been absolutely brilliant! I mean, you went to all that trouble just to unite a couple of complete strangers. You've been absolutely marvellous.' She turned to Rachel sternly. 'You've got a lot to thank Polly for, you know. There aren't many people who'd put themselves out to that extent, most people wouldn't have bothered to do anything. I think she's been tremendous, absolutely tremendous. Selfless, spirited, enterprising and –'

'Er, hang on, Pippa' I interrupted nervously. 'I haven't finished yet. You see, the thing is –'

'The thing is,' Rachel's head suddenly turned one hundred and eighty degrees to face us. It was a bit like something out of *The Exorcist*; any minute now we'd be in for a bit of projectile vomiting. Her face was grim, and her eyes almost disappeared into her face they were so screwed up with bitterness. 'The thing is that I didn't want her to find me at all. She's just a stupid, interfering old cow.'

'Oh now, look here!' said Pippa warmly. 'Talk about ungrateful. I mean –'

'No, Pippa. Listen to me,' I burst in. 'Adam wasn't looking for Rachel at all, he was looking for Jamie.'

'For Jamie?'

'Yes, for Jamie, the baby – this baby.' I jabbed my finger babywards. '*Their* baby.'

Pippa's eyes grew wide. 'Oh!'

I sighed. 'Exactly.'

'Oh! Oh gosh, how awful! You mean he just pretended . . . You mean he tricked you into . . . Oh!' She turned back to Rachel. 'So you didn't want to be found at all!'

Rachel declined to answer this, and gave her a look of such withering magnitude that most people would have been silenced for life, but Pippa was determined to get things straight in her head. 'So – so hang on a minute,' she persisted. 'This is like a tug-of-love thing, is it? You know, with the baby in the middle? The kind of thing you read about in the papers, is that it?'

Again this was deemed to be unworthy of response, and Rachel resumed her contemplation of the cherry tree in the garden.

Pippa looked at me, all rolling eyes and raised eyebrows. Oh my God, she mouthed. I nodded back miserably, agreeing wholeheartedly. Yes, oh my God.

'What are you going to do?' she whispered to me.

'I don't know,' I whispered back.

There was a profound silence. I looked at Jamie, who was sleeping peacefully in his carry-cot, oblivious to all the fuss and confusion surrounding him. He really was quite divine: all pink and white and chubby-cheeked with lovely little creases round his neck. Shame about the red hair, but if he turned out to be as good looking as his father, he'd be all right.

As for the mother – I sneaked a quick look at her grim profile – well, I had to say I still didn't remember her. She had a fluffy cloud of fair hair which not only needed a wash but, to my practised eye, could have done with about forty pounds'-worth of highlights; a pale, heart-shaped face with pointed features; and small, bluey-grey eyes with those rather unattractive blonde eyelashes. She was, I decided charitably, sweetly pretty in a little-girl-lost sort of way, but next to Pippa, who admittedly had a head start with the just-got-out-of-a-hot-bed-of-lust look, she scored about minus six on sex appeal. The big grey cardigan didn't help, because you couldn't really tell what sort of a figure she had, but I supposed she had a certain helpless attraction and would appeal to men of the caring and protecting per-suasion. I had a sneaky suspicion she was pretty damn tough underneath that oversized cardigan, though: she was certainly toughing this silence out.

'So what's your sto . . . I mean, what's the real story then?' I said as sympathetically as I could. I was beginning to feel a trifle irritated. After all, I'd tried my damnedest to help her. OK, I'd got it completely wrapped round my neck, but the least she could do was shed a bit of light on things instead of sitting there in supercilious silence like something out of a Botticelli madonna and child portrait.

'Rachel?' I raised my voice slightly. Still nothing.

Pippa coughed nervously. 'Well, of course you're welcome to stay here for a bit if that's what you'd like. I mean, I know it's not ideal but, um . . .'

Rachel continued to stare at the cherry tree and the tongue stayed hinged. Pippa looked at me and raised her eyebrows. I licked my incredibly dry lips.

'Well, Pippa, that's terribly kind. I think we'll say yes please, if that's all right with you and if, um, Rachel agrees . . .'

Suddenly Rachel turned towards us, she opened her mouth and – yes – she appeared to be contemplating a sentence. I for one was on the edge of my seat.

'Do you have anything stronger to drink besides coffee?' she asked. Wow! Not just a sentence, but a show-stopper of a sentence.

Pippa leaped up off her chair as if she'd been goosed, and was instantly hospitality itself. 'Gosh yes, of course. What would you like?'

'Could I have a gin and tonic?' It was getting better and better. In fact it was the first sensible thing she'd said since I'd met her.

Pippa raced off to the fridge and came back brandishing a frozen ice-tray, which she banged on the upturned coffee table spraying ice everywhere. Meanwhile, I poured three whopping great gins, adding a soupçon of tonic. We gulped them down thankfully and lit cigarettes. All at once a slightly less frosty, more conspiratorial atmosphere seemed to prevail.

Rachel put the sleeping Jamie in his carry-cot, crossed her legs and rested her chin in her hand. She sighed. 'OK. I'll tell you how I got into this mess.' Pippa and I leant forwards in unison, anxious not to miss a syllable.

'As you probably know, my father dragged me out of school just before my A-levels.'

'Gosh, how awful, why did he –' began Pippa.

'Sshhh.' I nudged her. For God's sake, she'd started, let her finish. 'Go on, Rachel.'

'Well, I was desperately upset, in fact when we got home I couldn't even bring myself to talk to him. I just locked myself in my room and refused to come out. I think that really shook him, so much so that when I asked if I could go abroad for a bit, amazingly he agreed, on the condition that I stayed with some friends of his in Boston. Well, I went, and that's how I met Adam, their son.'

So far so good, I thought.

She hesitated and took a long drag of her cigarette. 'Adam was – is, ten years older than me, good looking and very charming. I was incredibly unhappy, still rather shell-shocked, I suppose, and in dire need of a shoulder to cry on.' She shrugged. 'His was the obvious one: he offered it and I took it.' She paused for a moment and took another glug of gin. 'He was kind and sympathetic and, actually, great fun to be with. He made me feel a hell of a lot better, and we began to see each other practically all the time. Inevitably, of course, we ended up in bed.' She shook her head. 'God, when I look back now . . . You see, I was so ridiculously innocent, he was the first person I'd ever slept with, and I was so clueless that I didn't even think about contraception. I mean, I knew all about it, but I just didn't think.' She sighed. 'I got pregnant almost immediately.'

Let that be a lesson to you, Polly my girl, I thought. Keep taking those pills.

Rachel took another huge gulp of gin and continued. 'I

didn't tell him for a while because I was frightened of what he might say, but when I really couldn't squeeze into my jeans any longer, I did. He couldn't have been nicer. At one time I'd thought about having an abortion but was too much of a coward to go through with it, and Adam was appalled that I'd even considered it. To tell you the truth, he was thrilled about the baby, and determined we should keep it and get married.'

'Well, that's not so terrible!' I said. I imagined Harry's reaction to fatherhood would be to frogmarch me off to Harley Street where he no doubt knew of an obliging little clinic.

'No, I agree, and for a while things were great. We lived in his parents' house in Marblehead and I got bigger and bigger and felt reasonably happy about it. When I was about seven months pregnant, we rang my father and broke the news.'

'What!' I gasped. 'Didn't he go ballistic?'

Rachel smiled. 'He's not nearly as bad as you seem to think, you know.'

You could have fooled me, I thought.

'I mean, sure, he wasn't exactly thrilled to bits, but he came round eventually and, anyway, what could he do? I was due to have the baby in two months. Anyway, he came out to see me in America, met Adam properly, and everyone agreed that we should get married. Everyone, that is, except me.'

'Why on earth not?' said Pippa.

'Because' – Rachel struggled to explain – 'because I wasn't really in love with him.' She bit her lip and stared beyond us, almost as if she were thinking the whole thing through again as she spoke. 'I'd fallen for Adam when I was at a very low ebb, you see. I was depressed, miserable and lonely. I needed someone to turn to, and he just happened to be that someone. Looking back, I suppose it could have been anyone, within reason of course. D'you know, I think that even then, even right at the beginning when I was sleeping with him, in the back of my mind, I knew that I wasn't in love with him.' She looked up. 'Does that sound terrible?'

Pippa and I shook our heads vigorously.

'No, of course not!'

'God no.'

Oh yes, we'd both been there. We'd both had a few – ahem – liaisons, shall we say, with individuals who didn't altogether make our hearts beat faster.

'So you can see why I couldn't marry him?'

We nodded, but less vigorously this time. This was slightly trickier, since neither Pippa nor I had ever been on the receiving end of a marriage proposal. We would have liked to have been, but somehow those four little words had never cropped up in our earshot, and it was hard to say what our response would have been. None the less, we agreed wholeheartedly with the sentiment.

'Oh absolutely,' said Pippa.

'Oh God, I agree. Couldn't marry someone I didn't love,' I added. Unless, I thought privately, he was very *very* rich.

'Anyway,' Rachel went on, 'I prevaricated for a bit and said I'd rather wait for the baby to be born. After all, I was pretty enormous, and I pretended I wanted a proper white wedding.'

'Just playing for time,' said Pippa.

'Exactly. So two months later Jamie arrived, and actually we were OK for a while; I remember feeling reasonably happy. Then Adam started pestering me to marry him again. I put him off and put him off and we began to argue quite a bit. I was also desperate to get back to my music, I wanted to study some more – go back to college and get a nanny for Jamie. Adam was horrified – he thought I should stay at home; but eventually I persuaded him and in fact in the end he stayed and looked after Jamie because he could work from home. But things got worse and worse.'

Rachel rubbed her eyes with the back of her hand. She looked all in. 'Adam became incredibly possessive, questioning me endlessly about the boys at college, refusing to let me go for a quick drink after school with anyone; in fact, he took to waiting at the college gates in the car just to make sure I didn't. I even caught him reading my diary once. It was ghastly. I began to really resent him, and then of course, I began to hate him.' She smiled sardonically. 'You know what it's like. A little irritation can easily turn into full-blooded hatred.'

'Perhaps you should have gone on holiday together or something, just the two of you, without Jamie, tried to fall in love again?' said Pippa, who read lots of agony columns.

'But you see I never really *was* in love with him, that was the root of the problem.' Rachel sighed and ground her cigarette out in the ashtray. 'One night we had an absolutely furious row, a real humdinger, and the next morning I decided I'd just had enough. Adam had gone to Boston for a meeting, so I booked myself on a flight to London, packed a bag, left a note and went, taking Jamie with me.'

Pippa and I looked rather shocked.

'I *had* to do it like that,' she said emphatically, 'or I'd never have got away. You don't know Adam, he's just so determined.'

I did know Adam, vaguely, and I took her point. If she'd so much as suggested a separation she'd never have got across the doormat, let alone to the airport. I looked across at Pippa who was gripped, her mouth hanging open and about two inches of ash hanging from the cigarette in her hand. I grabbed an ashtray and held it underneath. Too late.

'So you went home to your father's?' she said, ignoring the pile of ash on the carpet.

'I had nowhere else to go. He was pretty shocked and tried to make me go back and patch things up, but once I'd sat down and talked it through with him, he came round, and in fact he said that in retrospect it was a good thing we'd never got married. The next day Adam telephoned, extremely drunk and extremely belligerent.' She sighed and took out another cigarette. 'He called me all sorts of names, threatened me with all kinds of hideous things, and said he'd never let me have Jamie. That happened about three times. He also threatened my father and said he was coming over to take Jamie back. I didn't consider it an idle threat either, because I know what he's like when he wants something. That's when Daddy and I decided I should go and live at his flat in the Temple. He's had that place for years, but he hardly ever uses it, and I don't suppose anyone even knows he's got it.' She lit her cigarette, blew the match out and crushed it in her hand. 'I liked it there. I felt safe.'

I looked down at my shoes and wondered which part of my body she'd imagined she was breaking into little bits when she savaged the matchstick. I had the feeling another apology might be in order at this point.

'I'm really sorry, Rachel,' I began. 'I had no idea –' but she interrupted me.

'It's OK. I dare say I was living in a fool's paradise anyway. He probably would have found me sooner or later.' I privately rather agreed with this, especially since her father's name was written in six-inch gold letters above the door.

'But surely,' said Pippa, 'surely with your father being a judge and everything, you could have held on to Jamie legally. I mean, couldn't you have got a court order or something?'

'Oh yes, legally; and that's what I intend to do; but that still doesn't stop Adam snatching him back and just getting on a plane to the States, does it?'

'Well what about,' Pippa went on, feeling her way carefully, 'what about if you had some kind of custody agreement, you know: you have him for a while and then Adam has him for a bit?'

'What, so Jamie spends his whole time to-ing and fro-ing across the Atlantic?' snorted Rachel. 'No thanks. Anyway, once Adam had him out there he'd never give him back, I know him too well.'

I couldn't think of anything to say. I'd been well and truly hoodwinked. And yet he'd seemed so straightforward, so . . . in love. Suddenly I plucked a thought from my brain.

'But there was a letter! A letter to Sally Lomax from you, saying what a terrific guy he was and how mad about him you were. Where did that come from?'

'Oh, come on,' scoffed Rachel, 'pretty easy to forge something like that, isn't it? I mean, do you know what my handwriting looks like?'

'No. No, I suppose not.'

Was I stupid or what? I'd sat at the Savoy making a complete prat of myself. I dug my nails into my hands in embarrassment. What a fool I'd been, and what a con man he was. I couldn't help remembering that bit in the letter about him being so good looking: he'd got quite a nerve to write that about himself, hadn't he? Quite a nerve. I stared into space, contemplating the magnitude of his gall.

Just then, Jamie decided it was time to wake up and exercise his vocal chords. He gave us the benefit of his extremely healthy lungs and – SCREAMED. I had no idea babies could cry quite so loudly. Pippa and I clustered round and bent down for a closer look as Rachel gathered him up in her arms. He stopped crying and Pippa held her arms out for a hold, but Rachel pretended not to notice. She obviously wasn't letting him out of her arms, let alone her sight.

Pippa straightened up and tied her minuscule dressing gown around her in a businesslike manner. 'You'd better stay here for a while, Rachel.' I could have hugged her. 'He's hardly likely to come looking for you here, I mean I don't know him from – oh well, you know.' She giggled, Rachel didn't. 'So you can have the whole of the top floor if you like: there are two tiny bedrooms and a bathroom.

It's not particularly spacious, but it's clean and reasonably tidy and, er, oh!'

Whilst Pippa had still been in mid-flow, Rachel had walked straight past us, into the hall and up the stairs. I felt hot with embarrassment. She was beginning to annoy me, a small thank-you here and there wouldn't go amiss. I waited until she was out of earshot.

'Thanks so much, Pippa, you're an angel. Sorry about that ungrateful cow. I mean, honestly, she's probably safer here than she was in the Temple.'

'It's OK. She's probably still upset,' said the ultra-tolerant Pippa, picking up the sofa cushions from the floor and gathering together what looked like a crateful of empty bottles. 'Oh, and you'd better stay too, of course.'

'Me? Why?' I said in surprise, gathering clothes from the floor and folding them up on a chair.

'Because, dick brain, what's the first thing Adam's going to do?'

I turned a pair of jeans the right way out and gave it some thought. 'Go to Judge Marsden's flat?'

'Right, and then?'

I dropped a full ashtray on the floor in horror. 'Go to my flat!'

'Exactly, employing whatever bully-boy tactics he feels are appropriate to pick your brains.'

'Oh my God!' I felt like Salman Rushdie. I was being persecuted – I needed police protection! I reached for my felt hat and pulled it down over my eyes, ramming my Ray Bans on my nose with my other trembling hand. I was not a very brave girl.

'What shall I do?' I whispered, sliding down into a chair. My knees felt rather weak.

'Just stay here and lie low for a bit.'

Oh, I would. I would lie very low. I would lie under that sofa if necessary, or, or down in the cellar where it was very low, I'd be so low you'd have to rip up the floorboards to find me.

I ran off to the hall to telephone Lottie. I told her the whole horrendous story and explained that she might have a visitor in the shape of one large ginger-haired Adam Buchanan ready and willing to wrench out teeth, hair and entrails in his search for his son. Lottie was totally unfazed by all this: her streak of yellow wasn't nearly as wide as mine. She said she'd pop over later with some clothes for me. All at once I knew who my friends were.

'Oh, and Lottie!' I screamed as she was about to put the phone down. 'Don't drop them all over the pavement, will you? Don't use a case, use a black binliner or something and – and look behind you to make sure you're not being followed. Remember whoever it is could be in disguise and, and – just be bloody careful!' I squeaked into the receiver, thinking of my own skin of course rather than hers.

When Pippa and I had tidied up and she'd shed her dressing gown for something more suitable, we all trooped off for a rather strange and subdued lunch in the Scarsdale. We were an unlikely bunch in the pub that afternoon: Pippa, Charles Stanley, Rachel – with Jamie asleep in a sling – and me.

We couldn't possibly tell Charles the whole story, but you could see his brain was working overtime as he wondered what this dolly mixture of girls was all about. Who was that white-faced one in the corner with the baby? And why did she and the one in the brown hat and dark glasses leap up and down every time someone came into the pub? Were they being followed? These and other unanswered questions clearly ran through his mind, but Charles, who was a good chap, said nothing and coped wonderfully – entertaining us, feeding us, plying us with drinks, and resisting all offers of payment.

It was rather as if Pippa had suddenly sprung a large and motley family upon him which he was expected to provide for, no questions asked. And wasn't he just taking it all in his giant stride, I thought, as I watched this long-legged hunk of man gaze adoringly at Pippa over his Guinness.

How would Harry have reacted, I wondered? He always enjoyed Pippa's company because she was so pretty, but I wasn't quite sure how he'd have coped with the anaemic waif and baby. I realized with a jolt that I hadn't thought about Harry for at least a day. Seeing Pippa and Charles so happy together made me miss him with an almighty great pang. I'd ring him later. Yes I would. Bet you anything he was wondering how I was. I was almost as good at lying to myself as I was to other people. Had he been trying to ring me, I wondered? At least he could reach me at the agency. I went cold. So could Adam.

'Pippa!' I squeaked, rudely interrupting Charles who was deep in the finer nuances of the latest French film at the Curzon, 'Pippa, he knows where I work! He'll be bashing down the agency door on Monday!' Pools of blood were swimming before my eyes as I imagined the nasty stains on the agency carpet.

'Yes, I was wondering about that,' said the altogether unflappable Pippa, obviously alive to the possibility before it had even filtered through my own fuddled brain. 'You'd better take the day off tomorrow and stay at home with Rachel. If he puts in an appearance, we'll say you've taken some leave: gone to stay with friends in the country for a couple of weeks or something.'

'Suppose he doesn't believe you!' I wailed.

'So what? What can he do? He might well believe it anyway; I mean it's quite likely really, considering he's after you.'

After me! Great Scott, someone was after me! I sank back in my chair in despair, nursing my gin and tonic. Perhaps I should change my identity completely, steal a passport, become a nun or something, emigrate to Australia perhaps.

Out of the corner of my eye I could see that Charles was looking more and more mystified. This latest outburst from the maniac in the hat had really got the cogs whirring in his brain. Ah yes, I was obviously on the run from my drunken, wife-beating husband – he looked at the empty ring finger on my left hand – common-law husband. He switched his gaze to Pippa. Pippa was obviously sheltering me, perhaps she ran a home for battered wives or something, or perhaps – yes – that was it, she was working for the Samaritans. He took her hand tenderly. That would explain the white-faced single parent in the corner. Perhaps white face was also a drug addict or a prostitute and Pippa had generously taken us all under her wing. He stroked her hand and his eyes shone with love and admiration. I drained my glass. Well, one good thing had come out of this saga. We were obviously doing wonders for Pippa's big-hearted image.

That evening, back at Pippa's, I weakened and rang Harry.

'Hi Polyester, how's it going? I've been looking for you everywhere, where have you been hiding?'

My knees buckled and I sat down very hard on the wooden chair by the telephone. A vase of flowers on the table next to it wobbled perilously. Harry had been looking for me?

'Well, I'm staying at Pippa's for a few days,' I replied in a somewhat dazed voice.

'Ah, so that's where you've been. I tried to ring you at lunchtime to see if you wanted a drink, but there was no answer from the flat.'

This time I had difficulty staying on the chair, in fact I had to grab hold of the banisters. 'You did?'

'Yes, I fancied a pint.'

'Oh! Well, what about tonight?'

'Oh God, I'd love to, darling' – Darling? – 'but I'm tied up now, I've got to work.'

It didn't matter, nothing mattered, he'd wanted to have lunch with me, he'd actively looked for me, no – no, he'd *searched* for me, oh joy!

'Listen,' he went on, 'I'm up to my eyeballs revising for this bloody stockbroking exam on Monday. I'll ring you in the week, shall I?'

Was he asking my permission? 'Yes, yes, fine!' I said, unable to keep the ecstasy from my voice.

'OK, take care.'

'And you . . .' I hesitated, dug deep for courage, and chanced it '. . . darling.'

I waited for the snort of derision; none came. 'Bye then.'

'Bye!'

I replaced the receiver and leaned weakly against the front door. Harry had actually phoned me on a normal, common-or-garden Saturday. He'd picked up the telephone and dialled my number because he wanted to see me. No, no, correction. He'd *missed* me. I salivated and tried to recreate the scene – yes, yes, that was it. First he'd missed me (Oh Polly, oh miss miss miss, oh where are you, Polly? Oh, I miss you so), and then, *then* he'd picked up the telephone (rush to telephone, must see Polly, must see Polly now) in order to ask me, to *ask* me (please Polly, please? If you're not too busy?) to meet him for lunch. Nothing mattered now, nothing at all. The whole ghastly Rachel and Adam business faded into insignificance.

With a shriek of joy I leaped two feet off the ground and skipped off down the hall, whooping and thumping the air as if I'd just won an Olympic gold. I ran slap-bang into Rachel, who'd been changing Jamie's nappy in the downstairs loo.

'Oops, sorry Rachel! Didn't see you there!' I couldn't wipe the silly grin from my face.

She ignored me and pushed past, taking Jamie upstairs for his bath. Oh God, she must think me a complete cold-hearted bitch, messing up her life and then whooping with pleasure. I went in search of Pippa who was in the kitchen. She was pleased for me, but not as impressed.

'Well, he damn well should ring you at weekends,' she said, shaking a wet lettuce round the kitchen. 'He should ring you every day, come to that.'

But nothing could dampen my spirits now. After a jolly supper with Pippa, minus Rachel, who said she wasn't hungry, I went to bed feeling absurdly happy and hugging my happiness to myself.

Later on that night I was awakened by Jamie crying for a bottle, and much much later on I was woken again. Only this time it wasn't Jamie's crying I could hear, it was Rachel's.

Chapter Eleven

When Monday morning arrived, it was beautifully sunny. I drew the curtains and hopped back into bed, pulling the duvet up around my chin. I lay there, staring out of the window at the Kensington chimney pots set against a bright blue sky, and watched the plane trees swaying in the breeze. I could hear Pippa banging around in her bedroom next door, getting ready for work, and for the first time in my life I actually felt jealous. What the hell was I going to do all day alone in the house with Rachel? Sit next to her in uncompanionable silence?

I would have helped her with Jamie, but she rejected all offers, and in fact positively discouraged me from having any sort of contact with him, which was irritating as well as insulting. It wasn't often I had the chance to get my hands on a real live baby, and I was just getting to the stage in my life when they were becoming vaguely interesting. Only vaguely. I had an idea that it would be rather pleasant to bounce one or two Harry look alikes around on my knee, help them with their finger painting (or did that come later on?) and watch the little darlings in the nursery-school nativity, dressed up as angels or shepherds (later still, perhaps?).

Anyway, I liked the whole concept of babies; what I wasn't so sure about was the having of them. This worried me. I'd even taken to prowling round Sainsbury's, browsing around amongst the frozen turkeys, looking at the eight- or nine-pounders. They were big bastards those nine-pounders, I can tell you. And that was the size of an average baby? And that had to come out of – well. It took my breath away just thinking about it; no wonder you had to go to classes and learn to breathe all over again. I really took my hat off to my mother and all the other mothers I knew. Talk about the camel going through the eye of the needle: knowing my luck, I'd probably have something about the size of a camel.

I'd read in a magazine somewhere that one of the Mitford sisters had been plagued by similar misgivings, and had asked her mother what it had felt like to give birth. 'Well,' her mother had said, frowning with concentration as she tried to remember, 'it was rather like having an orange pulled out of your nostril.' This awesome simile had stayed with me for a long time afterwards, and I crossed my legs and winced every time I thought of it.

I would have liked to have asked Rachel for her views on the subject, since she had first-hand experience, but she wasn't really the sort of girl you could sit down with for a cosy labour and contractions chat. She wasn't actually the sort of girl you could sit down with for a cosy anything chat, I thought, as she stomped moodily into the kitchen in a full-length Viyella nightie to give Jamie his breakfast.

'Morning!' I ventured cheerily, clocking the Viyella with amazement.

'Oh, uh, morning,' she mumbled back, as one might mumble to a slug.

'AY AY AY AAAAAY!' chirped Jamie, giving me a great big beaming smile. Now that was more like it!

'Woo Woo, Jamie!' I waved back and made a funny face; he laughed delightedly. Shame he seemed to be on permanent send at both ends, though, I thought, as a rather unpleasant smell began to pervade the kitchen. How could a baby as small as that produce smells so monumentally vile? Rachel shovelled Weetabix into his mouth, but he seemed more concerned with spitting it out than getting it in and – oh God, what was he doing now? Pushing it up his nose? Perhaps I'd take a rain check on babies, or maybe I'd adopt one when it had got past this rather messy stage. Pop down to the orphanage and pick out a clean one. When did they become clean I wondered; round about three? Or more like ten, perhaps?

Pippa appeared, dressed for work, and began spooning what looked like sawdust and milk into her mouth in her latest desperate bid to open up the bowels, an ongoing problem that occupied most of her waking hours.

'Still no luck?' I asked. Like most constipation sufferers, she liked to talk about it.

'It's been five sodding days now,' she mumbled back through the sawdust.

'Oh well, never mind, it's probably all that sex.'

'What d'you mean?' she spluttered, spraying me with milk.

'Well, it's bound to bung you up, isn't it?'

'Is it? Christ, so celibacy's the only answer, is it? The only way I'm going to get regular is to make sure I don't get it regularly?'

I giggled. 'Exactly, and the reason you have to eat so much bran is that you get too much oats.'

'God, imagine being a nun, you'd be on the bog all day, wouldn't you?'

We giggled. Rachel looked totally unamused.

'What will you tell Nick?' I asked, as another megaton of fibre found its way in.

'I'll just say you're sick,' she munched.

'Oh, OK. Just hope he doesn't ring the flat, that's all.'

'He won't – why should he? And if he does, you can just say you were asleep and didn't hear the phone, I mean, that's what you normally say when you skive, isn't it? Anyway, must go, bye.' She flung her spoon down and replaced it with her handbag.

'Bye,' I said dismally. 'Have a good day at the office.' I felt like the bored housewife already.

It wasn't as if it was high summer and I could lie in the sun all day, and it wasn't as if I had any money to go and play with. I shoved some toast in the toaster. Window shopping was no good. I just ended up feeling poor and envious, and then I had to indulge in a spot of retail therapy to make me feel better. That meant buying something cheap and cheerful and then realizing on the bus on the way home that a purple mini-skirt was a big mistake and wouldn't go with any of my other clothes. Then, of course, I'd have to spend the whole of the following lunch hour taking the wretched garment back to the shop. That involved endless imaginative lies about how I'd been high on valium at the time of purchase on account of severe depression following a close relative's death and therefore not in my right mind, or else I'd go through the rigmarole of putting a curtain ring on my finger and saying my husband didn't like me in purple (actually I got a vicarious kick out of this one), and then I'd have to spout out the same stories all over again when the dreary shop assistant called the manager.

'I'm not really supposed to do refunds, you'll have to speak to Mrs Meekins. Mrs Meekins, there's a lady here who says her husband's got a thing about purple . . .'

Some boot-faced old bat would appear and, together with Dreary, she'd inspect the garment thoroughly amid loud cries of, 'I hope it hasn't been worn, madam, only it seems rather *soiled*. I see a little stain here!'

'No, no, I think you'll find that's just the sheen of the cloth,' I'd say and – oh God, so it went on. An exhausting waste of time that could easily take up two whole days with absolutely nothing to show for it at the end.

No, shopping was definitely out. I'd just have to watch soap operas all day. I was on my way to the viewing room, wondering if nine-thirty wasn't perhaps a little previous for even the most bored of housewives, when the telephone rang.

'Hello?' I said gloomily into the mouthpiece *en passant*.

'Hi, Polly? It's Lottie.'

'Lottie! Hi, how are you getting on without me?'

'Oh I'll manage. Listen, I rang the agency and gathered from Pippa you were lolling around doing nothing, so are you free for lunch?'

'Free? I've never been so free in my life, that's a brilliant idea! I'll come to the City shall I?'

'Why not? I'll meet you in Corks at about twelve-thirty. OK?'

'Great! See you then, bye.'

I put down the phone. Things were looking decidedly upward. In fact, when I saw Rachel's stony face advancing towards me down the corridor, I felt as if I'd discovered the wooden horse. My escape was taking shape. Freedom was on the cards. I gave my face a look of friendly concern.

'Will you be all right on your own here if I pop out for a while at lunchtime?' I asked her.

'Of course.'

'Sure? Only I don't want to leave you if you feel nervous. I should lock all the doors, oh, and probably best not to answer the door, or even the phone.'

She didn't bother to reply and gave me a look of utter contempt. Who was I to tell her about safety?

I ran out of the house at eleven-thirty, and leaped the little wall at the front of the garden as if it were Colditz barbed wire. It was ridiculously early, but if I caught a bus it would take ages to get there, and I liked sitting on the top deck at the front. There's nothing nicer than taking a bus through London if you've got bags of time and nothing worse if you're late and desperate to get somewhere.

The number eleven chugged and spluttered its way slowly through the West End and out towards the City. As we trundled past the Bank of England and then rounded the corner, we passed Harry's office, as I knew we would. I peered in through the dark grey smoky windows on the off-chance that I might get a glimpse. Poor Harry. He was probably scribbling away at his exam at this very moment.

I arrived at Corks at bang on twelve-thirty, and sauntered down the stone steps to the cellar. The place was packed already, heaving with bankers and brokers braying loudly at each other and 'haw-hawing' with laughter. I began pushing my way past a million pinstriped backs, knowing Lottie would be late and arrive looking hot and bothered with tales of ghastly clients wanting advice who had kept her talking on the phone. I peered around the gloom of the dark cellar bar looking hopefully for a table that didn't already have a dozen city types jostling for position around it, and was surprised to see Lottie over in the corner, already in possession of this very rare commodity. What's more, she had a full bottle of wine in front of her. She looked pale and utterly worn out. Overworked and underpaid, I thought sympathetically: she should have stuck to shorthand and short hours like me.

'Hi! What's with the bottle of wine? I thought you people with proper jobs didn't drink at lunchtime?'

'I don't normally, but I thought we might need it under the circumstances,' she said a trifle grimly.

'Oh really?' I kissed her and sat down. Gosh, she really did look all in. Whatever was the matter? Lottie only cracked under the severest of pressure, unlike me, who needed a drink after a typing error. I peered at her through the candlelight.

'Are you OK? You look terrible, if you don't mind me saying so.'

'Had a bit of bad news,' she said, taking a swig of wine.

Oh poor Lottie, whatever could it be? Her home life minus a mother wasn't the happiest of places anyway. I hoped nothing had happened to her father, or Caro perhaps?

'What is it, Lottie, what's happened? Is something wrong?'

'Yes, it is actually, and in the absence of anyone else

coming forward to tell you about it, it seems to have fallen to me to be messenger boy.'

I felt an Arctic chill pass through my shoulderblades and down my spine. I knew at once that it wasn't her, it was me. I sat very still.

Lottie looked me in the eyes for the first time. She took a drag of her cigarette. 'Pour yourself a drink, Polly,' she said gently.

'In a minute. Go on, Lottie, just tell me.'

Lottie sighed. 'OK. Harry is seeing Caro.'

I let this bombshell of a sentence whistle through my ears, cruise into my brain, and crash into my heart. It exploded on impact and all my blood seemed to drain downwards into my feet. I found my tongue and licked my lips, except they didn't feel like my lips.

'He can't be,' I whispered.

'He is,' said Lottie brutally, knowing full well that brutal was what she would have to be.

'I don't believe it.'

She put her hand over mine and moved her face closer. 'Believe it, Polly, he is, I know he is.'

'But – but, he phoned me yesterday, he called me darling, he wanted to see me, he *asked* if he could ring me later – he *can't* be, Lottie, he just *can't* be!'

'Guilt?' said Lottie simply. Suddenly I knew she was right.

Lottie let me get used to the idea for a second. She poured me a glass of wine. I took a large gulp.

'Define seeing,' I whispered.

She looked down at the red-and-white checked table-cloth and picked a bit of candlewax off it with her fingernail. 'She spent Saturday night there and she was there last night too.'

I gasped in amazement. Somehow, what struck me more than anything was the luxury of two nights in a row. I'd never been afforded that privilege, not even in the early days. Harry was seeing Caro. Harry was *sleeping* with Caro. My guts seemed to be knotting themselves into a fierce ball of anguish. I clenched my fists and tried not to scream. It was a small wine bar and Lottie's local: it wouldn't look good. Try as I might, I couldn't resist imagining the scene. It was vivid. I saw Harry launching himself in all his golden glory from the diving board; I saw a *giggling*, squirming Caro, her perfect body naked on the Conran sheets, her perfect hair spread all over the pillow. My sheets. My pillow. My hand flew to my mouth. I wasn't going to scream, I was going to be sick. I gulped down the nausea and took deep breaths of musty, smoky air. He'd only met her in the flat about a week ago and already . . . I moaned softly.

'How long have you known?' I asked, keeping my sentences to the minimum. A certain amount of puke might well escape if I kept my mouth open for too long.

'Not long.'

'How long?'

'A couple of days.'

'How did you find out?' Details were important.

Lottie sighed. She looked wretched. 'Harry phoned me at work on Thursday for Caro's number.'

I stared at her, dumb with disbelief.

She squirmed and continued bravely. 'It's true, Polly, that's how much of a bastard he is. He telephoned *me*, your *best friend*, for Caro's *number*.' She spoke slowly, using TV presenter *emphasis* to try to ram the idea home.

'What did you say?'

'I told him to sod off. And I didn't tell you in case he'd just had one too many at lunchtime and thought better of it later. I rang Caro this morning. I wasn't going to mention Harry but I wondered if she would. She did. She was full of it, bubbling over, couldn't tell me quickly enough in fact,' she said bitterly.

I felt a brief pang for Lottie. Divided loyalties were awful, and she must be feeling ghastly, but it was only a very brief pang. Most of all I felt sorry for me because I was hurting like hell. If someone had whacked me round the head with a cricket bat I couldn't be more stunned. This must be how a man felt when he'd been kicked in the balls. I wouldn't mind kicking some at this very moment, actually. I looked around murderously for a spare pair of wandering balls; any pair would do, as long as they were male and firmly attached. I wondered if it would be possible to kill someone like that. I hoped so. I returned slowly from my homicidal depths and emerged with a raging thirst. I wanted more wine and I wanted it *now* and I wanted more details too. I wanted to cram my head full to bursting with Harry and Caro's indecent exposure and as many nasty, sordid facts as my head had room for, and then I wanted to take a deep breath and explode with self-pity. And boy, would I explode. I drained my full glass and filled it up again, hoping the cellars here could cope with my sudden insatiable thirst.

'I want to know everything, Lottie.'

She sighed. 'Not much to tell, really. Apparently he

eventually got her number from those friends they were discussing the other day, the people in Hampshire. Then he rang her up, took her out to supper –'

'Where?' It was important.

'Er, well, Le Caprice, I think,' said poor Lottie.

'*Le Caprice*!' Ouch! I caught that one right in the stomach. It fair doubled me up with pain. Never in my wildest dreams, and let me tell you, there had been some pretty wild ones – including holidays in Mustique, a clothing allowance at Chanel, and sapphire eternity rings – but never, *never*, had I ever dreamed that Harry might take me to Le Caprice. He'd always been dead against fancy – or should I say expensive? – restaurants on principle. All that money for a carrot cut into a flower? And all those ridiculous service charges just because we're sitting in Mayfair? Of course I'd been right behind him, thinking there were much more important things for us to spend his money on – like diamonds, for instance. Le Caprice! I recovered from the body blow and lit a shaky cigarette.

'Go on,' I gasped.

'Oh Polly, you don't want to know. I mean, it's obvious really, isn't it? Dinner, coffee, back to his place . . .' She tailed off miserably.

'But they definitely did it?'

'Of course they did it,' she said crossly. 'What, you think they might have played Scrabble until dawn or something? Of course they did it.'

All at once a little ray of hope scuttled across the dark horizon. 'Well – well, maybe it's just a quick fling? Perhaps he just fancied her rotten and felt like a spot of how's-your-father? Because – because of course I haven't been around much recently, you know, Lottie, I've been very busy. In fact he tried to ring me at the flat yesterday, but I wasn't there, but perhaps – perhaps now I'm back he'll drop her like a cup of cold sick and – and come running back to me? Maybe he just couldn't help himself? Some men are like that, aren't they? What d'you think?'

Lottie narrowed her eyes as she blew smoke across the table. 'Maybe.'

'You don't think so.'

She ground her cigarette out and sighed. She leaned forward, perhaps imagining that the closer she got to me, the easier it would be to drum some sense into my skull.

'Look, Polly, did he ever treat *you* as anything more than a quick fling? I mean, I know you wasted nearly a year of your life on him, but how many times did you see him? About twenty? Thirty? Think about it, did you ever see him at weekends? Did you ever meet his parents? Did you ever go away together, even for a day or two, let alone a holiday? Did he ever give you anything – flowers, a birthday present, security, happiness, love, anything?'

I was shrinking down in my seat under this rain of bullets, each one hitting the spot. She saw my tortured face and stopped, although there was more.

'I'm sorry, Polly, I don't want to make it worse, but you've *got* to believe it. You can't keep hanging on to someone who was never even there in the first place and hope that this nobody is going to come back in order to give you precisely nothing. Think about it, please.'

I couldn't. All I could think about was Harry and how much I loved him, had always loved him, in fact, from the moment I'd first set eyes on him. I vaguely remembered someone else saying that to me recently. Of course, it was Adam, waxing lyrical on the grim-faced Rachel at Boston airport. My heart went out to him for a millisecond. I drained my glass again and tried to get my head round this nightmare. Harry and I were no more. Harry was seeing someone else. I'd been dumped. His future no longer contained me.

We drank the bottle and ordered another, Lottie drinking much less than me. An hour later, I swayed out into the sunshine, blinking hard against the bright light, hoping I'd dulled the pain but knowing I hadn't. Lottie hugged me and shepherded me to a bus stop. She waited until a bus came along, then hugged me again and put me on it, handing me sixty pence for my fare as if I were a child. I clutched the coins and walked shakily up to the top deck. I walked down the aisle very carefully, holding myself together like a piece of broken china. If I let go, I might spill out all over the place. I made my way to the front and sat down.

London was still bathed in sunshine as we headed back West. Once again we passed Harry's office. I wondered how the exam had gone, and then remembered that it had been a lie. He'd been in bed with Caro. I got out my purse to pay my fare, forgetting that I was already clutching it. Harry's photograph stared at me from the credit card section. I took it out and rubbed some dust off with my finger. It wasn't even one that I'd taken: I'd found it lying around in a drawer in his flat and stolen it. He was lying on his tummy on a Greek beach, squinting slightly from the sun, laughing into the camera, brown and sandy and beautiful.

The tears began to fall. They started slowly at first, just a few trickles down the nose brushed hastily away with the back of my hand, and the odd catch in the throat that could be contained and might well be passed off as a touch of hay fever. But then the tears stopped being individual and became continuous rivers which flowed and flowed. I couldn't stop them, they got faster and faster and my hay fever got louder and louder until there was nothing I could do to control it. I was doing proper shoulder-shaking sobs now, heaving and gasping as I limbered up to reach fever pitch.

'Ooooooohhhhhh? . . . hagh-hagh-hagh? . . . oooohhh-hhoooo . . . hagh-hagh-hagh . . . ohohoooooooo . . .'

The top deck was full, but I didn't care. I let them have it, every single anguish-ridden decibel. The conductor avoided taking my fare, and I kept on shaking and sobbing all the way to Hyde Park Corner. Eventually a fat lady in a furry hat and tweed coat could bear it no longer. She came bustling down the gangway and plonked herself down next to me in the seat that no one else wanted. People were sitting on each other's laps, heads, feet – anything to avoid that seat.

She patted my hand and passed me a tissue. 'There, there, dear, it's all right, it's all right. You have a good cry.'

That's what I was doing, wasn't it? Christ, I was positively in overdrive, what on earth did she call a good cry? I was also at the talking-through-the-sobs stage now, wanting to share my grief with complete strangers, that kind of thing. It was lucky she'd volunteered to sit next to me, actually, otherwise I might have grabbed just anyone, like that terrified-looking teenager in the seat opposite, or the man next to him with his face hidden studiously in the newspaper. They could have been innocent victims.

'I-I-It's – hu hu, my bo-o-y frie – nd – hu hu, he's – hu hu hu hu hu he's –' I sobbed to Tweedy Lady, wondering if she could possibly stay on as far as my stop and then come home for tea.

'Your boyfriend, is it? There, there, dear, don't worry. He'll be all right, don't take on so,' said the lady, no doubt imagining horrific motorbike accidents or worse. 'Really now, he'll be fine, they can do marvellous things these days, what with medical science and that, don't you worry.'

Oh yes, he'd be fine, he'd be fine and dandy. But it wasn't him we had to worry about, was it? It was me. Would I make tomorrow? She rummaged in her oversized handbag and pulled out a crumpled paper bag.

'Here now, have one of these.'

She passed me a rather sticky peardrop. I took it, and as I sucked, my sobs seemed to subside slightly, rather like Jamie's did when he got to grips with his dummy. It was strangely soothing. I stared out of the window and she patted my hand saying, 'There, there, it's all right,' every now and then, which again was very comforting. They should employ ladies like this to tour the hospitals with their peardrops and their tweedy coats, patting the hands of people with real problems, like relatives of accident victims, girls whose boyfriends really had come off their motorbikes. Women like this should be available on the National Health.

When we reached my stop, I stumbled blindly down the aisle to the steps and realized that about forty pairs of eyes were trained eagerly upon me. This must be a little like getting married. A little. Except that this particular congregation were craning their necks to get a better look at the girl who'd had the screaming heeby-jeebies on the bus. I imagined the scenes all over London tonight, in pubs with friends, at home with mum and dad, in the kitchen with hubby. 'Cor, bloody hell, there was this girl on our bus today who had a *fit*, a real *fit*, she did, all shoulder shaking and 'ysterical-like. Ooooh, it was *awful*.' I reckoned I'd done my bit for street theatre.

As I walked home I realized I was heading for Tregunter Road by mistake. So what? I simply turned round and headed for Kensington. It would take about an hour but what the hell? I had the rest of my life to fill, didn't I? The rest of my life without Harry. I looked at my watch, it was only three o'clock. I'd be hard pressed to make it through the rest of the afternoon, let alone a lifetime.

I walked up the Fulham Road, looking at the shops but not seeing anything. On and on I walked, until the shops gave way to tree-lined avenues, the sort of avenues Harry and I were to have lived in. How crazy I'd been, living on dreams. How idiotic of me, and how presumptuous to think that I could have held him. As I walked past a garden square, I noticed the gate was open. I went in and walked around it three or four times. The wind rustled through the trees overhead, and the sun was streaming down through the leaves making a dappled pattern on the grass. I thought of all the times we'd had together; they seemed to be illuminated by the sunlight. I'd never hear his footsteps pounding up the stairs to the flat again, I'd never roar off to supper in his car, I'd never feel that excitement, that passion. But I'd hear about him. Oh yes, I was sure of that. I'd hear about his exploits with Caro, or whoever came after Caro. I'd hear about the parties he'd been to, the fun he'd been having, and I'd want to hear because that way I'd feel I was still a part of his life. I'd want to torture myself.

I walked round the garden one more time, then headed off to Kensington. It was a warm spring day and I'd walked for miles but I felt very cold.

When I reached Pippa's house, I realized I didn't have a key. I rang the bell and Rachel opened the door. She stared at my ashen, tear-stained face in astonishment. I ignored her and walked slowly upstairs. I lay on my bed with my jacket on for about an hour, not really thinking about anything in particular, just staring at the ceiling. I heard the clock down the road strike six o'clock; a few seconds later another one struck. Odd how church clocks could never seem to get it together.

After a while there was a tentative knock on the door. It was Rachel with a cup of tea. She didn't say anything, didn't even ask what the matter was. She just sat on my bed while I drank it and then took the cup downstairs again. People could be kind, I thought, as I turned my face to the wall. The wallpaper was cream with a light green trellis pattern around which roses grew. I stared at the roses winding themselves around the trellis. My eyelids felt heavy. I didn't think I'd sleep, but I dropped off almost immediately, absolutely exhausted.

Chapter Twelve

I arrived for work the next morning looking like I'd just gone fifteen rounds with Mike Tyson. My eyes were like a couple of jam doughnuts – little red holes in bloated puffs, my lips had swollen out of all proportion, and my cheekbones had risen a good three inches. Pippa marched me in like a boxing manager with a prize fighter, glaring at everyone and daring them to comment. She needn't have bothered, it was rather like the parting of the Red Sea the way everyone ran for cover – disappearing behind doors, filing cabinets and photocopiers like frightened rabbits, anxious not to get involved. Of course, as the morning wore on their curiosity got the better of them, and they crept out, sidling up to my desk to borrow a paperclip or a stapler, bending low and sneaking what they imagined was a surreptitious look at my distorted face. I felt like the bearded lady at the fairground, and rummaged in my bag for the trusty sunglasses.

Joss and Ron were among the first to slide their bottoms on to my desk. They could smell boy trouble at fifty paces.

Joss took my hand and stroked it. 'Poor Polly.'

Ron found my knee and stroked that. 'Poor poor Polly,' he echoed, 'but we did warn you, darling, didn't we?'

'Oh indeed we did,' agreed the other half, 'we warned you time and again. We said, whatever you do, Polly, don't play with boys, they're very dangerous. We did say that, didn't we?'

I nodded miserably.

'And do you know why they're so dangerous, my darling?' persisted Ron.

I shook my head wearily.

'Well, I'll tell you. It's on account of the one-eyed trouser snake. Are you with me, Poll?'

I sighed and smiled weakly.

'Ay yes, I think you are, and I think you've been playing with one, haven't you? And we all know what happens to little girls who play with trouser snakes, don't we?'

Joss nodded sagely. 'They get bitten.'

'How right you are, Joss my boy, they get bitten. Best to leave well alone.'

'Become a nun,' suggested Joss. 'I like you in black.'

'Or a lesbian?' ventured Ron eagerly, seeing himself perhaps in the role of managing voyeur.

'Either will do,' agreed Joss, 'but that's all by the by. What you need right now, of course, is some nice casual sex with no strings attached.'

'In a hotel of your choice.'

'My choice,' corrected Joss.

'Not Sussex Gardens again?'

'Why not? Very discreet, sheets are clean, a Teasmade in the bedroom, what more could a girl ask for?'

'A little bit of style, Ronnie boy, that's what! Dear oh dear, we're not talking about one of your regular scrubbers, you know. Polly's got class, she's probably even been finished off at one of those flower-arranging places in Switzerland – Mummy does good works you know, Daddy

237

plays bridge; she's not going to drop her drawers just any-where!'

Ron held my other hand as I eventually shook him off my knee. 'Don't you listen to him, darling. He's got no idea, and you'd never get your rocks off anyway, you'd be up all night waiting for the earth to move and it wouldn't even shudder. He's all gong and no dinner, that one. No, no, you come with me. Ronnie boy knows the ropes. We'll sneak off after lunch for a bit of afternoon delight – I know a nice little flat in Tregunter Road, actually. About four o'clock suit you?'

I smiled weakly; they were doing their best to cheer me up. 'Thanks boys, some other time perhaps.'

'I've never had any complaints, you know,' said Joss in a mock injured tone. 'I may not be as young as your Harry, but I'm just as athletic, and I can always be relied on to rise to the occasion.'

My face crumpled slightly at the mention of his name. Joss noticed and quickly lit a cigarette for me before putting it in my mouth. 'Breathe deeply,' he commanded. I sucked gratefully. 'Drink?' he offered, taking a hip-flask out of his pocket. I shook my head, that really was the slippery slope.

'Bit of a lad, that Harry, wasn't he?' mused Joss, light-ing one for himself and taking a quick swig of whisky. He had a faraway look in his eye and I detected a touch of admiration in his voice. 'Still, bit rotten of him to roger your flatmate. Too close to home.' I could tell he was deeply impressed. I sighed, Chinese whispers had started already.

'Not my flatmate, her sister.'

'Really? Oh, well that's all right then.' He sounded dis-appointed. 'Fair dinkum. What's she like?'

'Oh, you know, pretty, young, sexy, glamorous, big tits, nothing special,' I said bitterly.

Their eyes lit up. 'Really?' said Joss. Ron whistled softly. I looked up sharply. 'What a bastard,' he added quickly, shaking his head.

Nick strode through on his way to his office. 'James Hutchinson's coming in at twelve o'clock, so clear this place up, please. It looks like a pigsty.'

Joss and Ron raised their arms in Nazi-style salutes and goose-stepped back into their office. Nick reached his own door, then paused and came back to my desk. He took my sunglasses off and peered into the jam doughnuts.

'Jesus, not again, Polly. What have you been up to this time?'

'Gastric flu,' I said, snuffling hard and hastily replacing my glasses.

'Really? Gastric flu? Not alcohol-induced?'

I shook my head. My face wobbled violently: it seemed to be full of liquid. 'No,' I whispered.

'Well, shouldn't you be in bed then?' His voice was soft now, his face kind. Oh God, don't be nice to me, please don't be nice to me, I thought desperately.

'I'll struggle on,' I said bravely, digging my nails into my hand to stop myself from crying and wishing he'd revert to his usual SS tactics.

'I really think you should go home, you look awful. Shall I order a taxi?'

I couldn't reply to this without sobbing loudly and doing the nose trick all over the document in front of me, so I shook my head violently and hoped he wouldn't notice the tear, goddamnit, that had somehow escaped and was even now peeking out from behind my glasses and travelling down my cheek.

He noticed it. 'Harry?' he said simply.

I nodded briefly, surprised that he even knew his name, and not really feeling up to any more lying. I also hoped this would put an end to all the kindly concern and cause a few fuses to blow. It didn't. Instead he did something that reduced me to a shivering mass of jelly. He took a lovely clean white hanky out of his pocket, and wiped my tear away before handing it to me. 'Here.'

This sweet touch of humanity damn nearly did for me. I breathed deeply but it was no good: the inhaling part of the exercise was too shuddery. Great shaking sobs were building up in my breast and I clutched the side of the desk in horror. I must not break down, I must not break down! I thought hard about unemotional things like the Chancellor of the Exchequer and the Hanger Lane Gyratory System and – and the Middle Ages; anything, in fact, that would help to keep the waterworks at bay. Nick began to look rather alarmed at the prospect himself: the odd tear, fine, but a full-scale flood was clearly a different matter.

He straightened up quickly and sensibly wiped the concern off his face. 'All I really need today is a working lunch for my meeting. D'you think you're up to arranging that?' he asked briskly.

'Oh yes, of course,' I gasped between shudders, glad to be back to normal office-speak and glad to have something to do. 'I'm um, feeling much better already actually.'

I managed a wobbly smile. I'd feel even better if he could see his way clear to calling me a lazy good-for-nothing slut, but I supposed that was out of the question in his present mood.

'Good.' He nodded briefly and turned to go back to his office. He paused, and swept his hand around the room. 'Oh, and don't forget to do something about this hell hole.'

I breathed a sigh of relief. That was more like it, although a few more expletives here and there wouldn't have gone amiss. It was as if the hanky episode had never happened. This was the Nick I knew and – I hesitated. For some reason, 'hated' was too strong a word. I buried myself in my typing, wishing I'd never grown out of the dolls and ponies stage. Men were still such a mystery.

Mr Hutchinson arrived dead on twelve, looking even more rat-like than usual. He was panting slightly from climbing the stairs, but as I watched his mousy little chest palpitating up and down, I couldn't help wondering if he hadn't in fact just been for a nice little pedal in his wheel. His beady eyes darted around, taking everything in, especially, it seemed, my battered face. His whiskery nose twitched with excitement, and he actually stood on tiptoe to peer over my glasses. I straightened up to my full five foot three inches, which seemed to be more than he had to offer, and he lowered his heels admitting defeat.

'You're looking very mysterious today, Polly. Not trying to hide from me, are you?'

'Of course not, Mr Hutchinson,' I said, taking his paw which he'd held out for a shake. 'I'm just getting over the flu and my eyes are still a bit sensitive.'

Did one's eyes get sensitive? I always enjoyed such rude

health I could never quite remember which symptoms went with what ailment, but Ratty didn't seem to want to query this. I relieved him of his grey coat, grey scarf and grey umbrella, and wondered briefly if his underpants were grey too. At least I didn't have to relieve him of those. Suddenly I felt a bit peculiar and wished I hadn't thought about that. I showed him into Nick's office.

'Would you like some tea?' I asked as the two men shook hands.

'Naughty, naughty Polly!' he remonstrated, waving a little claw in my face. 'You know I only drink coffee, don't you!'

'Oh yes, sorry. I'm afraid we're out of filter, though. We've only got instant muck at the moment. Is that OK?'

Mr Hutchinson's face froze. Behind him, Nick shook his head in despair before putting it in his hands. The rat's eyes were narrowing.

'Well I'd better have some instant muck then, hadn't I?' he said nastily.

I groaned and clutched my mouth. 'Oh gosh! No, sorry – um, no – I didn't mean Special Roasty, that's not muck, that's delicious, no – I – I meant something else, something really horrid that's been sitting in the cupboard for ages – I'll get you some Special Roasty right now.'

I disappeared in confusion. When I returned with the tray I didn't look at either of them. I set it down on the desk and scurried away. After all, I didn't really have to look: I could feel Nick's icy glare freezing into the very marrow of my bones.

'Well, I've lost my boyfriend, I might as well lose my job,' I said gloomily to Pippa as we arranged the cold roast beef for lunch on a plate in the tiny galley kitchen.

'Never. He's much too fond of you,' said Pippa, throwing a salad together.

'Fond of me? Don't be ridiculous,' I scoffed, although a white linen hanky did make a brief, fluttery appearance in my mind's eye.

'It's true, he thinks you're wild and wacky.'

'Oh terrific.'

'What's wrong with that? It probably makes a refreshing change from all those sophisticated models and actresses he usually hangs around with.'

'Thanks very much,' I said dryly. 'You mean he thinks I'm gauche and stupid.'

'Something like that . . . Where's the knife to cut this cheesecake with?'

I rummaged in the drawer. 'We've got about a million spoons and forks and no knives – here, use this.' I handed her Ron's scalpel which he used for cutting up layouts.

'Polly, that's hardly hygienic –'

'Oh don't be silly.' I ran it under the tap. 'Here, give it to me.'

She handed me the cake and I cut it into slices.

We deposited the lunch in Nick's office amid deep and turgid discussions about brand shares and meal figures, whatever they were. Once again I thanked my lucky stars that I hadn't been born bright enough to be a career girl. I perched on Pippa's desk and cut the split ends off my hair, wondering if I'd ever be happy again.

'Oh, by the way, Adam was here yesterday,' said Pippa absent-mindedly as she typed away.

I gasped and dropped the scissors. 'No! Was he? What, here, in the agency? Pippa, why didn't you tell me?'

'I'm telling you now. You've been a bit preoccupied, you know.'

'What happened? Where was he, was he waiting outside? Pippa, stop typing and bloody well tell me what happened. It's all right for you; it's not your blood he's after!'

Pippa paused and swivelled round in her chair. 'Yes, he was waiting outside; well, pacing actually, stomping up and down like a caged animal, shaking that mane of red hair – incidentally, he's not my type at all, you know, you always get much redder pubes than you think you're going to with –'

'Go *on*, Pippa,' I urged. God, she always got so side-tracked.

'Anyway, he was pacing up and down, and – and shaking his head about like this' – she shook violently all over her word processor – 'like a rabid dog, in fact, and mouthing obscenities – well, what I assumed were obscenities. Honestly, Polly, if you ask me he's seriously disturbed. In fact he reminded me of a friend of my brother's who went really loopy when he came to stay with us one summer, started talking to himself and –'

'Pippa! What happened?'

'Oh well, eventually Mummy rang the hospital and the little men in white coats came to –'

'*No!* With Adam?'

'Oh. Oh, well, the moment I arrived he pounced. He'd obviously pounced on everyone else as well, but he grabbed my arm like this' – she demonstrated with a sharp pincer grip on my arm; I suppressed a scream – 'and asked me if I worked with you. I said I did and funnily enough

I'd spoken to you only last night. I said you'd telephoned to say that you wouldn't be in for a couple of weeks because you'd gone to stay with friends in the country.'

'Good girl. What did he say to that?'

'He grabbed my other arm like this' – more demonstrations – 'and asked me who the friends were and where they lived. When I said I didn't know, he said perhaps I was lying and secretly shielding you. I tell you, it wasn't very pleasant. Anyway, just as he was about to draw the silken cord from his pocket and wrap it around my throat, Nick came flying to my rescue.'

'Seriously, was Adam getting aggressive?'

'Well, maybe not aggressive,' said Pippa grudgingly, 'but I must admit I was jolly glad when Nick appeared. Adam had a pretty loony look in his eye – that guy is definitely barking, Polly. Nick thought so too.'

'OK, OK,' I waved aside Pippa's amateur psychoanalysis. 'So what did Nick say?'

'Well, of course he was slightly taken aback when he heard about your sudden departure to the country leaving him secretary-less.'

I groaned. 'Oh no!'

'But it was OK, he rose to the occasion beautifully and said how he wasn't really surprised because you'd been looking so tired recently and you probably needed a break –'

'Knowing it was a pack of lies?'

'I suppose so. I mean, he didn't look surprised to see you this morning, did he? Anyway, he was brilliant, he even said Adam could sit in reception and wait for you if he liked, but he'd be waiting there for a couple of weeks.

Of course Adam lapped it all up, coming as it did from a fellow man in a suit with a proper job rather than a mere secretary. I mean, talk about gullible. Anyway, he came up here just to make sure, had a good poke around, in fact,' she giggled, 'he even looked under your desk. Then eventually he sloped off, probably to slit his wrists; he looked capable of it.'

'Poor Adam. Did you tell Nick what it was all about?'

'Not really, I just said this guy was hounding you because he thought you were hiding his girlfriend.'

'What did he say?'

'He shook his head and sighed and said, "You know, it really wouldn't surprise me," in a kind of resigned voice.'

'Oh God. He thinks I'm mad,' I said miserably, tapping Ron's scalpel on the desk.

'Probably, anyway then –'

'Pippa, look at this.'

'What?'

'The scalpel, look!'

She looked and grabbed it from me. 'The blade's missing!'

'Exactly.'

We stared at each other for a few seconds.

'It must have fallen off when you cut up the cheesecake,' she said slowly.

'So where is it now?'

I jumped off the desk and bolted to the kitchen. I ran my hand over the work surface looking for a small, but potentially lethal, razor-sharp blade.

Pippa peered into the sink. 'It could have gone down the plughole, couldn't it?'

'Unlikely,' I said, feverishly shaking out tea towels and dish cloths. We faced each other again, at the same time facing the awful truth.

'It must be in the cake!' I gasped.

We ran as one, as if we were tied together in a three-legged race, to Nick's door, and pressed our noses up against the small square of glass. Luckily Mr Hutchinson had his back to us. Nick spotted us and frowned but carried on talking, no doubt trying to pretend that it was quite normal for us to take such a keen interest in client meetings.

The roast beef had been demolished, as had the salad, but the cheesecake was still mercifully intact. But not for long. Still talking, Nick handed Mr Hutchinson a side plate, and then pushed the cheesecake towards him.

'Say no, say no,' I breathed. But how silly, of course he'd want some, after all, it was cheese, wasn't it? The little claw came shooting out cakewards, but then, miraculously, paused in mid-plunge. It waggled around a bit as Mr Hutchinson no doubt decided it was time to put Nick straight on some highly important point, like how he was the client and it was his money so what he said went. Nick conceded, making a Prince Charles gesture with his hands and nodding his head. Mr Hutchinson sat back in his chair, pleased with his point, probably believing it was his superior intellect that had secured his victory rather than his dosh; at any rate, the cake was forgotten.

We breathed again, steaming up the glass somewhat. But too soon! Seconds later, those ratty little tastebuds were reasserting themselves and, with a swift dart of the paw, Mr Hutchinson lunged forward and helped himself

247

to the largest slice of the cake. It was too much for me. I flung open the door and in an equally swift movement removed both the cake from the table and the slice from Mr Hutchinson's hand. It was the work of a moment. Both men stared at me in astonishment, the client blinking away as if his life depended on it.

I laughed nervously. 'I'm so sorry, but it's off.'

'Off?' said Nick.

'Yes, it's bad, you know, gone off. Just had a call from the cake shop.'

Nick looked deadly. 'Polly, what on earth is going on?'

'It's past its sell-by date, you see – way past, in fact – months, years past. They forgot to tell me when I bought it, but they rang just now to let me know. So sorry! I'll take it back.'

'It can't be . . .' began Mr Hutchinson.

'It is, though. Weird, isn't it?' I gave him a synthetic little smile and fled, cake in hand.

Mr Hutchinson's voice trailed me. 'But it looks so delicious . . .'

I closed the door on him. OK, Nick was furious, but I'd rather incur his wrath than kill a client – just. I could see the headlines in *Campaign* next week. 'Secretary kills client – razor in cake.' I shuddered and ran into the kitchen, where Pippa and I inspected each slice like a couple of forensic scientists. We picked them over one by one and, sure enough, the last slice yielded a small, sharp, deadly blade.

'Thank God!' I cried, holding up Exhibit A in my fingers.

Just then the kitchen went dark. I looked up to see

Nick's large frame filling the doorway. I instantly dropped the blade in the sink.

'Have you gone quite mad?' he barked, striding over to me. I pressed the cake back into his hands, thus keeping a cake plate's distance between us. It was still too close for comfort. The glare from those eyes was enough to make me want to reach for my sunglasses again.

'Oh Nick, it was all a terrible mistake!' I blurted out. 'The cake shop just rang to say it wasn't our cake that was stale at all, it was somebody else's! They'd got it wrong, isn't that marvellous? So we can eat it after all!' I grabbed a piece and crammed it into my mouth. 'MMmmmmmmm, oh yesh, mmmmm, delishious!' I said, spitting crumbs all over the place and rolling my eyes to demonstrate its delectability.

Nick stared at me in disbelief, but I did wonder if around the mouth region there wasn't just the hint of a flicker of a ghost of a – no, perhaps not.

'I'll speak to you later, Polly,' he snapped. He turned on his heel, cake in hand, and marched back into his office, closing the door very firmly behind him.

I staggered back into the pit and fell reeling into my seat. I felt like I'd gone through a mangle. This was all I needed, today of all days. I hadn't even had much time to indulge in some serious self-pity, it had been so chaotic. Maybe I should take advantage of Nick's earlier suggestion and go home, stopping off *en route* to jump in the Thames. At least if I were dead he'd have to think of some nice things to say about me to my parents at the funeral. I sighed. I didn't really want to die, I just wanted to press a fast-forward button and be about two months, or two years, hence. I couldn't really go home, anyway: Nick was going away for two weeks on Thursday and there was still masses to do before he went. At least then I could have a break.

I switched on to autopilot and bashed away at the keyboard, wishing it was Caro's face. Perhaps I should have kept my suntan going? Had a few sunbeds? I'd been so brown when I'd met Harry, he'd liked that. Did Caro have an all-over tan, perhaps? I bet she did. I snarled and thumped the keys viciously, well on the way to giving her severe brain damage. I tried to look on the bright side. No need to have my hair highlighted quite so often, ease up on the leg waxing too, I thought. At least I'd be marginally richer – and marginally darker haired and hairier legged too. Yes, really attractive, Polly, just the right combination to catch a new man. But whatever was I thinking of? New man? Good Lord, no, I was in mourning. Odd though, how in the very, very back of my mind – and we're talking archives here – there was just the remotest, almost non-existent feeling of, how shall I put it – relief? Now why was that? Because I didn't have to jump every time the telephone went? Because I didn't have to arrange my life in such a way that everything could be cancelled at the last minute in case he called? No, surely not, it was – good grief, what on earth was that noise?

I looked up from the battering I was giving Caro and cocked my ear in the direction of reception. There was the most almighty commotion going on out there. Probably Josie the receptionist arguing with yet another salesman, I thought. I thought wrong. Because at that moment the door flew open and in strode Adam, looking, as Pippa had so rightly put it, seriously disturbed.

Josie appeared behind him, red in the face and flustered, her glasses slipping off her nose. 'I'm sorry, Polly, I couldn't stop him!'

Adam was terribly pale and hollow-eyed and his lips were thin and bloodless. It made quite a contrast with the red hair. He was almost unrecognizable as the healthy, sparkly-eyed, all-American jock of a week or so ago. A muscle in his cheek was pulsating away at an alarming rate, and I instinctively rose from my chair, realizing that a little fast running might well be in order.

He was over to my desk in a second. 'Where is she?' he said in a dangerously quiet voice.

'I – I don't know.' I whispered back, equally quietly, but not in a dangerous way, more in a bloody terrified way.

Adam slammed two large, freckled hands the size of meat plates down on my desk. It seemed to me that on the back of one hand was written the word 'Polly's' and on the other 'neck'. The fingernails were white with pressure, the same pressure which would soon, no doubt, be transferred to my swan-like. He was just limbering up. Pressure applied, my head would come popping off like an easy blackhead – one of those really ripe ones that's been brewing up nicely for a couple of days – just a little bit of a squeeze and – pop! Off it would come, highlights and all, and over the desk it would fly before landing neatly in that conveniently open filing cabinet over there – plop!

I sensibly backed away, self-preservation high on my list of priorities now, all previous ideas about throwing myself in the Thames long forgotten. I wanted to live. I forced my eyes up from the freckly, murderous hands to the cold bloodless lips.

'You bitch,' he breathed.

'Now don't be like that, Adam,' I muttered.

'You're going to tell me where she is, Polly. I know you know, and you're damn well going to tell me, because if you don't I'm going to break your fucking *neck*!'

I knew it, I just knew it would be my neck. I was frightened, bloody frightened. He had a clenched calmness about him that terrified me. I was also dimly aware that I should try and talk him out of anything untoward, that was the received wisdom on dealing with rapists and murderers, wasn't it?

'Now look here,' I squeaked, 'killing me won't solve anything you know. It's – it's pointless and futile and – and totally counter-productive, it's been proved many times and, and – well, it just won't get you anywhere!'

Adam's eyes glazed over. The thought had obviously not occurred to him as yet, but now it was right up there amongst the grey cells where I'd so thoughtfully lobbed it. Hmmm . . . murder, yes of course, that was undoubtedly the answer; thanks, Polly. To this end, one of the freckled meat plates inched forward on the desk and closed slowly round a rather sharp-looking paper-knife that I'd been careless enough to leave lying around. I whimpered. Oh God, yes – that was for my heart. Any minute now he'd raise it above his head and then plunge it into my breast with a Tomahawk screech – HAYACK!! I wondered how far the blood would spurt, over to the photocopier perhaps? As far as the window? And who would clear it up afterwards? Pippa? Josie? Probably Pippa, I decided, sobbing wildly.

Knife in hand, Adam took two slow steps to the left,

advancing round the desk. I mimicked him perfectly, but cannily took my two steps in the opposite direction, thereby keeping the desk well and truly between us. He took another to the left, I jumped to the right. We occupied diagonal corners now. He paused, then – three to the right! Off I went to the left! Then two to the left! I hopped to the right! Left! Right! Right! Left! I was squeaking with terror but keeping in step like a sort of manic Ginger Rogers. He was dancing up a storm, but I was with him every step of the way, my heart banging away like a demented dinner gong.

A small corner of my terrified mind wondered how the rest of the agency were taking this drama. A quick peek was enough to ascertain that they were taking it 'from behind'. Pippa and Josie were 'behind' the photocopier, Jason was 'behind' a large potted cheeseplant, and Ron and Joss were peering out from 'behind' their door. They could smell the blood all right but, understandably, didn't particularly want to get it on their hands. Thanks, guys, I thought grimly.

Adam and I paused briefly as we once again occupied diagonal corners of the desk. I licked my lips and addressed myself bravely to his steely stare, totally devoid of any of the old Savoy sparkle.

'Look Adam, can't we talk about this sensibly? I mean, it's crazy to behave like wild animals, anyone would think we were – Aaaah!'

I screamed as a mighty great hand came crashing down on the desk, sending papers flying and my fellow members of staff running for even more cover.

'CUT THE CRAP, POLLY, AND JUST TELL

ME WHERE SHE IS! OK? JUST TELL ME!' he bellowed at the top of his voice.

'I – I don't know, I really don't,' I yelped, experiencing a curious loss of confidence in the leg department: they were decidedly wobbly and I hoped fervently that all the dancing was over for today. I was also acutely aware that my deodorant wasn't all it was cracked up to be.

Adam leaned across the desk. 'You do know,' he said, softly now – I infinitely preferred the bellowing – 'and you're damn well going to tell me, because if you don't, I'm going to kill you. Do you understand?'

'She's – she's at her father's,' I lied.

'DON'T LIE!' Christ, he was quick, but then I've never claimed to be a good liar, just a prolific one.

'Well, OK, yes – yes, you're right. I just sort of said that really, she's not at her father's at all, she's er, she's er . . .' Yes, that was it, I'd just carry on saying 'she's er' and something would eventually crop up. He'd get bored, it would be time to go home, the phone would ring, the police would arrive, the building would collapse. 'She's er, she's er,' I muttered – and something did happen. He lunged across the desk towards me and grabbed hold of my hair, yanking my face towards him.

'AAAAAAHHHHHHH!!' I screamed with terror, loud and shrill, and as I did so, Nick's door flew open. There he stood, a veritable God of War in a Savile Row suit. If anything, he looked even more terrifying than Adam. I fervently hoped I'd die of shock and wouldn't have to experience the next ten minutes.

'WHAT THE HELL IS GOING ON?' he thundered.

Adam dropped my hair for a split second, but it was just split enough for me. I seized my chance and legged it, scuttling off in the direction of Nick's broad back. I just wanted to run up those grey flannelled legs, duck under the jacket, and scurry across the blue-and-white striped shirt until I got to the armpit where I would adopt the foetal position and snuggle down with my thumb in my mouth for the next hour or so. Instead I shot around the un-Adamed side of him and cowered behind his beautiful, broad, oh so welcome, grey-suited back. And there I stayed not glued, but welded.

'Please leave,' he said to Adam, in what would appear to an innocent bystander to be a reasonable voice, but which was in fact his most lethal. He walked forward. I walked too, shadowing his every move, although why we were going forwards rather than backwards was a mystery to me. He clenched his fists, I clenched mine – you see I'd lost my identity. We were one and the same now, Nick and Polly. A Nolly.

'Come on,' he said, jerking his head towards the door, 'out you go.'

'Not until I've talked to Polly,' said Adam, advancing towards us.

'PLEASE LEAVE THE BUILDING NOW OR I'LL CALL THE POLICE!' Nick strode towards the telephone, I strode too, it was poetry in motion, and as I went I admired the exquisite tailoring at the back of his jacket; anything to keep my eyes off Adam. I was riveted, never have I seen such stitching. Nick had his hand on the phone. There was an eerie silence. Eventually I dragged my eyes away from the grey flannel and took a peek at Adam.

His face was crumpled and wretched. He caught my eye. 'Polly, please!' he said, stretching out a hand and changing tactics dramatically. 'Please, just let me talk to you for a minute, just for a minute. I promise I won't hurt you,' he pleaded.

I felt for him, really I did, but what could I do? I had to stand by Rachel and, besides, I was yellow through and through. I averted my eyes, and in doing so caught a glimpse of the rat, peering out of Nick's office. His little nose was twitching away and his glasses were steaming up with excitement. This was probably the closest he'd ever got to a thrill in his whole life.

Nick picked up the receiver. 'I'm going to give you ten seconds to leave this office and then I'm calling the police. One, two, three, four –'

'OK, OK.' Adam raised his hands in defeat. 'I'm going. But you haven't heard the last of this, oh God no. I'll be back, Polly, you can be sure of that. I'll find my son, don't you worry, I'll find him whatever it takes!' His voice cracked with emotion.

He turned to go, raising his hands again in a despairing gesture. They fell limply to his sides. He looked utterly destroyed. I counted to ten before looking again, and was just in time to see his back disappearing out of the door. It slammed behind him.

A tense silence fell. Nick eventually broke it. He turned to Mr Hutchinson and smiled. 'I'm sorry about that, James. As you can see, Polly has an extremely persistent suitor on her hands, but I'm sure he's got the message now. Shall we continue?' he said, motioning him back into his office with his hand.

Mr Hutchinson reluctantly sidled back into the room looking hugely disappointed. No rape, no blood, no murder – shame. He'd have to revert to slowing down on motorways to view the accidents.

The two men disappeared but, as the door was about to close, Nick stuck his head around it and gave me a meaningful look. 'When I've finished my meeting, Polly, I want to talk to you.' With that he shut the door.

I clutched my desk, lowering myself carefully into my chair. Oh God, that was awful, truly awful. I felt positively ill.

My colleagues gathered around me now, like bees at a honey pot: exclaiming, commiserating, wondering, shrieking, gabbling; glad of a chance to tell me now how they'd been right behind me all the way, straining to hold themselves back from leaping to my defence. Indeed, it was a mystery to most of them how they'd managed to control themselves. I listened to their excited chatter in silence, taking the occasional swig of whisky from a hip flask and dragging a whole cigarette down in one. I wondered if I'd ever be the same again.

Josie was the first to mention the unmentionable. 'Do you think he'll sack you now, Polly?' she said, wide-eyed behind her specs. 'Do you think you've really done it this time?'

'I'd say it's probably a safe bet, Josie,' I said weakly. 'I wouldn't open a book on it, put it, that way.'

'I mean, this is probably the worst thing that's ever happened to you here, isn't it?' she persisted, eyeing my desk somewhat covetously, 'and in front of Mr Hutchinson too!'

I sighed. 'Yes, Josie, I think you're probably right – and

rest assured, you'll be the first to hear about it should my position become vacant.'

Eventually they drifted away and I sat out the rest of the afternoon in a daze while Pippa did all my typing for me in silence. It was bad news when she couldn't think of anything comforting to say.

At about four-thirty I showed Mr Hutchinson to the door, dressing him up once again in the grey ensemble. He lingered, keen to discuss the afternoon's events, but I shook him firmly by the paw and practically bundled him down the stairs. Then I walked meekly into Nick's office, head bowed, poised thus for the guillotine to fall.

Through the glass in the door I could see the gang assembling at my desk as they waited for the verdict. Ron had even rustled up a few bottles of red wine. Presumably this bevvy was intended to soften the blow, but they appeared to be cracking into it already. Josie had brought her knitting along; she sat in my chair, legs crossed, glasses slipping down her nose, clicking away like a true *tricoteuse*.

I sat down on one end of the sofa and stared at my shoes. Nick got up from his usual position behind his desk and sat down next to me, obviously favouring the softly-softly approach. He scratched his head and sighed, no doubt wondering how to phrase this without provoking a fresh flood of tears. He looked at his watch. 'Look, Polly, I haven't really got time to talk to you now because I'm supposed to be in a meeting outside the agency in a few minutes, but I'll tell you what. Book a table for lunch somewhere tomorrow and we'll talk about it then, OK?'

I looked up in surprise. 'Oh no, it's OK, that's not

necessary, really. Just do it now and I'll go, really, it's no problem.'

'Do what?'

'Well, you know, aren't you going to fire me?'

He looked exasperated. 'No, I'm not going to fire you. Not yet, anyway – don't tempt me. But what I would like to know is why you arrive at work looking like you've been beaten up, tell our most important client his product is shit, try to kill him with a razor blade in a cake, and then encourage some bulging biceped American to throw his weight around in here, frightening the life out of my staff, not to mention my clients!'

I opened my mouth to begin some form of convoluted explanation (oh God, he'd spotted the scalpel blade), but he held his hand up and shut his eyes firmly, staunching the inevitable flow.

'Not now! Not now. Please, Polly.' He opened one eye cautiously. 'Not now. Tomorrow, at lunch. Book a table somewhere.'

'But Nick –'

'Just do it, will you?' he said desperately, getting to his feet. 'For once in your life, could you please just do as I say?'

I stared at him, totally at a loss. A table? Lunch? Was this a stay of execution? And was the interview truly over? Had I somehow survived? I obviously had. Nick raced around the room grabbing documents, files, a pen, his coat, then he departed in a flurry of tweed, briefcase flying, leaving me sitting there to ponder my good fortune.

We were to have lunch tomorrow. Just the two of us, me and the man who loathed taking clients out to expense-account lunches, let alone members of staff. To talk things over, he had said, not to hand me my P45. I breathed again and, in a fit of gratitude, slipped off the black leather sofa and went down on my knees on the grey flecked carpet. I shut my eyes tight.

'Oh please God,' I whispered passionately, hoping He remembered me, 'please don't let me cock it up. Please let me get my story straight, don't let me get it all arse about tit as usual. I've lost my boyfriend – that's Harry,' I added quickly, in case He'd missed his brief appearances – 'but please, oh please, don't let me lose my job too. It's all I've got!'

There was a loud click as the door handle went down and I looked up from my position on my knees to see Nick's startled face peering round the door. He slipped his hand in, grabbed his umbrella from the hat stand, clocked the born-again Christian but, wisely, made no comment. Then he disappeared, shutting the door quietly behind him.

I sighed, got to my feet, and went in search of some communion wine.

Chapter Thirteen

That night I paid a brief visit to my own flat and gathered together everything Harry had ever given me. Needless to say, it didn't take long. Theoretically I was going to throw everything associated with Harry straight in the bin, thereby exorcizing him from my heart for ever – a cathartic exercise. Practically, of course, I didn't quite have the guts to go through with it, so instead I decided to parcel everything up, hide it away somewhere and completely forget about it. Then, one day in the far distant future, I'd be turning the flat upside-down, looking for something like my birth certificate – I'd probably need it to get married or something – and while I was searching I'd chance upon the Harry bundle and have a good old chuckle as I recalled my silly, lovestruck, misspent youth. That would be in about one hundred and fifty years' time. Right now, before I hid it away, I was going to have a good old blub over my pathetic little pile of memorabilia, and even I had to admit that 'little' was the word.

First, I dripped copious tears over the two paperbacks he'd given me for Christmas, stroking their covers and marvelling at the vast number of pages – he really could be quite generous. One was called *Cookery for Morons*, which I'd thought a huge joke, but which Lottie had insisted was about as subtle as an air-raid, and the other was *The Vogue Book of Beauty Tips*, which on reflection wasn't much better, especially since he'd inscribed the inside front cover with, 'Happy Christmas, Polly, Read, learn and have a go, especially Chapter Eleven! Love Harry xxx.' Chapter Eleven was entitled, 'Say Goodbye to Cellulite'. Charming. I sighed, placed the books neatly in the cardboard shoebox I'd enlisted to act as the coffin, and turned my attention to my one and only love letter.

This treasured missive had been hastily scrawled on a scrap of paper and slipped under the flat door one evening when I was out. It was short, but very sweet. It read: 'Called round on the off chance, sorry to have missed you, love Harry.' Now I have to admit that, as love letters go, it wouldn't stand up to too much scrutiny in an Oxford anthology, if there is such a thing, but as with most pieces of literature, there were two ways of looking at it. Oh yes. On the one hand you could read it straight, as I have just demonstrated; but the subtle, more imaginative, way was to fold it in half, thus eliminating the first nine words. This revealed something altogether more romantic, namely, 'missed you, love Harry', and since this was of course the deep, implicit meaning behind the note anyway, it really wasn't cheating at all. Funnily enough, this was my favourite interpretation, so much so that the note was in danger of falling apart, so often had I creased it down the middle.

I smoothed it out now and placed it on top of the books, remembering how Lottie had snorted with laughter when I'd seized it on our way in from the pub, jumping around the flat with excitement, the evidence of my man's love waving around in my hot little hand.

'On the off-chance of what?' she'd scoffed. 'On the off-chance that you might be on for a quick one?'

I sighed. Poor Lottie. She really did have a very cynical outlook. It must be something to do with being a solicitor.

I turned to my next piece of correspondence from Harry – golly, I'd quite forgotten what a prolific letter writer he'd been – a carefully chosen scenic postcard featuring a mountain range complete with chairlift. It read: 'Pissed again on the piste, chalet girls are brilliant . . . cooks! Love Harry.' Gosh he was funny. How I'd laughed when I'd received that. I placed it a trifle grimly on my motley pile, deciding on balance that the letter under the door was far more touching and much more – well, much more *Harry* really.

Then I turned to the jewellery collection. Surprised? Oh yes, Harry had given me jewels. The choice had been a little unfortunate, I admit, since the silver (hallmarked, I checked) earrings had in fact been designed to go through pierced ears, which I do not possess. Tainting the earrings even more was the faintly disturbing but highly unreliable piece of gossip that these very same baubles had once dangled from the pierced lobes of a previous girlfriend, which suggested to some people – but not to me – that the ex had left them behind in Harry's flat and he'd simply recycled them. The very idea! More unbridled cynicism. No, no, these earrings had been chosen for me, by Harry, with me and me alone in mind. OK, I couldn't wear them, but I could polish them, couldn't I? I gave them a quick rub on my jumper to prove it and placed them carefully in the box.

To this now burgeoning treasure trove I added the butt of the cigarette he'd smoked when we'd first made love – I'd retrieved it from the ashtray the next morning – and a cutting from his Busy Lizzie plant, which unfortunately had failed to re-root. OK, it had died, only I'd never liked to think of it in such bald terms before, in case it had been symbolic in some way; but what did it matter now? It had been lovingly pressed for posterity, and I laid it like a wreath on top of the correspondence.

Now there was, I'm ashamed to say, one last memento to add to this collection. A pickled kidney stone. Harry had passed it in acute agony in the loo at his flat about two months ago, amid rather a lot of unmanly screaming. I hadn't really thought about it at the time, but I thought about it now and, my God, he'd screamed. Anyway, once he'd passed it, he'd fished it out, washed it, and together we'd inspected it, marvelling at how such a small thing could cause such pain. He'd been about to throw it down the loo again when I'd piped up with the idea of keeping it, well – actually with the idea of *me* keeping it. He'd found the concept hugely amusing, but had graciously handed it over, and even gone to the lengths of providing me with an old jam jar and some vinegar to pickle it in. Unfortunately, within a matter of days it had gone rather a funny colour, what you might call diarrhoea yellow, and had disintegrated slightly. Perhaps I should have held out on the pickling front until I'd got home and used white wine vinegar instead of Sarson's malt. I hadn't liked to suggest it at the time for fear of sounding like a vinegar snob. I placed the jar carefully in the box.

Now that the collection was complete, I put the lid on and tied a red ribbon around it, sobbing quietly. Actually, my tears made a rather nice effect on the cardboard, and I squeezed out a few more, admiring the distressed – literally – look I'd achieved. Eat your heart out, Jocasta Innes, I thought as I placed it tenderly at the very back of my wardrobe under a pile of dirty washing. I was quite sure I wouldn't stumble upon it there for a very long time.

Now for the gallery. This consisted of five, or was it six? Yes, six enlarged photographs of guess who, arranged in a haphazard manner on the ceiling above my bed – it had been my way of kidding myself that I woke up with him every morning. There was Harry smiling, Harry pouting, Harry laughing, Harry working, Harry frowning (sexily), and Harry looking moody. I ruthlessly dragged them down, taking care not to damage any part of his gorgeous anatomy, and shoved them unceremoniously under the bed. I also removed the large black-and-white portrait photo from my bedside table and, devil that I am, even managed to flick a rather half-hearted two fingers at it before hurling it under the bed. I instantly regretted it and dragged it back out, pressing my face ardently to his and whispering – didn't mean it, didn't mean it, didn't mean it – before pushing it back under the bed again.

Safely back at Pippa's an hour later, I crawled into bed feeling exhausted. I'm ashamed to report that, during the night, I was ambushed by tears yet again. I tried to beat them back and failed, but at the end of the day it was no bad thing, because I woke up feeling so ghastly I resolved never to shed a tear over a man ever again. So when Jamie had a sobbing fit at the breakfast table and threw his Marmite fingers around the room, I sympathized, but didn't automatically feel like joining in as I had yesterday. A major step forward.

Buoyed up by my new attitude, I set off for work feeling a weeny bit tougher. Positive thinking was definitely the answer. One just had to think happy. Mind over matter.

Unfortunately, I was so engrossed in my positive thoughts that I clean forgot to book a table for lunch. It wasn't until twelve o'clock that I remembered and spent a frantic ten minutes ringing round all the local watering holes, desperate for a table. The only place that would agree grudgingly to squeeze us in was San Frediano's in the Fulham Road. Great fun though this teeming joint is, it's hardly conducive to impressing one's boss and hanging on to one's job, but it was the last resort, so I took it.

'What's this place like?' asked Nick as we walked down the Fulham Road twenty minutes later.

'Oh it's great, the food's good and it's got plenty of, um' – I groped for the right word – 'atmosphere.'

In fact the atmosphere greeted us right around the next bend, before we'd even set foot in the place. A taxi screeched to a halt outside and the driver flung open the door with a flourish, glad to be shot of his cargo of four or five half-cut secretaries, who tumbled out on to the pavement, shrieking with laughter. They pushed past us and poured through the restaurant door. Nick stood aside and raised his eyebrows, but didn't say a word.

He held the door open for me and a terrific barrage of noise hit us full in the face. 'Are you sure you booked, Polly?' he shouted, pitting his voice against the braying and shouting. 'This place looks full to bursting.'

'Oh, definitely,' I yelled back, grabbing the nearest laughing-cavalier waiter, complete with whiskers, by the arm.

'McLaren,' I yelled, 'table for two!'

He knew better than to waste his breath and compete with the noise level, but nodded and grinned widely before showing us to a table about the size of a postage stamp, right next to the very same typing-pool party we'd encountered in the street.

Nick lost his patience. 'Don't you have anything quieter?' he barked.

The cavalier grinned even more widely, and threw his arm demonstratively around the gobbling, gabbling throng, as if we might somehow have overlooked the crowd scene. 'So sorry, signor, fully booked!' he beamed, glowing with pride, lira signs shining in his eyes. 'But,' he added, tapping his nose conspiratorially, 'for young lovers' – I cringed deeply – 'I find more room. I find somewhere more private!'

With that, he took a firm hold on our postage stamp and moved it a good nine inches away from the hen party. 'There!' he said, standing back and admiring his handiwork as if he'd miraculously discovered a private room. 'Now you have plenny room to tell her how much you love her!'

I cringed some more and Nick sat down, resigned. 'Really, Polly, couldn't you have booked somewhere a little less "atmospheric", or do you have to live your life in a permanent disco?'

'Sorry,' I mumbled. 'I left it a bit late.'

I crunched maniacally on a bread stick like a demented rabbit. Not a very auspicious start. I also realized that I was unaccountably nervous, sitting here in what one might call a social setting, with my knees about a millimetre away

267

from my incredibly anti-social boss's. I tried to remember if we'd ever had a conversation that didn't begin with something like, 'Dear Sir, Please find enclosed . . .'

Nick's face was only about a foot away from mine, and suddenly I wished I was looking a bit more presentable. I bore a startling resemblance to Chairman Mao, what with the slitty eyes, puffy cheeks and greasy hair plastered attractively to my head: I hadn't washed it since Black Monday – what was the point?

I ran my hand through the limp curls, trying to fluff a bit of life into them, and knocked over our table arrangement with my elbow. A glass vase containing a solitary carnation smashed noisily on the floor. The hen party freeze-framed for a second, then burst into hysterical giggles, pointing and whispering.

The cavalier arrived and brushed it away, instantly replacing with another. 'You nervous!' he whispered in my ear. 'Ees OK, he love you!'

I blushed hotly and made a mental note never to patronize this restaurant again. Luckily Nick had missed this little aside, but he was beginning to look irritated. 'Polly, just relax, will you? What on earth's wrong with you? You're jumping around like a frog in a bucket.'

'Sorry.'

'And stop apologizing all the time.'

'Sorry.'

He shook his head in bewilderment and addressed himself to the menu as the waiter arrived. I ordered the cheapest salad available, not wanting to look like a lunch tart.

'Are you sure that's all you want? Just a salad?'

'Yes, thank you.'

'Well, I'll have a rare fillet steak please, with french fries, and we'll have a bottle of house red.' He handed back the menu.

'Now then.' He folded his arms on the table and leaned forward, which wasn't easy given the limited surface area. His brown eyes bore into mine, but they were kind and encouraging. 'Suppose you tell me what's been going on recently?'

I was afraid we might get around to this, but hadn't envisaged getting around to it quite so quickly. Couldn't we limber up with a bit of friendly repartee first, just to remind ourselves how it was done? Christ, I hadn't even got a glass of wine to slurp on.

'Oh, nothing really,' I said, shifting around miserably in my seat and doing a spot of origami with the paper napkin. What did he want to hear? And in my view that was all that mattered. It was no good getting all honest if it was going to backfire me down to the dole queue.

'Come on, Polly, I'm not that much of an ogre, am I?' I looked up from the shredded napkin and thought I hadn't seen a kinder face in a good long time. But it was no good. He was my boss, and we'd never enjoyed a think-of-me-as-a-normal-human-being sort of relationship, so how the hell did he expect me to start now? I shifted about a bit more, but the brown eyes held their unwavering beam and I knew he wouldn't be easily deterred. I reached for my comfort pack, lit one, and took a deep breath of nicotine.

'OK, where would you like me to start?' I ventured, thinking birth might not be a bad idea if he wanted a catalogue of disasters.

'How about starting with the obsessive redhead?'

Oh yes, him. Nick was obviously still under the impression that Adam was hounding me for my body. I suppose he was, in a way, except that he wanted to cut it up into little pieces and scatter them around the countryside. I could at least put him straight on that score.

I embarked on the Rachel and Adam saga, telling it exactly how it was with no exaggerations or embellishments or what other people call lies.

Nick listened intently, chewing thoughtfully on his steak. When I'd finished he paused and pushed a few peas around before looking up at me. 'That's quite a story, Polly.'

'But it's true!' I said indignantly.

'Oh, I believe you, don't worry.' He wiped his mouth with his napkin. 'Not even a consummate liar like yourself could make up something as outrageous as that. And don't look so miserable, it's not totally your fault, you acted with the best intentions. How were you to know there was a baby involved?'

'Exactly!' Whew. One tiny Brownie point.

'Bloody stupid to get mixed up in all this in the first place, though.' He had to spoil it, didn't he? 'Why couldn't you have left him to sort his love life out for himself? Did you fancy him or something?'

'Certainly not!' I said, bristling. 'I felt sorry for him, he struck me as – as an innocent abroad,' I added piously.

Nick threw back his head and roared with laughter. 'Oh God, Polly, you're so theatrical! An innocent abroad? That guy looked about as innocent as Crippen. Didn't you notice the murderous glint in his eye or the mean and twisted mouth? I suppose those little details escaped you at the time: no doubt you were quaffing buckets of champagne down at the Savoy, were you?'

'The champagne had nothing to do with it!' I said hotly. 'If you must know, I hardly touched a drop. I – I just helped him out of the goodness of my heart.'

'Ah I see, just another of your philanthropic gestures.' He grinned. 'OK, Polly, don't get in a bate, I'm just mobbing you up. So what are you going to do now?'

'Do? What d'you mean?' Was there still *more* I had to do? Why was it always *me* who had to do the doing? Couldn't someone else do something for a change?

'Well, she can't stay at Pippa's for ever, and neither can you. How long do you imagine that arrangement can tick along for?'

I sighed. 'I don't know, really. As long as Pippa will put up with us, I suppose. She's being very good about it, but it's playing havoc with her love life.' I thought of poor Charles.

'Doesn't Rachel have any plans?'

'Well, her latest idea is to go and live in Paris.'

'Why Paris?'

'Because that's where her friend Sally Lomax lives, the one I was telling you about who was supposed to have written the letter. Of course, she can't actually stay with Sally, because Adam knows where she lives, but she's asked her to find a flat for her.'

'That sounds like quite a good plan, but who would finance all this? Has she got money?'

'Oh, that's no problem, her father's loaded and she's an only child. Thing is, though, finding a spare flat in Paris takes time; people kill for accommodation over there. I could have her on my hands for weeks.'

'And the idea is to stay at Pippa's till then?'

'It's not ideal, I agree.'

'It certainly isn't. He's only got to follow you home one night, and you've had it.'

I didn't care for the macabre way this was put. Did he mean 'had it' in the sense that dead meat has had it?

'Have you got any better suggestions?' I snapped, irritated that all he'd done so far was put the fear of God into me.

Nick wiped his mouth with his napkin and stared into space, well, not space actually, more like the top of my head where I'm sure my dark roots were flourishing wildly, springing wantonly from my head, untouched by human hairdresser's hands for many a long month.

'Hmmm ... I'm not sure,' he mused thoughtfully. I waited meekly for the oracle to speak. I fidgeted a bit. He was taking his time and I can only be meek for so long.

'Look, Nick, it's nice of you to take an interest, but the fact is it's my problem and I'll have to deal with it. I'm sure I –'

'Hang on, hang on, you're always so bloody impatient. If you must know, I do have an idea. I'm just trying to work out how to orchestrate it.'

'Oh, really? What is it then?'

Nick finally dragged his eyes away from my roots and fixed me with his piercing beam.

'You know I have a house in Cornwall, don't you?'

Christ, what did this have to do with anything – and no, I didn't know actually, was I supposed to? Was it in my job

272

description or something: always keep a tally of the number of houses your employer owns. How the hell *should* I know, when he played his cards so close to his chest?

'Oh yes,' I mumbled, nodding inanely.

He went a bit misty-eyed. 'I grew up there, it's been in my family for years. It's nothing special really, just a rambling old farmhouse by the sea, probably in imminent danger of falling into the sea, it's so run-down, but I love it . . .'

He stared into his wine and I shifted about again. I mean, I was very pleased for him and all that, but what the hell did his idyllic Cornish childhood have to do with keeping wolf-man from the door?

'Tim, my brother, lives there during the week with his girlfriend, and I go down at weekends to make sure the farm's ticking over.'

'The farm?'

'Yes, I said it was a farmhouse, didn't I?'

'Yes, but I thought you meant a sort of converted one. I didn't imagine it had a proper farm attached.'

'Oh yes, in full working order. In fact, you're looking at the farmer.'

I gagged on my lettuce. 'You! A farmer? You must be joking!' Nick was about the most unlikely farmer I'd ever seen. I tried to imagine him leaning over five-barred gates sizing up the cattle, straw in mouth, briefcase in hand . . . I stuffed my napkin in my mouth to stifle a guffaw.

He grinned. 'I suppose that is quite hard to believe, seeing as you've only ever seen me in a suit at work; but I can assure you, I'm far more at home delivering a calf than I am sweet-talking old rat-face Hutchinson.'

I grinned. So Nick thought he was a rat too, eh? That was promising. 'But – but what's all this got to do with Rachel?'

Nick looked surprised. 'Oh, didn't I say? I thought she could go down there for a while. As I said, it's a big place, she'd have plenty of room and still be out of Tim's way, and this Adam character wouldn't dream of going down to Cornwall to look for her, so she'd be perfectly safe. What d'you think?' He calmly folded his napkin.

I sat there, bug-eyed with amazement. Nick would accommodate Rachel in Cornwall? In his house? I struggled to find my voice.

'Bloody hell, Nick, that's a marvellous idea, but we couldn't possibly, it's – it's much too much of an imposition. I mean, you don't know her or anything.'

'You didn't know Adam, but you got involved – and who knows,' he grinned, 'she might even be my type.'

'Highly unlikely, but Nick, why should you? I mean, it's terribly kind, but I just feel it's too much to ask.'

'You didn't ask, I offered.'

'Yes but –'

'Look, Polly,' Nick leaned forward. Suddenly he looked remarkably serious. 'I've been joking about this, but the fact is you're in a hell of a mess, to put it mildly. I saw that guy's face yesterday, and he's not going to stop hounding you until he finds his child. So far he's gone slightly mad in the process. You and Pippa are protecting the mother, which is all very fine and laudable but, frankly, dangerous. For one thing, he knows where you work, and is quite likely to turn up every day to terrorize you and pick fights with anyone else who gets in his way. Paris is a good idea but, as you say, it could take a few weeks to get it together. Now, it's no skin off my nose to have her to stay in Cornwall. It's a big house, so I probably won't even see much of her. I'm planning to go down for a couple of weeks as from Thursday, so I can at least keep an eye on her. Now, what I suggest is that you come down with her and stay the weekend so she's not completely fazed by a crowd of strangers, help her to settle in, and then, when she's found her feet, just leave her to have a peaceful few weeks by the sea until the flat in Paris is organized. Now, does that sound reasonable?'

He drained his glass of wine, sat back and lit a cigarette. My eyes and mouth were wide. Reasonable? It was the sanest thing I'd heard in days; it made complete sense. It was also incredibly kind. As for me going too, the idea of staying with Nick at his house initially filled me with horror, but on reflection, as I studied my employer over the table, I almost warmed to the idea. What bliss to get away from all the horrors London held for me – Adam, Harry, everything. I'd been to Cornwall before in the spring and it had been heavenly – brimming over with primroses and early daffodils. I turned the idea over in my mind, and the more I turned it, the more attractive it became.

'Will the daffodils be out yet?' I asked dreamily.

He laughed. 'Would you like me to ring and check before you make a decision?'

I grinned. 'No. No, the more I think about it, the more I think it's an absolutely brilliant idea. I just don't know how to thank you enough, really it's –'

'Not at all,' he said briskly, cutting me off in mid-gush. 'Of course Rachel will have to agree.'

I groaned. 'That's a point, grumpy old cow, I'd forgotten about her.' I had. I'd been skipping through the daffodil fields singing a happy tune, not a sulky face in sight.

'Well, give me a ring at home tonight and let me know,' Nick was saying, filling up my glass, 'because if she agrees, I suggest we set off tomorrow morning instead of waiting for Friday. No point in hanging around waiting for the mad axe-man to strike.'

'But what about work, haven't you got meetings tomorrow?'

'Only one, and Jason can handle that. It's about time he earned his keep.'

I giggled. Poor Jason was wildly intelligent in the academic sense, but totally useless in any other sense. Client meetings would send him into paroxysms of fear, his glasses would steam up with embarrassment, and he became paralysed with shyness, visibly palpitating whenever it was his turn to utter a few words. Occasionally a sentence would emerge, but when it did it would take him completely by surprise and he'd almost jump out of his skin, looking around wildly as if he half expected someone else to take the credit for saying it. Nick despaired, but was too soft to fire him.

'He'll cope better without you there. You frighten people.' By now my tongue was totally unhinged by alcohol.

Nick raised his eyebrows in surprise. 'Me? Frighten people? Don't be ridiculous; I don't frighten you, do I?'

'Well, no,' I said, thinking well, yes, and we're talking living daylights actually, 'no, not frighten exactly.' I wriggled uncomfortably and felt my colour rising. 'But you can be rather, you know, intimidating.'

'I'm sorry.' He looked genuinely surprised and even a little hurt. 'I don't mean to be.'

'Oh no, it doesn't matter,' I said quickly. 'It's quite nice really in a – in a forceful sort of way.' Christ, what was I saying? Forceful? I'd be on to thrusting next.

Nick looked even more surprised but hugely amused. I went about the colour of the tomato on my plate.

'Forceful, eh?' he said, grinning. 'Is that how you like your men?'

Now in my normal line of work I can take any amount of sexy banter and always come back with a witty riposte, but this was different, this was Nick, for God's sake. What on earth was he playing at? I squirmed about on my seat, gushing from every conceivable pore and wishing I was somewhere else, like in the Ladies'.

He watched me wriggle, then laughed and let me off the hook. 'All right, we won't go into your love life. I have a feeling that's an even bigger can of worms.'

No, just the one, I thought miserably, and even he's buggered off to a new mate. Happily the waiter appeared with the coffee, so I was spared making a reply. As I stirred my cappuccino it occurred to me that Nick had his own love life too.

'What about Serena, won't she be coming down?'

'No, she won't,' he said shortly. Too shortly. I was intrigued as well as relieved; I didn't particularly want to look at her gorgeous face all weekend.

I ploughed on nosily. 'Doesn't she normally go to Cornwall with you at the weekend?'

It was his turn to shift about a bit. He lit another cigarette. 'She's not mad about the place, to tell you the truth; more of a London girl, I suppose. Anyway she's filming this weekend.'

'She must be quite busy – I mean, as an actress?'

'Yes, quite.'

'So I suppose if you go to Cornwall every weekend, you don't see that much of her?'

'I suppose.'

'And of course you work so late during the week, that must put a strain on –'

'Polly, shall we just stick to sorting your life out for the time being?'

I grinned, mentally notching up marks for trying. Still, it was odd. They obviously didn't see a great deal of each other; perhaps he was still playing hard to get. She was quite a catch, after all.

Nick paid the bill and we left the still throbbing restaurant. Of course I'd drunk too much as usual, and the cold air hit me like a fridge door in the face. I felt a bit unsteady on my feet, and had a sudden desire to put my arm through Nick's strong, dependable tweedy one. I giggled and resisted it. Instead I shivered and pulled my ineffectual bum-freezer of a leather jacket around me. It was pretty damn cool in both senses of the word.

Nick regarded me dubiously as we started up the Fulham Road. 'D'you want my coat?'

'No, it's OK thanks,' I said between chattering teeth. Meanwhile he'd flagged down a passing taxi and I found myself being bundled, protesting, into the back.

'But we're only going up the road!'

'Never mind. I don't particularly want an invalid with pneumonia on my hands in Cornwall.' He pressed the heater button. 'And why don't you eat more? That rabbit food you eat won't warm you up. You're not dieting or something stupid, are you?'

'No.' I sulked in the corner. God, he was such a bully. What business was it of his whether I froze or starved to death? As it happened, for once in my life I wasn't dieting. I just didn't feel much like eating and my clothes were falling off me. It was the only compensation for having a broken heart, I thought wretchedly.

That night, I tackled Rachel on the subject of Cornwall. I picked my moment, waiting until she'd bathed Jamie, read him a story, put him to bed, made up his bottles for the following day, and eventually had a firm grip on a gin and tonic and normality. I topped the gin up for her and sat down beside her on the sofa. I explained about Nick's house, phrasing the plan carefully so she wouldn't think I was pushing her into it.

'Oh Polly, that's a marvellous idea, but won't he mind?' She turned to me with such eagerness it made me jump.

'Not at all, in fact he suggested we go tomorrow, if you don't think that's too much of a rush?'

'Of course not, the sooner the better, I can't wait to get out of London.' She leaped up from the sofa with hitherto unimagined alacrity. 'I'd better ring my father and let him know, then I'll pack a few things. Thanks, Polly!'

Thanks, Polly! Good Lord, had I found favour? Suddenly I felt a sharp stab of pity for her. I'd been so busy with my own private tragedies I'd forgotten about hers, which were, after all, on a much grander scale. Perhaps she'd been scared stiff on her own here every day, just waiting for Adam to swing through an upstairs window with a knife in his teeth. How awful not to have anyone at all to turn to. There were plenty of friends in the country to whom I could have escaped, but she didn't seem to have access to any. Some uncharitable little notions about how, if she made herself a tad more pleasant and accommodating, she might have more friends, were bubbling under in my brain, but I hastened them back down again.

I listened to Rachel's excited voice coming from the hall. '. . . It'll take a little while to get the court injunction served, won't it? And you know I've always loved Cornwall. It'll be so good for Jamie to get a breath of fresh air, and now I know Adam's in London I can't wait to get away!'

Perhaps the judge didn't feel so murderously inclined to me now. Well for once, Polly old girl, I thought, you've hit the jackpot. You've actually managed to get something right – or rather, I conceded magnanimously, Nick had. I waited until Rachel had finished and then dialled his number. I'd never spoken to him at home before, and the thought filled me with ridiculous nervous dread.

I practised a bit while it rang. Don't say hi, say hello; remember not to say, 'It's me'; try to sound intelligent. A girl answered, which completely floored me.

'Hello?'

Serena.

'Oh, um hi – er, is Nick there, please?'

'Who is it?' She sounded cross.

'Um, it's Polly – from work,' I said quickly, nearly adding, just a boring little secretary with dark roots; no competition at all.

'Hold on,' she said tersely. Charming telephone manner. Suppose I'd been Franco Zeffirelli in disguise, ringing up to offer her a part in his new film?

A second later Nick came to the phone and I told him we'd love to come. We agreed he'd pick us up in the morning at about nine a.m.

I put the phone down slowly and wondered what they were like together. Did they snuggle up on the sofa and watch TV? Did he run his fingers through her white-blonde hair and kiss her pert little nose? Did she trace his rugged features with her finger, a tantalizing little smile playing about her luscious lips? Did they walk upstairs together, arm in arm, giggling and kissing the while? Did they get undressed first, or did they still rip each other's clothes off and fall in a tangled shrieking heap on to the bed? Did they gaze into each other's eyes as they lay there, dark and blonde on the pillow before he reached out and gently stroked her – Polly, stop it! I thought, alarmed at the pornographic lengths my imagination could stretch to: what business is it of yours?

That night I dreamed I was drifting through a daffodil field, one hand brushing lightly against the nodding yellow heads, the other clasped tightly in darling Harry's hand. He smiled tenderly and bent down to pick me a flower, but when he straightened up, I realized it wasn't Harry at all, it was Nick. He raised the flower above his head and I looked up, just in time to see the daffodil turn into a meat cleaver. I glanced down at him in surprise but the eyes I encountered were not brown but blue, blue with cold and blue with hate. Adam. The meat cleaver was being raised higher and higher, the music from the shower scene in *Psycho* was screeching in the background, and with an Anthony Perkins maniacal smile on his face, he plunged it downwards, homing in on the small square inch of brow between my eyes.

I sat bolt upright in bed, shrieking like a Banshee and soaking wet. Christ Almighty, what the hell was happening to me! I flopped down on the pillow, my heart hammering around in my quivering ribcage. For God's sake, I thought miserably, reality was bad enough, couldn't I at least have some pleasant dreams?

Chapter Fourteen

The next morning, at nine a.m. sharp, the doorbell rang, piercing its way through my slumbering eardrums. I shot out of bed like a lunatic and ran, stark naked, to the open window. Without thinking, and still half asleep, I leaned out and peered down just as Nick was peering up. Our eyes met and he hastily averted his: more, I decided, backing away and looking in the dressing-table mirror, out of horror than decency. My hair was standing on end and my face was a riot of blotches and bags. Faced with such an obvious paper-bag job, he'd clearly been put off examining the bodywork.

As I slunk behind the curtain, I watched him on the pavement below, his hands thrust deep into his trouser pockets, his foot tapping away on the pavement as he gave his shoes a great deal of embarrassed consideration.

I dragged my dressing gown around me and stumbled out on to the landing in time to see Rachel appearing from her bedroom looking smug. She was not only washed and dressed, but packed – suitcase in one hand, baby in the other – and ready for the off. Why the hell couldn't she have given me a shout? Pippa put a tousled head round her bedroom door. She was wearing a T-shirt that just about covered the basics, but only just.

She rubbed her eyes and yawned. 'Nick's here,' she said sleepily. 'We overslept.'

Through the gap in the door I caught a glimpse of a naked Charles, stumbling round the room, picking up bras and pink knickers and dropping them again, in a vain attempt to find his own underpants.

'I know, tell him I'm just coming, will you?' I said as she stumbled downstairs to answer the door.

I raced around the bedroom, throwing on a skirt and a jumper and raking a comb through my knotted hair. There wasn't time for a shower, so I doused myself in Diorissimo instead, hoping it would drown, or at the very least compete with, any unpleasant odours. It had been a stressful night.

I thundered downstairs, rubbing blusher on my pale, wan cheeks, feeling late and foolish as usual. In the kitchen, Pippa was cooking bacon for Charles and Nick, and you could clearly see two inches of bum sticking out at the bottom of her T-shirt as she stood with her back to them at the stove, frying away. Every so often she'd give the pan a vigorous little shake, which had the knock-on effect of making other things shake vigorously too. The boys were chatting away amiably enough over mugs of coffee, but without ever looking at each other: both had their eyes firmly on the chef's behind, and Charles seemed to have no qualms about sharing the spectacle with Nick.

Rachel wandered in and declined breakfast on the grounds that she'd had hers much, much earlier – one got the impression we were talking dawn here. She went to sit in the drawing room, her case at her feet as if she were merely killing time as she waited for her chauffeur to finish his breakfast in the servants' quarters.

I grabbed a piece of bacon from the pan and sandwiched it between some stale Mother's Pride, then sat down and munched away, trying desperately to wake up. Every so often I shot a sneaky glance at Nick, who was laughing and joking with Charles and Pippa.

He looked a different man in mufti. His faded cords and baggy navy sweater gave him an altogether softer, younger look. His dark hair flopped into his eyes from time to time, and he pushed it away as he threw back his head and laughed at Charles's jokes. Without the granite grey suit to augment them, his craggy features looked blunter somehow, as if he'd taken a file to them, rubbing off the sharp edges. He was all smiles this morning, too, quite different from the snarling workaholic I usually encountered first thing in the morning.

He caught me staring and flashed a smile. I flushed unattractively and started clearing up the breakfast things to cover my confusion. What the bloody hell was he up to, smiling at me like that? Anyone would think he was human. But then, perhaps he was, I thought miserably, as I stood at the sink rinsing bacon grease off my plate; perhaps it was me. Pippa certainly didn't have any hang-ups about him, I reflected, as I watched her larking around, pulling blonde hairs off his jumper and holding them up in evidence. They were all shrieking with laughter now.

It must be me, I thought, as I dried my plate, stacking it in the cupboard above. I obviously took this employer–employee thing far too seriously. But we weren't at work now, were we? Hell no, this was supposed to be a break – a holiday even. I'd have to stop running around, doffing my cap at every conceivable opportunity, like some sort of secretarial Uriah Heep, if we were going to spend the weekend together. Yes, I'd be my own person, call a few shots even.

I turned round from the sink, put my hands on my hips and smiled confidently. 'Right, let's go then, shall we?' I said briskly, in my new, assertive voice.

Too assertive. The others broke off from their friendly chatter and looked up in surprise. Nick hurriedly shoved half a bacon sandwich in his mouth and stood up, abandoning his mug of coffee.

'Sure,' he said agreeably from the corner of a bulging mouth, 'I'm ready. Sorry, I hadn't realized you were waiting.'

Oh God, now I was just being a bossy old cow. What was the matter with me?

I traipsed miserably down the hall after him as he strode off to the car. We loaded it up together as Rachel stood watching. Most of the luggage seemed to consist of baby paraphernalia, which she was keen to have aboard but not too keen to touch.

As we drove away, Charles and Pippa stood at the front door with their arms around each other. They waved us off, looking like something out of a soap opera, except that Pippa still didn't have any knickers on, and when she raised her hand to wave, her T-shirt rose a good six inches. Nick swivelled his head around one hundred and eighty degrees to get a better look, and narrowly missed colliding with the milkman.

When we'd negotiated most of London and were heading out to the motorway, Nick looked at Rachel in his rear-view mirror and smiled. 'So how old is Jamie, Rachel?' he asked.

'Just over five months,' she mumbled inaudibly.

'Sorry? Did you say five months?'

'Mmmm.'

'Ah. And, is he – you know, good? Is he a good baby?'

'Yes, quite.'

'Doesn't cry too much?'

'Not really.'

'Oh well, that's a relief, he won't keep us up all night then!'

'No.'

'Good, good . . . I must say, he's a nice-looking little chap; solid, too: he'll be playing rugby for England soon, by the look of him – what d'you reckon, full back?'

'Sorry?'

'Full back – it's a rugby position!'

'Oh . . . oh right.'

At this point Nick gave up. A lesser man would have baled out sentences ago. Rachel's No Entry sign was firmly in position, and she sat in the back staring out of the window, pretending she couldn't really hear. It must take a certain self-confidence, I thought, to care so little about what people thought of you.

As we negotiated the final roundabout and roared off on to the motorway, I took over the role of question master.

'So how long have you had this house, then?'

'Oh, about two hundred years.'

I gasped. 'How come?'

He laughed. 'That's how long it's been in the family. Various generations of increasingly penniless Penhalligans have lived there since about 1790.'

'And now it belongs to you?'

'Yes, although my younger brother lives there at the moment while I'm in London.'

'So what about your parents, where do they live?'

'Well, my father's dead and Mum moved out when he died. Said it was much too big for her to live there on her own, and I think she found it rather spooky without Dad. Too many memories and that sort of thing.'

'Oh, I can imagine, how sad. So where does she live now?'

'Just outside a village called Gweek, which is about four miles away. She's converted an old barn there: we'll go and see her if you like. You'd like her,' he laughed. 'She's pretty batty!'

I gave this some thought. 'And is that why you think I'll like her? Because I'm batty too?'

He took his eyes off the road for a moment and grinned at me. 'I'd say you've got a lot of potential, although women only go truly batty at about forty. There's always a chance you'll be a bit previous though – say thirty-five?'

I grinned back, but secretly made up my mind to be a very late developer in the bats department. I thought of Serena. Serene Serena. That's how I would be all weekend. Very sophisticated, very elegant, very cool. If I had to laugh, I would tinkle rather than guffaw, and if I smiled it would be with the minimum of teeth and gum.

I crossed my legs, which were splayed out in front of me at an oafishly obtuse angle, and surreptitiously spat my chewing gum into my hand, noticing as I did so that I had a rather dirty plaster on my thumb which must have been there for at least a week. I deftly pulled it off and wrapped it round the chewing gum before depositing the nasty little bundle in . . . now, where on earth should I put it – ashtray? No, he might find it – ah yes, my handbag. As I snapped the bag shut, I looked up to encounter Nick looking hugely amused, having witnessed the whole operation. Bugger. Better laugh it off. I tried out my new tinkle.

'Cut myself while I was making supper last night – lobster thermidor actually! He-ya! He-ya!'

'What's the matter?'

'Sorry?'

'What was that noise?'

'What noise?'

'Just then, like a horse.'

'Oh! I was just laughing.'

'Really? Sounded very odd, like you had a pain in the tubes or something.'

I groaned inwardly. Christ, I couldn't win. I swiftly changed the subject. 'So who looks after the farm while you're away?'

'Oh, I've got a brilliant farm manager who runs the whole show, he's got a cottage on the estate.'

Estate! Bloody hell, where was I going, Balmoral?

He saw my look and smiled. 'Oh, don't worry, it's not smart at all, very much a working farm.'

I wasn't worried. I liked the idea of Balmoral. I mentally unpacked my suitcase – did I have the right gear? I thought on balance, yes, although I might need to do a little bit of light-fingering in Balmoral's cloakroom; a Barbour here, a pair of green wellies there – all country houses seemed to have enough to camouflage an army.

'But why keep it if you're never going to live there?'

'Who says I'm never going to live there?'

'Well, surely if you carry on running Penhalligan and Waters, you'll never actually live in Cornwall, will you?'

'Which is precisely why I'm selling the agency.'

My jaw hit my chest and my monosyllable was loaded with incredulity. '*No!*'

'Oh yes, definitely.'

'But why? Why on earth would you want to sell? It's going so well!'

'Exactly, and because it's going so well I should get quite a bit of money for it. It was only ever a means to an end, Polly. I needed the money to sort the house out and get the farm running smoothly. You've no idea how expensive it is to run a big house – the roof's caving in; we've got galloping dry rot, and wet rot too I shouldn't wonder; the heating system is archaic; the windows are all falling apart – it takes a lot of dosh to put these things right, you know. I'm just making a fast buck so I can pay for it all.'

'But – but you're so good at it!' I gasped. 'Won't you miss it? Don't you enjoy it?'

Nick threw his head back and laughed. 'Enjoy it? You must be mad. Enjoy entertaining revolting, slimy little toads like James Hutchinson, smarming up to him to make him feel important for five minutes, helping him to offload his rotten coffee beans on to an unsuspecting public? No, I don't enjoy it, in fact the more I consider what we do every day, the more I hate it. Think about it, Polly: we spend our time filling people's television screens with false images full of happy loving couples and perfect children, we make people believe that's how the other half live, with their big houses and their cars and their holidays, and we hold our hands up in horror when someone breaks into the local hi-fi shop and steals a video because they've seen it on the telly and think they have a perfect right to own one. Advertising stinks, Polly, and the more I see of it, the more I want to get out.'

'But – but what will happen to the agency?' I stammered. 'I mean, you run the place, it'll fall apart if you leave.'

'Course it won't,' scoffed Nick. 'And anyway, I'm not going to sell you all down the river; you'll all keep your jobs. I'm just going to sell out to Waters. I daresay he'll just employ another managing director to lick you all into shape.' He grinned. 'Who knows, he might take you to a few shoots, maybe even treat you to expense-account lunches!'

I smiled weakly. For some reason I felt unaccountably sick. 'So – when will all this happen?' I asked in a rather small voice.

'Oh, in about six months, I should think. Hopefully we'll win that dog-food pitch, which will add about half a million to our billings, and then I'll be off.'

He flashed his lights at a slow-moving truck in the fast lane; it moved over to let him by and he sped past.

I stared at the rather clean bit of thumb where my plaster had been and picked miserably at the few remaining bits of dirty, sticky thread with my fingernail. Whatever he said, the place just wouldn't be the same without him. He was the whole energy behind it, the driving force. If he went, everyone else would just go to the pub. As it was, I shouldn't think many people had gone to work today. Pippa had certainly looked as if she was heading straight back to the bedroom with Charles, and Joss and Ron were no doubt already stalking their prey in a South Ken wine bar.

I looked at the combination of square jaw, Roman nose and straightforward eyes sitting beside me. It was all very well saying we'd be OK, but not everyone had that sort of determination or strength of character. Mention a drink, or a day off, or a long lunch, and we were anybody's. He was deserting us, leaving us to our own loose morals and weak characters. I felt absurdly upset.

'Well, if you think advertising's so immoral and the people so ghastly, why did you decide to make your millions in it?' I snapped petulantly.

'I haven't made millions, and I didn't say all the people were ghastly: just James Hutchinson and one or two others like him. I know I sound like a hypocrite, and it's easy to take the high moral ground now I'm leaving, but I promise you, when I joined I didn't realize quite how much I'd hate it.' He turned and grinned. 'Which might explain why I'm so bad tempered in the office.'

'Oh, I wouldn't say —'

'Polly, I'm well aware that I'm a complete bastard to work for, and I apologize, but it's because I loathe what I'm doing. I've only stayed this long because I realized how much money I could make from it, and I'm not so high-minded that I was going to turn down the money for my new roof, or all the farm equipment we so badly need. All I'm saying is, I don't want to do it for ever.'

I sat in sullen silence. Well, for that matter neither did I, but what choice did I have? I didn't have a convenient farm to inherit. Everyone seemed to have plans except me. What about my life? What was I supposed to do? Hadn't anybody thought of that? I choked down the lump in my throat and tried not to feel too sorry for myself. I tried a different tack.

'Won't you miss London?'

'Not a bit. What should I miss – the traffic? The crowds? The underground? The carbon monoxide? The stress? The ultimate ulcer? Or are you perhaps referring to the gay social whirl?'

'Well, something like that,' I said uncomfortably. 'Yes, I suppose I am.'

Nick paused for a minute as he pulled over to let a Porsche go steaming by us at a million miles an hour. 'I honestly wouldn't care if I never went to another London drinks party ever again. All that tedious standing around, clutching a glass of fizzy white wine, talking to complete strangers about their dreary lives when you really couldn't care less because you know you'll never see them again. No thanks.'

'Surely there are people you like in London? Don't you have any friends?' I added maliciously.

'Oh sure, plenty, and I like seeing them for a drink after work or for supper, but what I don't like is spending an hour in a traffic jam trying to get to their bloody houses, and then coming out a few hours later to find my car's been broken into. Wait till you see what I'm swapping it all for, Polly: it might even make a city slicker like yourself want to head for the wide open spaces.'

'I doubt it,' I snapped. 'I don't suppose Armani has opened a branch in Helford yet.'

He roared with laughter. 'No, but then I don't have much use for Armani – I'd look pretty silly wading through the manure in a designer suit.'

I stared sulkily out of the window thinking life was a bitch. Speaking of which . . . 'What about Serena?'

Nick didn't answer, he stared straight ahead and a little muscle twitched in his cheek. Aha! I'd got him at last! Not so self-assured on that little point, eh, Mr Cool Dude? Mr I-Know-Where-I'm-Going?

'You said she doesn't like Cornwall!' I persisted eagerly.

'No, she's not too keen.' He narrowed his eyes and put his foot down somewhat.

'So will you stay together, d'you think?' Still no answer, but that didn't deter me. 'What d'you think?'

He laughed. 'God, you're like a battering ram. Quiz me on something else, Polly, this isn't really my best subject.'

Now what the hell did that mean? He wasn't good at talking about it or it wasn't going very well?

I stared out of the window and watched the fields and hedges flash by. Cows and sheep, cows and sheep. We ate up the miles and Phil Collins ate his heart out on the cassette recorder. 'And now we're living, se-ep-arate lives', he crooned. I gulped again. Separate lives. Me and Harry. Another gulp and a blink too. I was definitely upset. About Harry? Perhaps. Or about Nick leaving? Perhaps it was just the general feeling of rejection? Yes, maybe I didn't like being deserted on such a regular basis by one and all. I felt about five years old and back in the playground again – quick, run away, Polly's coming!

Nick's voice broke into my misery. 'I know it's a little late, but I thought we might stop somewhere for lunch. Is that OK?'

'Sure.'

It had been a good few hours since that bacon sandwich, and my tummy was doing a sensational job at accompanying Phil on the drum rolls.

We turned off the main road at Wincanton and tootled down a country lane, which led in turn to a series of increasingly smaller lanes until we seemed to be almost on a dirt track. I looked at Nick in surprise.

'I hope you know where you're going.'

'Don't worry, I've been here masses of times.'

The bumpy track, which was producing grunts of indignation from Jamie in the back, eventually came to a completely dead end. As I peered out of the window, I saw that we'd come to rest outside a very ancient-looking pub. It was thatched, with pretty bay windows and, surprisingly enough – seeing as it was in the middle of nowhere – there were quite a few cars parked outside.

'Where are we?' I opened the door dubiously and looked around nervously for cow pats and puddles before I ventured forth in my oh so casual, but oh so expensive, navy blue loafers.

'Welcome to the Dog and Duck. It belongs to a friend of mine.' And so saying, he whipped round to open Rachel's door. She yawned and stretched as Nick wrestled with the baby's car-seat.

As we ducked our heads to avoid the low-slung beam over the main entrance – yes, myself included – Nick turned to the left and led the way into a cosy little bar with dark, mahogany-panelled walls and an enormous fire roaring away in the inglenook fireplace.

Rachel and I made for it immediately, and stood toasting our bottoms while we looked around the room. The carpets and curtains were a lovely old rose pink, and the panelled walls were dotted with sporting prints. There was a comfortable old chintz sofa, and one or two ancient leather chairs which were sprouting horsehair at the seams, plus a few wooden tables and chairs. It was an effortlessly comfortable room, and looked as if it had been this way for ever, but I had a shrewd suspicion that a great deal of thought and consideration had gone into its well-worn antiquity. As I stared out of the leaded windows to the fields beyond, a shriek went up from my left.

'Nick!'

I swung round to see a ravishingly pretty girl framed in the doorway. She was small and as slim as a blade, with dark shiny hair cut in a bob, large almond-shaped eyes, and a wide sexy mouth which almost split her face in half as it spread into a smile of true pleasure. She squealed with delight and threw herself with gusto into Nick's welcoming arms. He swung her round in a massive bear hug, lifting her clean off her feet. Why did I feel just the tiniest bit proprietorial as she gave him a series of resounding kisses, two – no, three on his cheeks – followed by a severe hair ruffle? He held on to her, laughing as she squealed to be put down, before eventually setting her back on her feet again.

'Nick!' she spluttered breathlessly. 'You old goat, what the hell are you doing here?'

'Thought I'd surprise you – catch you out and see what mischief you've been up to. I must say you're looking pretty damn fit, Pen. Being a country bumpkin obviously suits you!'

'You're looking pretty tasty yourself for an advertising executive – but why the hell didn't you tell me you were coming? It might have been my day off, and I'd have killed you if I'd missed you.'

'Well, I had a feeling you'd be here – you know, watching for my car, waiting by the door . . .'

She squealed with mock rage and went to hit him as he ducked and pinned her arm down. He turned to us, laughing. 'This is Penny the publican! She runs this place with irritating efficiency and alarming success. Penny, meet Polly, Rachel and Jamie.'

We all smiled and said hi, it was impossible not to take to her immediately, she was so full of fun and life. I instantly recognized a kindred spirit, with her merry eyes and naughty smile; just the sort of girl who would go down extremely well in my neck of the woods.

Penny bent down to coo over Jamie, breaking off now and again to throw questions out to Nick. How was so-and-so? What were they doing now? Who was doing what to whom? How was the agency going? They obviously knew each other extremely well. How well, I wondered?

After we'd toasted our bums a bit and they'd done the preliminary chat, we followed her through into a pretty olive-green dining room, streaky with sunlight which streamed in from the bay windows. It was surprisingly crowded, and as we sat down at the only remaining table, I was surprised to see a fair amount of silver and a crisp linen tablecloth. This was no ordinary pub.

Penny declined to eat with us on the grounds that she was far too busy, but served us herself, pausing to chat as she piled our plates high with rare roast beef, baby sweetcorn, mange tout and the tiniest, sweetest little new potatoes I'd ever tasted. It was all absolutely delicious and I told her so.

She smiled. 'Well, that's all down to Tim, Nick's brother. He grows organic vegetables and delivers them here whenever he can. I must say I adore them, they really do taste quite different, don't they?'

They certainly did, and so did the summer pudding with great dollops of clotted cream which followed. I sat back, full to bursting, as she brought our coffee and pulled up a chair to join us.

I studied her carefully as I sipped the piping-hot coffee. This was no country bumpkin. What on earth was a beautiful girl like this doing running a little country restaurant, albeit a very attractive and obviously successful restaurant, in the middle of nowhere? Shouldn't she be charging down Sloane Street looking for that elusive but crucial little black number to wear to some crumpet-filled Chelsea drinks party tonight?

Nick and Penny chatted about old friends and old times, all of which meant nothing to me, but I listened carefully, waiting for interesting snippets to fall by the wayside.

'So how are you and Serena?' asked Penny, dropping me the very snippet I was looking for. 'Still throwing plates and gin bottles at each other?'

I tried to look casual as I stirred my coffee, but my ears felt like Mr Spock's, pricked to distraction.

Nick smiled, lit a cigarette – funny how the mention of her name made him do that – and blew the smoke out thoughtfully. 'Well, let's just say we've reached a stage of armed neutrality.'

Curiouser and curiouser, what the hell did that mean?

'You mean you're both standing by your guns but you're not using them?'

'Something like that.'

'So whose guns are the biggest?'

Nick laughed. 'Ah well, that would be telling!'

Well, we wouldn't want to do that, would we? Hell, no. Would someone please tell me what they were talking about? I love gossip – thrive on it actually – especially, I thought, looking at Nick, in this case.

Nick expertly manœuvred the conversation away from his love life and round to the restaurant, giving advice when she asked for it, and praising her for everything she'd done. Rachel and I joined in with equally effusive praise. When lunch was over, we wandered back through the rickety corridor and out under the low beam of the front door into the sunshine.

Nick and Penny kissed each other goodbye with, to my practised eye, a great deal of unnecessary hugging, and we all piled back into the car. She stood at the door, smiling and waving until we were out of sight.

I was burning with curiosity, but managed to hold myself back until we'd at least negotiated the bumpy track and were whizzing down the country lanes again.

'So how d'you know Penny?' I asked casually.

'Oh, she's just an old friend.'

'Looked like a pretty good one to me.'

He grinned. 'OK, a pretty good, old friend.'

'Why on earth is she running a pub out here in the middle of nowhere?'

'She likes it, I suppose.'

'But it's so . . . quiet.'

He smiled. 'That's why she likes it.' He turned on the cassette recorder but I wasn't dissuaded that easily.

'Have you known her long?' I persisted.

Nick caved in. 'Penny's an old girlfriend. We went out together, years ago. It was just after I came down from Cambridge. I was living in Cornwall at the time, and she lived there with me. When we split up, she went back to London and found she couldn't bear living in the city any more; she really missed the country. I scouted around in this area and helped her find the pub. She'd been left a bit of money, and the rest she borrowed, and she's been here ever since, making a very decent living. Her boyfriend owns the antique shop in the village and, as far as I know, she's extremely happy – is that so strange?'

It was to me. 'No, no, not at all!' I lied, thinking I'd go stark raving mad stuck out here in the country, miles from anywhere. So Penny was an ex-girlfriend, eh? That explained all the kissing and cuddling.

'Are you on such good terms with all your exes?'

He laughed. 'I suppose I am, although there haven't really been that many, only Penny and –' He broke off and pretended to look at a signpost, although he must have known the way blindfolded. And who? Who couldn't he bring himself to talk about? God, he was mysterious.

I resigned myself to the fact that no more blood was going to come out of this particular stone at present, and contented myself with staring out of the window, watching the countryside slip by.

Little by little, the scenery was changing. The fields seemed to be getting smaller, the hedges taller, the hills steeper and the lanes narrower. The hedgerows at the side of these tiny lanes had gone quite berserk; primroses and bluebells were jockeying for position on the steep banks, and all the flowers seemed to have the same death wish as their heads were inevitably knocked off by cars as they swept past.

The lanes were so thin that there came a point when we seemed to go backwards more than forwards, as we reversed to let other cars, or more often tractors, pass in the opposite direction. It was impossible to see into some of the fields now, the hedges were so high, but every so often I caught a glimpse of a beautiful lush green meadow, or saw a flash of yellow as a field full of glorious daffodils shot by.

I sat up eagerly, like a child waiting to see the sea. Now and again a village – or perhaps even a hamlet: they were so small, it was hard to tell – would whizz by. If you blinked, you'd miss the irregular smattering of low, white-washed cottages, their heavy thatched eyebrows frowning over tiny latticed windows, all clustered around a small, mouse-grey church. I opened the window and leaned right out, shutting my eyes and letting the wind sweep through my hair.

Nick laughed. 'What are you doing?'

'Giving my diseased lungs a taste of this wonderful country air – you're right, it is lovely here.'

A broad grin spread across his face. I'd pleased him. How touching to be so proud of a little patch of England. I couldn't quite imagine feeling the same way about Esher. Even Rachel, who'd been asleep, was now sitting up in the back, pointing out cows and sheep to Jamie, who was gurgling appreciatively. Suddenly I felt almost happy. There was a definite holiday atmosphere in the car, a real sense of adventure and camaraderie – any minute now, I'd break into a spirited rendition of 'Green Grow the Rushes Oh'.

As we hurtled down a particularly narrow lane at breakneck speed, with Rachel and I squealing in mock terror, Nick suddenly changed dramatically from fourth to second gear and swung the car left through some crumbling white gates. We trundled over a cattle grid and down a narrow, pitted drive. It was long and windy with woods on either side, through which the sun flashed intermittently, as if someone were shining an almighty great flashlight at us. Seconds later, the woods parted, and a sweep of lawn rose up before us. Straight ahead, looking out proprietorially on to this sylvan scene, was a large and ancient grey stone house.

It was long and low, with large sash windows at the front and an imposing arched front door surrounded by a sweep of grey stone. Covering almost half of the house was a giant wisteria, which looked about as old as the house itself, and, as we drew nearer, I could see what looked like a stable block behind, with a bell tower peeping out over the rooftops.

I caught my breath with delight. 'Oh Nick,' I breathed. 'It's beautiful!'

'Isn't it just!' echoed Rachel.

Nick beamed with pleasure, looking like the Cheshire Cat. 'It is rather a decent-looking place but, unfortunately, as you'll see on closer inspection, it's falling to bits.'

We got out of the car and wandered up – and I did see. The brickwork was literally crumbling to the touch in places, and most of the windows were rotten, hanging in their frames at precarious angles.

Nick strode ahead and pushed through the giant wooden door, leading us into a large creamy hall which looked remarkably like the National Gallery. The walls were crawling with ancestors, and a very gloomy crowd they looked too. Most had piggy brown eyes and big noses, and were swathed in what looked like velvet and ermine. They also appeared to be sporting quite a few sizeable baubles, notably around the head and neck region. What was going on here: was Nick related to royalty or something? Was I in fact in the presence of a Young Pretender, the last of the Cornish Plantagenets, perhaps? One of the old codgers on the wall certainly bore an unnerving resemblance to that king with the hunchback and the dodgy leg who does a lot of Shakespeare. He gave me the creeps and I decided to keep well clear of him. I could do without being followed around by those piercing, judgemental eyes.

'Tim? Where are you!' yelled Nick. 'It's me!'

I heard voices coming from behind the double doors opposite, and a shout of recognition went up. Nick pushed open the doors and, as he strode through, a smaller, thinner version of Nick leaped up from an armchair, scattering pieces of the *Independent*, and sending an ashtray flying.

'Nick!' he vaulted over a sofa to get to us. 'What the devil are you doing here? I didn't expect you till tomorrow!'

He slapped Nick on the back, who slapped him back, grinning, and then they slapped each other a bit more, as men seem to do.

While the Morris Dancing was going on, I noticed a

pretty girl with curly brown hair and freckles get up from a chair in the corner. She put down her book and took her glasses off, smiling shyly. Nick took two giant strides to get to her and kissed her smartly on both cheeks.

'Sarah! It's good to see you. How are the stables? Still up to your knees in it?'

She laughed. 'They're fine, thank you, and you'll be pleased to hear I change my jeans when I come over here, so no more manure jokes, please.'

'Glad to hear it, especially if you're sitting on my chairs . . . Oh, this is Polly, and Rachel, and Jamie. Sarah Mansfield, Tim's – revolting word – fiancée.'

She grimaced. 'Isn't it just, but I suppose that's what I am. Hello.' She turned to Rachel. 'What a beautiful baby, can I hold him?'

Jamie was duly bundled into her arms with a smile from Rachel. Sarah cooed and tickled him, and I wondered if she'd been briefed – be nice to the scared-looking one with the baby who looks like she's just got out of Belsen. Jamie took hold of her finger and squeezed it in his fierce little grip.

'Oh! Aren't you sweet!' she cooed. 'I've got a little nephew just like you, but not nearly so good looking!'

Rachel looked proud, and they knelt down by the fire talking babies. Rachel looked positively happy. I supposed this must feel rather like reaching Switzerland after escaping from Colditz. Nick offered to show me the house and, as we were on our way out, Rachel turned to him, eyes shining.

'Thanks, Nick!' she blushed. 'I mean, for driving me here, and – and everything.'

'No problem,' said Nick, 'just make yourself at home. I thought you and Jamie could have the pink room at the top. It's got its own bathroom. Tim will show you where it is.'

Tim nodded, 'Sure.' He was staring at her intently as she sat huddled by the fire in her outsized grey cardigan, thinking, I'm sure, what most people think when they meet her for the first time: how small and lost and vulnerable she looked. He poured her a large drink, and Nick and I disappeared to look around the house.

As we wandered from one vast, high-ceilinged room to the next, I realized why Nick was so desperate to keep it. It was just as pretty inside as it was out, but again, in a precarious way. I felt that a sudden gust of wind breezing through an open window could sweep all the fragile pieces of china off their shelves, whisk the soft silky curtains from their few remaining threads, and break the legs on all the spindly little pieces of antique furniture. Everything was beautifully pale and washed out, too, rather as if someone had turned down the colour on the telly. The floors were very pale oak, the Persian carpets were so faded you could hardly see the pattern, and the walls had lost most of their original colour and were those lovely soft, muted shades that paint manufacturers would kill to recreate. It was indeed beautiful, and it occurred to me, as I ran my amateurish, *Antiques Roadshow* viewer's eye over it, that it all looked rather valuable too.

I casually picked up a pretty blue and white plate which weighed about half an ounce, and put it down hastily as I realized how eminently breakable it was.

'Couldn't you sell some of this?' I ventured timidly,

gesturing around at the treasures. 'I mean, if the house is costing so much to repair, surely you could get quite a bit for the furniture and, um – china?' Was china the right word? Somehow it sounded too much like the ground floor of Peter Jones.

'I could, I suppose. I daresay the porcelain' – the very word I'd been groping for – 'would fetch quite a bit at auction, but I don't want to. I grew up with all these things – they're like family to me. Anyway,' he grimaced, 'it wouldn't be enough. Holes in roofs make pretty enormous holes in pockets.'

We wandered into the dining room and encountered a vast mahogany table, heaving with silver. An enormous candelabra stood in the middle, surrounded by lots of little silver animals: pheasants, foxes, ducks . . . I picked up a little hare and turned it over in my hand.

'Oh! How pretty!' I exclaimed. 'Where did you get them from?'

'I'm not sure,' said Nick, scratching his head. 'They've always been here. I suppose Mum would know, but they were probably here when she arrived on the scene too.'

Of course, how stupid of me, people like Nick didn't buy their own silver. I wondered how many more cringe-makingly naff remarks would fall from my lips during the course of the weekend. Any minute now I'd be demanding to know why there wasn't a fluffy little mat on the loo seat, or how come the front door bell didn't play 'Jingle Bells' when you pressed it.

Nick showed me the rest of the house. I smiled a lot and nodded admiringly whenever I deemed it appropriate, but said little. Surely smiling and nodding couldn't be wrong?

As we went back through the hall, though, I couldn't help enthusing about a dear little walnut table which stood at the foot of the stairs. It was terribly delicate and intricately inlaid, just the sort of thing I'd kill to have by my bed one day. On it stood a tiny bowl of primroses which were just dropping a few of their petals on to its smooth walnut veneer.

'Oh look!' I breathed. 'Isn't it divine? What a beautiful little table!' I ran my finger over its smooth, highly polished surface.

'It's pretty, isn't it? It was a Christmas present, actually.'

'Really? How incredibly generous. Who from?'

Nick looked slightly uncomfortable. 'From Serena.'

'Serena? Gosh!' I recalled my own, I'd thought, incredibly generous Christmas present to Harry – one navy blue cashmere scarf – and realized I was well out of my depth here.

'How kind,' I muttered.

'Wasn't it?' agreed Nick. He stooped and picked up a few petals that had fallen just by my feet. His hand accidentally brushed my shoe. He straightened up and smiled. 'Nice legs.'

I flushed with pleasure, thrilled that he'd noticed one of my undoubted assets, set off, rather attractively today, by black Lycra tights. I lowered my eyelids and smiled coquettishly.

'Yes, I love the way they bow, ever so slightly, at the bottom,' he went on.

I gasped with horror. Who was he calling bow-legged! Bloody hell! I intercepted his gaze and followed it back to the walnut table – oh! Oh, yes I see, OK. I nodded vigorously, hoping he hadn't noticed my flaming face.

'Oh I agree, I um – I like them like that, sort of – curvy.' I followed him meekly back into the drawing room, feeling decidedly disappointed. Tim and Rachel were sitting by the fire, chatting away in what I have to admit was quite an animated fashion. I even heard Rachel laugh once or twice, and at one stage I could have sworn she came close to completing a paragraph.

Tim was listening intently, egging her on and encouraging her to reveal yet more of her wildly attractive personality. He seemed intrigued by her, willing to spend time and energy coaxing words to flow from her mouth. And flow they did, albeit in a somewhat jerky fashion. Perhaps a combination of these kind, friendly people and the country air was getting to her, and perhaps now, finally, we could all relax a bit, I thought, flopping down thankfully into a nice squashy sofa.

Sarah had gone back to the local riding stables which, I gathered from Tim, she ran practically single-handed. It sounded like a pretty labour-intensive job, and not one I particularly envied. I always like to slip into a nice tight pair of breeches and some black leather boots if there's anyone around to admire the effect, but I'm damned if I want to get near the beastly creatures, and as for working in a stables – imagine the pong! But Sarah returned a couple of hours later looking flushed and happy, and reeking, not of manure, but of job satisfaction.

'Two new pupils today!' she said cheerfully, helping

herself to a glass of wine. 'And they've both signed on for a course of ten lessons!'

'Excellent!' beamed Tim. 'If you keep going at this rate, I can retire! Keep at it, work harder!' he cried, cracking an imaginary whip. 'What's for supper, by the way?'

She threw a cushion at him, laughing. 'You'll be getting it yourself if you're not careful, but since you ask, beef bourguignon. I'll just go and see how it's doing.'

And so saying, this capable girl whizzed off to the kitchen to put the finishing touches to her dish, wisely waving aside my feeble offers of help – for feeble is what they would have been. Beef bourguignon was the sort of thing I ordered in restaurants: I'd certainly never attempt to recreate it.

Supper that night was a happy and relaxed affair. After Tim and Nick had dispensed with the preliminary farm chat, with Nick asking questions about crop yields and lambing, and Tim prefixing his answers with words like 'high', 'excellent', and 'bloody good considering', all of which made Nick beam with pleasure, we got down to the interesting bits, like me asking who owned what – surreptitiously, of course.

The house and most of the land apparently belonged to Nick, who had obviously inherited the lion's share, but Tim owned a certain amount of acreage adjacent to Nick's estate, which he also farmed, but in a purely organic way. There was apparently a cottage on the land, too, which Tim and Sarah were painstakingly restoring so they could eventually live there.

'Probably in about the year 2000 at the rate we're going!' said Sarah, laughing; but she looked pretty happy about it, and Tim blew her a kiss over the table.

'Don't you worry, I'll be struggling over the threshold with you long before that!'

'Oh!' I said breathlessly, seizing on a subject that was close to my heart. 'When are you getting married?'

'Next year,' said Sarah happily, 'at the church in Manaccan. It's so pretty, you must come and have a look at it.'

'I'd love to!' I said, jumping at the chance to talk flowers and bridesmaids' dresses and wedding lists. I wondered if the London stores would take on a wedding list this far away? No doubt it was a problem she'd already wrestled with, but I supposed there were obvious compensations attached to a country wedding: a picturesque setting; off to the reception in a pony and trap; perhaps a dance in a marquee in the evening . . . I sighed wistfully.

We laughed a lot that night. The beef bourguignon was ambrosial, the claret flowed, and Nick showed the sort of form I wouldn't previously have thought possible. He and Tim had us in stitches as they played a couple of Cornish yokels, affecting deep country burrs and clowning around in a ridiculous manner, egged on by the shrieks of laughter from us girls. As I watched him larking around with his brother, he turned suddenly and caught my eye, smiling, and raising his eyebrows inquiringly. 'All right?' he mouthed. I nodded and smiled back, hoping he wouldn't notice that there were tears in my eyes. Recently I wasn't used to anyone bothering to find out if I were happy or not.

That night, I left the curtains open and pulled the bed-clothes high up under my chin as I stared out at the vast black sky. An owl hooted way off in the distance. A lamb bleated for its mother, then there was quiet. I breathed deeply, savouring the cool night air. I smiled. How comforting it was to know that in the morning I'd wake up – not to an alarm clock, followed by a rushed breakfast, followed by the underground – but to those enormous oak trees swaying in the breeze outside my window, and a field full of sheep with their spring lambs. I snuggled down further in the bed and closed my eyes, letting the dark night wash over me. This was the nearest I'd come to happiness in a good many days.

Chapter Fifteen

At breakfast the next morning, over great platefuls of bacon and eggs, expertly cooked by Tim, Nick suggested we all had a look at the farm. My heart sank deep into my Docksiders. I had visions of myself, up to my designer-jeaned knees in cow pats and manure, miserably swatting flies with my handbag.

'Sorry, I'm far too busy, got to get the beans in today,' said Tim, helping himself to more toast and mopping up his fried egg. He grinned at his brother. 'Some of us have to work, you know!'

'Well, you're lucky you can do it down here rather than in London. How about the wife-to-be, or are you keeping her nose to the grindstone, too?'

''Fraid so,' said Sarah. 'I've got a new pony arriving at about ten o'clock. Maybe I'll catch up with you later, though.'

'Rachel?'

She sighed. 'I'd love to, but unfortunately Jamie will have to have another sleep in about an hour, so I'd better stay here with him.'

Nick made a face. 'God, I'd no idea this mothering lark was such hard work. Having you and Jamie around certainly makes me think twice about throwing myself into parenthood.'

'Ah yes, but you'd only be a father, wouldn't you? That

doesn't come with quite so many occupational hazards,' said Rachel darkly.

That's pretty rich, I thought, considering Adam's moving heaven and earth to take on those hazards, but I wisely held my tongue.

Nick turned to me with a smile. 'Looks like we're on our own, then – how about it?'

For some reason, my heart stopped lurking sulkily in my shoes and rocketed swiftly back into position again. 'Yes, I'd love to see the farm.'

'Sure? You don't have to be polite, you know, you can do what you like.'

'I should think the last thing she wants to do is trail round a smelly old farm,' said Tim. 'If I were you, Polly, I'd catch a bus into town and check out the only boutique in Helston.'

'Don't be silly, there's nothing in that ghastly little shop that would interest Polly. Why don't you come to the stables with me?' suggested Sarah. 'I'm only doing half a day today, we could go and have some lunch in a pub when I've finished.'

'Oh no, that's very kind, but I'm not desperately fond of horses and, anyway, I'd really like to go with Nick!' I said eagerly. Far too eagerly. The phrase 'really like to go with Nick!' seemed to hang, echoing in the air. I felt it needed a little explaining. 'You see,' I stammered, 'I'm . . . I'm terribly interested in farming!'

'Really?' Nick looked up from his bacon and eggs in surprise. 'Polly, I had no idea!'

No, neither did I, and hopefully he'd forget I'd said that, but he showed no signs of doing so just yet.

'Which particular areas are you interested in?' he asked.

'Um, d'you mean – which particular areas, in particular?' I faltered, playing with some crumbs on the tablecloth.

Nick looked confused. 'Well, yes, I suppose I do mean that.'

'Oh. Oh well, all sorts really.'

'All sorts?'

'Yes, but, um, if you want to get specific, I'd say particularly animal, vegetable and, er – mineral.'

By now Tim, Sarah and Rachel had all put their knives and forks down and were looking at me in astonishment.

'Animal, vegetable and mineral?' inquired Nick, his mouth twitching slightly.

'Yes, you know, cows, sheep, er – hay, straw . . .' I racked my brains. What else did they have in these bloody places? One of Jamie's animal books sprung helpfully to mind. 'Oh yes, and chickens, horses, zebras –'

'Zebras!' cried Sarah in astonishment.

'Oh, er – did I say zebras? Oh well, perhaps not in this country, but certainly in Africa. Yes, there are a hell of a lot of zebras out there, and of course I'm interested in farming on a very global scale – you know, global farming.' I seized this concept gratefully.

Tim snorted with derision. 'But zebras are wild, they charge around on game reserves. People don't farm them!'

'Oh you'd be surprised, Tim,' I said, nodding sagely and wishing I too was safely charging around on a game reserve in darkest Africa. 'Some of those tribesmen will stop at nothing.'

'Have you spent a lot of time in Africa then?' asked Sarah in wonder.

'Well, perhaps not a lot, but certainly a bit, yes, I'd say a fair bit.'

'Really? Whereabouts?'

'Whereabouts? Oh, all over really, but mostly – mostly East, you know, East Africa.'

'What – Tanzania? Kenya? Or further up?'

'Mmmm . . . yes, mostly – I say, I love that jumper. Did you buy it locally?' I snatched desperately at the first handy distraction to catch my eye.

'What, this old thing?' said Sarah dubiously, staring down at what indeed was a very old thing, a sort of dirty grey Shetland wool affair with bobbles of wool where it had been rubbed and patches on the elbows. She gazed at me incredulously. 'This is the one I wear to the stables. D'you like it?'

'Very much.' I nodded vigorously, chewing hard on my bacon and staring at the truly repulsive jumper which had absolutely nothing to recommend it. I waved my fork in its general direction. 'Everyone's wearing them like that in London. It's quite the thing this season, especially with the elbows patched. Goes with the ripped jeans, you see. Rachel's got one, haven't you?'

'Have I?' asked Rachel, wide-eyed.

'Yes, except it's not quite a jumper is it? More of a cardigan, really, that lovely baggy grey thing you wear all the – quite a lot.'

'Oh that! God, I wasn't aware it was fashionable.'

'Oh, very, very,' I said, still nodding furiously, lips pursed, and I have to admit, warming wickedly to my theme. 'I know girls who'd kill for a cardigan like that – kill. You can't move for them in the King's Road at the moment.'

Out of the corner of my eye I caught a glimpse of Nick, who seemed to be stuffing the tablecloth into his mouth and making strange hiccuppy noises.

'Really?' Sarah looked dumbfounded. 'I had no idea that sort of thing was trendy, but then it's so long since I've been to London – oh well, I've got hundreds more like this. In fact there's a mauve one upstairs which is so threadbare it's unreal. You can borrow it if you like. I'll run and get it.' She put down her napkin and made to go upstairs.

'Oh er, no, Sarah, it's OK,' I said, polishing off my bacon and eggs in one huge mouthful and jumping down from the table. 'I don't think I'll wear a jumper today. I find it frightfully warm for the time of year, don't you?'

I fanned my face with my napkin, which was suitably flushed with the exertion of so many verbal gymnastics, and beat a hasty retreat upstairs to the safety of my bedroom and my beautifully smooth, unbobbly lambswool jumpers.

I threw myself thankfully on the bed. I felt exhausted already, and it was only half-past nine. Why did I have such a propensity to dig whopping great holes for myself and then proceed to clamber inexpertly out of them in front of a vast audience? Ah well, never mind, at least the agenda for today was looking good. A whole day on the farm with Nick – now why was that such a treat? I declined to answer, afraid of all the mighty implications it could throw up.

'Don't think about it,' I instructed myself, jumping off the bed. I opened my suitcase and pulled out a whole heap of clothes, throwing them into a huge colourful pile on the bed.

Now, for someone who's more at home in South Ken than South Cornwall, 'A Day on the Farm' was a tricky brief, but I rose gleefully to the challenge. What it called for, I decided, was something that would ease me gently into the part without looking too contrived. In the end I settled on a pair of brown corduroy jodphurs, a yellow and red checked shirt which leant on the lumberjack side, and a pair of brown leather riding boots which were serious but sexy. I studied the overall effect in the mirror. Hmmm. Whilst not exactly looking at one with nature, at least I didn't look as if I'd been born in a wine bar.

As I bounced downstairs in a jaunty, country girl manner, I saw Nick waiting patiently for me at the bottom. He was leaning against the hall table reading an old copy of *Country Life*. He looked up and smiled as I came down. I smiled winningly back and skipped on down; then, warming to my jaunty theme, decided to jump the last few steps to display a certain amount of fresh-faced athleticism. A huge error. As I took off I realized – too late – that five steps and a shiny wooden floor as a landing pad was, to say the least, ambitious. As I plummeted through the air, I had just enough time to catch the look of alarm on Nick's face as I hurtled towards him. Nine-and-a-half stone of blonde lumberjack cannoned into him and sent him crashing to the ground.

'Oooof!'

'Sorry!' I gasped.

'Christ, steady!' he cried in alarm, as he was sent sliding towards the front door, pinned to his ancestral floorboards by my tremendous weight. As we shuddered to a halt, perilously close to Serena's fragile little table, he struggled desperately – too desperately, I felt – to free himself from my bone-crushing bulk.

'Sorry!' I gasped again, as I clambered to my knees. 'Lost my balance!'

Nick was on his feet before I was and he pulled me up. 'So it seems. What were you trying to do, kill yourself? Or kill me, perhaps. Are you OK?'

'Fine,' I lied, wincing from a shooting pain in my ankle and the embarrassment of it all. What must he think of me? Did he think I was being incredibly forward or something? Did he imagine I was literally flinging myself at him? I blushed to my dyed roots.

'Sure you're all right?' he asked with concern, still holding my arm as I gingerly tried my ankle. 'Can you walk on it?'

I hobbled around. 'Yes, honestly, I'm fine, sorry about that.'

'It's OK. Just warn me next time you're feeling energetic, and I'll lay on some trampolines or something . . . Christ – what's that terrible pong?' He sniffed the air suspiciously.

'What pong?'

'That funny smell, like rotting cabbages or something.'

'Oh that,' I cringed deeply. 'It's called Country Girl. Just something I put on to make the cows feel at home.'

'You mean you bought it? In a bottle?'

'It didn't smell too bad in Boots,' I muttered.

'Jesus. Well let's hope it doesn't knock the cows out. Come on, let's go.'

He marched off, farmyard bound, and I hobbled along after him, nursing my pride and my ankle.

As it turned out, the farm was immaculate: hardly a cow pat to be seen, and certainly not a pebble out of place in the cobbled yard. The barns were spotless, and everything that could shine did. In fact, the milking equipment looked like it had been on the receiving end of a passionate love affair between Mrs Mopp and Mr Sheen. I half expected doormats as we inspected the outbuildings.

'Hope my shoes are clean,' I muttered as we entered a huge Dutch barn, 'I had no idea farmers were so house-proud.'

Nick laughed. 'It's just been cleaned up, actually, but I agree, we keep the farm in better nick than the house. Sometimes I think it would be more comfortable to sleep in the haybarn than in my bedroom, where the windows don't fit and the plaster's falling off the walls. The thing is, though, the farm's always got to come first. It's our livelihood.'

Our livelihood? I wondered who he was planning on sharing it with.

We looked in on the cows in their five-star accommodation. It was cool and dark in the shed, and the cows stood in a long row, pulling at hay nets and stamping their feet. They turned their heads briefly and stared at me insolently before going back to their rhythmical munching, swaying their heads and rotating their jaws. I felt as if I'd interrupted some kind of religious sect chanting a mantra. I patted one gingerly on the bottom. She stamped her foot and swished her tail around in irritation. I backed off smartly.

'Sorry,' I muttered.

'They're waiting to be milked,' explained Nick. 'They get a bit jumpy with strangers.'

One of Nick's farm hands appeared and started to fix them up to milking machines, so we left him to it, emerging out into the sunshine again, blinking against the bright light.

Just then a hearty male voice hailed us. 'Hello, hello! I can't believe you're the new cow girl, but if you are, things are looking up!'

I swung around to see a rather attractive man smiling at me from the other side of the post and rail fence. Although he was the wrong side of forty, he had obviously been extremely good looking once, but was now steadily going to seed. His bright blue eyes sported terrific bags, and his handsome face was lined and ruddy; the result, I suspected, of a combination of fresh air and too much alcohol.

'Good Lord, Nick, how did you manage to entice such a delightful creature into your barns. D'you think she'd like to look at mine too?'

Nick grinned. 'Polly, this is Jack Crawley: neighbour, stud farmer, womanizer and piss artist.'

'Come now, dear boy – "*bon viveur*" is much more to my liking . . . Enchanted, my dear!'

He grasped my hand and put it to his lips. I smiled delightedly, keen to make the acquaintance of someone who would flatter me rotten in front of Nick. He ran his rather sexy, bloodshot eyes over me appraisingly, and held on to my hand for a second longer than was absolutely necessary.

'Been showing you the equivalent of his etchings, has he? Want to see mine?'

I grinned. 'Are they up to scratch?'

Jack roared with laughter and, as he opened a gate to let

us through, took my arm and whispered in my ear, 'So I've been led to believe, but who am I to say? Women tell such terrible whoppers. Come and see the horses anyway and then we might find time for a little mid-morning tipple . . . Got time, Nick, or shall I take her myself?'

'I think I can spare a couple of minutes,' said Nick with a grin. 'You're incorrigible, Jack.'

We followed the delightful Jack through his lush green fields towards the stable block in the distance. Over by the far gate were a few brood mares with their foals. The foals frolicked around in the sun, bucking and kicking, trying out their spindly new legs. Every so often they would return to their mothers for a reassuring nuzzle before shying off to test-drive their legs again. The mares, meanwhile, munched contentedly at the grass, or just stood staring into space, basking in the early spring sunshine, resting a back leg and swishing the occasional fly away with their tails. It looked a peaceful sort of life.

One elegant bay mare trotted over, and I stroked her velvety nose as she blew warm, sweet air into my face. She seemed to like me, so it was with a new enthusiasm for horses that I went to the yard to meet Sorcha, Jack's prize stallion.

There were quite a few boxes in the yard, most of which were unoccupied, but there was a great deal of stamping and snorting coming from the one in the corner. I wandered over and leaned over the stable door, peering in to see what all the fuss was about. Suddenly Sorcha's enormous chestnut head came looming out of the darkness, eyes rolling, teeth bared, like Jaws emerging from the depths.

I yelped and jumped backwards, dodging the teeth as

they went to take a chunk out of my nose. He'd obviously got a whiff of Country Girl and couldn't believe his nostrils, but I must say I was mildly insulted.

'Jesus, he's a bit wild, isn't he?'

'It's nothing personal,' laughed Jack, 'he's just a dreadful old misogynist, I'm afraid.' He patted his nose, and Sorcha nuzzled his hand like a pussycat.

'Doesn't bode well for the brood mares, does it?' I said doubtfully.

'Oh, he's keen enough when it comes to sex, he just can't be doing with the social niceties.'

'Hmmm, I've known a few like that,' I muttered darkly.

Jack laughed. 'Oh, the mares don't mind, they've been so revved up by the teaser he could pick his nose while he was on the job for all they cared.'

'What's the teaser?' I asked, wondering if it was some kind of sexual aid for horses, an Ann Summers equine tickler perhaps.

'Here's the teaser,' said Jack, indicating a small and rather scruffy looking grey in a nearby stable. He was circling round and round, neighing his head off in a demented manner. 'Meet Roger.'

'Poor old thing,' said Nick, patting his neck. 'His only role in life is to sniff around the mares and make sure they're in season. He gets them thoroughly sexed up and, just when he thinks he's going to get his wicked way, the mare will be led away for the likes of Sorcha or one of the other stallions to service.'

'So he never actually gets to do the business himself?'

''Fraid not, poor old Roger.'

'That's a singularly inappropriate name, isn't it?'

Nick laughed. 'It's Jack's warped sense of humour, I'm afraid.'

I watched, fascinated, as Roger was indeed led out to inspect a mare. He sniffed and snorted and rolled his eyes, prancing around her in a provocative manner and evidently pronouncing her to be not only in season but ready for anything. After a great deal of flirting and circling and, just as the poor old boy thought he was getting somewhere, the by now thoroughly over-excited mare was abruptly led away to the covering yard for bigger and better things.

At this point Sorcha was led out of his box by a stable boy. He strolled casually over to the covering yard, looking, I have to admit, devastatingly attractive: tall, dark, and not a hair out of place on his gleaming chestnut coat. His muscles rippled, he tossed his arrogant head, and the poor, mystified grey mare went weak at the knees, all thoughts of Randy Roger completely forgotten.

It reminded me of a haunt of mine in the King's Road, a nightclub where quite a few pretty girls go to dance round their handbags and get picked up. Invariably some spotty no-hoper of a guy would do just that. Having made contact with a girl, he'd ply her with drinks, dance his little socks off, shouting above the disco to make himself heard and, just as he'd be about to pounce, lo and behold, his good looking coolie friend – six foot two and not a spot on his chiselled, smouldering face – would stroll up and take over. Coolie would claim just one dance – usually a slow one – before disappearing into the night with her, leaving spotty no-hoper to gnash his teeth and chew the dashboard of his second-hand Mini.

Like a lot of these cool Chelsea guys, Sorcha had no

manners whatsoever and didn't know the meaning of foreplay. He walked nonchalantly around the back of the mare, and heaved himself on board without so much as a friendly neigh in her general direction. Having said that, I have to admit he did his stuff with one of the most impressive pieces of kit I've ever seen. It was enough to make your eyes water, and the little grey mare looked pretty impressed too, if her eyes bulging out of their sockets were anything to go by.

'Make sure it's in deep, for God's sake!' yelled Jack to the stable boy, who had the mammoth task of guiding Sorcha in.

At this point I had a violent attack of schoolgirl giggles, and had to move away, stuffing a hankie in my mouth to muffle the snorts. The whole thing was titillating enough anyway, but somehow, standing next to Nick made it even worse. I felt ridiculously embarrassed.

I went off to comfort Roger, who was thrashing around in his stable looking thoroughly pissed off, chewing anything he could get his teeth into: stable door, bucket, manger – anything to relieve the frustration. I hastily moved away, just in case he decided it was time to bury those enormous yellow teeth into harmless human flesh.

When Sorcha had finished and the mare had been led away to recover and ponder her good fortune, Nick and Jack wandered over.

Jack rubbed his hands together. 'Well, hopefully that's another prize winning foal in the bag. Where did you get to, Polly, you missed the best bit!'

'Didn't want to put him off his stride. I thought he might perform better without too much of a gallery.'

'Don't you believe it, old Sorcha likes an audience. Got time for a swift one back at the house, you two?'

'Some other time, Jack,' said Nick. 'I promised to show Polly the rest of the farm, and then I really must get down to some work.'

'Ah, that's your excuse, is it? Fair enough, I know a couple of love birds when I see them. Run along and frolic in the cornfields then. See if I care!'

Nick laughed. 'You've got a one-track mind, Jack. See you tomorrow, possibly – come up to the house.'

'Will do. Bye, Polly.' He winked. 'Watch him now, he's one hundred per cent pure beef, like the rest of his herd!'

By now my face was puce pink, but I laughed gaily and shook hands, rather unaccountably at a loss to know how to react to this sexy banter. The natural thing would be to tell Jack he'd got the wrong end of the stick, but on the other hand . . .

Nick and I climbed the fence and strolled back towards his farm again. It has to be said there was rather a telling silence. I'm not very good at silences, telling or otherwise.

'He seems like a nice chap,' I said lamely.

'Jack? Oh he's great fun. Got a brain the size of a pea, though and he keeps it between his legs.'

I laughed. 'Yes, he did seem a little – obsessed.'

Nick opened the gate to his yard. 'Well, let's face it, he runs a stud farm, so it's all he ever thinks about. He lives and breathes sex, does Jack . . . Jump in, I'm just going to check on the cows.' He indicated an open-topped Land Rover standing in the corner of the yard.

I obeyed, quietly relieved. My shiny brown boots were already caked with mud, and my legs were beginning to ache from all this exertion. A minute later, Nick jumped in beside me. Now you're talking, I thought, as we zoomed off, my hair streaming away from my face like corn in the breeze, or so I liked to think. This was much more my scene.

As we charged around the farm, Nick pointed out his woods and fields and, in the very, very far-flung distance, boundaries where neighbouring farms began. He seemed to own half of Cornwall, and it occurred to me to wonder whether he wasn't in fact Prince Charles in disguise. That would certainly explain all the regal looking portraits in the hall.

We roared off down a particularly bumpy track, which seemed to be going nowhere. All I could see in the distance was bright blue sky. The bumps were getting larger, and I folded my arms protectively across my chest, fervently wishing I'd had the nous to invest in a sports bra before embarking on an all-action weekend like this. All of a sudden, Nick slowed right down and we came to a shuddering halt. He turned the engine off.

I wondered why we'd stopped, there didn't seem a great deal to see, but I got out obligingly. We were at the very edge of a cornfield and, as I walked to the edge, I caught my breath. The cornfield sloped away to green fields below, and below that, to what I'd originally perceived to be the sky, but which was in fact a great expanse of sea. I stared down at the sparkling chasm that had opened up in front of me. It was dotted with tiny boats which bobbed jauntily around, their sails fluttering in the breeze. The water was as smooth as a mirror, just tilting now and then to offer up a different angle for the sun to reflect. Far away, on the opposite shore, I could make out a cluster of tiny white cottages basking in the sunshine.

I turned to Nick in amazement. 'This is absolutely beautiful. I had no idea we were by the sea!'

He laughed. 'Really? Well, I suppose technically we're not. This is a river, actually. It runs up to Gweek which is a few miles in that direction, and out to sea the other way. Over there is Frenchman's Creek – see?' He pointed out a dark and narrow inlet overhung with trees and heavy foliage.

'Oh yes – is it really? How romantic!' It was one of the few books I'd read, and I could quite imagine the dashing young Frenchman snaking up there in his boat to treat his aristocratic lady friend to a bit of *je ne sais quoi* behind some ancient oak tree.

'The village you can see over there is Helford,' said Nick pointing to the white cluster in the distance. 'If you like, we'll take the boat over there tomorrow and I'll show you around. It's really pretty.'

'You have a boat?' Was there anything this man didn't have?

He laughed. 'Well, it would be pretty silly to live here and not have one. Do you sail?'

Now I don't actually 'do' anything that one is supposed to do, like ride, ski, sail, hunt, or even cook, and the only time I can answer a 'do you?' question in the affirmative is when the next word is either drink or smoke; but having come up against quite a few of these tricky little inquiries in my time, I go armed with a set of stock replies. I smiled up at him. 'No, but I'm very good at lying around in a bikini waiting for the sun to pass over the yard-arm.'

He laughed. 'I bet you are, but I'm afraid there's no deck to speak of on this little dinghy. It's more of a ropes and reef-knots affair. What are your knots like?'

'Oh, I do a lovely sheep shag,' I said with a smile, and then realized that wasn't quite what I'd meant at all.

Nick roared with laughter. 'Well, you've come to the right place for that. There's a whole flock in the next field who'd be only too pleased to oblige! Perhaps I'd better let you off the actual sailing part, though. You can just sit at the back and look decorative. I must say I like the sound of the bikini.'

He gazed down at me speculatively from his dizzy heights. I met his eye fleetingly, but instantly looked down and dug up an ear of corn with my toe. Good Lord, was he flirting with me? Surely not. I looked up again and saw the brown eyes still twinkling away in my direction. A smile played around at the corners of his mouth. I immediately returned to my ear of corn. Christ, he was, and what's more the shock had completely taken the wind out of my normally flirty little sails. This was most out of character for both parties. Surely he should have warned me? Sent me a memo or something?

To Polly: Just to inform you that on Friday 12 April there may be a brief and uncharacteristic flirtation on my part in the large cornfield overlooking the Helford River. Please be ready to anticipate just such an eventuality and respond accordingly. Nick

Yes, that would have been much more in keeping. As it was, I was struggling to remember just one of the well-honed lines that would normally trip straight off my tongue in this sort of situation, and which had ensnared the likes of Harry Lloyd-Roberts and plenty more before him. I bit my lip.

'Wind . . . that's your problem,' Nick muttered.

I gasped with horror. Wind? Christ! Had I, in my nervous confusion, inadvertently expelled some vile and evil-smelling gases? How unspeakably ghastly!

I looked up in alarm, but he wasn't looking at me any more. In fact, he seemed to have totally forgotten about my existence. I followed his gaze out to sea. He was watching an unfortunate windsurfer who was struggling to stay on his board, collapsing repeatedly into the water.

'You've got to have a bit of wind to keep the thing upright,' he went on, shading his eyes against the sun and monitoring the sailor's progress. 'It's absolutely hopeless in this sort of weather, can't think why he's even bothering.'

'Oh! Oh yes, crazy . . . on a day like this,' I managed.

I tried to pull myself together. I realized now of course that Nick's reference to the delights of my bikini had just been small-talk. Yes, that was it. A casual pleasantry designed to please and perhaps even flatter, but nothing more than that. I, of course, had overreacted as usual, and had taken it to mean that he couldn't wait to take me in his arms and bowl me over in the cornfield.

I breathed deeply. How hugely disappointing. Hang on a minute – hugely what? Disappointing? Good grief, whatever was happening to me! Wasn't I supposed to be heartbroken? Hadn't I more or less decided that, since I couldn't have Harry, I was through with men and would probably remain celibate for the rest of my life? What on earth was I thinking of? I had a quick mental flick through my file of Harry pictures and found the pre-launch diving-board one, an old favourite. I studied it carefully. Good gracious. How extraordinary. Surely his eyes hadn't always been that close together? And wasn't that mouth just a tad on the pinched side, and was it possible that his hairline was – heavens above – receding?

Shocked to the core, I filed the picture away again and looked up at the one beside me. Wide-apart eyes, generous mouth, plenty of hair. Oh no. This could not be happening to me. My toes twitched nervously in my boots.

Of course, I reasoned, it's bloody hard to be cool and objective when you're up to your knees in corn, gazing out at just about the most beautiful sylvan scene in Christendom, and standing next to the dashing young owner of all that the eye can see. Confused? Who wouldn't be?

The windsurfer eventually called it a day, and swam back to shore dragging his board behind him. The sun disappeared behind a cloud. I shivered. Suddenly the sylvan scene didn't seem quite so peaceful and serene. In fact it seemed full of danger.

'Cold?' asked Nick, noticing my shiver.

'Mm, a bit chilly.'

Nick looked at the sky. 'I have a feeling it's going to rain, actually, which would be no bad thing. We could do with the water. Come on, let's go back, I could do with something to eat, apart from anything else.'

We climbed back into the jeep and sped off across country again. As we bumped along by the side of the field, I surreptitiously studied Mr Many-Acres sitting beside me. One arm was resting on the door, the other was casually guiding the wheel, his shirtsleeves rolled up to the elbows, exposing already brown, muscly forearms. He hadn't shaved that morning, but that did nothing to detract from the strong chin and the classic jawline.

I looked away, wondering how many other girls had fallen for his rural charms down here: not that I had of course – yet – I mean at all, and nor would I, but I just wondered. It was, after all, interesting to muse, wasn't it? How many others, exactly? According to him, not many. Penny I discounted on the grounds that she was a historical figure and very much a mate now, but Serena. Ah Serena, she was a different matter. She was not only very current but very beautiful. I bet she looked great, flat on her back in a cornfield. For some reason my teeth seemed to grind together when I thought of this, and my top lip curled in an unattractive manner.

Where was she at the moment? Ah yes, filming. Dangerous job, filming. All sorts of accidents occur, so I'm told; falling lights, masonry, scaffolding, that kind of thing. I wondered if anything untoward would befall her this weekend. Not that I wanted it to – dear me, no, nothing serious anyway. But perhaps if a piece of scenery did collapse – not too heavy mind, just a tree or something – and if she were to suffer, not a permanent injury, but something that would put her out of action for a while, briefly incapacitating her for, say, a couple of months? A broken leg maybe? And perhaps an arm too? Oh, and a touch of facial bruising, I added quickly, thinking she'd still look darned attractive lying in a hospital bed in plaster unless the face was, temporarily of course, disfigured.

Well then, that would clear the way a bit, wouldn't it? Give me a bit of time. For what, Polly? What exactly did you have in mind? Goodness, I thought, shaking myself, sometimes I even managed to shock myself.

Chapter Sixteen

As Nick had promised, we spent the following day in true Enid Blyton style. Five Go Sailing on the Helford River: Nick, Tim, Rachel, Jamie and me. It was a fine, blustery morning, and we seemed to rocket across the river in record time. I'd always imagined sailing was a slow, rather sedate form of travel, but both Nick and Tim seemed to be speed merchants when it came to boating, doing their damnedest to get as much wind into the sail, and leaning right out over the side on a frighteningly dangerous rope affair, appropriately called a trapeze. I forced a jolly smile on to my rather green face, but was secretly extremely glad when we hit *terra firma*. I had a feeling it would take me a while to find my sea legs; if, indeed, I had any to be found.

We tied up the boat – or moored, as I'd come to call it, by the jetty on the Helford side and strolled up to the conveniently placed pub which overlooked the water. We laughed and chatted as we went, and I relished the prospect of crab sandwiches and ice-cold lager. This place was having a curious effect on me: I seemed to be permanently hungry. As we walked in, we greedily surveyed the list of goodies chalked up on the blackboard, licking our lips at the prospect of a boozy, slap-up lunch – at least, three of us did. Once we'd secured a table outside and sat down, Rachel declared that she wasn't in the least bit hungry, and was going for a walk with Jamie. 'Sometimes,' she announced, with more than a touch of the Greta Garbos, 'I just want to be on my own – you know, to think things through a bit.'

She bit her lip and stared wistfully out to sea. Greta was now playing *The French Lieutenant's Woman*; all she needed was a hooded black cloak.

She sighed mournfully and turned back to us, 'I don't want to be rude, it's just – well, I've got so much on my mind at the moment. I just need a little time alone.'

Don't we all, darling, don't we all? But we don't make a big song and dance about it, do we? We don't sell tickets. We just creep off when no one's looking and lick our wounds in private, and when we return to the fold, we fervently hope that nobody noticed our absence, and if they did, we pretend we got stuck in the loo or something. But not our Rachel.

'It's just that – well, it all gets a bit much sometimes, and I have to get away,' she whispered, clutching Jamie to her breast, a pained expression on her peaky little face.

'Of course you do,' said Nick, looking concerned. He stood up and put a protective hand on her shoulder. 'You've been through a hell of a lot recently. I don't know how you've coped.'

Rachel sniffed a bit.

'Poor you, it must be awful,' agreed Tim. 'Shall we look after Jamie for you?'

'No, no,' she clung to him, chin up now, a brave little soldier look on her face. 'I'll carry him in his sling. I – I hope you don't mind, though, me going off like this?' Her eyes were wide and anxious.

'Not at all, not at all!' I chirped. 'Bye!'

'But will you be all right on your own?' asked Tim.

Would she be all right? For Christ's sake, she was going for a walk, not a bungee jump off the nearest suspension bridge – more's the pity. Of course she'd be all right.

Rachel bit her lip and nodded furiously, as if she didn't quite trust herself to speak.

I certainly didn't trust myself. Over the last couple of days it hadn't escaped my notice that, in her own quiet way, Rachel Marsden was one hell of a drama queen. She spent most of her time having long and meaningful discussions with Tim, the majority of which were conducted in huddled whispers by the drawing-room fire. He would gently prod and probe, asking her questions about Jamie, Adam, her father, and she would stare into space, twiddling a piece of hair around her finger before eventually muttering a monosyllable which you needed a hearing aid to catch.

This scintillating repartee would come to an abrupt halt if anyone was foolish enough to also want to sit by the only fire in this large and freezing-cold house. She would break off in the middle of one of her riveting replies such as, 'Um, I'm not sure,' or, 'Yes, perhaps,' and stare moodily into the flames, until the offending intruder got the hint and tiptoed off into another, colder room, at which point she would resume the halting discussion, pausing now and then to look up at Tim shyly from beneath her eyelashes.

It made me want to run to the nearest loo and stick my fingers down my throat, it all seemed so unbelievably phoney, but I wisely kept my counsel, not wanting to appear the arch bitch.

Tim found her fascinating and delighted in 'bringing her out of her shell', as he called it. He was patience itself, and regarded every muttered utterance on her part as a major breakthrough. Nick told me that Tim had always been brilliant in this respect, particularly with animals. I'd guffawed at the time, thinking this was a bit rich even with regard to Rachel, but I knew what he meant. He had a way of coaxing the timid and the shy, and Rachel certainly seemed to be opening up to him, but it occurred to me to wonder what Sarah thought about all this opening up while she slogged her guts out at the stables.

So here was our tragic heroine once again, standing on the sea front, baby clasped to bosom. 'See you a bit later,' she whispered, and off she drooped, cardigan flapping in the breeze, hair straggling down her shoulders, head bowed against the elements.

'Bye-ee!' I trilled.

'Poor little thing,' muttered Nick.

'She just seems so . . .' Tim struggled for the right word. If it turned out to be 'vulnerable', I decided I'd have the screaming heeby-jeebies and throw myself headlong into the river, tearing my hair out *en route*. '. . . defenceless,' he finished.

This was almost as bad. I ground my teeth together to stop them from seizing Tim's arm and shaking it like a dog.

'Hardly defenceless,' I said in what I hoped was a cool and level voice, but which I suspected had a touch of madness in it, 'I mean, she's got you two socking great lads running round in circles, ready to defend her at a moment's notice.'

'Well, if she needed us of course we'd be there,' Tim

336

agreed staunchly, failing to notice the shovel-load of irony I thought I'd piled on.

He folded his arms and leaned towards me over his pint. 'I must admit I find her fascinating. How well d'you know her, Polly?'

I sighed. 'Not well at all, she wasn't a friend of mine at school or anything.'

'So you only got to know her because of all this Adam and Jamie business?'

'Yes, and I'm quite sure our paths wouldn't have crossed otherwise,' I said with feeling.

Tim shook his head and looked thoughtful. 'You know, I get the feeling there's a lot more to Rachel than meets the eye. She's obviously extremely intelligent and very highly strung. I'd like to find out more about her, but it's so difficult to get her to talk, although I must say she's certainly started to chat a bit more since – Jack!'

He broke off in mid-sentence to jump up and slap Jack Crawley on the back. Jack, by some miraculous stroke of good fortune, had appeared at our table, grinning from ear to ear and swaying violently. He was definitely the worse for a gin and tonic or six. I'd been groaning inwardly as Tim had opened up yet more discussion on the topic of the fascinating Rachel, so I was immensely pleased to see him.

'Hello there, one and all!' he boomed, clutching the table for support.

'Jack! What the devil are you doing here!' Nick quickly slipped a chair beneath his bottom as it headed floor-wards.

Jack sat down heavily. 'Oops! Thanks, old man – just

been to a drinks party at the yacht club, hell of a good do, you know, can't think why you weren't there. Christ, they make a mean Bloody Mary, though; nearly blew my socks off. Thought I'd pop in here on the way home and see if you reprobates were propping up the bar as usual, and here you are! I say, it's the gorgeous Polly again!'

He slipped a lecherous hand on to my knee, and leered into my eyes. I giggled and brushed him off.

'Been showing you round the haybarns again, has he?' he asked with a grin, winking towards Nick. 'Can't see what a sophisticated girl like you sees in a chap like that. You'd be much better off with me, you know!'

The hand reappeared on my knee, and the other one went around my shoulder. 'How about a little drinkie over at my place tonight? Slip into something a bit more comfortable, preferably diaph –, diaphan –, diaphanous – oops! Bit of a tongue-twister that one, when you've had a few. Anyway, you know what I mean, black netting, or chiffon or something, and come round at about, ooh, nine o'clock? That suit you?'

I giggled. 'That's way past my bedtime, Jack.'

'Splendid, splendid! Couldn't be better! 'S way past mine, too, so that's where I'll be, in the bedroom – you can't miss it, top of the stairs, second on the left. I'll be the wildly attractive one lying on the square flat thing in the corner with not a lot on, now what d'you say? Eh?'

And so he went on, flirting outrageously, falling over his words and making us scream with laughter as he recounted what I suspected were mostly apocryphal tales of his love affairs with what seemed like the entire female population of Helford.

It only took Nick or Tim to prompt him with, 'And what about that blonde one, Jack?' or, 'Whatever happened to Sue?' and Jack would be weeping with laughter into his pint as he recounted yet another romp in the hay, the back of the Land Rover, the stable, or even – so he claimed – the covering yard.

We spent an entirely happy hour or so, laughing and joking and trying unsuccessfully to stop Jack pouring yet more drink down his throat. Eventually he admitted defeat and got unsteadily to his feet.

''S no good, y'know, I can't sit here all day chatting to the likes of you lot. Some of us have got work to do. Some of us have got mares to service!'

Just then Rachel appeared around the corner.

'And speaking of mares, here's another pretty filly!'

Tim got up quickly and gave her his seat. 'Rachel, this is Jack Crawley, a neighbour of ours. Jack, Rachel.'

Jack took Rachel's hand and held it to his lips, as was his wont. 'Enchanted,' he murmured in his practised manner.

Rachel frowned and pulled her hand away as soon as was politely possible.

'Rachel's staying with us for a while, with young Jamie here,' Tim explained as she sat down.

Jack chivalrously pushed her chair in for her and made an exaggerated sweeping bow. He lost his balance and staggered slightly on the way up. 'Delighted to hear it. The more girls the merrier, I always say!'

Not in this case, I thought grimly.

Rachel smiled thinly, looking at his bloodshot eyes with distaste, clearly deciding he wasn't worth even the briefest of hellos.

'So this must be young Jamie!' Jack roared, undeterred by the chilly reception he was getting. 'I say, what a fine-looking chap, look at those rosy little cheeks! How are you, young fella?'

He leaned, or even lurched across the table to tickle his face, and no doubt poor Jamie got covered in an entire brewery's worth of fumes, but Rachel's reaction was, none the less, unforgivable.

She swept Jamie away out of Jack's reach and turned to him with a look of utter loathing. 'Keep your hands off my baby, you disgusting old drunk!' she hissed.

Jack drew back in alarm, retrieving his hand as if he'd been burned, his mouth wide with disbelief.

There was a moment's shocked silence as this gratuitous attack was digested. Rachel, pink with fury, stared defiantly at Jack, who was rooted to the spot. It was probably the stillest he'd managed to stand all lunchtime.

Nick leaped in quickly and put his arm round Rachel's shoulder. 'Jack didn't mean any harm, Rachel, he's a friend of ours, he wouldn't hurt Jamie!'

''Course he bloody wouldn't!' I added staunchly, rage pouring from my nostrils.

'I say, certainly not,' muttered Jack, puce with embarrassment. 'Most awfully sorry and all that, didn't mean to frighten you or anything.'

Tim looked at her kindly. 'I'll get you a drink, shall I? You're just a bit overwrought, that's all.'

Rachel looked at the shocked faces assembled around the table and burst into tears. 'I'm sorry,' she sobbed. 'It's just – I have to be so careful, I hate anyone coming near him, I'm so sorry!'

340

'There now, it's all right,' soothed Tim. His hand covered hers on the table. 'Of course you feel like that, it's only natural after what you've been through, but old Jack here wouldn't hurt a fly, you know.'

Old Jack was doing a good job at catching them, though, as he stood facing her, wide-mouthed and incredulous. 'Lord, no, 'course not!' he mumbled.

'I know, and I'm so sorry, I do apologize, I totally over-reacted,' managed Rachel at last, between sniffles. She looked up at him. 'I'm – I'm just a bit nervous about any-one touching my baby at the moment, you see.' She blew her nose noisily into a hankie.

'Quite understand, quite understand,' said Jack, who clearly didn't. He shook his head vigorously. 'Can't be too careful these days, can you? Best forgotten now, though, eh?'

Rachel nodded and smiled briefly. 'Yes, absolutely.' She turned to Tim. 'I think I will have that drink now, Tim, if you don't mind.'

'Sure,' he got to his feet. 'Gin and tonic?'

'Please. I'll just go and wash my face.' Rachel got up and headed towards the Ladies'.

Jack turned to me and raised his eyebrows. 'I say, what about that?' he said quietly. 'I don't mind drunk, or even disgusting, but old!' He looked at me in horror and I giggled.

Jack polished off his pint. 'Might just slip off, though. Don't want to catch the sharp end of that one's tongue again. One always knows the women one can and can't charm, and I couldn't charm the shoes off that one, let alone the pants. Bye all!' and with that he donned his flat cap and hastily withdrew.

Rachel returned looking composed but, I was pleased to see, slightly shamefaced. As she sat down there was an awkward silence, and I for one was determined not to break it. I hoped it was killing her.

Tim took pity and smiled, handing her her drink.

'Before Jack arrived, I was about to ask Polly how you two knew each other. I gather you didn't bump into each other much at school?'

Rachel took a sip of her gin and visibly relaxed. 'No, Polly was a few years above me, but I knew of her of course. Everyone at school had heard of Polly, she had quite a reputation!' She smiled at me and I tried not to fall off my stool.

Heavens! Could this be for real? Was Rachel paying me a compliment? I beamed graciously at her. Ah yes, it was true, of course, I had been a bit of a lad. A bit of a one for the dastardly deeds – shimmying down knotted sheets from dormitory windows, putting salt in the headmistress's tea – all pretty mundane stuff in retrospect, but jolly daring at the time.

'Oh yes,' Rachel went on, warming to her theme, 'there are so many stories about Polly, I hardly know where to begin!'

I was keen for her to begin wherever she felt like it, if it was going to make me look terrific.

'Most of them apocryphal, I'm sure,' I said bashfully, lowering my eyes and playing with a beer mat to keep me from rubbing my hands together with glee, 'or, at least, exaggerated,' I added quickly, lest anyone should think the daredevil stunts Rachel was about to recount were entirely make-believe.

'What sort of things?' asked Nick, intrigued.

Yes, what sort of things, Rachel? I was on the edge of my seat. I was vaguely aware that I'd been regarded as a bit of a coolie by the lower forms, but I'd no idea I'd gone down in the annals of schoolgirl history as some kind of wild and abandoned folk heroine. A sort of Joan of Arc of the Upper Fifth.

'Well, let me think now . . .' Rachel frowned as she tried to remember some of the more hilarious anecdotes.

I leaned forward eagerly, wishing I could prompt her, but realising that might look a bit keen.

'Oh yes, I know!' she said.

Oh goodie!

'What about that time you were caught handing out drugs to everyone. D'you remember that, Polly?' Rachel turned to me with wide, innocent eyes.

Drugs! The word hit me hard in the face and seemed to stick there, slap in the middle of my forehead, written up in red. I caught Nick's rather shocked face out of the corner of my eye, and nearly gagged on a slice of gin-soaked lemon as my elbow went into overdrive, chucking it down my throat. Christ! What the bloody hell was she up to? I retrieved the lemon from my tonsils and brushed the gin off my chin in what I hoped was a nonchalant manner.

'Oh well, hardly drugs eh, Rachel?' I said lightly, cranking up a smile. 'I mean a few magic mushrooms mixed with the leaves of what I thought was a marijuana plant, but which in fact turned out to be an Aspidistra – I mean, that hardly constitutes hard drugs, does it? No one's going to mainline on Aspidistra leaves and mushrooms, are they?'

Nick and Tim roared with laughter. Phew. What a relief.

'Oh God, Polly,' said Nick. 'I can just see you chopping up Aspidistra leaves and cramming them furtively into little plastic bags!'

'Was that all it was?' Rachel looked disappointed. 'Oh, I'd heard there was more to it than that. I thought the police were called in and –'

'Good Lord, no!' I cut in hastily, 'No, no – nothing like that!'

There had, admittedly, been a brief interview with the headmistress in her study on account of the wooziness of one or two faint hearts in my dorm, and yes, this particular interview had in fact taken place in the presence of one Police Constable Moore from the local constabulary, but one piddly little village constable hardly amounts to calling in the police, does it? I mean, come on, Miss Marsden, we're not talking *Miami Vice* here, are we? And anyway, once I'd explained that I'd merely been attempting to make some herbal tea and had distributed it around the dorm on the grounds that it might be a soothing bedtime relaxant, all had been forgiven and forgotten, as I sincerely hoped it would be now.

'You see, that's how these little stories get exaggerated!' I cried, laughing nervously and taking a slug more gin: my throat was inexplicably dry. Come on, Rachel, get off the subject of drugs and police and on to some of my more amusing escapades, like the time I streaked naked through the village for a bet, or what about when I –

'Oh yes!' she announced, raising her index finger.

Oh good, I thought with relief. But it was oh bad.

'What about that dreadful business when you were caught cheating in your history O-level – looking at someone else's paper or something. D'you remember that, Polly?'

I did, and I didn't like the taste of sawdust in my mouth or the nasty glint in her eye. This was most definitely below the belt; so far below that I felt my knees sag in my leggings.

Of course I hadn't cheated. The very idea. No, it was all perfectly simple. Sophie Maxwell, sitting next to me, had dropped her paper and I'd merely picked it up, pausing, of course, to glance at it and to check that – well, to check that her name was at the top of the paper and that it was in fact hers, before handing it back to her. Wouldn't anyone? Anyone, it appeared, except the ghastly invigilator who hauled me out of the exam room and accused me of nicking Sophie's dates. The historical kind of course.

I narrowed my eyes at my new accuser. 'That was all a big misunderstanding,' I said slowly, sounding, I hoped, rather like Margaret Thatcher, 'a total misunderstanding which was cleared up very quickly. There was a full inquiry, and I'm pleased to say I was fully vindicated.'

'Ah,' said Rachel thoughtfully, 'I wondered. I mean, after all, you didn't pass, did you? So it wasn't as if you even benefited. Am I right in thinking you were the only girl to leave St Gertrude's with absolutely no qualifications whatsoever? What a scream!'

Not nearly as much of a scream as you'll make when I get my hands round your throat, I thought savagely.

'But am I right?' persisted Rachel. 'Did you get any?'

I ground my fingernails into my rather damp palms, thinking that it must surely be time Rachel went for another walk, along the clifftops perhaps, perilously close to the edge.

Nick looked confused. 'Oh no, no, that can't be right, can it, Polly? Because on your CV it says you got six O-levels, I distinctly remember.'

Which in turn distinctly reminded me of something I'd temporarily forgotten. This was my boss we were talking to, or rather, Rachel was talking to. Surely there were rules about this sort of thing? Unions to complain to, punishments to hand out. Surely she couldn't get away with it without a life sentence to contend with?

'It was six, wasn't it?' repeated Nick.

My eyes glazed over and my mouth opened bravely. What on earth would come out of it? I marvelled at its courage. What form of words would it deem appropriate? I sat waiting, as they did too, for my lips and tongue to surge into action.

'That's right, six. I took them at a crammer,' I spluttered. Brilliant! Absolutely bloody brilliant! Who needs O-levels when your mouth can say things like that, eh?

'Which one?' piped up Rachel, but she was fighting a losing battle. No one was terribly interested in which crammer I'd gone to.

'Which one? Oh, one in Oxford,' I said vaguely, 'can't remember the name of it. Would anyone like another drink?'

'No thanks,' said Tim, draining his glass. 'We'd better be getting back, I've got work to do.'

And so have I, I thought savagely as we sailed across the river ten minutes later. It was called murdering a fellow house-guest in cold blood without anyone noticing. If only I'd read more Agatha Christie. Perhaps I could just slip her over the side? I peered into the water. It looked pretty deep and cold, eminently suitable, but this was a very small boat and I didn't think I could subtly up-end her into the murky depths without drawing attention to my actions and ending up in deep water myself. I would bide my time, I thought, grinding my teeth to pulp. Revenge, they say, is a meal best eaten cold.

I was still quietly seething when we got back to the house. Nick disappeared to tend to his sheep, so I made for the only warm chair in the house, the one Rachel usually bagged by the fire. I found a little footstool for my feet, and arranged the intelligent bits of the Sunday papers decoratively around me, although of course in reality I was shaping up to an hour or two's uninterrupted kip.

Rachel curled up on the rug by my feet. I shut my eyes and thought how amusing it would be if my leg had one of those involuntary spasms that sometimes occur when you're almost dropping off to sleep, and I inadvertently kicked her in the teeth. My foot twitched eagerly but I held it back. It might, after all, look a little too obvious.

I drifted off into a glorious dream in which I was quite the heroine of the hour as I singlehandedly delivered twin lambs. It was late at night and Nick was in the Dutch barn, where he'd been struggling for hours with a heavily pregnant ewe who was groaning in agony as she tried to give birth. Alerted by all the noise, I appeared in a rather fetching little nightie, and because my arm was thinner than his, was about to stick it up the sheep's whatsit and deliver the lambs. (I knew, of course, that in reality this would have been absolutely impossible because at the merest hint of blood I'd have been heaving and chucking all over the place, but happily, of course, in dreams, one can ride rough-shod over little details like that.) Anyway, suffice to say, Nick was absolutely delighted, beaming at me and showering me with compliments and praises, in fact – yes, that's right, he was hugging me, giving me a great big bear hug when, all of a sudden, Tim's voice piped up in the distance.

'Come on, Rachel!'

I opened one eye. He was over by the grand piano, patting the stool in an encouraging manner. 'Come on, come and give us a tune, it's about time we heard you play!'

I groaned softly. Oh God, we were bringing out Rachel again. I shut the eye and snored softly, hoping to suggest that I for one did not relish the prospect of being hauled from the Land of Nod by Rachel doing her party piece.

'Oh no, I couldn't,' said Rachel.

I couldn't resist a peep. She was huddled by the fire, smiling shyly and twiddling her hair.

'Oh come on,' urged Tim. 'We'd all love to hear you!'

Speak for yourself, I thought grimly.

'Oh no, really, not now . . .'

'Oh please do,' said Sarah, who had just arrived back from the stables. 'No one ever plays that piano unless it's to bash out "Chopsticks" or something.'

'Oh no, I don't think I could.'

'Oh, please.'

'No, really.'

Just as I was about to rise up from my chair like a woman possessed, charge across the room and single-handedly ram the entire grand piano into her mouth, she demurred.

'Oh well, OK. I'll just play a bit of Bach.'

She shuffled over to the piano and sat down. I braced myself. She flexed her fingers around a bit, and then she played. And I have to say it brought a lump even to my cynical throat. As the music filled the room, full of sadness and heartbreak and loss, I listened and stared, mesmerised. She certainly had a gift, a real talent. It was almost as if she'd become a different person. I blinked. That surely wasn't Rachel Marsden over there, venting all that passion and emotion, was it?

It was a long piece, but we were all on the edge of our seats, and when she finished, there was a moment's silence. Then we all clapped like mad, even me, which I thought was big of me.

'Bravo! Bravo!' shouted Tim.

Rachel smiled shyly. 'Thanks,' she whispered, looking down at her hands. 'It really wasn't awfully good, you know.'

She slipped off the stool and slunk over to the fire again to resume her hunched, gnome-like position once again. All emotion had gone, all passion was spent. Rachel, the tight-lipped little mouse was back *in situ* again.

Tim was in raptures, falling over himself to praise her. 'But that was fantastic, Rachel! I've never heard anyone play like that and, honestly, I may strike you as a philistine, but I have been to quite a few piano recitals. You really should take it up professionally, you know, I'm quite sure you're good enough. I honestly think you could be a concert pianist or something.'

'Oh well, one day maybe,' murmured Rachel.

'You really should try, you know, you've got so much talent. Don't you think so, Polly?'

'Definitely,' I muttered.

After this, of course, there was no stopping her, and with more encouragement from Tim, she performed for Nick when he arrived back from the farm. All the pieces she played were serious and melancholy, and marvellous though it all was, I felt ready to slit my wrists at the end of it. I also realized, with a dull thud of my heart, that it was time to go home.

I sighed and pulled a train timetable out of the bookcase, flipping through it miserably. I looked at the clock. God, at this rate I'd be back in London at about three a.m; I really must go and pack and get someone to take me to the station. The idea of leaving Cornwall filled me with doom and gloom. Who would have thought I'd want to swap the bright lights for cow pats so quickly? Of course, that wasn't the whole story, it had more to do with finding a different set of bright lights, namely the ones shining in those dark eyes over there. They met mine as I looked up from the timetable, and advanced towards me. I gulped as Nick sat on the sofa beside me and instinctively lifted my thighs up a bit to make them look thinner.

He took the book from my hands and snapped it shut. 'Is there any real need to go back tonight?'

Oh heavens, he was going to be all masterful. My knees began to wobble with excitement, and I had to abandon the raised thigh position.

'Well, no, I suppose I could go back in the morning – but I'd be a bit late for work.'

'And who would be there to care?'

I took his point, but wanted to appear conscientious. I frowned. 'There's quite a lot to do, you know,' I said piously, 'all the scripts for the Din-Din's Dog Food pitch have to be typed up, not to mention the entire presentation.'

'Well, I've yet to write it, so it can hardly be typed.'

'Even so, the work will be piling up.'

'Rubbish. I'm not there so why should you be? You might just as well stay here for a while.'

For a while? My heart did a backward flip-flap and danced merrily around in my ribcage. He wanted me to stay! He really wanted me to stay – or, to put it another way, he simply didn't want me to leave him! Of course. Yes, it was obvious. Over the last two days he'd become totally besotted with me, and whereas previously he couldn't bear to have me *in* his sight, he now couldn't bear to have me *out* of it. What a funny old world. I tried my voice.

'I'd – I'd love to . . .' too high. I coughed and tried again. 'I'd really love to stay, I – I really would, I just love it here, it's all so beautiful – the countryside, the house, the animals and oh – just everything. I haven't been as happy as this for ages!' I gushed.

Steady Polly steady, don't overdo it. I took a few deep breaths and tried to calm myself.

'Good!' He tossed the timetable over the back of the sofa. 'That settles it, then. To be honest, I really can't be fagged to drive you to the station.' He grinned.

I winced, but managed to smile back as I caught the body blow. Ouch. It had hurt quite a bit actually, but not enough to entirely dampen my spirits. If you really wanted someone to leave, you'd move heaven and earth to get them to the station, wouldn't you? I mean, if someone was really getting on your tits, a little forty-minute car ride would be a breeze, wouldn't it? Absolutely. I realized, though, that I might have to review his besottedness in the light of this comment. Later. Much later. For the moment I was happy just sitting here on the sofa, close to him – really quite close to him indeed. I'd say there was no less than, what – three inches between our respective buttocks?

He flung his arm along the back of the sofa, fixed me with his liquid browns and talked about the farm. I sighed happily and thought about the farmer. Blissikins.

'Sorry, am I boring you?'

'What? No, of course not! Why?'

'I thought you yawned.'

'Did I? Oh! No, just a sigh. I was just thinking – well, I was just thinking how nice it is to be staying on, um, for a bit – not long of course, just a bit.'

'Stay as long as you want,' he replied with a dazzling smile.

'Thank you,' I whispered, staring into his glorious deep brown eyes and wondering if we were talking weeks, or months, or even . . . No, don't be silly, Polly. I gave myself a little shake and listened attentively as he spoke of crop yields and lambing figures, nodding intelligently and asking pertinent questions, as any good farmer's wife, I mean, secretary should.

Chapter Seventeen

The next few days flew past. Rachel and Jamie stayed mostly at the house, and Tim and Sarah went back to work, which left Nick and me. We walked for miles, sat in quiet little pubs eating crab sandwiches and treacle tart and talked endlessly. When we weren't walking, talking or eating, we were either rowing or sailing – depending on the wind – up and down the river.

On one particularly sunny morning, as we drifted slowly up Frenchman's Creek, I lay back in the boat and pulled my straw hat down over my face. Through the holes in the straw I could peer at Nick without being observed. His black hair was tousled and his face, if not brown, was certainly ruddy after just a few days in this early April sunshine. All week, his increasingly tanned forearms had stuck out of an array of denim shirts and baggy jumpers, and today it was the turn of a rather countrified checked number to expose him to the elbows.

I stared at his strong hands as they gripped the oars tightly, expertly guiding the boat around rocks and over-hanging branches, and tried to remember what they'd looked like when they'd held documents and files and protruded from the sleeves of a pinstriped suit in an office in South Kensington. Then I tried to imagine all of him back in South Kensington. Funny, it seemed like another world, and one that he didn't belong to at all. Did I belong? Where was my world?

I shut my eyes and imagined for a moment that it was here. And not just in a small way, but in a mighty big way — so big, in fact, that within a twinkling I was mistress of Trewarren, wife to Mr Nicholas Penhalligan and mother of his — ooh, let's see, five, no — six children. It was the work of a moment. And within another moment, I'd pictured myself in Trewarren's kitchen, up to my elbows in cake mixture, singing away tunefully as I baked a cake for tea.

Now and again I'd smile down indulgently as my black-haired, brown-eyed babies frolicked around at my feet, happy with their finger paints and their Play-doh, and with none of that unnecessary shouting and screaming that seems to accompany most children's games. They were certainly the most angelic of babies, and one or two of them — or perhaps even all of them — were capable of changing their own nappies, had done so since birth, in fact; and they'd never been sick in their lives. But I digress.

As I poured my Victoria sponge mixture into a baking tin, the kitchen door opened, and who should appear, fresh from the fields, with the smell of corn in his hair and a special kind of wife-hungry light in his eyes, but my husband, the farmer. I wiped my floury hands on my apron, and greeted him with a tender kiss. Filled with a passion that hadn't wavered for a moment during four wonderful years of marriage — hang on, how many children did I say? Well some of them were obviously twins, er — yes, all of them, actually, three sets of twins — anyway, filled with this passion, he seized me firmly around the waist and pulled me, quite roughly really, towards him.

Under his coarse, tweed jacket which tickled my face, I could feel his hard, muscly body rippling against me, simply aching to take me upstairs, or perhaps – yes, that was it, what he really wanted to do was to ravish me right here and now on the kitchen table.

'How about it?' his eyes seemed to say. I glanced down at the children. 'Not now,' my own eyes seemed to say, a smile playing around my luscious lips, 'later.'

Panting hard, but somehow managing to control himself, he gazed deep into my sapphire eyes and planted a long lingering kiss on my full, rosy lips, marvelling, for the umpteenth time, at his supreme good fortune in finding himself such a terrific wife, who was not only effortlessly capable and ran the house with sizzling efficiency, but was also devastatingly attractive and downright saucy in the bedroom.

I frowned under my hat. Would the capable and efficient bit be a problem? I scratched my chin thoughtfully. I dare say I could learn, but – wait a minute, why bother? Why on earth should I be immersed in cake mixture? Surely I'd have a cook? Yes, of course. I wouldn't be in the kitchen at all, I'd be in the morning room!

Quick as a flash there was a speedy scene change and I was transported to the morning room, seated at my writing desk with the sun streaming in behind me through the huge bay window. Now, what was I doing? Ah yes, planning the menu for a forthcoming dinner party. Such a bore, but one must entertain the locals occasionally: the

Master of the Hunt, the neighbouring farmers, etc. they expected it, and of course I did it so well.

I took off my diamond bracelet – a wedding present from my husband, but so incredibly heavy it made writing difficult – and jotted down the courses: watercress soup, followed by salmon en croute, followed by raspberries and cream. There, that should do it. Oh, and I must remind Jenkins to get the appropriate wine from the cellar – or would Nick do that? I wasn't sure.

Anyway, I got up from my desk, pausing only to smooth a few wrinkles out of the wonderfully understated navy blue Armani dress I was wearing, and adjusted my pearl choker – another wedding, no, anniversary present from my husband. I caught a glimpse of myself in the mirror. The pearls looked so good around my throat, gleaming away against my Christmas-in-the-Caribbean suntan.

As I passed by the window I spotted my delicious children being either pushed in prams or carried around the immaculate gardens by a tribe of uniformed Norland nannies. I opened the window and blew them all a kiss – 'Co-ee darlings!' They waved back adoringly.

I drifted on into the kitchen in search of my cook, Mrs Bridges – no all right, too obvious – Mrs, um, Smith.

'Ah, Mrs Smith there you are. You'll be pleased to hear I've finally decided on tomorrow night's menu.' And so saying, I'd sink languidly into the large wheelback chair by the Aga and cross my slim, silk-stockinged legs.

'Very good, M'am,' she'd say, wiping her floury hands on her apron (*her* floury hands, note – not mine), and giving me her undivided attention. Would she curtsey? No, of course not, don't be stupid, Polly.

I leaned forward and fixed her with my capable, efficient eye. 'Now, as you know, Mr Penhalligan is very partial to watercress soup so I thought –' Just then, just as I was in the middle of briefing my cook, the door flew open and in strode my husband – fresh from the fields, smell of corn in hair, wife-hungry look in eye, etc., etc. Without pausing for a moment, he strode over to the chair, took me in his arms and – oh, just *before* he took me in his arms, Mrs Smith suddenly got an urgent telephone call from the butchers, saying the joint she'd ordered was ready and would she please come and pick it up *immediately* because, um – because otherwise it would go off. So off she rushed, and as soon as the door had closed behind her, he strode over to the chair, corn in hair, wife-hungry look, and took me in his arms. His breath was roaring away in my ears. 'Oh my darling!' he murmured, 'I want you so badly!' He kissed me hungrily, then he lifted me into his arms and strode to the table where he set me down, and roughly but gently, but firmly but roughly, he –

'What on earth are you doing?' My hat flew off my face at the very best bit and I looked up to see Nick, my boss – friend at most, but certainly not my husband – staring down at me, a puzzled look on his face.

'Are you all right?'

I sat up guiltily. 'What? Yes, of course. Sorry, what was I doing?'

'Well, you've been muttering and sort of squirming and wriggling. At one point you started moaning, quite loudly actually, about watercress. I thought perhaps you were having a nightmare, except you seemed to be rather enjoying it.'

'Ah! Yes – well, you're right, you see I was dreaming! I fell asleep and – and had this awful feeling that great clumps of watercress were bearing down on me, like – like the Triffids. It all came rising up out of the river and got me round the neck, like this!' I demonstrated, clasping my throat hard. I shivered. 'Phew, lucky you woke me when you did. That was no joke, I can tell you!'

'You look rather hot, your face is terribly red.'

'Is it?' I fanned my flaming face with my hat. 'That's probably because I thought I was being strangled, all the blood probably went to my face.'

'Are they always so vivid?'

'What?'

'Your dreams.'

'Oh! Oh yes, always. God, sometimes I cry out and . . . and thrash around. Once I even got up and walked downstairs. I've got such a terrific imagination, you see, and it all seems so real. I'm hell to sleep with.'

'Really?' Nick raised his eyebrows.

I fanned my face even harder as it got hotter and hotter. 'Well, no, having said that, no I'm not, I'm pretty easy to sleep with actually – easy in the sense that, well in the sense that I'm not difficult . . . I mean, no one's actually ever complained – not that there have been many who would – complain, I mean, simply because there really haven't been that many, if you see what I mean.' Things were getting decidedly out of hand here.

Nick roared with laughter. 'Polly, you are hysterical. I really couldn't care less how many people you've slept with or whether or not they've complained. It's none of my business.'

'Well I haven't,' I said crossly, indignant now, and keen to set the record straight, 'slept with many, that is, and the few that I have haven't complained either, so there.'

I childishly turned my back on him and stared down into the water, furious with myself for behaving like an idiot, and furious with him for not wanting it to be any of his business. I could feel my face heating up the river. God, I was a moron.

Nick rowed on, and I couldn't see his face but I was sure he was laughing at me. Determined not to turn around, I let my hand drift along in the water, grabbing at reeds and bulrushes and pretending I was thoroughly absorbed by the ripples.

The silence was deafening but I wasn't going to break it, he would just jolly well have to be nice to me for a change, and he'd have to make a real effort. How dare he laugh at me like that and – and how dare he be so rude? He needn't think he could get round me with a couple of glasses of cider and a ploughman's lunch either, oh no, he'd have to do better than that.

'Polly?' said Nick after a while.

'Hmm?' I responded sulkily. Whatever he wanted, the answer was no.

'I thought I might go to Gweek this afternoon. It's about time I looked in on Mum; she'll think I'm avoiding her. D'you want to come?'

'Oh yes please!' I spun around eagerly. 'I'd love to come!'

'Good. I'll give her a ring when we get back.'

Sulk? What sulk. It was high time I met my mother-in-law.

And so it was that a few hours later I found myself being driven off to meet Mrs Penhalligan. I mean surely. Come on. He could quite easily have gone on his own, couldn't he? It would have been much more natural to say, 'Hope you don't mind, but I must go and see my mother, can you amuse yourself this afternoon?' But no. No, it was important that I came too.

As we whizzed along in the Land Rover, I unclenched my nervous hands and smoothed out the skirt of my Laura Ashley dress.

Nick had looked highly amused when I'd waltzed down the stairs in this particular number, but there was no doubt in my mind that it was absolutely perfect. To capture the essence of this dress, one really has to refer to it as a 'frock', a sort of spriggy cotton muslin affair with daisies and an itsy-bitsy collar and a flouncy skirt. Twee, I grant you, but it's only ever worn on 'meet the parents' outings, and it's never failed me yet. Eminently suitable.

I tucked a little lace hanky into the sleeve for good measure, and gave Country Girl just one more chance, restricting it this time to wrists only and not backs of knees, neck, or other assorted pulse points.

Now. Chocolates? Flowers? Daffodils would be a little like coals to Newcastle, I decided, so I settled for chocolates and ordered Nick to stop at the village shop. He obeyed, and looked even more amused when I reappeared bearing a large box of fudge.

'Who's that for?'

'Your mother, of course.'

He exploded with laughter at the wheel.

'What's so funny?'

'Nothing, it's just that that's what all the plebby tourists buy to take back to Purley or Dagenham. Look at the label.'

I turned it over and saw, 'A present from Cornwall' in olde-worlde writing surrounded by gnomes and fairies. I sighed and tossed it into the back seat. I knew I should have gone for the clotted cream.

As we rounded the corner into Gweek, I was pleasantly surprised to see that it had a rather refreshing, business-like air about it. Helford was undoubtedly prettier, but it was very much a holiday homes and cream teas village. Gweek, on the other hand, was a village where real people lived and worked. No cutesy cottages here; in fact, the only one I saw was right on the edge of the village, perched on the top of a hill. It was whitewashed and thatched with honeysuckle rampaging around the front door and clematis winding its way around the windows. A large tabby cat sat sunning herself on the doorstep.

'That's Mum's place,' said Nick as we sped past.

'Oh! How pretty!' I nearly twisted my head off in an effort to catch a glimpse. 'But why aren't we stopping?'

An icy hand gripped my heart. Had he got cold feet? Had second thoughts? Couldn't bring himself to introduce someone as gauche and stupid as me to his undoubtedly highly sophisticated, elegant mother?

'Because she won't be there, she'll be in here.'

We rounded a corner and scrunched to a halt on the gravel drive of a pub just outside the village.

'Oh!' I was deeply shocked. You wouldn't catch my mother in the Fox and Hounds on Esher High Street on a Thursday afternoon. The Conservative Party Bring-and-Buy sale, perhaps, but not the Fox and Hounds.

'Has she got a problem?'

My vision of the immaculate Mrs Penhalligan, dressed in twinset and pearls and deftly arranging chrysanthemums in a crystal vase in her drawing room, was plummeting fast in the direction of a whisky-swilling bag lady, pub-crawling her way round southern Cornwall.

Nick laughed. 'Good God, no, I mean she certainly likes a drink, but it's not a problem.' He held open the door for me.

'So what's she doing in here in the middle of the afternoon?' I asked suspiciously as I ducked to avoid a low beam.

'This is where she gets her inspiration.'

'Inspiration? For what?'

'You'll see.'

My eyes took a while to adjust from the bright sunshine outside to the near darkness of the saloon bar, but when they did, Hetty Penhalligan was the very first person I saw.

She was sitting in the corner by an open window which shot the only beam of light into the gloomy room, surrounding her in a faint halo-like gleam and lighting up the unmistakable Penhalligan features.

Although I recognized her instantly, she was totally unexpected. I'd somehow assumed that the boys had inherited the Roman nose and square, determined jaw from their father, but in fact they sat very well on her strong, chiselled face. Her black hair, now streaked with grey, was cut in a sharp, geometric bob which complemented her striking features. She was a handsome woman.

I fluffed up my skirt and set my face in a sweet girlie smile as I followed Nick over to her but, as we got closer, my sweet smile froze and I had a violent urge to tear my frock from my back and run to the nearest Oxfam shop.

For that is undoubtedly where Mrs Penhalligan bought her clothes. Over a pair of baggy blue mechanic's overalls – or was it a boiler suit? Yes, it was a boiler suit – anyway, over this she was sporting a man's tweed jacket with the sleeves rolled up to her elbows. Around her neck was a spotty red handkerchief and on her feet were a pair of what looked like hobnailed Doc Marten boots. The whole ensemble was splattered with paint as if someone had systematically flicked the entire contents of a Dulux factory at her.

She didn't look up as we approached, but kept her eyes firmly on an old man sitting opposite her, staring at him in a peculiarly penetrating way. His eyes were staring equally fixedly into his pint.

As the penny dropped, it activated my jaw, which swung open with surprise. A painter! Propped up in front of her was a canvas, to which she added a couple of quick daubs, and, to her left, a glass of white wine which was rather an odd colour. It became apparent why, when she absent-mindedly dipped her paint brush in it, mistaking it for the water.

'Damn!' she bellowed, 'I keep *doing* that! Barney, get me another drink, will you? This one's gone Prussian blue again.'

She waved the offending glass at the barman, and then caught sight of Nick. 'Darling!' she cried, in a crackly, gin-soaked voice, 'What a lovely surprise!'

Nick kissed her. 'Hi Mum, thought I might find you in here.'

He settled himself down next to her.

'And who's this charming little flower?' she asked, her eyes roaming over the itsy-bitsy frock.

'Oh, this is Polly McLaren, a friend of mine.'

'Hello, Mrs Penhalligan,' I said, holding out my hand and smiling.

'You must call me Hetty, everybody does,' she said, taking my hand. 'Oh look, how silly of me, now you've got paint all over you. Here,' she handed me a piece of oily rag and I wiped my hand.

I felt absurdly self-conscious in my frock, and faintly irritated that Nick hadn't warned me. It wasn't as if I couldn't have looked the part, too: I had a whole collection of arty-farty clothes back at the house just aching for an outing. There was that lovely French peasant's smock and the pedal-pushers and, oh, all manner of bohemian gear. I whipped the lace hanky out of my sleeve and hitched the ghastly skirt up a bit when I sat down.

'Barney, for Christ's sake!' she roared, making me jump out of my skin. 'It's like the bloody Gobi desert in here. Line up three gin and tonics, will you, there's a love.'

Barney grinned good humouredly from behind the bar, put down the glass he'd been wiping, and hastened to oblige his customer. It had to be worth his while, she was a pretty colourful asset for any pub – cheaper than buying a fruit machine, I thought to myself.

'So how's it going, then?' asked Nick, straddling a stool next to his mother and peering over her shoulder at the picture. 'Been discovered yet?'

''Course I bloody haven't,' she boomed – this seemed to be the only volume her voice could manage – 'the philistines around here wouldn't know a decent canvas if they stuck their heads through it. All they want is chocolate-boxy pastoral scenes or little children with tears running down their cheeks. Ugh. No, I'm afraid I'm just going to have to kill myself. Nothing like a dead artist to send prices soaring through the roof.'

'Or cut your ear off?' I suggested tentatively.

'Might work,' she agreed, 'bit messy though.'

I looked at the painting. It was a riot of blotches and blobs and I could quite see why the locals weren't too enamoured. I thought it was dreadful. But I also knew, from my experiences at private views in London, that what I thought were unspeakably bad pictures were usually deemed to be extremely good.

'It's awfully good,' I lied creepily.

Nick guffawed loudly. 'Looks like someone's been sick!'

Hetty ignored her son and addressed herself to me instead. 'Thank you, my dear. Yes, it is rather, isn't it?' she agreed calmly. 'But then it helps to have a sitter as ugly as Arthur here. Bags of character.'

I glanced quickly at poor Arthur and hoped he was deaf as well as ugly. Hetty's voice had a certain resonance about it which made it hard to miss. Luckily he appeared to be not only deaf but brain dead too, as he sank further and further into his pint.

'Thank you, Arthur!' she yelled at the top of her voice, prodding him in the arm. 'That will be all for today!'

He waggled a bony hand in acknowledgement and raised his watery old eyes briefly from his beer.

I smiled at him. Sweet old man. It took me a few seconds to realize that he wasn't a sweet old man at all. He leered nastily at me and, rolling over on to his left buttock, let rip with a fart of such asphyxiating intensity it left me positively reeling. I gasped. Something had obviously crawled up and died inside him.

Hetty fixed him with her steely glare. 'I said thank you, Arthur, that will be all.'

But Arthur seemed unwilling to leave the cosy little gathering and join the rest of his cronies in the public bar. He sat resolutely still, leering into his pint.

Hetty sighed and got to her feet. 'Let's go and sit in the garden. It's much too stuffy in here anyway.'

Stuffy was the mildest possible way to describe the putrefied atmosphere that prevailed, courtesy of Arthur, and I followed her with alacrity as she headed off through the back door.

She stuck her head round the bar as we left. 'Oh, and Barney, we'll have three rounds of sandwiches and some of Mabel's lovely bread-and-butter pudding, please, when you've got a moment!'

This command was greeted with much mock forelock-touching amongst the bar staff, and one of them caught my eye and winked. I giggled.

'Your mother's very imperious,' I whispered as Hetty strode on ahead.

Nick grinned. 'That's nothing, you should see her when she's feeling bossy!'

We walked through the garden carrying our drinks. It was no more than a field really, the grass was long and full of wild flowers, and strewn here and there were one or two rugs for the customers to sit on. We found a sunny spot and sank down happily amongst the flowers.

Hetty sat next to me. 'Aah . . . that's better, I can't bear being inside that smelly old pub for too long. Have to get out in the fresh air.' She turned to me. 'Are you a country girl, Polly?'

'Oh yes! Well, I mean, at heart I am. I live in London but my parents live in Esh . . . in the country.' I knew from experience that not a lot of people considered Esher to be the country.

Hetty took hold of my chin and turned my face at an angle. 'Hmm . . . you've certainly got a fresh, country look about you.'

I wasn't quite sure how to take this. Did she mean in the bumpkin sense, I wondered?

But Hetty was nodding appreciatively now as she turned my head this way and that. 'Marvellous profile . . .' she muttered. 'Love to paint you some day.'

Thrilled to bits, I sucked my chin in and lowered my eyelids. This was definitely to be encouraged. I let her manhandle my face for a while, hoping it would give Nick a chance to stare long and hard and realize just what it was I'd got that Serena hadn't. And just what was that? I wondered, recalling Serena's Helen of Troy-like perfection. I also recalled that Hetty had found Arthur's profile pretty marvellous too. Laughing nervously, I rescued my face from her vice-like grip on the pretext of lighting a cigarette.

'Terrible habit,' said Hetty, getting one out herself. 'You'll end up with lungs like mine, shot to bits I shouldn't wonder. I keep telling the boys to lay off the ciggies but they won't listen to me: they don't listen to anything I say these days.' She turned to Nick. 'How's the farm going?

Did you interview that chappie I told you about? The one I said would make a good farm manager? I suppose you didn't take my advice on that score either.'

'Tony? Oh no, I hired him. You were right, actually, he seems pretty good. I had a long chat with him the other day and we appear to be doing much better than we were this time last year. I think he's quite shrewd, but time will tell.'

'You see!' Hetty was pleased. 'I told you he was all right. Old Bob Hawkins said he was a marvellous manager. So you do listen to your old mother occasionally! Got to keep an eye on him though, it's no good letting him have his head too much. Remember all the trouble Dad had with that dreadful chap – whatsisname – Reg Parker – remember?'

She reached out suddenly and touched my arm. 'Sorry, farm talk. Boring for you, I know, but I do like to keep in touch.'

I smiled. 'Oh no, don't worry about me, I'm perfectly happy.' I lay back on the rug. 'I'll catch up on my suntan while you catch up on the farm.'

I shut my eyes and they chattered on. Every so often I'd catch a sentence or two, but it wasn't long before I was back playing dinner parties in the blue Armani dress. Except that I'd progressed to a rather beautiful pink silk Versace number now, and I wasn't hosting a dinner party, I was opening the local fête, or – yes, agricultural show. Well, they were bound to ask me, weren't they? I was, after all, the modern equivalent of the squire's wife.

I frowned. If I had to cut a ribbon or two I would prob-ably need quite a selection of hats, and hats were always a problem. I had quite a big head and they never seemed to fit properly. Ah yes, of course, I'd have them specially made; silly of me not to think of it before. I'd whisk up to Herbert Johnson to be measured or – no, I'd go to Paris! Yes, one or two trips to Paris every year would be a very good idea. I mean the country is undoubtedly lovely, but one wouldn't want to take root, would one?

Yes, I'd spend a couple of weeks every year viewing the collections. I rather fancied the idea of perching on one of those spindly little gilt chairs in the front row of a fashion show, with – oh, I don't know, Princess Caroline on one side and Jackie Onassis on the other? I'd probably saunter in a bit late, and of course a million heads would turn and then the whole place would be buzzing.

'Who's that?' they'd whisper.

'Don't you know? It's Nicholas Penhalligan's wife.'

'Ah . . . I'd heard she was a beauty, but I had no idea . . .'

'They say he's absolutely besotted, hates to let her out of his sight for even a moment.'

'Well, I can imagine . . .'

And so it went on, getting more and more outrageous and out of hand. I was just agonizing over what I was going to wear to dinner at Kensington Palace, and wondering how I would manage without a cigarette between courses because of course Diana is very anti, when I heard a snippet of real-life conversation that made me open my eyes and sit up.

'How's Tim, married Sarah yet?' Hetty was asking.

Ah ha. Cows and sheep were off the agenda and marriage was on. This was just my tipple.

Nick laughed. 'Don't you think the news might have

filtered down your way if he had? I mean, I know he plays his cards close to his chest, but I think he might tell his own mother.'

'Can't think why he's hanging around till next year,' grumbled Hetty. 'Why not do it now? Seize the moment, go for it. He's so bloody prudent it's ridiculous. All this talk about money and where they're going to live – what does it matter? Why don't they just go and shack up in a rented flat or something? A lovely girl like Sarah will be pinched from right under his nose if he's not careful.'

Atta-girl, Hetty! I mentally applauded like mad. This was fighting talk and I was right behind her. Why pussy-foot around when you're in love? This woman certainly had her heart in the right place. She obviously wasn't the sort of mother who couldn't bear for her sons to let go of her apron strings either. All of this boded well for the future.

'Well, you tell him, then. It's no good talking to me about it!' laughed Nick.

'I will,' promised Hetty, 'and while we're on the subject, what about that uppity little actress bit you were seeing. I hope the emergence of young Polly here means that that's all over and done with.'

She put a friendly arm around my shoulders and raised her eyebrows quizzically at Nick. 'Am I, perhaps, sitting next to your latest girlfriend?'

I sat bolt upright, rigid with delight, hardly daring to breathe, and the little bit of breath that did escape was well bated, I can tell you. Yes, Hetty, I thought gleefully, are you perhaps? I resisted the temptation to raise my eyebrows too.

He laughed, obviously quite used to her blatant nosiness. 'Mind your own bloody business, Hetty,' was his disappointing answer.

Hetty sighed. 'They're both the same, I'm afraid, these boys of mine. They won't tell me a thing. I should have had a daughter, they're much more forthcoming.'

It was on the tip of my tongue to venture that a daughter-in-law might do just as well, but decided that, even with Hetty's obvious penchant for straight talking, it might be considered a little previous.

'So tell me, my dear,' asked Hetty turning her beady brown eyes on me. 'What do you do? You don't throw yourself about half-naked on film sets, do you?'

'Certainly not,' I said priggishly. 'I'm a production assistant.'

Nick's eyebrows shot into orbit. 'You're a what?'

I was so used to lying about my job I'd forgotten for a moment just who was listening in. 'Oh, er – I mean a personal assistant,' I said quickly. Nick's eyebrows lowered very slightly.

'Well actually,' I said humbly, coming completely clean. 'I suppose I'm just a secretary really.'

'Oh no, I'd say you were definitely a personal assistant,' said Nick, grinning.

I grinned back. Just then a young girl walked through the field towards us armed with great platefuls of sandwiches and bread-and-butter pudding. She set them down in front of us; my mouth watered greedily.

'A secretary, eh? So what's your boss like?' asked Hetty, passing me a sandwich.

'A bastard to work for, but totally divine out of the

office.' I gave Nick a huge smile, what did I have to lose? He had the grace to blush.

'Just like you, I bet!' said Hetty, prodding Nick's arm with a bony finger. 'I'd hate to have to work for you, I bet you're thoroughly bad tempered.'

'He is,' I said truthfully. 'You see, it's Nick I work for.'

'There you are, what did I say!' She threw back her head and roared with laughter. 'So I was spot on! How hysterical. Well, don't you take any nonsense from him, Polly. Lick him into shape. He needs a firm hand, you know.'

'I'll see that he gets it!' I said gleefully.

'Must be difficult, though,' said Hetty, tucking into an enormous roast beef sandwich. 'I mean, with the baby. I suppose you have a nanny, do you, or does it go to a child-minder or something?'

She sounded so sure of herself that for a moment I wondered if perhaps I did have a baby and had temporarily forgotten about it, tucked it away in a drawer or something. I am incredibly absent-minded, but not normally on such a mammoth scale. I was pretty sure I'd remember giving birth, too. It was, by all accounts, pretty bloody painful. I racked my brains. No, I definitely hadn't given birth.

'I don't have a baby,' I said carefully.

'You don't?'

'No.'

'Oh.' Hetty frowned and looked perplexed. Was this a problem, I wondered? Did she like her future daughters-in-law to come complete with babies? Was there a breeding problem with the Penhalligans?

She turned to Nick, winking broadly. 'Darling!' she drawled, 'What a hectic life you lead.'

'Come on, Mum,' said Nick, getting cross. 'What the bloody hell are you babbling on about?'

Hetty finished her sandwich and got out a cigarette. She lit it and puffed the smoke out thoughtfully. 'Well, I thought Polly here was someone else, you see, another of your female friends.'

'Who?' he said impatiently.

'I don't know, do I? I've obviously never met her, whoever she is.'

'Christ, Mum, what are you on about?'

'Well you see, yesterday I was sitting in the pub painting, when this chap came in and asked at the bar for Mrs Penhalligan. I popped up my hand and he came over. We chatted away for a bit, he said he'd seen one of my pictures in London and had really liked it and because he was on holiday down here, thought he'd seek me out – load of bullshit, of course, but you know me, I'm a sucker for compliments.'

'Oh, do you show your paintings in London then?' I asked.

'Er, well, no, I don't actually, not yet anyway.'

'Exactly,' said Nick grimly, 'go on.'

'Anyway, he bought me a drink and said he knew you,' she nodded at Nick, 'said he saw quite a lot of you in London, and that he was in advertising too and that's how you'd met. Then he asked if you were down here at the moment, and if so did you have a girl with you, with a baby. I said I had no idea, because if you were here you certainly hadn't managed to stagger down to Gweek to see your old mum and, anyway, I never really knew whether you were in London or Cornwall. Well, that's why, when you walked in here with Polly, I assumed she was the girl he was talking about.'

She put her hand on my shoulder, 'Especially in that dress, my dear. It's the sort of thing you wear when you've just had a baby.' She smiled kindly and patted her tummy. 'Hides the paunch.'

I tried to answer, but my mouth was so dry it felt as if someone had just given it the once over with a hairdryer.

'Who was this friend, exactly?' said Nick quietly. 'Did he say?'

'Oh no, I've no idea what his name was, darling. He might have said, but you know me and names. He was quite a big chap, though, burly, with red hair. American, I think, rather cute actually.'

Chapter Eighteen

My first reaction was one of horror. Nick and I exchanged shell-shocked glances in the wake of this exploding missile. Christ Almighty, he'd found us already! I reached for my tongue, but it was sensibly staying put on the roof of my mouth, glued on with a mixture of terror and bread-and-butter pudding. I left it there and abandoned myself to my second reaction which was, I'm ashamed to say, fury. Bloody Adam and bloody Rachel – damn them! Here I was having a half-decent holiday for the first time in months, with a thoroughly decent man, and they were doing their best to ruin it for me. I was tempted to suggest we simply reunite the surly mother with the aggressive father and push them out to sea in a leaky boat, hoping they'd sink without trace, but I could see that Nick was determined to take a more conscientious line.

He was questioning his mother closely. 'When exactly did you see him?'

'I told you, yesterday.'

'Yes, but what time of day?'

'Around lunchtime, I suppose, yes, about twelve o'clock. He said he'd been over to the house earlier and there was no one there.'

'We were all out yesterday, thank goodness, but you didn't actually say I was in Cornwall?'

'No darling, why should I? I didn't know you were here,

you never let me know what your movements are. In fact, I distinctly remember telling him that, since I hadn't heard from you, I imagined you were probably in London.'

I relaxed slightly. That was something, surely? Maybe Adam had somehow heard that Nick had a house in Cornwall and had come down purely on the off-chance, just to check it out? And, on finding it empty, he'd headed back to London? But how on earth had he rumbled the fact that Nick was even remotely involved? Just a hunch? Or was he slightly better informed? None of this boded well.

Nick chewed his bottom lip thoughtfully. 'I don't suppose you have any idea where he's staying, Mum?'

'I do actually, he's renting one of Mrs Green's cottages in Manaccan, that little white terraced one in the middle of the village, I think. I've got her telephone number in my address book if you want it.'

Oh Christ, renting. That sounded a bit too permanent for my liking, but there weren't, I supposed, too many five-star hotels around these parts, and a bed and breakfast would be a bit *infra dig* for our Adam.

'So you definitely didn't say we were here, or were expected down soon, or anything like that?' persisted Nick.

'Darling, do stop banging on, I told you, I simply said I had absolutely no idea where you were,' said Hetty petulantly, her eyes wandering somewhat: she'd got rather bored with this interrogation. 'Oh look, there's Arthur!'

Sure enough, out of the back door came Arthur, roaring along on his Zimmer frame.

'Darlings, may I leave you to fend for yourselves now?

Only I must finish Arthur this afternoon, I fear he's not long for this world. Arthur! Co-ee! Arthur, you're not going home yet, are you? Where are you off to?'

Arthur pointed to the outside loo and made an obscene gesture to indicate his intention on reaching it.

Hetty sighed. 'He's quite repulsive, of course, but what can I do? He's such a marvellous sitter, so still and corpse-like. Honestly, the sacrifices I make for art's sake. I'll intercept him on his way out – must fly!' She gathered her cigarettes and lighter together and got up to go.

Nick grabbed her arm. 'OK, Mum, but listen, if you see this guy again, don't mention you've seen us, will you? Oh, and hang on, the phone number.' Nick pushed a scrap of paper and a pencil under her nose and she jotted it down.

'Bye, my darlings!' She blew us a kiss. 'Have fun – oh, and if you fancy another little drinky-poo, just tell Barney to put it on my slate, all right?' And with that she disappeared.

I felt my insides curdling. 'Will we have to go back to London?' I whispered miserably, selfishly thinking of my own happiness as usual.

Nick was staring into space, eyes narrowed. He didn't answer for a moment. 'No . . .' he eventually said, slowly, 'I don't think so. In fact, the more I think about it, the more I think we'll just stay exactly where we are. In fact . . . yes, I want him to know that we're down here.'

'But you just told Hetty not to say anything if –'

'I know,' he said impatiently, 'but I've changed my mind. We'll face him head on this time. I'm not being ousted from my own house by one lousy American, nor am I going to run around England like a fox with the bloody hounds behind me.'

'What – so we just stay put and wait for him to pay us a visit? I mean, he will find us, Nick, there's no doubt about that, and he's not going to politely knock at the front door either. He'll probably smash his way through the french windows – or, or through my bedroom window most likely!' I gabbled, frightened out of my cowardly little mind. It was all very well, but Adam definitely hated me more than anyone else in the whole world. I was number one on his hit list without a shadow of a doubt. Nick was silent.

'Well?' I squeaked.

'Hang on, Polly, I'm thinking.'

'But you've seen what he's like, he's a nutter! In fact he's probably clinically insane by now, he'll stop at nothing – and – and anyway, what about Rachel and Jamie?' I added charitably but desperately.

'Don't worry, I'm not abandoning them at this stage, although God knows, sometimes I think Rachel deserves all she gets. No, we'll just have to think of a way around this.'

'But what if –'

'Polly, for God's sake shut up, will you? I'm trying to think!' he snapped.

Ah. I pursed my lips and sat back, folding my arms. I recognised a flash of the old Nick there: hadn't taken long to surface, had it? Nevertheless, I obediently shut up and waited for my next order. I didn't wait long.

'Come on, hurry up.' Nick got to his feet and drained his pint.

'Where are we going?' I scrambled around, looking for my handbag.

'Back to the house, of course. Thank God Tim and Rachel have gone into Helston this afternoon.' He strode off.

'Oh! Right, hang on, just coming.' I drained my glass, scooped the last of the bread-and-butter pudding into my mouth, and ran after him.

Nick was already half-way across the garden. 'Bring the glasses will you, Polly?' he yelled over his shoulder.

I dashed back meekly to pick them up. Odd how in a crisis we'd suddenly reverted to our more usual roles of servant and master.

I panted back down the garden after him. 'In a couple of weeks we'd have been shot of her, she'd have been in Paris and we could have told him to sod off. Oh, why did he have to come now?' I grumbled, breathlessly running to keep up as he strode round the side of the pub to the car park.

He didn't answer but, without pausing to open the door, vaulted neatly into the open-topped Land Rover and revved up the engine. It was a cool, effortless move straight out of the movies.

Suddenly I felt a little twinge of excitement. After all, here we were, bang in the middle of what the tabloids would call a tug-of-love scenario, protecting the mother, and ducking and weaving from the vengeful father: we were a team, a duo – yes, we were partners. We moved as one, we thought as one, we stood up for justice, we protected the weak, we leaped into jeeps – I took a little run up, grabbed the top of the door and jumped – about two inches off the ground. Nowhere near. I tried again, run and – hup! Gosh, how on earth did he do it? Panting with exertion, but determined to crack it, I stepped back for another try. I charged towards the door just as he, simultaneously, leaned across and swung it open to let me in. It caught me full in the stomach.

'Oooofffff . . .' With a loud, yob-like moan I fell back on to the gravel, bent double and clutching myself like a footballer who's been kneed in the privates. As I lay there, moaning and rolling around in a heap of Laura Ashley, he came running round to retrieve me.

'Gosh, I'm really sorry, I had no idea you were still leaping around out there. Are you OK?' He helped me up.

'Sure,' I croaked, staggering to my feet and clutching what was left of my stomach. 'My fault, really, showing off as usual.'

Would I ever be able to have all those babies now, I wondered? Wasn't that where all the important tubes were? I nursed what remained of my abdomen, wincing and gingerly feeling around for signs of blood. None, unfortunately.

Nick heaved me bodily into the jeep, slammed the door and ran round the other side. With a screech of tyres and a great deal of flying gravel, we shot out of the drive.

We sped off in silence, and I was loathe to break it, knowing from experience that whatever I said would be wrong. He was either hatching a master plan, or so pissed off he couldn't speak. At last he did.

'Right . . .' he said slowly, 'now listen, Polly, this is what we're going to do.'

'Yes?' I whispered. Surely yes couldn't be wrong?

'First of all, we're going to send Rachel and Jamie away,

get them as far away as possible from the action, some-where safe.'

'Like where?'

'Like Penny's. Tim can take them, he often goes to deliver vegetables anyway. He's pretty quiet on the farm at the moment, so he could probably stay a few days and surreptitiously play bodyguard, make sure they're OK. There's no way Adam will find them there.'

Don't be too sure, I thought grimly, he found us here; but I had to agree, it wasn't a bad plan.

'Will Penny mind?'

'Not a bit, she's got bags of room at this time of year, and she's always glad of some company.'

'OK, and meanwhile?'

'Meanwhile, I'll telephone Adam and invite him over for a drink.'

'You'll what!'

'I'll ask him over for a drink.'

I was bug-eyed with amazement. 'Well, don't mind me, but I'll just be down at the nearest travel agent negotiating a one-way ticket to Australia!'

'Listen, Polly, if we seize the initiative we might just get away with it. I'm not prepared to sit around and wait for him, and I think it makes sense to catch him off-guard. The last thing he'll expect is a friendly telephone call.'

'Well I'm not crazy about being a sitting duck, either, but what happens when he accepts our offer and turns up keen to stage the Cornish Chainsaw Massacre?'

Nick paused as he slammed down a gear and negoti-ated a tricky hairpin bend. 'We tell him a little story,' he said softly.

'Oh really? And what might that be?'

'We tell him that the strain of being caught in the middle of this ghastly situation – you know, looking after Rachel, leaving your flat, and not being able to come to work, not to mention splitting up with your boyfriend – left you feeling absolutely exhausted.'

'Too right,' I said with feeling.

'You were totally drained, emotionally and physically, so much so that you almost became ill – basically you were in dire need of a break.'

'Dire. Dire need.' I nodded emphatically.

'So, I suggested that a little holiday in Cornwall might do the trick. You agreed, and here we are.'

'What, just the two of us?'

'Why not? After all,' he took his eyes off the road for a second and gave me a most dazzling smile, 'we are having an affair, aren't we?'

I gulped, getting my oesophagus in a serious twist. 'An – an affair?' I stammered, through twisted tubes.

He grinned. 'Yes, an office romance – you know, dipping the pen in the company ink and all that. Goes on all the time. But of course, it couldn't be conducted in London for all the agency to witness, so we came down here for a bit of peace and quiet.'

'I – I see,' I faltered, recognizing a somewhat familiar fantasy here, 'and what about Rachel?'

'We have absolutely no idea where she is now, neither do we care. The last we saw of her was when we dropped her off at her father's house.'

'Oh come on, that's very weak. Adam will have been

watching the house in Kensington like a hawk. He'll know she's not there.'

'Exactly, he'll know we're lying, and he'll pounce on that immediately. That's when we deliver the red herring. Under extreme pressure – and I mean extreme pressure, let him stamp around a bit and flex his muscles, maybe even exert a few bully-boy tactics – you eventually admit that you heard her on the telephone inquiring about homes for unmarried mothers.'

'Christ, we'll have him breaking down every hostel door in London!'

'So what? They're quite used to lunatic fathers raising merry hell, they'll just get the police on to him. Good thing too.'

'Suppose he doesn't believe us?' I quaked.

'Well, what does it matter? He won't find them if he decides to search the house, and then what can he do – kill us? He a frustrated father, Polly, not a mass murderer.'

'Don't be so sure,' I muttered nervously, recalling those giant freckled paws, which in my mind's eye had already grown Mr Hyde-like claws. 'So do we tell Rachel all this?'

'Christ no, she'll be terrified if she knows he's down here, we don't want her panicking all over the place. I'll have a quiet word with Tim, explain the whole story, and get him to ask her if she'd like to go up to Penny's for a few days.'

'She'll smell a rat, though, won't she? I mean, why should she go to Penny's?'

'Because Tim will tell her we want to be alone to conduct our illicit affair in private.'

'Oh God, you mean she's going to get the story about us having a ding-dong too?'

'Why not? He'll tell her we're both feeling rather self-conscious and we'd like a little time to ourselves, just a couple of days, of course. Once we've seen Adam and we think the coast is relatively clear, they can come back,' he grinned, 'to the hotbed of lust and passion!' He threw his head back and laughed, no doubt at the sheer outrageousness of it all.

'Oh yes, I see, very good!' I said faintly. I threw back my own head and added a merry little chuckle of my own, but it was awfully hollow, principally because I couldn't quite see the joke. What was so side-splittingly funny about us being lovers, I wondered? He was still guffawing loudly. Was he going to be sick?

As he coughed and spluttered over the steering wheel, I considered the joke from Nick's point of view. Good-looking, successful, loaded young blade, with beautiful, highly desirable actress girlfriend, risks all to nip down to Cornwall for a bit of how's your father with gauche, dyed blonde, overweight secretary. I squirmed uncomfortably. Yes, well, put like that I could see wherein lay the mirth.

I stared miserably out of the window. The hedgerows reared up and waved at me as we flew past; grasses and flowers waggled their heads knowingly: it was as if they were laughing, mocking me, and who could blame them? I'd been living in a dream world these last few days. Nick would no more fall in love with me than sell the farm and become managing director of ICI. And why should he? He had a perfectly good girlfriend back in London. I stared out of the window. Yes, she was all the way . . . back in London.

I was feeling low, very low, but not low enough for this last, indisputable fact to escape me. The girlfriend was, indeed, a long way away, and I was, indeed, right here. She was three hundred miles up the M4, while I was all of three inches. She was over six hours from his presence, while I was half a moment. What's more, we were to be alone.

A small window of opportunity presented itself. It was about the size of a cat-flap with about as much visibility, but still, it was there. I mean, there's a great deal to be said for being on the spot, isn't there? If only in the sense that it's better than not being on the spot. I gave myself a little inward shake. Atta-girl, Polly, where's that famous McLaren spirit? Rally it fast, please.

It wasn't as if I'd really turned on the charm yet either – OK, yes, I'd been trying, but not very hard, not as hard as I could. I hadn't, for example, fixed him to any of my smouldering hot looks, I hadn't got as far as the come-hither eyes or the sexy suggestive smiles, and I hadn't even begun to turn him on with my wardrobe. And my golly, I had some pretty lethal gear with me one way and another: the leather mini-skirt, the clinging cross-over top, the blue silk shirt with most of the buttons undone, the tight black leggings – he didn't stand a chance. And of course, once I'd hooked him, winding him in would be the work of a moment. I smiled smugly, secure in the knowledge that I may be a talentless little secretary, but at least my snogs were up to scratch.

As we turned the corner and swept through the gates of Trewarren, I felt a little better. So you think it's all a big joke do you, Mr Penhalligan? Well, we'll soon see about that.

As soon as we got back to the house, Nick buttonholed Tim in the cow shed. I left him to it, unwilling to be deafened by the bellows of laughter, or to witness the side-holding and thigh-slapping that would undoubtedly occur when the incredible Nick-and-Polly fantasy was raised.

It had already been decided that Tim, of the famous animals-and-oddballs touch, would speak to Rachel but, until he'd done so, I couldn't let her out of my sight. Odd, I thought, that I could be so allergic to Rachel but still not want to see her baby wrenched from her arms. I shadowed her around to the extent of following her into the tiny downstairs loo while she changed Jamie's nappy.

She frowned up at me as she knelt on the floor, a half-dressed baby wriggling around between her knees. 'Did you want something, Polly?'

'Noo, noo nothing,' I laughed nervously, 'just interested really. Oh, I see, those disposable things just have sticky tape at the front, do they? No pins?'

'Polly, you've seen me do this millions of times.'

'Have I? Oh well, I must have forgotten. Anyway, I might have a baby of my own one day, so I need all the practical demonstrations I can get.'

'What, you look after a baby? Do me a favour.' She snorted with derision.

'And why not?' I said hotly. 'I'll have you know I'm extremely maternal; I'd be a brilliant mother.'

386

'You might be maternal, but you're hardly responsible, are you? Babies are one hell of a commitment, you know, you can't just look after number one all the time.'

I fumed silently, steam pouring from all orifices. Ungrateful cow, if only she knew. She was one hell of a responsibility, and I was shouldering her pretty well at the moment. I waited until most of the steam had subsided. No point having a row with her now.

I shrugged. 'I suppose I'm just a bit bored, really.'

'Well, d'you think you could move slightly to the right, only I need to spread this plastic mat out?'

'Oh yes, right.'

There wasn't much room, so I put the lid down on the loo and stood on that instead.

Rachel looked up at me in alarm. 'Are you sure you're OK?'

'Fine, fine . . .' I gave my face a vacant expression and stared up at the cracks on the ceiling, biting my thumbnail, swaying slightly and humming to myself. Hopefully she'd just think I'd gone a bit mad and ignore me. I was making Jamie laugh, anyway. I rolled my eyes and pulled faces as he gurgled up at me.

'Rachel?' Tim shouted from the corridor.

'In here! Come in, everyone else has.'

Tim poked his head around the door. He looked up at me in wonder. 'Don't tell me – number of people in a downstairs loo? *Guinness Book of Records*?' He leaped up beside me. 'Three! Four with Jamie!'

I giggled and jumped down, closing the door behind me. No, I thought grimly, bodyguard to the sulky and undeserving. I wandered off to the kitchen in search of calories. Instead I found Nick, prowling around, locking doors and windows.

'Don't do that!' he snapped, as I opened the larder and made for the light switch. I jumped and snatched my hand back.

'Sorry!' Was he possessive about his chocolate biscuits? I knew the feeling. 'Just felt a bit peckish,' I stammered guiltily.

'Fine, go ahead, but don't turn the light on!' He came over and put a hand on my shoulder. 'Sorry, didn't mean to snap, it's just that while Rachel and Jamie are still here we've got to be so careful. If Adam is prowling around outside, we don't want him to think there's anyone here. When they've gone, which hopefully will be soon, it doesn't matter, but just for the moment let's keep all the doors and windows locked, turn the lights off and keep away from the windows, OK?'

'OK,' I whispered. Anything was OK if he kept his hand on my shoulder like that. I'd creep around on all fours if he liked.

'Did you speak to Tim?' I asked, trying to keep him talking, trying to keep the hand on the shoulder and prolong the ecstasy.

'Yes I did, he's talking to her now. I hope they're going to leave as soon as possible. Tim was planning on delivering some vegetables tomorrow, anyway, so it's worked out quite well.'

Footsteps approached the kitchen. The hand disappeared like lightning.

'Well!' said Tim, rubbing his hands together and smiling as he came in. 'Rachel thinks it's a great idea, don't you?'

Rachel was right behind him. 'Yes, I'd love to go. It'll be a nice change and, of course, it'll give you a break, Polly.'

Her mouth twisted into an unattractive little smirk as our eyes met. Ah yes, of course, she'd heard about the Polly-and-Nick affair, the one that was so unspeakably sordid it needed acres of space in which to be conducted. It couldn't come within miles of another living soul, so shameful was it. She obviously thought I was a right little tart, too. Only a few days ago she'd dished out tea and sympathy as I'd lain prostrate on my bed, distraught at Harry's desertion, and now here I was throwing myself at Nick.

Well for your information, *dear*, I thought glaring at her, it's all an elaborate hoax laid on for your benefit, purely to save your anaemic little skin. I conveniently forgot that it would be fine by me if the fantasy we'd cooked up turned into reality; for the moment I was concerned only with her deeply hypocritical smugness. I mean, didn't she just take the biscuit? It was only because of her little indiscretion with a man she didn't love that we were all running round in circles now. Oh yes, it's all very well taking the high moral ground with me, Miss Marsden, but if you hadn't jumped into bed with Adam, we wouldn't be going through with this idiotic charade now. I glared back at her.

'Er, good!' beamed Nick, ignoring the sparks that were so obviously flying between the women. 'That's settled then. You'll enjoy staying with Penny, Rachel, the food's infinitely better than it is here, and you get room service thrown in too. I must say I envy you, I could do with a few days of being waited on hand and foot!'

'Oh, I'm sure you'll survive,' purred Rachel. 'After all, you've got Polly to look after you.'

Nick blushed. 'Oh, er – yes, well of course. Um – tell you what, let's all have a quick drink before you go. It had better be a quick one, though, because I expect you'll want to get off while it's still light.'

'Oh, there's no rush is there?' said Rachel. 'I thought we might go after supper. It only takes a couple of hours to get there, doesn't it?'

'Er, yes, but Penny might be expecting you for supper – oh God, that's a point, I'd better ring and tell her you're coming!'

Rachel looked puzzled. 'She doesn't know? But I thought she invited us?'

'Oh! Yes, she did! Rang this morning actually. No, what I meant was, I'll just let her know when you're leaving.'

'So she can have some supper ready,' I added soothingly.

'But – but I thought you said she was expecting us for supper?'

'Oh she is, she is!' said Tim quickly. 'But it's always as well to remind Penny, she's so absent-minded, we don't want to turn up and find she's closed the restaurant, do we!'

'It's hardly likely, it's only five o'clock now!'

God, she would go on, wouldn't she?

'Is that all!' Tim looked at his watch. 'I had no idea it was so early – to tell you the truth, Rachel, I'm absolutely starving, and I just want to get to Penny's as soon as possible so I can get stuck into some decent food! A man could die of starvation in this place.'

'Oh, right.' She looked reasonably convinced. 'Oh well, I'll just go and pack. I won't have a drink, thanks, I'll just get my things and organize Jamie.'

She shuffled off to her room and the three of us headed thirstily for the drawing room where the gin bottle beckoned.

'Christ!' Nick flopped down on to a sofa nursing his drink. 'All this lying is really taking it out of me. I didn't realize it was such hard work. I must say, you're awfully good at it, Polly.'

'Years of practise,' I said without thinking. 'Er – well, you know, I've been in one or two tight spots before.'

'I can believe it.' He twinkled knowingly at me.

I squirmed uneasily. Now what was that supposed to mean? As I sipped my drink, I brooded on its implications.

A few minutes later, Rachel reappeared laden down with baby gear. The boys sprang up to help her. Tim drove the car round to the back door where there was more privacy. They loaded the car, sat Jamie in his car seat, Tim and Rachel climbed in the front, and with a scrunch of tyres on the gravel, the Wincanton party sped off.

Nick and I watched from the window, peering out from behind a curtain. I for one heaved a huge sigh of relief. Thank God. I'd just about had it up to here with that ungrateful little hussy, and was very much in need of a sabbatical.

As the car reached the end of the back drive and turned the corner out of sight, I gazed out at the view. It was a beautiful afternoon. The sun was still bright but it was quite low on the horizon, and the countryside was bathed in a golden, soupy glow. The trees that lined the drive cast long skinny shadows across it at intervals, like an erratic railway track. Up in the sky, a few clouds raced along in the blue, as if they'd been separated from the rest and were dashing to catch up. Just outside the window, the daffodils were bobbing around like billy-o, trying to keep their heads up in the breeze. I sighed dreamily. This was England at its very best, at its most beautiful. And I was alone with Nick.

He was standing next to me by the window, holding the curtain open a crack. Our shoulders were close. I turned to him and gave him one of my most turning-on smiles.

'So what shall we do now they've gone?' I murmured. 'It's such a beautiful evening, why don't we take the boat out on the river? Or go for a walk along the cliffs?'

'We'll do neither,' he said grimly. 'We'll ring Adam Buchanan.' He turned on his heel and made for the telephone in the hall.

'Oh.' My heart sank down into my espadrilles. 'Yes, I'd forgotten about that.'

He turned and looked at me in amazement. He shook his head. 'Sometimes, Polly, I wonder what planet you're on.'

He marched on, telephone-bound. I trudged meekly after him. Well, I thought gloomily, I'd like to be on a wildly uplifting planet, or even over the moon perhaps, but unfortunately someone keeps bringing me right back down to earth.

Chapter Nineteen

I sat down at the bottom of the stairs, hunched up and hugging my knees like a little gnome. Any minute now, Adam would be on the other end of that telephone. I shivered. Suddenly there seemed to be a nasty east wind whistling through the very marrow of my bones, and yet it was such a beautifully warm day. These old houses were unbelievably draughty. I pulled my jumper right down over my hunched-up knees as Nick picked up the telephone.

'Shall I go away?' I asked. 'Would you be better on your own?'

'No, stay,' he licked his lips nervously, 'I need moral support.'

Any time, I thought dreamily, studying his Docksiders as I sat at his feet; moral support, physical support – my eye was roving up his blue-jeaned legs – surgical support . . .

Nick took a crumpled piece of paper out of his back pocket. He telephoned Mrs Green and got the number of the cottage in Manaccan.

'Right,' he said replacing the receiver, 'ready?'

'As ready as I'll ever be to invite a madman for a drink.'

He grinned. 'Courage, Polly, courage!'

He dialled the number. There was a long pause as it rang at the other end. Please God, please let him be out – my huge yellow streak was well to the fore as usual – please let him be out and I promise I'll go to church when I get back to London; Matins, Evensong, confession, happy-clappy tambourine time – you name it, I'll be there. God had heard it all before. Adam was in.

'Mr Buchanan?' Nick raised his eyebrows, I held my breath. 'It's Nicholas Penhalligan here, I saw my mother this afternoon, she said you were looking for me, is that right . . .? Yes, of course, no problem, but I can't help you much, I'm afraid. I gather you're looking for Rachel and Jamie . . . No, no, they're not . . . No, I've no idea where they are, I'm afraid . . . Polly? Well no, she's not in London, she's down here with me . . . Yes, staying here. She's sitting right next to me, actually.'

He glanced down and winked. My hands started to sweat, I dug my nails into my palms.

'Well, let's not go into that right now, shall we? Why don't you come over for a drink, then we can all have a civilized chat about it . . . Yes, why not? . . . Seven o'clock? . . . Finc, we'll see you then . . . Goodbye.'

He replaced the receiver. I wiped my sweaty hands on the stair carpet and looked up anxiously. 'Well?'

'That's it. He took the bait, and he's coming over.'

'How did he sound?'

'Perfectly normal.'

Perfectly normal. That's how people always sound when they're about to do something perfectly atrocious. Everyone always says so afterwards: the neighbours, the greengrocer, the stunned and weeping mother. 'Oh, he seemed perfectly normal that day, right as rain. He was always such a good boy, such a comfort to me, I can't think why he suddenly took it into his head to let loose with a Kalishnikov and mow down two innocent people in cold blood.' Yes, it was always thus. Suddenly I felt awfully scared.

'Could I perhaps stay in another room while you speak to him?' I ventured timidly. 'I mean there's no need for me to see him, is there? Three's rather a crowd, isn't it? You could tell him our little story and I could be getting on with something useful upstairs. Maybe I could clean out the attic or something? Would that be a help?'

He laughed and kicked his shoes off, changing into one of the many pairs of wellingtons that lay in a jumble in the hall. 'Polly, it's all going to be fine, stop worrying. He's just coming for a friendly chat.'

'But – but I might say the wrong thing, cramp your style, you know.'

'I wasn't aware that I had a style. Anyway, you don't have to say anything much if you don't want to.'

'But – but what are you going to tell him? Shouldn't we get our story straight? Synchronize watches? That kind of thing?'

'Don't worry about me, I'll just wing it!' He grinned, grabbed his Barbour from the banisters and headed for the front door. Where the hell did he think he was going? I grabbed his arm in alarm.

'Where are you going?' I squeaked, hanging on like a limpet, feet almost off the floor. 'Take me with you!'

'I'm just going to check on the cows.'

'I'll come with you,' I gasped. 'The dear, darling cows, haven't seen them for ages!'

'Don't be silly, it's getting dark so you won't see much,

and anyway they don't like to be disturbed. I won't be long. Pour yourself a nice big drink and turn on the telly. This will all be over before you know it.'

He patted my hand abstractedly, then prised the fingers one by one from his arm before wandering off to the relative calm and comfort of the cow shed.

It's all very well for you, I thought miserably, dragging my feet back to the drawing room; you've got your ruddy cows, what have I got?

I curled up on the sofa and tried to watch the television, maniacally switching from channel to channel and staring blindly at the flickering cathode rays. I seemed to be sucking a cushion. I started to play 'what if?' with myself. What if he didn't believe us? What if he turned nasty? What if he had a knife? I stuffed the cushion further into my mouth and nearly gagged on the tassel. It was quite conceivable, though, wasn't it? I mean, OK, I had Nick to protect me, but what if Adam was armed: there wasn't an awful lot Nick could do against a sub-machine-gun, for instance, was there? And Americans carried guns as a matter of course these days, didn't they; it was in the Constitution or something. In fact, I had a feeling it was compulsory for all American males over the age of twenty-one to carry a gun.

Suddenly I knew what I had to do. I reached for my handbag, pulled out a pencil and rummaged around for a piece of paper. I found my bank statement, which I never open and which therefore always serves as a handy note-pad. On the back I began, in a shaky hand, to pen my final instructions.

Dear Lottie,

*In case I never see you again, I want you to know that I leave you
my compact-disc machine and all the cassettes. Please also take
whichever clothes you fancy and offer the rest to Pippa. I'd be
grateful if you didn't give any to Caro. My legit jewellery had
better go back to my parents, but by all means make free with the
Butler and Wilson. I want you to know that you've always been a
terrific friend and ally over the years, please think of me fondly
from time to time, your dear, most probably dead friend, Polly.*

*PS. Please ensure that Harry hears of my demise and gets an
invite to the funeral.*

Ah yes, the funeral. Death does have its compensations
doesn't it? I sucked my pencil thoughtfully. I wondered
where it would be. Probably in that nice little church off
Pont Street, yes, that would be quite smart, quite – you
know, social. Handy for a wake in the Admiral Coddering-
ton afterwards. Funny how my fantasies always seemed to
revolve around churches. I'd been up and down this particular aisle on a number of occasions – vertical, of course,
and dressed in white. This time I'd be horizontal and dressed
in, well, in a shroud, I supposed. Were they white too?

I could see my coffin, laden with flowers as it proceeded
slowly down the aisle. The church was packed – naturally –
so much so that some people had to stand outside. Harry
was a pall-bearer, as was Nick (if he wasn't dead too, of
course), and there they stood, side by side in their dark
suits, heads bowed, breasts heaving with emotion, united
in their grief. They stared down at my coffin which lay at
the front of the church.

'There'll never be anyone quite like Polly,' whispered Harry between sobs, hanky dabbing wet eyes. 'How could I have been such a fool? My own little Polyester – gone for ever!'

Nick simply couldn't speak, his face was contorted with emotion, he wrestled with pent-up tears. Eventually, of course, his grief got the better of him and he broke down, flinging himself at my coffin, beating on the lid with his fists and crying, no – better still, shrieking – 'Polly, Polly! My only true love, come back to me, don't leave me! I can't bear to go on without you! I just can't bear it!' I sucked my pencil thoughtfully. Was that too over the top? Too – you know, nancy-boyish? I hesitated. Nah, for God's sake, I was dead, wasn't I? He was entitled to be over the top.

Anyway, eventually he was prised from the mahogany by other mourners who tried to calm him, but he pushed them all away and stumbled outside, blinded by tears, unable to face the rest of the service; unable, in fact, to face the rest of his life.

At the bottom of the church steps was Serena, looking remarkably unattractive for her, actually: greasy hair, one or two spots, bags under the eyes. 'Nick – darling!' she called out, but Nick brushed her aside, quite roughly, before staggering off under the weight of so much emotion, to be alone with his memories. Or, wait a minute – yes, perhaps Serena should look absolutely stunning and *still* he brushes her aside. Yes, that would be even better.

I doodled on the envelope. Should I jot down a couple of hymns in case Lottie didn't know any real tear-jerkers? I wanted nice dreary ones to set the mood and get the weeping under way. I was just wavering between 'The

Lord's My Shepherd' and 'I Vow to Thee My Country', when Nick walked in. I stuffed the letter in my handbag. No doubt the police would find it there later and pass it on to Lottie, and I dare say I could trust her with the order of service. She had, after all, been to a convent.

Nick looked calm and relaxed. 'OK?' he queried, raising his eyebrows.

'Sure, fine actually,' I bleated, with a brave little smile. 'Much better in fact.'

'Good girl.' God he was gullible. He sank down in front of the television with a sigh. 'God, I'm knackered.' Then he sat up a bit. 'Oh great, *Dad's Army* – it still makes me laugh, even after all these years.'

And laugh he did, quite a lot actually, was this man human? I had a go, just to show willing, but it sounded like a pregnant hen being strangled. He looked at me in alarm.

'It's going to be fine Polly, really. Don't worry about it.'

I nodded dumbly, feeling very sick all of a sudden. My tummy was churning and rather a lot of bile was rising up from it *en route* to my throat. Just at that moment the doorbell went. Coincidentally I completely lost my bottle. I shrieked and ran out of the room.

'I really don't think I can cope with this, Nick, please don't make me!' I pleaded from behind the door. 'I've got this terrible pain in my tummy, I really think I ought to go and lie down, I've had it before and if I don't lie down I'm generally sick all over the carpet!'

'Don't be silly.' Nick dragged me out from behind the door. I dug my heels in but he was too strong for me. I slid along the shiny floorboards.

'Would you just sit down and relax? Here.' He steered me, like a professional ice-skater with a beginner for a partner, towards the sofa. 'Now stay there while I let him in.'

I looked doubtfully at the sofa. He gave me a little push. 'Sit.'

My knees creaked as they bent unwillingly into it, my buttocks clenched with terror as they sank down towards it.

'It'll be an absolute breeze, I promise,' he lied, and with that he sallied forth to answer the door.

I whimpered quietly as I heard Adam's unmistakable transatlantic drawl getting closer and closer. A moment later, Nick was ushering him into the room. He seemed to fill it. Everywhere I looked there was a piece of Adam – an arm here, a leg there; I'd forgotten how big he was, and how red. I cowered back in terror, watching his enormous shadow lurk along the curtains.

'Hello, Polly,' he said in a strained but civil voice.

'Hello,' I whispered.

'Drink?' asked Nick.

'Please. Whisky and soda, if you've got one.'

He sat down at the other end of the sofa, but I felt as if he'd sat on my lap. Christ, there were plenty of other chairs in the room, weren't there? I scrambled right into the corner, holding on tight to the arm. Adam crossed his legs and leaned back, flinging his arm along the back of the sofa. I flinched as his freckly hand landed inches from my head. Bastard. He grinned, rather menacingly I thought.

'Don't worry, Polly, I'm not going to bite you.'

'That's what I keep telling her,' said Nick over his shoulder from the drinks cupboard, 'but she won't have it. She thinks you've come round to bump her off.'

Adam grinned. 'Not unless I'm severely provoked!'

'Don't provoke him, Polly,' warned Nick. 'I don't want to have to pick up the pieces. Ice?' he asked Adam.

'Please.'

Oh terrific, I thought grimly, glaring at Nick. Gang up on me now, won't you? Be Adam's buddy boy, laugh at silly old Polly. Well, wait till he chases you round the table with six inches of cold steel at your throat, because he undoubtedly will: see how funny you find that. I looked furtively at Adam's jacket, looking for bulges that might indicate a jack-knife or a gun. Nothing was glaringly obvious. Perhaps in his socks; people often kept knives in their socks, didn't they . . . ? I dropped my cigarette packet and bent down to pick it up, meanwhile scrutinizing his footwear.

'I'm not armed, if that's what you're wondering,' said a sarcastic voice in my ear.

I breathed in sharply and jerked upright to find ice-cool blue eyes boring into mine. Of course, he was telepathic, I'd quite forgotten. Somehow this was more frightening than any arsenal he might have secreted in his socks. I scrambled back to the relative safety of my corner again, bringing my knees up to deflect any body blows.

'Just dropped my cigarettes,' I mumbled, taking one out of the pack with a shaky hand.

A gold Cartier lighter flicked silently into action under my nose. The flame was bright and steady. I dipped my trembling cigarette into it and sucked hard.

'Thanks,' I muttered.

'How are you finding Cornwall?' asked Nick as he handed Adam a whisky.

Adam's eyes narrowed. 'Look, I'm not about to beat the shit out of anyone, but let's cut the crap, shall we? Cornwall's fine, but I didn't come here to pick wild flowers, I came to get my son.'

'Well, in that case I'm sorry, but I'm afraid you've come all this way on a wild goose chase. It seems you had too much faith in Polly's sense of responsibility. Jamie's in London with Rachel, we left them up there. They're fending for themselves now.'

'So you said on the telephone,' said Adam grimly, 'but I'm not entirely convinced, I'm afraid.'

'Look.' Nick sat down opposite Adam. 'D'you mind if we look at this from our point of view for a minute? Get things into perspective a little?'

'Sure, if you must.'

'I must, because you don't seem to realize that you're not the only one in a tight spot here. Polly feels very guilty about the mess she got Rachel into –'

'You mean the mess she got *me* into,' interrupted Adam fiercely, jabbing his chest with his finger, no doubt to indicate the size of his massive pectorals which were soon to partake in the dismembering of my body. He glared at me. I whimpered and threw more gin down my throat and, oddly enough, my jumper.

'All right, all right, the mess she got you into, have it your own way,' sighed Nick. 'I'm not prepared to go into whose side she should have been on, because the point is that she shouldn't have been put in the position of having to pick sides in the first place. I mean, none of this whole

ridiculous business had anything to do with her, did it?'
He turned to me. 'In fact, it still beats me why you ever
got involved in all this in the first place.' He shook his
head with genuine incredulity. I hung mine in shame.

'Anyway,' he went on, 'that's another story, and we
won't go into Polly's inability to mind her own business
right now; but believe me, when she told me all about it
my immediate reaction was one of absolute horror. I
couldn't believe she'd got mixed up in all this. I told her in
no uncertain terms that she should extricate herself from
the whole affair, tell the pair of you to bugger off, and let
you fight it out between yourselves. As far as I was concerned, there was no reason why she should dig herself in
any deeper – I mean, it's not as if she even knew either of
you, for God's sake. It's one thing to help out old friends,
but complete strangers? Come on. She'd done more than
enough.'

Too right. I rather enjoyed that little speech, it had a
nice protective ring about it. Adam looked thoughtful. He
cradled his whisky in his fingers and swirled it around a
bit. He didn't say anything.

Nick leaned forward. 'The whole situation was becoming totally absurd. She couldn't go home to her own flat in
case you were waiting for her there, she couldn't come to
work in case you followed her and attacked her –'

'Oh come on!' said Adam. 'You make me sound like an
animal. I had no intention of attacking her –'

'Oh really? Well that wasn't the impression we got. You
come charging into our office, brandishing knives and
scaring the pants off everyone – what are we supposed to
think?'

Adam shrugged, he looked a little shame-faced. 'OK, OK, I admit I acted a little crazy that day, but I was – well, I was desperate. I'm sorry, I apologize for all that, it's totally unlike me, I hate violence – really, but I've been under a hell of a lot of strain lately, as you can probably imagine. I guess I just lost my rag.'

Nick shrugged. 'Well, fair enough, it happens, but you can see my point. We weren't to know that you'd just temporarily "lost your rag". Polly really thought her number was up.'

Adam shook his head and sighed. 'This is crazy, you know. I'm not trying to hurt anyone, or even frighten anyone. I just want to find my son.'

'Fine, I realize that, but all I'm saying is that, at the time, we weren't to know that your threats were idle. Polly was scared out of her wits, and I was pretty worried myself, I can tell you. Anyway, that's why I suggested' – he paused and let a hint of a smile play around his lips – 'with, I have to admit, something of an ulterior motive, that she come down here and stay with me for a while. To get away from it all and to – well, to have a holiday.' He grinned. 'I've been trying to drag her down here for some time, actually. In a way this was the perfect excuse.' He shot Adam a quick, half-embarrassed, half-cocky look, and then turned to look out of the window, letting this sink in.

I was impressed. Talk about the gifted amateur, this was the work of a seasoned liar, not a total beginner. Perhaps he'd been taking notes from me.

Faced with Nick's back, Adam swung round to me for confirmation. I'd done nothing but look permanently shifty for the last five minutes, and it was a demeanour which suited this revelation right down to the ground. I shifted some more.

Adam's top lip curled into a knowing sneer. 'Well, well, what do you know? Looks like I've stumbled in on a bit of a love nest here, doesn't it? Well congratulations, you guys, I hope you'll be very happy together,' he drawled.

'Thanks very much,' said Nick with a grin. 'I'm sure we will.' He got up to pour himself another drink, and paused *en route* to take my hand. He gave it a quick squeeze; it instantly broke out into a muck sweat. He looked casually at Adam. 'Another drink?'

'Sure, why not?'

'Polly?'

'Mmmm!' I nodded furiously, and gulped hard, hoping nobody was expecting me to say anything more than that. Just breathing and drinking were proving to be enough of a struggle at the moment.

'Well, Polly,' smirked Adam, 'you've certainly changed your tune, haven't you?'

'What d'you mean?' I said quickly. Too quickly. As usual my mouth had responded before my brain had had time to engage. I didn't want him to tell me what he meant at all.

'Well, as I recall, a little over a week ago, Nick here was not exactly your favourite guy. And certainly not what you might call dream-boat material. In fact, if I remember rightly, you went so far as to write him off as a total jerk, am I right?'

I tried hard to erect a dam at the top of my neck to stop the red-hot blush from spreading on to my face, but it was no good. 'Don't be ridiculous!' I spluttered. 'I would never say anything so – so absurd!'

'Ah, but you did!' said Adam, enjoying himself. 'In fact, I remember your very words. You called him – not a jerk, but that marvellously English insult – a git!'

Nick threw back his head and hooted with laughter. 'Well, thank you, my darling. A git, eh? That's not what you said last night!' He tapped me playfully on the nose as he handed me my drink.

I fumed at Adam, puce with embarrassment. What must Nick think?

'How dare you! It – it's outrageous of you to repeat a private conversation. I remember now that I'd had a bad day at work and was feeling a bit miffed with Nick over something silly, I don't remember what, and – and I might have said something to you in the heat of the moment about how I was a bit, um, irritated with him, but I certainly wouldn't have called him a git!' I gabbled.

Adam and Nick were both grinning widely. Nick sat on the arm of the sofa, threw an arm around my shoulders and hugged me towards him.

'Don't worry, darling, he's teasing you. Anyway, I know what you used to say about me, I dare say I've said a few uncharitable things about you in the past, too, but that's all forgotten now, isn't it? And of course you know what they say: there's a very thin line between love and hate!'

'Yes – yes, they do say that, don't they? D-darling,' I stammered. I was positively dripping with perspiration, and we hadn't even got to the difficult bit. Perhaps I could go and clean the attic now? The only consolation was that Adam had loosened up a bit, obviously enjoying my discomfort.

He smiled sadistically. 'Well, hey, I'm sorry if I've put a spanner in the works. I guess you'll have fun kissing and making up when I've gone, though. I must say it's fascinating to hear yet another chapter in Polly's somewhat chequered love life.'

'Chequered?' I spluttered. 'There's nothing chequered about it. I'll have you know it's always been extremely straightforward!'

He laughed and held up his hands. 'OK, OK, I'll take your word for it. Anyway. We digress. Let's not get too sidetracked by your incredibly "straightforward" love life, shall we? We don't want to lose sight of the point of my little visit.'

He swilled his whisky around in his glass. For a moment I'd completely forgotten what the point was. He hadn't.

'Polly, where's Rachel?' he asked, in a soft but deadly voice, raising his eyebrows at me.

I shrank back. Did I say he'd loosened up? I felt the blood drain away from my face. Victoria plum to sheet white in less than five seconds; quite an achievement, really. My eyes caught on his like Velcro.

'I really don't know,' I whispered.

Nick strengthened his grip on my shoulders. 'Look, Adam, we haven't a clue where she is now, but there's no harm in telling you that we dropped Rachel off at her father's house before we came down here.'

'Oh, come on, d'you really expect me to believe that? There's no one at that house except the judge and the housekeeper. D'you think I haven't been watching?'

'Well, maybe she's not there now, but I can tell you, we dropped her off there last Thursday morning, plus Jamie and half a ton of baby gear. That's the last we saw of them, and we haven't heard from Rachel since.'

Adam shook his head. 'No way.'

'Take it from me, it's true. Maybe they were only there for an hour or so, perhaps they moved on almost immediately, I don't know. I'm just telling you that that's where we bow out of the story. That's where we left them.'

Nick looked Adam straight in the eye. Adam hesitated. My toes were creaking with suspense. He must have heard them, he turned to me.

'You spent a few days with Rachel, Polly, you must have talked to her. Did she give any clues as to what she was going to do? You must have discussed it with her. What were her plans?'

'I really don't know, she didn't say.'

'Oh come on, she must have said something!'

'She didn't – really, she kept very much to herself.'

'You know, you really shouldn't tell lies, Polly.'

'But it's true! Honestly, it's true, she – she didn't say a word!' I stammered nervously, no acting required.

Adam stared at me for a moment, then he rubbed his eyes and sighed deeply. He scratched his head. He didn't look in the least bit menacing now, he just looked tired.

'Look. I can quite understand why you don't want anything more to do with this business, but just listen to me for a minute, the pair of you, will you?'

I nodded dumbly. Did we have any choice?

'I'm not going to try to snatch Jamie away from Rachel.'

I looked at him suspiciously. 'You're not?'

He shook his head. 'No. Now I admit that originally I was so incensed that all I wanted to do was to find the pair of them, grab Jamie, and take him back to the States with me; but I've had a lot of time to think recently.' He leaned forward and rested his forehead in his hands, staring at his shoes. 'I've sat in quite a few hotel rooms, or rented houses, staring at walls trying to get things straight in my mind, and I've come to the conclusion that in the long run, it wouldn't get me very far. Rachel and her old man would have the police on to me in seconds. I'd just spend the whole time running and hiding. It would be pretty horrific for Jamie, too.'

'It certainly would,' agreed Nick.

'Yeh, yeh, I know, don't worry, I've worked it all through now. I know I'm on a hiding to nothing. All I want to do is find Rachel, talk to her, and see if we can't sort something out like a couple of sensible adults. There must be some kind of custodial agreement we can come to without going through the courts.'

'But she's too frightened to see you now, she won't speak to you,' I said.

Adam held out his hands in despair. 'But why? For God's sake, why won't she speak to me? There's no rhyme or reason why she should be scared. OK, in the heat of the moment when I was absolutely furious – and blind drunk incidentally – I made a couple of stupid telephone calls to her father's house, but she knows me well enough to know that I'd never hurt her, or Jamie. She's making out that I'm some kind of maniac, some kind of homicidal nut-case – it's crazy! What have I ever done to her, apart from love her, have a child with her, and ask her to marry me? Is that so terrible? Well, apparently it is, because d'you know what she did? Without any warning whatsoever, without even giving me an inkling of what was on her mind, she just up and left one day, taking our son with her. She left a little itsy-bitsy note – about three lines long, it was – on the kitchen table and, cool as anything, walked out. Can you believe that? She just packed a bag, tucked Jamie under her arm, and got on a plane to England. And now she won't even speak to me – don't you think that's a little strange after all we've been through together? Wouldn't it drive you a little crazy if you were in my position? My whole world has collapsed and everyone's acting like I'm the lunatic, like I'm the one who's acting irrationally!' He shook his head in disbelief.

'Look, Adam . . .' began Nick softly, but Adam went on as if he hadn't even heard him. It was as if we weren't even in the room.

'But you know what? D'you want to know the craziest thing of all? In spite of all she's done, I still love her. I'd marry her tomorrow if she'd have me. We had a child together, my son, who I love more than anything in the world. That's what's important. That's what I keep hanging on to.'

He paused and ran his fingers through his hair. He looked terribly tired. Nobody spoke for a moment. At length, Adam continued. His voice had a crack in it.

'Now, I realize she doesn't feel the same way about me. I'm coming to terms with that, and I daresay one day I'll even accept it. People fall out of love all the time, and I just happen to be the injured party, that's all. OK, fine, but Christ, she owes me some sort of an explanation, doesn't she? Jesus, just to get on a plane and take off to another country like that without a word, taking Jamie with her.'

His voice all but collapsed here; he fought to control it. 'I mean, whatever you think of me, you've got to admit, she owes me some kind of access to my son. She owes me the right to see him from time to time, doesn't she? Am I asking so much of her?'

I stared out of the window. I was surprised to discover I had tears in my eyes. I blinked. The curtains hadn't been drawn, and while we'd been talking it had got quite dark. A black, starless sky hung over us. The wind had dropped completely and all was still and quiet. There wasn't even a rustle in the trees, or a distant bleat of a lamb.

Of course he wasn't asking too much. She did owe it to him, and she owed him a lot more besides. I tried to imagine what it must be like to come home from work one day and find that your family has disappeared. We were well and truly caught in the middle here, and more and more I realized where my sympathies lay. I wanted to tell him where she was. I wanted to blurt it out – say that he'd find her holed up at a little pub called the Dog and Duck just off the Wincanton Road. All the same, I knew I couldn't. I was supposed to be feeding him the unmarried mothers line. I looked in desperation at Nick. He too looked pained, and shifted about uncomfortably on the arm of the chair. I wondered if he was thinking the same thing as me.

'Nick?' I whispered.

Adam pounced, misinterpreting my appeal. 'Nick, is there anything you can tell me? Something you know?'

Nick hesitated. 'No – no, not really . . .'

'For pity's sake, please!' Adam urged him.

'Well – well, actually she did mention something . . .'

'Yes! Yes – go on.'

'No Nick, don't,' I said softly.

He put a hand on my arm, 'I think we should, Polly.' I gulped and stared at the carpet. This was going to be more convincing than we could have possibly imagined, and I couldn't bear it. I couldn't look at Adam's eager face.

'Go on?' he leaned forward eagerly.

Nick sighed. 'Well, it's just that, while the girls were staying with Pippa, before they came down here, Polly overheard Rachel on the telephone.'

'Yes?'

'Well, she got through to one of those hostels, a home for unmarried mothers . . .'

A light seemed to go on inside Adam's tired, dull eyes. I turned away. 'A home? You mean like a shelter, that kind of thing?'

'That's it. I don't suppose she was thinking of staying there on a permanent basis, perhaps for a week or two, I don't know, and I'm afraid I've no idea which one.'

Adam shot me a look. I shook my head vigorously. 'No,' I whispered, 'no, she didn't say.'

He stood up slowly. 'An unmarried mothers' home. Yeh, we have those in the States, I know what you mean.' He walked to the window and looked out at the black night.

'You won't get in,' I said quickly – somehow I couldn't bear to think of him beating his way into these places to no avail – 'and – and they'll just get the police on to you if you try.'

Unwittingly I'd managed to seal it. He drained his whisky. 'Will they indeed?' he said grimly. 'Just let them try.'

He turned to face us. His freckles stood out harshly on his pale, determined face. His eyes were wide and staring now. He put his glass down on a table.

'Thanks for the drink,' he said curtly. He nodded to us and turned to go. As he got to the door, he hesitated, his hand on the handle. He turned back. 'Thanks. I realize you didn't have to tell me that. I'm grateful. Thanks, Nick. I guess you can understand a little of how I feel.' With that, he opened the door and walked out.

Nick and I sat in silence. I heard the front door close behind him, then I heard a car door slam. An engine turned over and roared into life. There was a crunch of gravel as the tyres spun on the drive, a familiar rattle as the car crossed over the cattle grid, and finally a distant roar as it sped off, no doubt heading for the London road. Still neither of us spoke.

Chapter Twenty

Eventually Nick sighed heavily and got to his feet. He crossed over to the fire and kicked one of the logs savagely, sending sparks flying on to the hearth. I felt like kicking something myself, but I'd had so much to drink I didn't think I was capable of standing up, let alone raising one leg off the ground and taking aim. Instead I sat in a booze-sodden heap, feeling seriously depressed. Nick threw a couple more logs on the fire, and stood brooding down into the flames. Then he turned, warming the backs of his legs. He saw my dejected face and shook his head.

'It's no good looking like that, Polly. We did what we had to do.'

I sighed. 'I know. It just seems so unfair, though. Why do we have to take her side?'

Nick shrugged. 'Why do we have to take any side? It's a bloody ridiculous situation. Here we are, being forced to manipulate the lives of two people we hardly know, sending one off on a wild goose chase, and playing bodyguard to the other.' He shook his head grimly. 'I tell you, the sooner this is all over, the better.'

He turned back to the fire. We watched the flames for a while.

'Poor Adam,' I said eventually. 'He'll be banging on all the hostel doors in London tonight.'

Nick turned on me angrily. 'Well, that was what you wanted, wasn't it? It's no good saying "poor Adam" now!'

'I know, I know, but – well, I just feel so awful, I almost wish we'd told him where she is!' I blurted out, feeling close to tears.

Nick looked at me, exasperated. 'God, Polly, sometimes I just don't believe you! What did you expect me to do, for God's sake? Dig out a road-map and trace a route for him from here to the Dog and Duck? Wave him on his way and let him charge up the motorway and go storming into the pub without giving Tim, Penny or Rachel any warning? Is that what you wanted?'

'No but –'

'Well, what then? And anyway, who's to say that he's telling the truth? Who's to say that he wouldn't just grab Jamie and take him back to America: how would you feel then? You'd be saying "poor Rachel" then, wouldn't you? Well, wouldn't you?' he demanded angrily.

'Yes, I suppose so,' I whispered.

I blinked hard. It had been a tough evening, and I really didn't think I could cope with anyone else having a go at me. Tears were literally poised on the precipice. I bit a very wobbly lip and looked away, but he saw the wobble and immediately sat down next to me, contrite and full of remorse.

'Oh Polly, I'm sorry, don't cry. It's not your fault, I'm just letting off steam. I know I shouldn't take it out on you, but to tell you the truth, I'm fed up with being in such a bloody awful position. It's really beginning to get me down.'

My chin wiggled dramatically as I fought with the water-works. He sighed and ran his fingers through his hair.

'And I know why I'm angry. Because for what it's worth I feel the same way you do now. The more I hear about this saga, the more I think that Rachel acted abysmally, but that's not the point, is it? The point is, we promised we'd look after her, and we can't just abandon her now. You do see that, don't you?'

I gulped. 'Yes, I do, and I know you're right but – but it just seems so rough on Adam. He's not such a bad chap really, is he? A little impulsive, I grant you, but who wouldn't be under the circumstances?'

He laughed drily. 'I must say you've changed your tune. Half an hour ago he was public enemy number one.'

'I know, but everything looks different now. He's been so hurt, and for what? I mean, as he says, all he's ever been guilty of is falling in love with a girl, getting her pregnant, wanting to marry her, and wanting to look after her and the baby. That's not so terrible, is it?' I gritted my teeth and clenched my fists. 'If you ask me, Rachel Marsden is a complete and utter bitch!'

Nick grinned. 'Feel better for that, do you?'

'I do, actually.'

'Polly, I agree with you, and the whole thing is very frustrating, but there's nothing we can do about it. Let's just try and forget it. We've got rid of Adam, and in a few days we'll get rid of Rachel, too. Then it'll all be over and you can relax. OK?'

I smiled weakly. 'OK.'

'In the meantime,' his voice softened considerably,

'why don't we just forget the pair of them and try to enjoy what's left of this little holiday?'

Now I know a seductive tone of voice when I hear one, in fact I can detect one at twenty paces, and I could have sworn I'd just heard one. I looked up in surprise. Nick smiled, and – good gracious, yes – the brown eyes were most definitely soft and encouraging. Like two deliciously gooey chocolates, they seemed to be beckoning me on.

'Oh yes, please,' I whispered greedily. 'I mean, yes please, let's enjoy ourselves. I'm all for enjoyment, aren't you?'

I gave him what I hoped was my most smouldering, sexy smile, but which could well have been taken for a pissed leer. He smiled back. Suddenly everything was so still, I could hear my heart beating. I waited, rigid with excitement. *Something* was definitely going on here, *something* was about to happen. I held my breath and sat quietly. Nick's smile turned into a steady gaze which seemed to envelop me completely. I bathed in it wantonly, not daring to move.

Overhead, a lone seagull wailed mournfully as it circled the house; the long case clock ticked away steadily in the corner; the fire crackled cosily in the grate. Other than that, there was just a highly charged silence. It was killing me, and so, for that matter, was my head. An intoxicating mixture of gin and desire was sending it into something more usually associated with the final spin-dry of a washing machine. How maddeningly inconvenient. I shut my eyes briefly in an attempt to arrest the cycle. A fatal mistake. Even though I was sitting down, I swayed violently. I opened them immediately.

'Are you all right?' asked Nick, whose come-hither gaze had turned to one of concern.

'Fine, fine, really. What were we saying?'

He smiled warmly. 'Something about enjoying ourselves.'

'Ah yes,' I murmured, and smiled back, even more warmly.

The washing machine abated slightly as every conceivable nook and cranny in my body tingled with anticipation. My heart went into overdrive, thumping away as it sent red-hot blood steaming around my body, pumping it into places that didn't normally require it. Even my toenails seemed to be throbbing, charged up to the cuticles with the stuff. Please hurry, I willed him silently, please hurry *up*!

But still he sat there, silent and watchful. Eventually, after what seemed like a century but was probably three seconds, he turned his body in towards me slightly and rested his hand on the sofa behind my head. Yes, yes, *yes*, I urged silently, go for it. GO FOR IT! He didn't take his eyes off me. His hand rested softly on the back of my head. He stroked my hair gently and smiled.

I met his gaze, but was aware that my nostrils were flaring dramatically. I seemed to have far too much breath, I didn't know what to do with it. Out it came in short, chuggy bursts, and then in went gallons more. Where did it all come from? The more I tried to disguise it, the more I chugged and snorted. Now his hand was on the back of my neck, stroking it gently, making my hair stand up on end, making goose pimples break out in the oddest places, and all the while, he fixed me with those deep brown eyes.

I wasn't used to such slick, subtle moves. Most of the

men I'd had close encounters of the sexy kind with would have had their tongue round my tonsils by now and be grappling with my bra strap. This hair-stroking lark was a new one on me, but it certainly sent the pulse rate soaring.

I chugged and snorted a bit more. We were close, but not that close. About twelve to eighteen inches of Cole-fax and Fowler chintz upholstery was still most definitely between us. There was no doubt that either a quick lunge or a surreptitious sidle would have to be made by some-body. But not you, I told myself sternly. Don't be fast and vulgar. For once in your life, be slow and tasteful. Just concentrate on sitting very still and he'll do the rest.

But when? He stroked and smiled, and stroked and smiled, and suddenly I could bear it no longer. Slow and tasteful be damned, I'd be dead soon. In one swift, jet-propelled move, I launched myself across the eighteen inches of sofa and flew into his arms.

He ricocheted slightly on impact, and out of the corner of my eye I caught a hint of a raised eyebrow, but no mat-ter. Hating myself for my highly previous nature, but unable to control it, I lifted my face and – yes, he was low-ering his. In an instant we were locked in the most divine, the most passionate, the most, oh so exquisite kiss I'd ever experienced. On and on it went, getting sweeter and sweeter, and deeper and deeper by the moment. I could have stayed there for ever, but breathing difficulties were becoming apparent on his part, and so at last, like a couple of deep-sea divers, we came up for air. Locked in his arms, I gazed up to see what effect all this passion was having on the geometric features. They'd softened considerably. He looked pleased, if a little surprised.

'Well, well, well,' he said softly, gently tracing my mouth with his finger. 'Who would have thought . . .'

'Yes, who would have thought!' I whispered back breathlessly.

Who would have thought what? That I could be such a brazen hussy? That he could have lowered himself to the depths of snogging his secretary? Or that it could all be so deeply wonderful? Who would have thought what? I longed to know but, more than that, I longed for more. Unfortunately my head was against it. Once more it had switched into spin-dry mode, and I had to steady myself on his shoulder to stop the room from spinning round.

I held on tight and breathed deeply. It was important to take very deep breaths and on no account to shut my eyes. I concentrated like mad on the fire, I watched the flames as they licked greedily around the logs, and then, when I deemed it safe to move my head, I looked up. Nick frowned down at me as I span.

'All right?' he inquired.

All right? What – the kiss? Was he asking me? 'Oh yes! Fantastic! One of the best – the best in fact!'

Nick seemed to find this a puzzling response. He frowned some more. What a thoroughly sexy frown, I thought dreamily as it swam in and out of focus. What can he be thinking about? Whatever it was obviously required a great deal of thought. Ah yes! I know, he's wondering where we should go from here! Only literally, of course, we know in theory where we're going, but where should the action take place?

Was he the kind of man who had to do it in a bed? Or would that mouth-wateringly appetizing Persian rug in front of the fire do just as well? Still he frowned. The location was obviously not to be chosen lightly. Of course! He was probably considering the hay barn! Hadn't he mentioned only the other day that he'd like to sleep in it? Now if that isn't a broad hint, I don't know what is! I helped him along.

'Are you thinking about the barn?' I whispered.

'Sorry?'

'The barn, is that what you're thinking about? Because if you are, I want you to know that I think it's a very good idea, very – you know, rustic!' I gently nudged his gloriously hunky shoulder with my head and winked in a knowing fashion.

Nick looked even more puzzled. Then suddenly he disentangled himself and got up. He went over to the fire, crouched down and poked it thoughtfully. I sat up. Gracious, this seemed to me to be an entirely retrograde step, what on earth was going on? It didn't take that much thought, did it?

'Only joking about the barn,' I mumbled. 'I'm easy.' God, that sounded awful. 'About – about where we go, I mean.' Even worse. I flushed and looked down at my hands.

More frowning, and more fire maintenance followed these brazen confessions. I bit my lip. I felt decidedly out of my depth here. These decorous periods of inactivity might be highly civilized, but they puzzled the hell out of me. After all, the first kiss had been planted, intent had been established, action should be taking place. Shouldn't we even now be thundering upstairs, tearing each other's clothes off, and launching ourselves at the double bed in a frenzy of excitement? Even the restrained hair-stroking was preferable to this malarkey. I thought hard. No Polly, no, you're wrong as usual. This was obviously how civilized people made love. Of course! How silly of me: fire-poking was probably the ultimate in erotic symbolism. After all, he had been to Cambridge, hadn't he? And I hadn't been exposed to such high-minded love-making before. Up to now it had all been very – well, very red-brick. Even polytechnic at times.

I watched eagerly as he rooted away in the grate, excitement growing within me – oh yes, I see, I see! The more he poked, the more excited I got, I was really catching on now – God, this was thrilling! But how should I respond? Join him at the fireside? Throw on a lump of coal? This was all new to me; how taxing it was!

I racked my brains. Come on, Polly, think, think. Suddenly it came to me. I would dance towards him. Yes, of course, a dance – what could be more erotically symbolic than that? And I was a good dancer too.

'Nick?' I whispered eagerly.

'Yes?' he turned around.

'Ready?'

'Er . . . yes.'

I got unsteadily to my feet, pulled a lock of hair over one eye, and fixed him with a sexy, penetrating gaze. I put my hands on my hips and wiggled them seductively. Then I rotated my shoulders, slowly. Next I concentrated on the wrists, twirling them around, seven veils-fashion, stretching out the fingers – oops, there went an ashtray, crashing to the floor, spilling ash everywhere – no matter, I was well away now. I really began to move. I swayed towards him, flashing my eyes from under their lashes, and giving the sexy smouldering smile yet another outing. Atta-girl, I thought to myself, atta-girl! This will rock his socks off.

He watched, in wonder and in a little too much amazement, as I shimmied towards him, hips snaking, arms twisting. The more I shimmied, the wider his eyes grew: he was totally captivated. I was right above him now as he sat crouched, a trifle nervously perhaps, by the fireside. I really let him have it. I threw back my head and twirled and snaked and twisted and writhed and –

'Oops!' – tripped over the rug, toppling headlong towards the fire.

'Watch out!' yelled Nick as he grabbed me, rugby-tackling me away from the flames.

'Oof, sorry!' I landed, rather heavily it has to be said, in his arms. OK, so it wasn't the most graceful of landings, but there I was, where I most wanted to be. I smiled up at him dreamily as both of his rather fuzzy heads separated for a moment and then came together again. All I had to do was lie here and wait. Any minute now he'd pull me roughly towards him, and envelop me in the most passionate embrace, kissing me madly the while. I shut my eyes in an ecstasy of anticipation.

Nick cleared his throat. 'Right. Bedtime I think.'

He just couldn't wait, could he? 'Oooh, yes please!' I wriggled gleefully, then reached up and pulled his head down towards mine, lips parted, eyes shut – one for the road, eh?

Lip contact was never made. I opened my eyes. Nick seemed to be disentangling my arms from around his neck. 'No, Polly, separate bedtime.'

He stood up, hoisted me to my feet, turned me around and pointed me in the direction of the door. 'Go on,' he said softly. 'I'll see you in the morning.'

I stood there, swaying incredulously. My mouth opened wide, my eyes boggled. I turned back. 'Separate beds?' I echoed dumbly.

'Separate,' he affirmed decisively.

My insides curdled, my jaw slackened. I was amazed, incredulous, uncomprehending. Separate beds? That's what he'd said all right, but was he serious? And if so, what did it mean? That I'd got it all wrong? That I'd read his signs wrong? Surely not.

I frowned, pondering the mighty implications of it all. Then, quite suddenly, it dawned on me, crashing over me in a tidal wave of shame and embarrassment. Oh my God. Of course! I'd failed the kiss test.

Now, I freely admit to having failed a lot of tests in my time. Scores of O-levels, a smattering of A-levels, Grade Three piano, cycling proficiency and life saving, to name but a few, but never, *never*, have I failed the kiss test. Let's face it, I've had too much practice. In fact, without wishing to sound immodest, I generally pass with flying colours and leave the lucky recipient begging for more. But to fail! I hung my head and felt my face flame. How deeply shameful.

What could it be, I wondered? Galloping halitosis? Or something more sinister like a nasty little cold sore at the corner of the mouth? I put up a tentative hand and felt around gingerly. Nothing seemed to be glaringly apparent; it must be lurking nastily beneath the surface.

But, on the other hand, maybe it wasn't that at all.

Maybe – and this was a real shaker – maybe he just didn't fancy me. Perhaps he'd thought it might be quite fun, a bit of a laugh, but when it came to the crunch he'd found it – well – rather nauseous; repulsive even. After all, he already had a girlfriend, didn't he? And a jolly pretty one at that: why should he mess around with the likes of me? I was mortified. How could I have been such a fool? I felt a bit of a lip tremble coming on. I stiffened it instantly. Bear up, Polly, bear up. We'll have none of that, thank you.

I raised my head and met his eye. 'Right-o then!' I said in a cracked little voice, desperately trying to force a hockey stick into it. 'I'll be off to bed. You're right, I am rather tired actually – cheerio! See you in the morning!'

Smiling bravely, I turned and crossed the room in a reasonably straight line, although I have to admit, I lurched the final yard or two and had to grab hold of the door frame to steady myself. Every moment in this room was unbearable now.

I was aware that he was following me. I could feel his eyes on my back as I made it through the hall to the bottom of the stairs, albeit with a bit of wall-hanging along the way.

'Are you OK?' he asked anxiously as I began, gingerly, to mount the stairs.

'Sure!' I croaked, raising my hand in a backward wave to reassure him, and quickly replacing it on the banister as I nearly lost my balance. Sure. Only about eighteen inches tall now and getting smaller by the minute, but other than that, fine, just dandy.

The stairs seemed to go up and up for ever; higher and higher they went, like something out of a 1940s

Hollywood musical set, and all the time he would keep standing at the bottom watching my unsteady progress. I looked back. Yes, he was still there – Christ, what a long way down! I grabbed the banister as I stumbled: how extraordinary, I seemed to be suffering from vertigo.

I bit my quivering lip. Don't cry, I thought with rising panic. Don't cry yet. Not yet. And don't, whatever you do, look down. I climbed the last step, turned left, realized my mistake in an instant – lightning reflexes – and turned right instead. I stumbled blindly down the dark passage-way, feeling my way in the dark.

At last I reached the right door. Now you can cry, I thought as I stumbled in. I shut the bedroom door behind me and leaned heavily against it. Now you can cry all you like. I threw myself on my bed and buried my face in my pillow. The floodgates opened. I sobbed and sobbed, for about – oh, a couple of minutes probably. Because after that the strangest thing happened. Instead of sobbing long and hard, and on and on, into the small hours, as I'd rather imagined I would, almost immediately, I fell fast asleep.

Chapter Twenty-one

When I awoke the next morning I was almost blinded by the light. The window and the curtains were wide open and a sixty-watt bulb was glaring down at me above my head. I blinked and rubbed my eyes. How very odd. Why on earth was the light on? Had it been on all night? I raised myself up on to my elbows. A huge mistake. A wave of fresh spring air surged through the open window and hit me full in the face. I moaned low and sank down on to the pillow again.

I felt awful, really awful. I lay still for a minute as I tried to get the measure of this. Something deeply unpleasant was going on here, mostly in the head region. My brain seemed to have expanded overnight and was fighting for accommodation, bashing away against my skull in a painful, frenzied fashion. My tongue had swollen out of all proportion and had grown fur, like some ghastly Caliban festering in its cave. What on earth had I been up to last night to surface in this sorry condition?

I frowned and cast my mind back a few hours. Slowly, the penny started to drop. It landed with a resounding clatter and the whole horror of the night before slotted into place. I stuffed the sheet into my mouth. Oh my God! I'd tried to seduce him! I'd leaped into his arms! I'd – I'd, oh horror of horrors, I'd danced! Had I really? Yes I had! I pulled the sheet right over my head and groaned. Suddenly

I went cold. Had I – and here I had trouble even suggesting the notion to myself – had I, perchance, danced naked?

I sat up, terror-struck, and had a swift glance round the room. Happily, most of my clothes could be accounted for. There was my skirt on the lampshade, my shirt on the bookcase, my jumper hanging out of the window, my bra – where was my bra? I glanced down. Oh. How odd. I frowned at my chest. I seemed to be wearing it. Oh well, at least it hadn't come off; but what other face-flushing atrocities had I committed?

With a heavy sigh I lay down again and turned on to my side. As I did so, I realized there was something wrong with my feet. I couldn't move my toes. I tried to wiggle them, it was quite an effort. Ah yes, of course, I was obviously paralysed. I'd heard of people being paralysed with embarrassment before; clearly it had happened to me. Paralysed from the – let me see, I tried an unsuccessful ankle wiggle – yes, from the knees downwards. What a shame, I was rather fond of walking. I peeped warily under the bedclothes and spotted my cowboy boots still clinging to my person. Ah. That explained it. How peculiar, I usually remembered to take my shoes off.

At least that was all of my clothing accounted for, except – except my knickers! Where the hell were they? Draped over a lampshade in the drawing room? Hanging over an ancestral portrait in the hall? Decorating the banisters, perhaps?

I jumped out of bed, clad fetchingly in a bra and cowboy boots like something out of a Soho sleaze joint, and stared wildly round the room. Ah! Thank goodness. There they were in the washbasin. I fell on them gratefully and hugged them to my bosom. At this point I experienced a certain amount of head rush and had to steady myself on the washbasin. I shouldn't have leaped out of bed so quickly. I took a deep breath, counted to ten, then crawled back to bed and shut my eyes tight.

After about half an hour I realized, with a glance at my clock, that it was already ten o'clock and if I left it any longer *someone* might breeze in full of pity and find me in this hideously unattractive state. Some sort of repair job would have to be done on the face before such an eventuality. Apart from that, a raging thirst was beginning to get the better of me. I had to get up.

I staggered to the washbasin and glugged desperately at a running tap, wet hair streaming down the plughole, but it was no good. A hosepipe turned on full blast was needed to quench this sort of thirst.

I gazed in the mirror above the basin. How strange. Someone rather like me but much uglier was gazing back. Same shaped face and same hair, but with tiny, slitty little eyes which were only being kept open by the weight of a huge pair of pendulous bags which dragged the bottom lids down. The complexion was pasty and pallid and the mouth enormously swollen. Swollen heart, too, I thought mournfully as I brushed two inches of fur off my teeth. That was the worst of it, and something I could only just bring myself to contemplate. He didn't want me. He'd rejected me. If I was the last woman on this earth he'd emigrate to Mars. And I loved him.

It hit me full in the face like a runaway train. I loved him. The ugly face in the mirror began to quiver perilously and the piggy little eyes looked alarmingly moist. Don't cry!

I commanded the face sternly. It shuddered obediently to a halt and the eyes blinked back their tears. For God's sake. You're ugly enough as it is, don't make things worse.

I showered long and hard and dressed slowly. Then I spent about half an hour on my make-up, to no avail. It was quite clear that on this particular morning I had the choice of looking like a prostitute or a battered wife. Initially I went for the prostitute look, then got half-way downstairs and ran back to wash it all off again. If I looked like a tart it might remind him that I was one. No. Barefaced cheek was the order of the day.

With freshly scrubbed cheeks I crept down into the kitchen. There was no one about. Nick had obviously breakfasted long ago, up at five with the cows, no doubt. I opened the fridge and greeted the orange juice like a long-lost friend. The muesli was a different matter. I toyed with it limply and stared out of the window. Where was he? Hiding in a barn? Ringing Tim and Rachel, begging them to come back and rescue him from the hands of a nymphomaniac who'd taken the whole charade seriously and had tried – unsuccessfully, mind – to get into his jeans? I groaned. Oh, the shame.

The muesli was making me retch so I poured it down the sink, clogging up the plughole. Suddenly I looked up – I could hear footsteps on the path outside. Oh God, it was him, and before I even had time to decide what sort of an expression I would have on my face, he was opening the back door.

'Hi!' he greeted me cheerily, looking fresh-faced and windswept. His hair was tousled, his eyes were shining, and he looked utterly divine. How could I ever have thought he'd be mine?

'Hi!' I managed to gasp in response. The expression my face had chosen for me was of the timid, cowering, puke-making variety. I hovered by the Aga; should I stay? It would be too rude to leave immediately, and yet I couldn't bear to make small-talk with him.

'Had some breakfast?' he asked conversationally as he sat down and pulled his boots off.

'Oh, yes thanks.'

There was a silence. I cast around desperately for something interesting to say.

'Have you?' Pathetic, Polly. Truly pathetic.

'Yes, I had mine hours ago. Been up since six.'

'Ah.'

It was so hard to talk, and yet recently it had been so easy. I stared miserably at the kitchen floor.

'What have you – um, been doing then? I mean this morning?' I faltered.

'Oh this and that, been out with the sheep mostly. Oh, incidentally, I telephoned Mrs Green.'

'Oh yes?' I tried to sound interested, but really I couldn't have cared less. I was fed up with other people's lives.

'And she said that Adam left last night. Just paid the rent, packed his bags and shot off, saying he was going back to London. He was in quite a hurry apparently.'

'Oh well, that's good. Gosh, that's good. What a relief!' I said unconvincingly. I stared at my fingernails. I must go on saying ordinary things.

'Everything – um, all right on the farm front, then?'

'Yes, fine, one of the ewes had twins which is always a bonus. I'd got her down as a singleton, but she popped two little ones out first thing this morning.'

'Oh good.'

'Yup, and they both seem to be doing well. Oh, and the lamb whose mother died seems to have been fairly successfully adopted by another ewe who lost a lamb, so things are looking up.'

'Great!'

A silence ensued. It had to be filled. I felt myself blushing. The whole room seemed hot.

'And – and the cows?' I faltered.

He grinned. 'The cows are fine, thank you, and I'm sure they'll be pleased to hear you've been asking after them. Shall I give them your best?'

He was laughing at me. I bit my lip. I could feel tears gathering behind my eyes. I turned away and lifted the top of the Aga, putting the kettle on to boil. It boiled almost immediately and I poured myself a coffee. Still I couldn't bear the silence. I had to fill it, however clumsily, however stupidly. I must seize new, harmless topics.

'I wonder how – how they're getting on back at the agency! Without us, I mean – well, without you.'

Nick looked at his watch. 'Oh, I should think they're probably all in the pub by now, don't you? I mean, it is ten-thirty. That's where you all normally congregate when I'm away, isn't it?'

'Er, well, not always, now and again, I suppose. Yes, we do have the odd drink.'

He grinned, 'Well, why not? It's different when you're

working for yourself, of course. Time spent in the pub is money lost as far as I'm concerned.'

'Yes, yes, I suppose it is.'

Another silence. This was gruesome, truly gruesome, I'd never felt so uncomfortable with anyone in my whole life. I had to get away. I sidled towards the door clutching my coffee. Nick struggled to pull his second boot off, threw it on the floor and grinned up at me just as I'd reached the door.

'So how are you feeling?'

I turned. 'Me? Oh fine, fine.'

'Really?'

'Really. Well, no all right, ghastly actually. Got a bit of a headache.'

He laughed. 'I'm not surprised! You were drinking for England last night!'

'Was I? Oh, yes, well perhaps I did have a bit too much.'

'A bit? Polly, you could hardly stand!'

Really, this was hardly chivalrous, was it? To remind a girl the following morning of a totally uncharacteristic over-indulgence the night before?

'Well, yes, perhaps I didn't – you know, pace myself very well.'

Nick got up and went to the sink to wash his hands, but it was full of muesli. Without a word, he scooped it out by the handful and threw it in the bin. I stared at his back as he rinsed his hands. It was no good. At some point I would have to make reference to last night, and I might as well do it now while I had the advantage of addressing his back rather than his face.

I took a deep breath. 'Nick, I'm sorry about last night,' I burst out.

He grabbed a towel to dry his hands and turned to face me. 'What d'you mean?'

Oh God, this was too much. What did he want me to do, rewind last night's spool and run through it again for him?

I blushed. 'Oh well, you know. Throwing myself at you and all that. Can't think what got into me.'

'A litre of gin, perhaps?'

I grinned. 'You're right, I was a bit pickled.'

He sat down at the kitchen table and looked at me as I hovered by the door. 'Polly?'

I met his eyes.

He held out his hand. 'Come here,' he said softly.

'What?'

He beckoned me over. 'Come over here.'

I sidled gingerly across to the table. 'What, right over here?'

He grabbed my arm and pulled me down on to his lap. 'Yes, right over here!'

'No, I'm too heavy!' I squeaked. I kept one foot firmly on the floor, hoping it would take most of the weight. What was this – corporal punishment time? Was he going to put me over his knee and spank me for my outrageous behaviour last night?

'Now listen to me. There's no need to apologize for anything you did last night. I loved it.' He grinned. 'Especially the dance!'

I hung my head in shame.

'But you were so pissed, so unbelievably steaming, I just

had to send you up to bed on your own. I honestly think you would have passed out if we'd risked any funny business, either that or thrown up. I mean, you probably don't remember this, Polly, but at one stage you were rambling on about barns. You kept talking about wanting to go to a barn, d'you remember that?'

'Um, vaguely,' I muttered. I flushed to my toes.

'At that point I thought you'd got serious alcohol poisoning.'

'Sorry,' I mumbled.

'Don't be sorry, it doesn't matter. God, we've all been in that state. I just didn't want to respond too eagerly in case I got my face slapped in the morning.'

I struggled to make sense of this earth-shattering turn of events. 'Oh! So you mean – you weren't necessarily that averse to my, um – you know, advances?'

He smiled. 'Not necessarily that averse, no.'

'Oh! So, so – oh. So . . .' I stumbled on, vainly trying to get my dehydrated grey matter around this revelation, and wondering what it signified. 'So, what you're saying is, that in a way, you almost liked them. My advances, I mean.'

He threw back his head and roared with laughter. 'Yes, I think we could safely say that I almost liked them, most certainly, Polly, yes.' He stopped laughing and just smiled, rather tenderly in fact. 'To tell you the truth, I've been thinking about them for some time now.'

I gulped. He looked utterly serious.

'Really?' I breathed.

'Really.'

I wanted to say I'd spent every waking moment thinking about his advances too, but that would have sounded silly. I sat as still as I possibly could on his knee. A silence enveloped us, but I couldn't fill the gaps any more, couldn't think of any words. I just felt dumb with longing.

In the event, no words were necessary. Nick gazed into my red-rimmed eyes which must have looked remarkably like road maps. I held my breath. He cupped my face in his hand and tilted it towards him. And then he kissed me. Softly and gently. At length, we parted, and as I breathed again I realized I'd been kissed like that once before. Of course, last night. As he held me tightly against him, I was relieved to hear his breath roaring in my ear. At least this time I wasn't the only one with respiratory problems.

'So,' he whispered, puffing a bit, 'shall we go upstairs?'

I opened my mouth to answer, thought better of it, and nodded. Surely if I just stuck to nodding I couldn't cock it up too comprehensively?

We climbed the stairs hand in hand. Those stairs had seen a lot of action one way and another. Twelve hours ago they'd borne me up in the depths of despair, now they bore me up in ecstasy. I felt as if any minute now someone might appear from behind a curtain, snap a clapperboard in front of my nose and cry, 'Right! Take three, Miss McLaren, let's try those stairs one more time, but this time we'll do the despair again, shall we?'

But no. We reached the top and walked hand in hand down the passageway that led inevitably to his bedroom.

But once inside I hesitated. I felt suddenly shy and awkward. My face was a mess and I had none of the gung-ho, alcohol-induced courage of the night before. I looked at him apprehensively. I did hope he wasn't just being kind. Charitable even.

'Nick, I do hope we're doing the right thing. I mean, it would be a shame to spoil our – you know – our friendship and everything, shouldn't we –'

But my heart wasn't in it, and anyway, whatever else I'd been going to say was lost as he took me in his arms and kissed me very firmly on the mouth.

'For once in your life, would you just shut up?' he asked reasonably.

What was a girl to do? I demurred, and let him kiss me again.

We were just inside the bedroom door. Still we kissed. Filled with a sudden desperate greed, and impatient as ever, it occurred to me that we still had a lot of floor space to cover before we were to make contact with the double bed and enjoy the pleasures of the horizontal, but I needn't have worried, Nick was alive to this. He wisely rejected carrying me, but steered me gently towards the bed. Still locked in each other's arms, and indulging in yet more passionate lip contact, we sank down on to the duvet with awesome choreography. This was obviously meant to be. As he went on to address my ear, my mouth and my neck and ultimately, of course, my buttons, he whispered tenderly in my ear.

'Sorry if I smell of cow shit.'

I giggled, delighted that someone else was feeling disadvantaged on account of their slovenly ways.

'Couldn't matter less. Sorry about the bloodshot eyes, the dog breath, the sweaty palms . . .'

'I love it . . . all of it,' he muttered back.

It was quite some time before we muttered again. When we did, he was lying on his back, one arm around my shoulder, and I was nestled up against him, my head resting on his bare chest and my arm thrown across it.

'Happy?' he murmured.

'Delirious,' I muttered back.

He smiled and stroked my hair. I studied his chest as it rose gently up and down, centimetres from my eyeballs. It was a pale, biscuity-brown colour with a discreet little smattering of dark hairs growing in a clump in the middle. I wondered how well I would get to know that clump. My eyes travelled up along his neck, and came to rest on his chin, which jutted out dramatically above me. It looked like the Rock of Gibraltar from my vantage point. I traced round it with my finger and smiled, 'Well, who would have thought?'

'Who would have thought what?'

'Exactly.' I grinned and shifted up on to my elbow to look at him. 'You don't remember, do you? That's what you said to me last night and that was exactly my reaction. Who would have thought what?'

He laughed. 'I suppose I must have meant, who would have thought this could finally happen.'

'Are you happy about it?' I asked tentatively, not wanting to spoil anything, but needing to know that it hadn't been a horrible mistake on his part and that he wasn't even now plotting how to get me on the next train to London.

He reached up and pulled me down towards him. 'You bet I am.' He kissed my nose. 'You're beautiful, Polly.'

I smiled, hugging the words to myself. I wasn't beautiful. I was rather overweight, my features were not desperately regular, and this morning did not find me at my best, but if he said it, I could feel it. He went on staring at me and, oddly enough, instead of squirming away and hiding behind my hair, the more he looked, the better I felt.

We lay there, locked in each other's arms, and would no doubt have embarked on a stream of tender pillow-talk for the next hour or two if my tummy hadn't decided it was time to register a protest. It had, of course, rejected the muesli some time earlier on the grounds that it might not have stayed put, but now it was rumbling noisily and clamouring to be given a second chance.

Nick laughed. 'Something tells me you need some blotting paper to mop up last night's excesses.'

I smiled ruefully. 'I suppose I am a bit hungry, but I'll survive.'

There was no way food was coming between me and pillow-talk. I snuggled up to him. My tummy had other ideas. Mount Vesuvius eat your heart out, I thought, as it rumbled again.

Nick laughed. 'Bloody hell, you'll erupt in a minute . . . Come on, let's eat, you're in danger of wasting away.'

'That'll be the day. I always used to wish for anorexia at Christmas when I got the wishbone.' I sighed. 'But you're right, I'm starving. I'll get up and get us some breakfast – or lunch even.' I glanced at his bedside clock. It seemed to be twelve-thirty.

He kissed my shoulder. 'Let's have it in bed.'

'Oh yes, let's!'

How unlike Harry he was, who had always wanted to get up as quickly as possible and get on with the important things in life, which had never included me.

I threw back the covers and climbed out of bed. He

pulled me back down again. 'I'll get it, you stay here. I want to come back and find you exactly as you are.'

I sank back down on to the pillows again. My whole body seemed to be wreathed in smiles. Oh joy! A man who actually wanted to do things for me! I was totally unused to this; it was a long time since I'd been out with anyone who wasn't a complete and utter bastard.

Nick got up and I was treated to a quick glimpse of his broad brown back before he pulled on his jeans and a shirt. He smiled down at me as he tucked the shirt into his jeans.

'You look fabulously wild and dishevelled. Don't move an inch. Just stay exactly like that and I'll be back in five minutes complete with tea and toast.'

'I won't move a muscle,' I said in a ventriloquist's voice, without moving my lips.

He grinned and leaned down to plant a kiss on my forehead. 'Peanut butter or Marmite?' he murmured.

'Peanut butter.'

And off he went, thundering noisily down the stone stairs. I heard him singing along to the radio as he clattered around in the kitchen, getting out mugs, boiling the kettle, making toast. I stretched luxuriously, feeling like the cat who's not only got the cream but the whole dairy too. I couldn't have been happier. He thought I was beautiful. Wild and dishevelled, eh? If only he knew how easy it was to look like that; it was sophisticated and elegant that caused the problems.

How wild, I wondered? I nipped out of bed and stole across to the oval mirror propped up on a chest of drawers. My face was quite attractively flushed and my eyes had widened considerably; there was a definite sparkle about them, too. Not bad, I thought appraisingly, not too bad at all considering the very raw material of first thing this morning. My hair was all over the place, but that apparently was no bad thing, and thank God I'd washed all that make-up off. It would be decorating his pillows by now.

I hopped back into bed and drew the sheets up under my chin. My feet took it upon themselves to do a little jig of joy under the duvet. So. Here I was at last. In Nick's bedroom. I took a good look around the room. It was perfect. Not like Harry's with its silly futon and oh-so-tasteful minimalist bits and pieces, but cluttered and lived in and – yes, welcoming.

The walls were Wedgwood blue with an indistinct criss-cross pattern, and the carpet a darker blue and very worn, with a series of reddish Persian rugs strewn over it, probably hiding a few holes. The bookcase underneath the window was crammed with books, which jostled each other for space and spewed out on to the floor, and the drawers in the huge chest on which the mirror sat were mostly open, with clothes falling out of them. A series of hunting prints covered one wall, and on another there were a few old maps. Above the bed was a rather modern, and quite good, painting of the house.

The room was untidy, but not massively so. Of course it had nothing on my sluttish tendencies, but it definitely showed promise. The bedside table, for instance, was covered with a thin film of dust, and in one corner of the room a pair of dirty jeans, some old socks, and a jumper lay festering in a heap. A nice touch, I thought. There were no photos either. Good. I liked a man who didn't wear his heart in his picture frames.

Balancing on top of the curtain pelmet were a few old Airfix planes. They brought a lump to my throat. He really had grown up in here. I wondered if he'd made the planes with his father. I wondered what he'd been like. Suddenly I wanted to know everything about him, about his parents, his childhood – everything. That was the joy of it all. We were at the beginning, with so much to find out about each other. I smiled to myself. Happiness flooded through every vein.

I plumped up the pillows and arranged myself decoratively upon them, with my hair spread out like a fan around my face. Then I set about my cleavage with a vengeance, draping the duvet seductively so it just covered my boobs but left quite a lot protruding voluptuously over the top. I positioned my arms to wedge the duvet in position, but made sure they didn't actually touch my sides or they'd look fat. I looked down. All was in order. Thus arranged, I waited. He'd been gone at least five minutes now, hadn't he? What was he doing, making the bread? Picking the tea? I smiled to myself. No. He was probably doing something terribly sweet like picking flowers for the tray. I'd pretend to be really surprised. 'Nick! Daffodils, how gorgeous!' I'd cry as he pressed a large bunch into my arms.

But wait a minute? What was that? Was that Nick's voice? Yes, it was, who on earth was he talking to? I frowned. There was another voice down there too. Female at that. Rachel? Surely she wasn't back already! No, it couldn't be Rachel, it must be – yes, of course, it must be Sarah! Sarah, over from the stables for a break and a cup of coffee. Of course. Hopefully Nick would get rid of her, tactfully. We could always ring her later of course, ask her over for a cup of tea. If we weren't indulging in a spot of afternoon delight, that is. I allowed myself a quiet little squeak of excitement – eeeeek! It really was all too thrilling!

The next minute I heard heavy footsteps bounding up the stairs. Goody-goody! I gave the duvet a last-minute adjustment and smiled eagerly. The door flew open and Nick came in. He stood in the doorway. His face was pale and drawn and the muscle in his cheek was bobbing up and down. The sweet, tender look of ten minutes ago was nowhere to be seen. He didn't say anything for a moment.

'What is it? What's happened?' I whispered in alarm.

Nick came over and sat down on the edge of the bed. He ran his hands through his hair. He looked shattered. 'I'm afraid we'll have to postpone our lunch, Polly, we've got a visitor.'

'Why? Who is it?'

He looked down at the duvet. There was a terrible silence. I felt my heart pause in mid-beat, then it started hammering away somewhere in the vicinity of my mouth. What on earth was going on?

'Nick, who is it? Who's downstairs?'

Funnily enough I knew the moment I'd said it. Nick merely confirmed my fears. He looked up and met my eyes.

'It's Serena,' he said quietly.

Chapter Twenty-two

'Serena!' I sat bolt upright.

Nick looked wretched. 'She's just arrived, I'm afraid. Look, Polly, I'll try and explain –'

'Darling? Darling, are you upstairs?' A strange bird-like trill interrupted us, warbling up from below, shrieking down the passageway, careering round the bedroom door, and hitting me full in the face like a runaway train. Those were Serena's dulcet tones, all right.

'You'd better go,' I whispered, suddenly filled with panic at the thought of her venturing upstairs and appearing at the door in all her Armani glory to witness this sordid little scene. 'Go on, quick. She might come up!'

Nick looked at my stricken face and took my hand, giving it a reassuring little squeeze. 'I'll explain everything later, Polly. It's just that – well, she's terribly vulnerable at the moment, and I really don't want to hurt her if it's at all possible. You do understand, don't you?'

He looked at me beseechingly and I nodded bravely, understanding precisely nothing. Hurt her? How about hurting me? Vulnerable, eh? Yes well, if you must know, I felt about as vulnerable as an open wound. An open wound that's just been on the receiving end of a Bruce Lee kung-fu kick, one of those flashy sideways ones that comes at you out of nowhere – ha-ya-ho! – and leaves you doubled up on the floor, spluttering and gasping for breath.

'Dar-*ling*!' There it was again, that voice; shrill, clear and confident, ricocheting off the bedroom walls.

Nick dropped my hand hurriedly and disappeared.

I lay there for a second feeling numb. Then I crawled slowly out of bed and fumbled around for my jeans and jumper. A tear dropped on to the Persian rug as I sat down to pull on my socks. I blinked hard. You silly little fool, I thought savagely, did you really think you were meant to be that happy? Don't you know the story of your life by now? What made you think you could start rewriting it at this late stage?

I found a comb and pulled it through my hair, looking in the mirror. The same mirror that moments earlier had revealed a flushed, excited, happy Polly. Now it revealed a white-faced, scared little creature with wet eyes and a trembling jaw.

I faced my reflection and addressed it sternly in a stage whisper. 'Pull yourself together, will you? OK, so the girl-friend who you'd both conveniently forgotten has arrived – it had to happen some time, didn't it? And just remember this, he's very, very fond of you. No one, *no one*, could have pretended like that back there – I eyed the crumpled sheets meaningfully – without being very, very, well, fond.' Ghastly word. One could be fond of a ham-ster, but one wouldn't necessarily want to spend the rest of one's life with it. I revised my adjective. 'Special, then. You're very special, OK?' I commanded my reflection. Somehow it didn't look convinced. What seemed to me to be more convincing was the blatant truth, but could I take it?

I eyed myself menacingly. 'OK, try this one for size, wobble-jaw. Nick Penhalligan is madly in love with the extraordinarily beautiful actress Serena Montgomery, who, unfortunately, is too busy attending to her glittering career to be with him for much of the time, so out of sheer frustration, and on the spur of a mad and lecherous moment, he bonks his secretary, Polly McLaren, of whom he is reasonably fond.'

I gulped hard. It certainly rang true. My reflection nodded back dumbly. Yes, that seemed to be much more like it. In which case, where did that leave me now? I felt panic rising within me. What was I doing upstairs? Tidying the airing cupboard? Dusting the bedrooms? Just making myself useful? What did concubines do, I wondered?

I buried my face in my hands, but only for a second. Then I shook myself. No, there was no doubt about it, she had to be faced, but this time – I flew out of Nick's room and ran down the passageway to mine – with war paint on and guns blazing.

Feverishly, I slapped on a protective coating of blusher, eyeliner, mascara and lipstick, then, suitably masked, I marched downstairs, summoning up as much of the old Dunkirk spirit as I could possibly muster. OK, I was going down, of that there was no doubt, but I wasn't going down without a fight.

However, all ideas of fighting Serena on the beaches disappeared in a little puff of smoke as I walked into the drawing room. My guns gave a brief splutter, a windy little fart, and died. She was sitting, or should I say, reclining, on the sofa, armed up to the eyeballs with beauty, poise and, what's more, a glass of white wine and a cigarette. Here she had me at an immediate disadvantage – what I wouldn't do for a cigarette, I thought, eyeing her pack enviously – but it was her staggering beauty that had me disadvantaged in a much more serious manner. We're talking crippled, actually.

How could her eyes be as green and sparkling as that? And did those cheekbones seriously shoot off into her temples in such a breathtaking manner? And was her complexion really so clear and peachy? What the devil was Nick up to, playing around with a flaky old yobbo like me when he had this devastating creature in tow? Was he insane? Or blind? Or perhaps her beauty intimidated him? It certainly intimidated the hell out of me.

As I came in, she ran a hand through her ash-blonde hair and stood up; not, you understand, out of any sense of politeness, but purely to give me the benefit of her devastating figure. The long, long legs seemed to take an eternity to unfurl and straighten and, as they sauntered towards me, clad in brown suede and topped with a cream silk shirt, I realized that, whereas I in my pancake make-up and tight jeans looked just wrong, she, on the other hand, looked just right. Not too glamorous for the country, but stunning enough to put anyone else to shame. In fact, come to think of it, she reminded me of a beautiful young filly: long-limbed, beautifully groomed, and gleaming to perfection, even down to her shiny little feet, shod as they were in expensive Italian leather and gleaming like newly oiled hooves.

There was simply no competition. I know when I'm

beaten. This was Nick's girlfriend all right, she had it written all over her.

I shuffled towards her, forcing a smile and feeling like
somebody's mother. 'Hi,' was all I could manage.

'Well, hello,' she said, raising her eyebrows as she extended
an icy white hand complete with immaculate red nails.

I took it gingerly, then dropped it hurriedly as Nick
appeared in the doorway with a tray full of coffee. I wasn't
standing next to her for comparison, no siree. I shuffled
off to my basket in the corner and curled up on a cushion.
I knew my place, and it was low, very low. Definitely floor
level.

Serena evidently knew her place, too, and it seemed to
be reclining on the arm of the sofa, head back, legs
crossed, arm flung out along the back of the sofa with all
her assets to the fore. If truth be told, it was an old trick
of mine, but one she did with a lot more style.

Nick set the coffee down and had the grace to look
sheepish. He turned to Serena. 'You remember Polly,
don't you?'

'Of course I do.' She swivelled the green headlamps in
my direction and smiled benignly. 'Goodness only knows
where you'll turn up next, though! One minute you're
behind a typewriter, then you're floundering around in a
freezer, and now you're lolling around down here! I mean,
really, whatever next?' She gave her silly, tinkly little laugh.

'Yes, that's me,' I muttered darkly. 'Ubiquitous.'

She frowned. 'What did you call me?'

'When?'

'Just then, you said you – something-or-other, what was
it?' she sounded angry.

448

'Ubiquitous. It's an adjective, not an insult.'

'Oh.' She frowned again and I saw Nick suppress a smile.

Actually, an insult was what I really would have liked to have hurled at her, along with some incredibly heavy pieces of furniture, like that mahogany chest over there, or those thumping great fire irons in the grate. I didn't like her sneering manner, nor did I like the freezer reference or the secretary tag. I flexed my not so much bitten as tapered nails, feeling well out of practice, and looked searchingly at her as if her face temporarily escaped me.

'. . . and it's um, Selina, isn't it?'

She looked taken aback for a moment, then her eyes narrowed and the lips tightened. 'Serena,' she hissed. 'Serena Montgomery!'

'Ah yes, of course, sorry.'

I smiled sweetly and wondered what my next mode of attack should be, but my heart wasn't in it and I felt weary already. Cat fights weren't really my scene; I didn't have the nails for it. Anyway, let's face it, why shouldn't she be angry, if not livid? She was, after all, the incumbent girlfriend – although let's not mention that: she might think I was suggesting she had bandy legs – and here was I, a usurper, lolling around, as she so eloquently put it, her boyfriend's house. Sorry, seat. Well, yes, that too.

'So how long will you be with us for, Polly?' she enquired, neatly ramming home the fact that she and Nick were very much an 'us', a couple, and since three was surely a crowd, should I not perhaps be thinking about boarding the very next train back to London?

'Oh, I don't know really, not very long. Haven't really

thought,' I muttered miserably, thinking – just as soon as I've stolen your cigarettes.

'Sweet of Nick to ask you down; he said you needed a break. I do hope you're feeling better?'

I glanced at Nick, but he had his back to me as he poured the coffee. So that's what he'd said by way of explanation. The benevolent employer was treating one of his menials from the workhouse to a holiday. Some poor deserving wretch, who did nothing but bash away at a word processor all day until her hands were red and raw, and who had eventually fallen on her screen in a state of nervous exhaustion, had been magnanimously rescued by her big-hearted boss, who'd whisked her away to breathe some clean, country air at his stately home. Services to shorthand no doubt. I glanced beseechingly at the back of Nick's head. Couldn't he just turn around for a second? Give me a little look to say, Don't worry, Polly, everything's going to be OK? Apparently not.

'Yes,' I sighed. 'Very good of him.'

At that moment there was a tap on the window. One of Nick's farm hands was standing outside. Nick went over and opened it.

'Sorry to disturb you, Nick,' he said, sticking his head through, 'but there's a ewe out here I'd like you to have a look at. She's cut herself quite badly on some wire. It's a pretty nasty wound, we might need the vet.'

'Damn.' Nick set his coffee down. 'There's too much of that bloody wire around; I thought I'd asked you to clear it all. All right, Larry, I'm coming.' He took a cigarette from Serena's pack and swept out through the French doors.

I watched him go. He strode purposefully through the garden, smartly vaulted the fence, and marched off towards his sheep in the far field. Well, thanks a bunch, I thought bitterly. When the going gets tough, the tough go shepherding. It briefly crossed my mind to follow suit and head for the wide open spaces myself, leaving Serena to bitch away to the fireplace on her own, but as usual my nerve failed and I stayed rooted to the floorboards, looking up at her expectantly like a subservient first-former waiting to see if the head girl would be handing out detention today.

'You're bound to feel better soon,' she tinkled on. 'This place is such a marvellous tonic. I always come down when I'm feeling a bit – you know, rough.'

What was I supposed to be, a drug addict going through cold turkey? A drying-out alcoholic? What sort of garbage had Nick been feeding her?

'Actually, I'm perfectly all right,' I said in a level voice, adding, with an uncharacteristic show of spirit, 'in fact, there's nothing wrong with me at all, never has been. Nick just invited me down for a holiday.'

She ignored me and carried on as if I hadn't spoken. 'The sea air will do wonders for your complexion, of course. You must get Nick to take you sailing: he has a darling little boat, and Frenchman's Creek is absolutely magical at this time of year.'

All my complexion needed was a day or two off the juice and eight or nine hours uninterrupted sleep, thank you very much, and anyway, on closer inspection I decided that a great deal of hers was out of a bottle. I also realized that she wasn't quite as young as I'd originally supposed;

she definitely had three or four years on me. I revised my previous description from filly to mare and felt about a millimetre better.

I wondered if I could slip away now, run upstairs to my bedroom and hide under the duvet, or slink off to the stables for a chat with Sarah, but as I tentatively tried to raise myself up from the floor, Serena fixed me with her beady eye and warbled off in her stagey voice again. I fell, winded, pinned and gasping beneath the weight of her mighty RADA monologue.

'. . . Yes, I come down here whenever I can, I simply love it, it makes me feel human again. People just don't realize how bloody hard acting is, they really don't. The hours are simply appalling for a start, up at dawn for make-up, and then shooting all day, usually in the blistering heat of some sub-tropical jungle or desert. I mean, people think it's glamorous, but it really isn't. They see us scampering around in foreign locations and think, Wow! What a fantastic life; but what they don't realize is that I'm sweltering away under the weight of some ghastly seventeenth-century costume and positively dripping under my make-up and those hellish lights. And the people! Ugh, I can't tell you. Sometimes I'm convinced I'm doomed to be surrounded by morons, you know.' (Here she gave me a searching look and I wondered if perhaps I'd just become chief moron, a walk-on part only, of course; chief, spear-carrying moron.) '. . . If it's not some idiot of a director telling me how to read my lines, it's some goon of a lighting cameraman – usually foreign because our ridiculous union rules dictate that we have to employ a certain amount of natives – telling me where he wants me to stand, as if I don't know by now. Some of them don't even speak English, you know! I can't tell you how frustrating that is. It happened to me in Delhi just the other day. Some cretin of a native tried to tell me my job, and he couldn't even speak the lingo! I mean, really. They say travel broadens the mind, but as far as I'm concerned it just reinforces prejudices, d'you know what I mean?'

I'd been staring fixedly at a matchstick that was wedged between a gap in the floorboards. I pushed it down with my fingernail and it slipped through, down to the bowels of the earth. I longed to slip down with it, but I managed to raise my aching eyes and murmur, 'Oh, yes, quite, absolutely.'

'No no, give me good old England any day,' she warbled on gaily. 'You know, sometimes I literally have to just close my eyes and – as the expression goes – think of England. I do, really I do. I'll be playing some ghastly love scene with some revolting ham actor with bad breath, and I try to imagine I'm back here on the farm with Nick. I imagine I'm helping with the baby lambs, or – or that we're drifting up the river together, lying back in the boat in the sunshine, my hand skimming along in the water as we row quietly up and down. It's my way of preserving my sanity, do you see?'

I nodded. I was wilting steadily and I had a nasty sicky feeling in my stomach. I had a shrewd idea she was playing a very clever game.

'I picture we're gently floating up Frenchman's Creek. I see the glistening water, the overhanging willow trees, I hear the sound of the seagulls circling overhead –'

'Yes, I've been actually,' I said, with a sudden flash of bravado.

'Oh, really?'

'With – with Tim and Sarah,' I added, coward that I am.

'Ah yes, you'll know all about it then. It is utterly divine, isn't it?'

'Oh yes, utterly,' I mumbled. This RADA lark was catching, but I couldn't help wondering where the eulogy on Frenchman's Creek was getting us. She didn't keep me in suspense for long, bless her.

'I simply adore it, it's quite my most special place.' She put her head on one side and gave me what I can only describe as a Dame Edna smile. 'Of course, you know why, don't you?'

'Er, no.' I felt like a rat in a trap.

The eyebrows shot up. 'You mean, he didn't tell you?'

'Tell me what?'

'That that's where he proposed to me, of course! In Frenchman's Creek!'

I gasped audibly. 'Proposed!'

'Yes, didn't you know?' There was a nasty glint in her eye and she glowed with triumph. 'In his dear little boat. Down on one knee he went. God, I remember it so clearly, we were wobbling around all over the place, in fact we nearly capsized – I promise you it was priceless!'

Her tinkly laugh homed in on my nerve centre and it seemed to me that I was being slowly but surely electro-cuted.

'He was so sweet, I'll never forget how he asked me. He didn't say, "Will you marry me", or anything boring like that, he said, "Serena, would you do me the honour of becoming my wife?" – isn't that just too divine? Of course I spoiled the dignity of the whole occasion by leaping up and crying, "Yes! Yes! Yes!" I was so excited! Then I just fell on him, simply covering him with kisses, and then of course the whole thing got totally out of hand and we ended up in a tangled heap at the bottom of the boat, giggling hysterically as the boat rocked perilously from side to side – I tell you, we were lucky not to go in!'

I wondered if I could just quietly be sick in that potted begonia without her noticing – or perhaps, yes, perhaps the coal bucket by the fire would stand up to my projections a little better. There might be rather a lot of it. I nodded, biting back the bile.

'Anyway, when we'd, you know, straightened ourselves out a bit – because actually the river isn't *all* that private and you never know *who's* going to cruise up beside you; there are all kinds of nosy parkers around – anyway, that's when he produced the most darling little ring from his pocket – look!'

She thrust her hand under my nose and wiggled her finger around. A very pretty antique gold ring with a jade stone winked up at me.

I gulped. 'V-very pretty.'

'Of course, it's only a makeshift ring, until I find something more suitable – you know, diamonds or sapphires maybe, but I think I'll always wear it anyway. It's charming, isn't it?'

'It certainly is,' I managed.

'He said he bought it because it matched my eyes.'

'Yes, yes it does,' I whispered, clutching a handy Queen Anne chair leg for support.

'Lord knows when we'll find time to get married, though. We're both just so busy. I've got this new film coming up, and Nick's got to tie up the agency – you know he's selling out, don't you?'

'Yes, yes I know.' This at least was one piece of news that didn't come as a total shock.

'So anyway, it could be a while, but at least we've made the commitment. I think that's so important, don't you? So many people these days don't make that commitment, and I think it's a mistake, I really do.'

I mumbled a suitable response. I'd collapsed in a little heap now, and the more I paled and wilted, the more Serena seemed to exult and billow and triumph.

She lit yet another precious cigarette, put her gleaming blonde head on one side, and smiled that caring little smile again. 'I do hope you won't take this the wrong way, Polly?'

I gulped. All sorts of things seemed to be going down the wrong way, one more surely wouldn't make much difference.

'Fire away,' I said bravely, and didn't she just.

'It's just that, well, I met Jack Crawley on the way over here, and he said you'd been making a bit of a fool of yourself, one way and another.'

I gasped. 'What d'you mean?'

Serena held up her hand to stop me. 'Now, there's no need to explain, really. I can quite understand how it happened. I know that Nick is a very attractive man, and I don't blame you for falling for him, but the point is that – well, he's finding it all just a teensy bit embarrassing.'

'That's not true!' I could feel myself going scarlet.

'Oh, I can assure you it is,' she said in a steely voice. 'Why d'you think he rushed off to deal with his sheep like that? Larry was quite capable of sorting out that little problem, but Nick was just glad of an excuse to get away. He's fearfully embarrassed about the whole thing. You really do moon around after him, you know.'

'I do not moon around!' I flushed angrily.

'Oh, but you do, everyone's noticed it. Why, Jack told me you follow Nick around like a little dog. Honestly, Polly, I'm only telling you this so you don't make a complete idiot of yourself. It was wrong of Nick not to tell you we're engaged, but perhaps he thought you wouldn't be able to take it.'

I stared down at my shoes, wishing I was a million miles away. I wanted to tell her where we'd been when she'd arrived, what we'd been doing, but I hadn't the nerve.

I licked my lips. 'Has Nick said anything?'

'I'm afraid he has. Of course he blames himself, he knows he should never have been so weak, but I am away an awful lot and it's terribly difficult for a man when a girl – well, when she throws herself at him, d'you know what I mean? Especially when he's been – well, doing without it for a while. One can understand how he might just – you know, go for it.'

I caught my breath. The bastard, how could he? I didn't trust myself to speak, and carried on staring at the fascinating top stitching on my shoes.

'Now, Polly, don't look so glum. You know as well as I do that boys will be boys. The poor dears find it so frightfully difficult to control themselves, and when the cat's away' – she shrugged – 'well, look what happens. Now, I'm not suggesting he's totally blameless, but I think you'll admit that most men would find it pretty hard to resist when it's handed to them on a plate like that.'

Please, could I just die quietly now? Don't let me live any longer, God, please! Had he really told her? Or was she just guessing wildly? I daren't look up. There was a long pause. My face was flaming as it faced the carpet. Any minute now it would surely just melt and drip steadily through that rug into the floorboards.

'Anyway,' she said at length, 'I don't want to make a big thing of it, I just want you to know that I'm not a fool and I know what you're up to, OK?'

My eyes remained glued to my shoes.

'And I don't want to be brutal, but you must realize that hanging around here is doing you no good at all. You're just making everyone feel uncomfortable: Nick, me, all of us. You do see that, don't you?'

I nodded miserably.

'The trains to London are pretty frequent, you know. I could give you a lift to the station if you just wanted to slip off quietly? There's no rush, of course.'

I met her eye with difficulty. 'Don't worry. I won't be hanging around making things uncomfortable for you. I'll be off just as soon as I've packed – and I'd rather walk to the station, thank you very much.'

She smirked, 'You'll find it's rather a long way, I'm afraid, but as you wish.'

She ground her cigarette out in an ashtray, and brushed her hands together lightly as if that little piece of business had been successfully concluded. Having made mince-meat of me, she turned her attention to the house. She got up and glided round the room, pausing here and there to wipe dust from a picture frame or rearrange a piece of china. Her eye swept around proprietorially.

'I really must do something about this room. Honestly, when I'm not here the place just goes to rack and ruin. These ghastly covers are finally falling to bits: a blessing in disguise, I think; perhaps Nick will finally get some new ones.' She fingered the lovely faded old chintz on the sofa. 'And as for these dirty old rugs, they've been here for ever.'

I was tempted to suggest that this was entirely their charm, but decided against it as she kicked the beautiful Persian rug with her expensive Italian boot. I didn't want to be on the receiving end of that toe-cap. No doubt in her mind's eye she already had the whole place carpeted wall to wall in off-white shag-pile.

She strolled towards me and I shrank back in terror, wondering what adjustments she had in mind – a biff on the nose perhaps, or a nice black eye – but no, she was making for the begonia. She fingered the soil in the pot and I fervently wished that I'd stuck to plan A and thrown up in it. She shook her head, tutting loudly.

'You see, no one even bothers to water the plants. If I'm not here to do it, they just keel over and die. I must talk to Nick about getting someone to help out here: a daily or, even better, someone to live in. This place needs a good seeing-to. If we're going to live here when we're married, I won't be able to see to it all on my own; I'm simply not used to that sort of thing. I must have some staff.'

She looked down at me, curled up as I was in a pathetic, squirming little bundle at her feet. She put her head on one side and eyed me speculatively. Good grief, was she sizing me up as a potential cleaner? Was she wondering if

I wouldn't in fact do nicely? Why not? I was already on the pay roll, I could just change my position. From secretary to char in one swift little demotion. I had a sudden, powerful urge to grab her elegant little ankles, rugby tackle her to the floor and kick her smartly in the teeth. Unfortunately I controlled it and, instead, in a totally shameless manner, blurted out my most overpowering need.

'D'you think I could possibly have one of your cigarettes?' It couldn't be helped. Unless I got some nicotine into these gasping lungs, they'd seize up.

She was all concern and benevolence. 'Of course!' she purred, pressing the packet into my hand like Maundy money. 'Take the packet. Goodness, your hand's shaking, you poor thing.'

'I don't want the packet,' I said petulantly. 'I've got some somewhere, I just can't remember where I've put them, that's all.'

'Of course you can't,' she said consolingly, 'you must be in a terrible muddle at the moment. I bet you don't know if you're coming or going!'

'Oh, I've got a pretty shrewd idea I'm going,' I muttered darkly, 'but don't worry about me. I'm fine,' I said, grabbing a box of matches and lighting the cigarette. It wasn't easy, as the match wobbled alarmingly in my hand. I sucked the nectar down to my boots.

'Really? Are you sure you're all right?' She glided over and sat down next to me in the Queen Anne, crossing her elegant ankles. 'Only, I hope you don't mind me mentioning it, but I hear Nick's not the only man you've fallen for recently. You've got rather a tangled love life at the moment, haven't you? Mmmm?'

'What d'you mean!' What on earth did she have up her sleeve now? A jack-knife? An anaconda? An Exocet missile? I kept a tight hold on my cigarette in case I needed to jab her in the eye with it.

'Well, I hear your last boyfriend gave you a rather rough ride. It was Harry Lloyd-Roberts, wasn't it?'

My jaw dropped. 'How on earth did you know about that?'

'Oh, everyone in London knows Harry, he's part of the scene. In fact, I even had a bit of a dalliance with him myself once, but he bored me after a while. He was frightfully upset when I dropped him, kept turning up at the studios uninvited, making a fool of himself; then he used to sit outside my flat in his car for days on end, just waiting for me to come out. He's dreamy looking, of course, but there's absolutely nothing at all between the ears. No substance whatsoever. You're much better off without him, you know.'

Was there no end to her charm? Would she just go on and on like this until someone put a bullet through her brain? Please could it be me? I'd heard about girls like this, read about them in the problem pages of women's magazines, real live bitches who took pleasure in pouring salt in wounds. Well, now I'd met one. Only this time, I thought with a small degree of satisfaction, she was wasting her time. She wasn't hurting me at all. I couldn't give a damn if she and Harry had bonked for Britain. The very thought was registering absolutely zero on my Richter scale of pain. Not a pang, not a twinge, not a sausage. Sorry, Serena.

I felt just a weeny bit stronger, but not enough to stand up, so when the telephone rang it was Serena who strolled off to answer it. Well, anyway, it was her phone, wasn't it? I lay down on the floor and gasped, glad of the chance to catch my breath. When she came back she looked rather annoyed.

'It's Tim. He wants to speak to you or Nick.'

'I'll take it,' I said, sprinting past her, desperate to talk to a normal human being. I grabbed the telephone.

'Tim?'

'Hi, Polly, how are you?'

'Oh er, OK. You?'

'Yes, I suppose so.'

'What's wrong? You sound a bit down.'

'So do you, come to that.'

'Well . . . I s'pose I am a bit.' Riveting stuff, eh?

'Listen . . .' he said, coming slowly to the point. 'Rachel and I thought we might come back, if the coast's clear, that is.'

'Oh yes, well clear. We saw Adam last night' – was it only last night? It felt about a year ago – 'and he swallowed the whole story. We did it rather well, actually. Nick checked with Mrs Green yesterday, and apparently he shot off back to London pretty sharpish.'

'Oh good, we'll come back then.' He sounded relieved. Was there a problem? Had Svengali and his pupil fallen out already? It wouldn't be hard, I admit, her sulky moods would try the patience of a saint; but Tim really was a bit of a saint on the quiet, and he'd been so keen to bring her out. Perhaps he'd just discovered there was nothing worth exposing.

'See you later then.'

'Yeh, see you, bye.'

I took the scenic route back to the drawing room, pausing *en route* to spend a couple of hours lying down on my bed. I was too upset to cry. Despair overwhelmed me. I just lay there looking at the ceiling, listening to my clock ticking. He was engaged to her. Engaged to be married, and I'd had no idea. I'd done it again, picked another bastard, and once more it was too late to do anything about it, I was head over heels in love with him. Oh God, what was I going to do? Go home pretty damn quick, that was for sure, either to London or to my parents, as long as it was far away. As soon as I'd got my strength up. I shut my eyes. To think I'd been presumptuous enough to imagine anyone in Nick's class could fall for someone as gauche and stupid as me when he had Serena – first-class bitch, granted, but beautiful and famous none the less – hanging on to his arm. How could I have been so ludicrous?

Chapter Twenty-three

I lay like that for an hour or more. Not crying, just staring into space, looking at the cracks in the ceiling. I could feel myself shaking a bit, so I pulled the duvet over me and hugged the pillow for comfort, burying my face in it. In actual fact I felt rather numb. I couldn't quite believe it was all true. I shut my eyes to block out the misery, and I suppose I must have dropped off, God knows I was tired enough, because the next thing I knew, I was opening my eyes and someone was knocking loudly on the door.

I reached out my hand and grabbed the clock by the bed. Ten past three. I must have been up here for ages. Who was at the door? Was it Nick? Had he come to find me? I sat up eagerly.

'Come in!'

Tim's head appeared around the door, followed by his body.

'Oh hi, Tim, you're back.' I tried not to sound disappointed.

'Yep, just arrived. I came to tell you lunch is ready. It's gone three o'clock, but no one seems to have eaten, so Sarah's rustled up a fish pie.'

'Thanks, I'll come down.'

Damn, I couldn't escape now. I'd have to put in an appearance at what would undoubtedly be one of the most grisly meals of my life. Tim turned to go, but lingered at the door, fiddling with the handle. He didn't look quite right somehow, his normally jolly, open face was pinched and haggard. He turned back. We both spoke at once.

'Are you all right?' we said in unison.

He laughed and I mustered a smile. He came over and sat on the side of the bed. I sat up and hugged my knees.

'What's wrong?' he said, peering into my face. 'You look absolutely terrible.'

Men never seem to learn that, even if we girls feel like death, we don't like to be told we look like it.

I grimaced. 'Oh, nothing.'

'Come on, what is it?'

Could I tell him? Right now I needed a friend extremely badly, but Nick's brother? And for all I knew he might be Serena's number one fan.

'I've just got a horrendous hangover, that's all. Totally self-inflicted. How about you?'

'Oh, er – well, yes, the same.' He looked shifty.

'Really? But you don't even drink, not properly, anyway.'

'Well, perhaps that's why I got so plastered, not used to it, you see.' He avoided my eyes and studied the wallpaper. Being such an accomplished liar myself, I can spot a porky pie a mile off. I reached out and put a hand on his arm.

'Tim? What is it? Is it Rachel?'

His face puckered up when I said her name, and I knew I'd hit the spot. They'd obviously fallen out in a big way.

'Have you had a row? Is that it?'

'Oh no,' he shook his head, 'nothing like that. Quite the . . . quite the reverse, really.'

The reverse? Quite the reverse of having a row? Well, what the devil was that then? They'd got on too well? Impossible. They'd got on so well that something untoward had happened? They'd got on so well that they'd ended up . . .

'Oh my goodness, Tim!'

Tim's shoulders sagged. He ran his hands through his hair and put his head in his hands. A guilty man if ever I saw one. I was staggered.

'Tim, you mean?'

Tim nodded into his hands, still avoiding my eye.

'Oh my God. You and Rachel? I just don't believe it!'

'Neither do I, now,' he whispered. 'I really can't believe it happened. But I promise you, Polly, at the time I felt absolutely powerless. I simply couldn't resist her. She was so . . .' he shook his head as he struggled to find the words, as well he might. 'Well, she was just so – so captivating, so, I don't know – irresistible, I suppose. And it all happened so quickly. One minute we were sitting downstairs chatting, and the next minute – the next minute we were in my bedroom. It was extraordinary, I just – I just couldn't help myself.'

Rachel? Captivating? Irresistible? Hang on a moment, did we have the same girl in mind here? Frumpy old, miserable old, bag lady Rachel? I struggled to get my mind around this one. Was he trying to tell me that that grumpy little heap of mouse droppings had, in the space of just one night, lured him away from his lovely, sparky, pretty girlfriend and succeeded in bewitching him to such an extent that he'd – had he?

'Did you?'

'What?'

'You know . . .'

He ran his hands through his hair and nodded. 'Yes, of course.' He'd ended up compromising himself wildly. Well, blow me, you had to hand it to her, didn't you? And here he was now, this handsome hunk of a man, reduced to a shivering pulp, eaten up with what I fervently hoped was remorse and not more desire.

'Do you regret it now?'

He wrenched his head out of his hands and groaned. 'Of course I bloody do, it was a stupid, irresponsible, idiotic thing to do, but I promise you, Polly, I just didn't stand a chance! I was putty in her hands, you can't imagine how – well, how downright sexy she was!'

I tried. I tried really hard, but no, he was right, I just couldn't imagine. It made you think, though, didn't it? I mean, all these years I'd been dousing myself in Chanel, pulling my necklines down, hitching my skirts up, endlessly crossing and uncrossing my legs, throwing back my hair, pulling it over one eye, practising smouldering looks in the mirror, cultivating a sexy voice, and do you know what I should really have been doing? I should have been taking piano lessons, twiddling my hair round my finger, sitting in a heap in a nasty grey cardigan and occasionally, for extra sensuality, donning a pair of tortoiseshell National Health spectacles. And there was I thinking that those spectacles were just another form of birth control, along with acne and bad breath. Ah well, we live and learn.

I was woken from this mind-boggling reverie by Tim, who was up to his elbows in confession. Once he'd started, he was determined to finish, as Magnus would say. He was over by the window, staring out at the fields, frantically unburdening himself to the sheep, the cows, the trees – anyone and anything that would listen.

'And yes, OK, I suppose I'd had a couple of glasses of wine, three maybe, which is more than I'd normally have, but that's no excuse, I certainly wasn't pissed. It just seemed so right, so natural. There we were, having supper in Penny's candlelit dining room which, as you can imagine, is pretty conducive to a little dinner *à deux* . . .'

Now this I could imagine. Penny's dining room would be magical in the evening, with its dark green walls smothered with oil paintings, and its cosy little alcove tables laden with silver; little hideaway places where two people could sit in relative privacy, their faces flickering in the candlelight, a cosy log fire crackling away in the grate beside them . . . Yes, I could imagine it would make quite a seduction scene. In fact, I made a mental note to reserve a table the next time an eligible young man wanted to take me out to a little country – oh well, forget that. There was never going to be a next time. It was the nunnery for me.

'Are you listening to me, Polly, because I can tell you this isn't the easiest story to tell.'

'Sorry, go on.'

'Over dinner, she started to tell me a bit about herself. I was really pleased, because you know how shy and withdrawn she can be, don't you?'

I ground my teeth together, dug my nails hard into the palm of my hand and nodded.

'She told me all about her mother dying when she was young, and how she grew up with just a father and a housekeeper, not even any brothers and sisters, and d'you know she wasn't even allowed to go out or have friends round?' Tim shook his head. 'Terrible. Then, of course, this Adam chap appeared on the scene. Just what she didn't need; I mean, he just sounds like a complete head-case. As far as I can gather, the man's completely barking. He was incredibly possessive, followed her around the whole time, wouldn't let her make her own friends – rather like her father actually. You know, one way and another, she's had a really hard time, Polly.'

'I know, I know, just get to the point,' I said quickly. 'Then what happened?'

I wanted to move this monologue on apace, I really didn't think I could stomach any more of Rachel's hard times on top of my own heartache and hangover.

'Well, we chatted on and on for ages. It's a long time since I've had a good chinwag, I'm always so bloody busy. She seemed really interested in me, asked lots of questions, and I told her all about Dad dying, something I realized I hadn't talked about for years. She was really sweet and sympathetic; well, she'd lost her mother, of course, so she knew how I felt. Then I told her all about the farm, and how I was determined to make it work, even though everyone assures me that organic farming is an economic disaster area, and she didn't say that. She was really supportive and encouraging.'

Well, she would be, wouldn't she? And come to that, wasn't Sarah too, who slogged away on his farm at the weekends after a gruelling week at the stables? Or was it only candlelit support that mattered? I bit my tongue.

Tim sighed. 'Well, I suppose after a while we'd exhausted

nearly every channel of conversation, and we just ended up looking at each other. You know how it is, Polly.'

I nodded, a woman of the world of wine bars. 'You exchanged a few meaningful looks?'

He sighed, 'Yes.'

'She looked down shyly, then up into your eyes again?'

'Well, yes.'

'She put her hand on the table?'

'Er, yes.'

'You covered it with yours?'

He looked surprised. 'Yes.'

'Your eyes met again, and this time you both held the gaze for a fraction longer than was absolutely necessary?'

'How on earth did you know that?'

I sighed. God he was naïve. 'Let's just say I recognize the signs. Then you paid the bill in silence while Rachel sat gazing at you, elbows on the table, her face cupped in her hands. You both got up slowly from the table, she took your hand, you walked out of the restaurant and, without another word, went upstairs?'

Tim looked miserable. 'I had no idea it was all so predictable.'

'Only thus far. It's the next bit that intrigues me. I mean, it could all have ended with a reasonably chaste, albeit lingering kiss on the lips at her bedroom door, after which she smiles sweetly, thanks you for a lovely evening, and slips into her room and then into her winceyette. On the other hand . . .'

'Er, yes, on the other hand?'

'You tell me, Tim.'

'Must I? You do it so well.' He sighed. 'OK, we did go

upstairs, and we did, you know, pause at her bedroom door because – well – I wanted to give her the opportunity to get rid of me if she wanted to. I even said goodnight.'

I nodded.

'And she didn't. Get rid of me I mean. She just strode on past, still holding my hand, until we got to my door. Then she took the key out of my trouser pocket – which was a hell of a turn on in itself, I can tell you – opened the door, and, well, naturally, in we went.'

I raised my eyebrows. 'Naturally.'

'Oh no, Polly, she wasn't pushy at all, it was so obviously going to happen anyway.'

'Maybe, but notice how it's Rachel who takes not only the initiative, but your hand, and the key to the door.'

My goodness, she was a smart cookie. She'd had her eye on him right from the word go, and nobody, certainly not Tim, had even suspected it. She'd had him for breakfast.

'How d'you feel about her now?' I asked.

He shrugged. 'Oh, I'm fond of her, of course,' I flinched at that word, 'but if truth be told it was just a one-night stand really, probably from her point of view, too. Don't get me wrong, it was great at the time; yes, it was really' – his eyes glazed over – 'great.'

I coughed.

'Oh, er, sorry, what I mean is, it was fun, but it didn't really mean anything, not in the heart department anyway. For goodness' sake, let's be grown-up about this, these things happen, don't they? Well, you'd know all about that, wouldn't you, Polly?'

'Thanks,' I said grimly

'Oh God, I didn't mean it like that. What I meant was,

you're not stupid. You know as well as I do that it's easy to get carried away, or rather, you know how easy it is for men to get carried away.'

Don't I just? I tried to banish his equally errant brother from my mind and listen to what he was saying.

'The problem is, I feel so wretched about Sarah. I wouldn't dream of hurting her, and there's no way anyone could ever take her place.'

'Well, that's a relief. Look Tim, the best thing you can do now is just forget it ever happened. Don't, for God's sake, decide to purge yourself and run off confessing to Sarah. Believe me, she may not be quite so reasonable about it.'

Tim scratched his head. 'The only problem is, Sarah might find out.'

'Why?'

'Because Penny came into my room the next morning with a cup of tea.'

'Oh no! What did she do?'

'Well, she looked pretty shocked and left, of course, but she slammed the door behind her. She and Sarah are very close.'

'How did Rachel react?'

'Pretty calmly. I leaped out of bed in a complete panic and started throwing my clothes into a bag, but she just sort of lay there smiling to herself.'

I bet she did.

'Well, then I rang you to say we were coming back. I couldn't bear to stay there a moment longer. I didn't see Penny again, not that I actively tried to find her. She was probably avoiding me, too. Polly, d'you think she'll tell Sarah?'

I sighed. 'Hard to say really, Tim. Female loyalty's a funny thing. Whereas boys probably wouldn't dream of spilling the beans, we girls tend to think it wouldn't be fair to let a friend go on believing that her man is whiter than white. Stupid really. On the other hand . . .' I hesitated. Lottie had told me about Harry's indiscretion, and in the long run I was glad she had, but then Harry was a louse. Tim, on the other hand, wasn't, and it would certainly be better if Sarah wasn't told.

'I think you should ring Penny and ask her not to say anything. Tell her you were drunk out of your mind, it was a huge mistake, and you're still absolutely bonkers about Sarah.'

Tim brightened considerably. 'D'you think that would work?'

'It might. On the other hand, it might not. She might insist you tell Sarah yourself.'

Tim banged his fist on the bedside table in fury. 'Women! Christ, you're all so bloody smug, aren't you? Do this, do that, don't do anything naughty because if you do we'll tie you up in knots before you can even apologize. It's almost like they're lying in wait for you. I mean, it was just a quick bonk, for Christ's sake, can't we leave it at that? Apparently not, no, we have to pick it all over, examine my motives, make me feel a complete and utter bastard, and where does that get us? I mean, what is the point?'

He was feeling nice and sorry for himself. A quick bonk, eh? This, from the lips of sensitive, caring, organically and politically correct Tim. Perhaps he'd thought a quick bonk would bring her out? Perhaps he'd thought he was behaving in a social, caring manner? Ah yes, that must be it.

'Well, I can't help you then, Tim,' I said quietly. 'I've told you what I think you should do. If you don't want to take my advice, you can sort it out for yourself.'

Tim blushed and looked at his shoes, instantly contrite. 'Sorry, Polly. That was infantile of me. It's all this guilt creeping out, I'm afraid.'

I looked at his shoes, too, half expecting to see the guilt seeping out all over the carpet. I wondered if Nick was leaking as well. As we watched his shoes glumly, both lost in our own private misery, Serena threw her best operatic voice upstairs.

'Lunch-is-rea-d-y!'

Neither of us moved.

Up it came again. 'Yoo-hoo, lunch-is-rea-dy!'

Tim sighed. 'We'd better go down. Thanks for listening, Polly, sorry I've been such a pig. I do feel a bit better actually.'

Terrific, I thought gloomily, as I dragged myself out from under the covers. I'm glad somebody does.

Chapter Twenty-four

It goes without saying that lunch was an unmitigated disaster. Sarah was the only one in high spirits, which in itself was unbearable. She'd heard that Tim had come back early, and had immediately dropped everything and raced over from the stables. In the space of about ten minutes, she'd thrown together a delicious lunch for us all and was obviously hoping for a jolly reunion party. She smelled outrageous, and I was longing to shower her in Dior to overcome the horsy fumes, but she couldn't have cared less. As she rushed around, helping us all to enormous platefuls of fish pie, she positively bubbled over with enthusiasm and happiness, chattering away, and not seeming to notice that no one really uttered back.

I couldn't bear to look at her, and I couldn't bear to look at Tim. Come to that, I couldn't bear to look at Rachel, and I certainly wasn't going to look at Nick. As for Serena, she was totally out of the question. That left Jamie. Luckily I was next to him. This was generally regarded as a bad seat, but today I was thankful. I gave him my undivided attention and concentrated on catering to his every whim; picking up his spoon whenever he dropped it; smiling gamely when he poked his sticky little fingers in my eyes, and indulging in fascinating lunch party repartee which involved lots of enthusiastic nods and smiles on my part and lots of shrieking and food-spitting on his.

Only Serena and Sarah were capable of eating the fish pie; the rest of us pushed it round our plates in a desultory manner. I toyed limply with a prawn, and Rachel stared dreamily into space. Occasionally she would flash a knowing look at Tim, who would flush guiltily and look away before shredding his napkin, apparently unaware that it was cotton and not paper.

Nick glowered into his wine glass, as if the answer to all his problems were somehow floating in a sea of Frascati.

Only Serena seemed equal to the situation. She sat at the head of the table and presided over lunch like the officious table monitor she had once so obviously been. She suffocated any attempts anyone else might have had at conversation by regurgitating a ceaseless flow of drivel about her latest film. It appeared to have a cast of thousands, and all concerned had their names dropped at regular intervals.

'. . . and as I said to Anthony when we were in make-up the other day –'

'Anthony who?' asked Sarah, right on cue.

'Andrews, darling,' came back the delighted reply, and then, in case anyone had failed to link up the Christian name with the surname, 'Anthony Andrews,' and then, in case anyone had been living in a cave in Outer Mongolia for the last ten years, 'he was in *Brideshead*, remember?'

'Yes, yes, we know who you mean,' said Tim, 'get on with it.'

'Well, it's just that he was saying how glad he was that he still had a base in England, and I couldn't agree more.

You see, it's terribly tempting just to up sticks and go and live in Hollywood. I mean, let's face it, that's where all the work is, so that's where all the money is, but is it worth it? I mean, OK, it's great fun, what with the parties and the fantastic weather and everyone paying you so much attention all the time; but really, there's more to life than that, isn't there? I mean, yes, sure, I've been tempted to stay: I remember one particular occasion when an absolutely divine director offered me the most amazing part – God, I was tempted – but it was a long TV series which would have taken for ever to film, and at the end of the day I just had to turn him down. No, I said, no, Roland, I'm sorry, but I'm going home, right? England is my home and home, as they say, is where the heart is, right? Well, of course he was flabbergásted, but what could he do? I mean, after all, it's my life, isn't it? I'm the one that's got to live it, right?'

She finished this string of platitudes with a triumphant flourish of the fork, and looked around expectantly as if awaiting applause. Most people appeared to be contemplating the table-mats, but someone must have raised their aching eyes for a moment and murmured an assent, because she ploughed on.

'I mean, sure, yes, LA is very exciting – it's fast, it's glamorous – but you know what? It's artificial. No, really, it is.' She nodded sagely as if perhaps we didn't believe her. 'Whereas,' she went on, waving her fork, 'whereas here, in dear old England, everything is – well, it's so *real*, isn't it? D'you know what I mean?' She cocked her head on one side. 'Hmmm? And you know, there's so much I miss when I'm in the States. Oh, I could bang on for ever

477

about the countryside and the history and everything, but you know what I really miss? Hmmm? People. Because when all's said and done, it's people that count, isn't it? And there are so many characters here. In LA everyone seems to be out of the same mould, they're all – well, they're plastic, right? Yes, lots of little plastic people!'

Her tinkly laugh rang around the dining room, and then her green eyes fell proprietorially on Nick, who was sitting next to her looking slightly mad about the eyes. He was maniacally smearing fish pie around his plate.

She leaned in close and ruffled his hair. 'I know what you're thinking, darling, and no, I haven't forgotten you. It goes without saying that when I'm away I miss you most of all,' she purred. She took his chin in her hand and turned his face towards her, going on in a baby voice, 'and I don't think you'd have been very happy in LA, would you, Pusskins?' she murmured, rubbing a bright red nail down his cheek. 'Hmmm? Not your scene at all really, is it?'

'Hardly,' said Nick grimly, jerking his head away and resuming his contemplation of his fish-smeared plate.

She turned back to her audience. 'Let's face it,' she said, as if some of us had been having difficulty, 'it's a fantastic place, but only in small doses, right? I know it's hard to believe, but one can get terribly bored with the rather self-indulgent lifestyle.'

'I don't find it hard to believe at all. I think it sounds a perfectly dreadful place and I know I'd be terribly home-sick,' said Sarah defiantly, desperately attempting to embark on some sort of discussion to rescue us all from this weighty, oppressive, cliché-ridden, minor-movie-star monologue. Alas, to no avail.

'Oh it's not *dreadful*, darling, it's great fun! But it is rather fast, and yes, if all you want to do is muck out stables, then you'd probably hate it. But I will say one thing,' she said, waving her fork around again and not entirely shutting her mouth as she masticated the fish pie. 'If you're not careful, you can end up losing your identity, d'you know what I mean?'

'Not entirely.' Sarah looked puzzled, as well she might.

'Well, you know how it is, darling, one's constantly being entertained and fêted and flattered, but some people make the great mistake of believing all that crap. You mustn't. You must stand still for a second, stand back from the whole scene and say – hey, now hang on a minute, what's going on here? Who am I – you know? I mean, what's it all about? Who are all these people? Are they for real?'

Well you certainly aren't, I thought, pushing half a ton of potato around my plate. I'd never met anyone so utterly phoney in my whole life.

'Don't you agree, darling?' She nudged Nick, who'd got bored long ago and was discussing crop rotation with Tim who was on his left.

'What? Oh yes, definitely.' He turned back to his brother.

'So that's why I decided to come home,' she concluded with a triumphant smile, as if anyone had been wondering. 'I just got fed up. I woke up one morning, packed my bags, and got a taxi to the airport.' She scraped her plate clean, put down her fork, and delicately patted her perfect cherry lips with a napkin. 'And here I am.' She turned to Sarah. 'Incidentally, Sarah, that fish pie was very good, but just a teensy word of advice. I always put a bit of parsley in mine: it makes all the difference. And perhaps a little less milk in the potato, it was slightly on the mushy side, wasn't it? I know you won't mind me mentioning it, because if you're anything like me, you'll welcome constructive criticism, right?'

Not only phoney, but poisonous too, I thought, almost with relief. What on earth does he see in her?

She leaned towards Nick and rested her head on his shoulder, although actually it was more like his back, because he'd almost completely turned around to talk to Tim.

She nuzzled into him as best she could. 'You couldn't believe it when I rang to say I was getting on the next plane back, could you, darling? Darling?'

'What?' Nick broke off his conversation.

'Honey, when I'm talking to you, you might at least listen. I can't talk to your back.'

'Sorry.' He resumed his discussion with Tim.

Serena turned back to address the rest of her equally unwilling audience. 'Anyway, apart from anything clsc, I just knew I had to come back to sort this place out. It needs so much attention. The roof is full of holes, for a start, and that's going to cost a fortune. Darling, did you speak to anyone about the roof? Darling? *Nick!*'

'Sorry, what?' He sounded irritated.

'I said,' began Serena, hissing through her teeth, 'did you talk to anyone about mending the roof?'

'No, I didn't, I'll get round to that when I've got some more money, all right? Sorry, Tim, what did you say?'

'Well, you know, that might just be too late; those holes aren't going to get any smaller. You really must get someone to give you an estimate. Apparently there's quite a good chap in Helston. He's just started up, so he might be glad of the work and give you a good price. And the windows are a disgrace, they're just falling off their hinges. I mean look at that one!'

She flung her arm dramatically towards the dining-room window. We all turned our heads obediently, except Nick and Tim, who were drawing diagrams on the back of an envelope now, their dark heads bent together.

'I mean, that just isn't going to survive another winter, is it? It's completely rotten, and if we get any more rain, it'll just crumble. We'll have water coming in and the carpets will be ruined. Not that there's much to ruin – look at this old thing – but Nick, you must get hold of a carpenter, really you must. Nick? Nick?'

She stared at the broad back that faced her. Still the brothers conferred. There was a terrible pause.

'NICK!' Serena flung down her napkin, scraped back her chair, and stood up. Everyone looked up at her; even Nick and Tim paused from their calculations.

'WILL YOU LISTEN TO ME!' she shrieked. Her face was white and she was shaking slightly. Suddenly she picked up her empty plate, raised her arm, and sent it crashing to the ground where it broke into a thousand tiny pieces. Then, with a stifled sob, she ran from the room.

There was a startled silence. Eventually Nick sighed, got up from the table, and with a look of resignation went after her.

We all looked down at our laps. I fiddled with my napkin. Rachel sniggered nastily.

At length, Sarah spoke up hesitantly. 'Don't take her too seriously. She can be – well, rather theatrical at times, I'm afraid.'

'Artistic temperament and all that,' muttered Tim, looking embarrassed.

'And I think,' went on Sarah, 'well, I think she's rather unhappy at the moment.' She looked at me briefly, not in an accusing way, but I flushed to my dyed roots none the less.

'Ah well, that gives her a perfect right to behave badly, doesn't it?' said Rachel sarcastically.

There was an embarrassed silence.

'I really must get back to the stables,' said Sarah, slipping down from her chair. 'I'm late already.'

'I'll come with you,' said Tim, throwing down his napkin and following her hastily. That left Rachel and me.

'Acting, of course,' said Rachel, licking her fork. 'She's just a spoilt little brat.'

It's hard to believe, but at that moment I felt a certain amount of sympathy for Serena, mainly because I felt such loathing for Rachel. I looked at her smug, self-righteous little face and felt myself coming up to the boil.

'And who are you to talk about behaving badly, Rachel?' I asked quietly.

She looked surprised. 'What do you mean?'

'Well, who exactly is behaving badly around here, eh? Answer me that one.'

'What are you driving at, Polly?' She narrowed her eyes warily.

'Tell me, do you feel even the slightest twinge of guilt when you sit next to Sarah? I mean, you are boffing her boyfriend, aren't you? So do you feel just the slightest bit uneasy about passing the time of day with her and eating her food, or does that hypocritical stuff come naturally to you? I assume you know they're getting married? How easy is the old adultery lark, do tell?'

She narrowed her eyes even more until they were just two little grey slits. 'I don't know, Polly, you tell me. You're the expert.'

I sat back in surprise. 'What d'you mean?'

'Well, how easy do you find it to sit next to dear Serena? After all, you're "boffing" – as you so elegantly put it – her fiancé, aren't you?'

I gasped in horror.

Rachel smiled. 'Spot on. Well, that was a shrewd guess, wasn't it?'

I gulped.

'Oh, don't look so surprised, it's quite obvious to anyone with half a brain cell. You haven't been able to take your eyes off him all lunchtime and he looks absolutely racked with guilt and remorse. So tell me, how do *you* sleep at night? When you're not with him, I mean?'

I bit my lip and looked away.

'Nothing to say, Polly?' she said quietly. 'Try taking the plank out of your own eye before you start complaining about the splinters in other people's.'

I took a large slug of wine and lit a cigarette with a shaking hand. Of course, to anyone but the educationally subnormal, the similarities between Rachel and myself would have been obvious long ago. But recognizing the obvious, especially the painfully obvious, has never been my forte, and when my brain is addled up with wine, lack of sleep and heartache, it's even more difficult. However, Rachel's acute observation pierced through the fog and left me reeling.

I licked my lips and tried to think of something to say. But what was there to say? She was right. I was no better than her, no better than Caro, and no better than any other cheap little slimeball who went around stealing other people's men. Serena and Nick were engaged to be married. I listened to her sobs coming from the kitchen and, not for the first time that day, felt sick. But this time with myself. Why shouldn't she rush down here to warn me off, waving her little green ring under my nose? Why shouldn't she point out the structural changes which were to occur under the forthcoming Mrs Serena Penhalligan regime? Of course she wanted to know when I was going: she wanted my claws out of Nick and back in London as soon as possible.

And what, after all, did I mean to Nick? Much the same as Rachel meant to his brother? A one-night stand? It was becoming more and more apparent that our one and only morning of passion had been a rather amusing indiscretion – perhaps even a charitable act – on his part.

I heard Nick's voice coming from the kitchen, soothing her, comforting her. Gradually her sobs subsided and there was quiet. No doubt he was kissing the tears away.

Not before time, I too slipped down from the table. I didn't look at Rachel, because I knew the sort of smile she'd have on her face. I just ran. At least I could do that. I could run away.

Upstairs, I tore around the bedroom like a lunatic, throwing things into a suitcase. Red shirt, leather skirt, little black dress, riding boots – all those well-thought-out outfits had done the trick all right, but where had the trick got me? In one hell of a mess, that's where.

The tears were streaming down my face by now, and I made no effort to check them, I just bunged on my sunglasses. I loved him so much, but I mustn't think about that because I'd go mad. The best thing I could do would be to slip away quietly and let him breathe a huge sigh of relief when he discovered the empty bedroom.

The only problem was, I couldn't do my case up. As always, I seemed to have twice as many clothes as when I'd arrived. I sat on the blasted thing and bounced up and down, but even my colossal weight couldn't close it. Eventually, in desperation, I took out a couple of jumpers and a pair of shoes and shoved them under the bed. I just had to get away.

I stole downstairs as quietly as one can steal with a two-ton case in tow, looking around feverishly for any sign of life. No one seemed to be about. Nick and Serena were probably still in the kitchen at the back of the house, Rachel and Jamie were no doubt up in her bedroom by now, and Sarah and Tim were at the stables.

I tiptoed quietly across the great hall, dragging my case, which luckily had those nifty little wheels at the back. I was just about to have the solid oak front door open, when the telephone rang.

Christ! I dropped my case and ran to it in a frenzy, terrified that someone else would hear and come running. I managed to grab the receiver just after the first ring. I put my hand over my mouth to muffle my voice.

'Yes?' I whispered.

'Hello?'

'Yes, hello, who is it?' I hissed rudely.

'Oh, er, sorry to disturb you. I was just wondering, is Polly McLaren staying with you by any chance?'

I sat down heavily on the bottom step. I'd know that voice anywhere.

'This is Polly,' I said quietly.

'Is it? Polly! God, it didn't sound like you at all. It's Harry!'

'I know.'

'You sound a bit odd, are you all right?'

'I'm fine. Fine. Hang on a minute.' Harry! It was no good, I had to have a cigarette. I dropped the receiver for a second, ran to the door, dragged my case back and punched it open. I rummaged desperately, flinging clothes out all over the parquet floor, found my ciggies, lit one, and inhaled deeply. Harry. Harry ringing here, looking for me. No wonder my hand was shaking. I picked up the receiver again. 'Hello?'

'You still there? I thought you'd done a bunk!'

'Er, no, I'm still here. What d'you want, Harry?'

'I rang to apologize, Poll.'

'Oh yes?'

'Yes, and to, well, to tell you I miss you.'

'Oh!' I was shocked to the core. I took another drag of nicotine and found my voice. 'But what about Caro, Harry? Isn't she keeping you company?'

'Oh Polly, don't be like that, I can explain, really I can. I just – well, I just got carried away, and I didn't think you'd find out, which I know is an awful thing to say and no excuse at all but – honestly, Poll, Caro was just a flash in the

486

pan; ships in the night and all that, you know? I can't tell you how much I regret it now. When I heard you'd buggered off like that, I just didn't know what to do. Honestly, I was tearing my hair out. Please forgive me, darling, please!'

My mouth was open. I didn't know what to say. I didn't know what to think.

'Say something, please Polly!'

'I . . . don't know what to say, Harry.'

'Oh, Polly, don't be like that, you sound so cold and hostile. Please don't go all hostile on me, just tell me you understand, I promise you it'll never happen again.'

'Oh, really?'

'Oh God, you're really pissed off, aren't you? Are you pissed off?'

I sighed. 'I honestly don't know.'

'Don't be, please don't be. It was such a mistake, such a ghastly, never-to-be repeated mistake. For what it's worth, it only happened once. She's so childish, she drove me up the pole after just one day. I know that doesn't make it any better, but I promise I've been regretting it ever since. I'm sorry, really I am, I can't tell you how awful I feel about it now. I've been all this time trying to trace you, none of your friends would tell me where you were.'

'So – so how did you find me?' I stuttered in disbelief.

'I worked on Pippa and she cracked eventually. Polly, I've got something very important to say to you.'

'Oh yes,' I croaked.

'It's not easy, because to be honest I've never said it before, but I've done a lot of thinking while you've been away, and I've come to a pretty staggering conclusion. You see, I reckon I'm in love with you.'

I gasped and reeled back against the stairs, grabbing the banisters for support. The receiver slipped from my nervous grasp. I fumbled to retrieve it.

'Hello? Hello? Polly, are you still there?'

'Y-yes, I'm here.'

'Look, I know this must come as a bit of a surprise. I mean, I know I wasn't exactly the model boyfriend, and I didn't treat you particularly well, but – well, I just took you for granted in London. You were always there. It was only when you went tearing off to Cornwall that I really began to miss you. And once I'd started, I couldn't stop. Please come back. I really need to see you.'

I couldn't believe this was happening. Harry missed me? Harry needed to see me? Harry – hang on, brace yourself for this one, girls – Harry *loved* me? I gaped into the receiver.

'Polly . . . ? Polly . . . ? This must be a really bad line, I can hardly hear you.'

'It's OK, Harry, I can hear you. Look, the thing is, I'm on my way back right now actually.'

'You are? Great! That's terrific! What train are you catching, shall I meet you?'

'Er, no, it's OK, I'll get a taxi. I'm not sure what time the trains are.'

'Oh, OK. Well, when you get to London, why don't you get the taxi straight round here.'

'Straight round where?' I said stupidly.

'Here, to my place. We could grab something to eat and then well, you know,' he laughed. 'Get to know each other again!'

I stared into the mouthpiece. He shouldn't have said

that. He really should not have said that. It was a big mistake. It not only made my skin creep, it made my toes curl up in their boots. Get to know each other again? Me and Harry? The diving board and futon nonsense all over again? In bed? With no clothes on? Embarking on a sexual marathon? With perhaps a little short back and sides thrown in for good measure? The very idea repulsed me. Oh no, I couldn't go back to that, not when I'd tasted the real thing. I thought of Nick. No, I could never go back to Harry.

I leaned back on the stairs, relief flooding over me. A colossal weight seemed to be lifting from my shoulders. I was shaking off my chains, I was free, and it was the most wonderful feeling. He meant nothing to me. Harry Lloyd-Roberts was history. Hoo-bleeding-ray.

'Polly, I think I'd better ring you back, I can't hear a word you're saying.'

'That's because I'm not saying anything, but I'm going to say something now, Harry. Are you ready?'

'Er, ready,' he said uncertainly.

'You're absolutely right.'

'I am?'

'Absolutely. You did take me for granted in London, and you're right, there is no excuse. Not only weren't you the model boyfriend, you weren't even a boyfriend. Far from it. If you really want to know, you were a pig. And I've been doing some thinking too. I've been thinking that I've actually got along quite well without you down here. I'm sorry, Harry, but our few days apart have obviously brought us to entirely different conclusions. You see, I'm over you. I hate to be brutal, but I'm afraid you're just too late. Sorry and all that.'

I heard a few distant splutterings at the end of the line. Without waiting for a reply, I gently replaced the receiver. Then I gathered my clothes up from the parquet floor, stuffed them back into my case, sat on it, snapped it shut, and dragged it over to the door again. With an almighty heave, I lugged my belongings over the threshold and staggered off down the drive towards the Helford Road.

Chapter Twenty-five

As I panted down the sweep of gravel to the gate, dragging my case behind me, I went over the extraordinary conversation again in my mind. It was incredible, what on earth had brought about this sudden change of heart? A little over a week ago he'd been indifference itself, now he was all over me. Did people change their minds as dramatically as that? I suppose they did. I mean, look at me, a couple of weeks ago I'd have flown back into his arms and been the happiest girl in the world, but not now. Not after Nick.

Nick. He'd changed too, hadn't he? And even more rapidly, come to that. Only this morning he'd told me – well, what had he told me, after all? Nothing very much when I came to think about it – that I was beautiful, yes, but that was just pillow-talk; he hadn't said anything truly heartfelt, had he? My own heart lurched as I thought of what he was telling Serena now. That he loved her? That he wanted to marry her more than anything in the world? That I'd been nothing more than a – what had Harry said about Caro – a ghastly mistake?

I sobbed audibly, and dragged the wretched case over the cattle grid at the gate, tears streaming down my face. It didn't help matters that I had three-inch heels on: I'd changed my shoes before lunch in a desperate attempt to make myself look a bit taller and perhaps even to come up to Serena's tummy button. I cursed my black crumpet-catchers now as I wobbled around precariously on them, tottering off in the direction of the river.

I had to get the ferry across to Helford before I could even begin the epic journey to Helston, and I had no idea when there'd be a boat. Did one just sit and wait, or did I have to hail one like a taxi? I struggled along the bumpy road feeling none too dry under the arms, and then turned off left and lugged the case down the bumpy track to the river. It bounced along behind me, steadily gaining momentum down the steep slope, forcing me to go faster and faster, so that when we eventually arrived at the bottom I was running pretty fast and very much out of control. Luckily I careered into some white railings on the jetty, which saved me from going in the water, and I sank down gratefully in a crumpled heap to wait for the boat, glad of a chance to get my breath back.

'You hopping on luv, or what?' said a voice.

I looked up. A little boat was bobbing around in front of me, packed full of people. They all seemed to be staring at me.

'Sorry?'

'I said are you hopping on?' said the voice again. It appeared to belong to a man with a blue cap and a wide grin. ''Cos if you are, you'd better get a move on, we're leaving any minute.'

I stared at the little boat. 'Oh! Is this the ferry?' Somehow I'd been expecting something much bigger, something more like the cross-channel jobbies that go over to France. This was just a little dinghy.

He grinned again. ''Tis as far as I know – and I should,

I've been ferryin' it there and back for more 'un twenty years now!'

I jumped up with alacrity. 'Oh! Oh well, yes please, don't go without me.'

'Give me that, luv.' He reached over and took my case. Someone else stretched out a friendly hand and helped me aboard. I sank down gratefully into the last available seat and, with a shrill whistle and a little blast of steam, we chugged off.

We were packed in like sardines, and I was jammed between two large women with enormous tweedy bottoms that cushioned me nicely on either side. It was really quite comfortable. I studied my fellow travellers. They were mostly sensible-looking women with empty shopping bags, off to do the weekly shop, no doubt. Their brown, wrinkled faces viewed me with interest and their kindly eyes twinkled. I tried hard to twinkle back but my face seemed to be locked into the forces of gravity which continually pulled it downwards. I'd twinkle later, I decided, when I needed to ask them the quickest way into town.

By now my feet were killing me. I decided to risk it and swap the ridiculous heels for a pair of espadrilles. My case was at my feet and I snapped it open, threw in the accursed shoes, and pulled on some heavenly flat ones. I crammed the lid down again, but of course once opened, the damn case wouldn't shut again, at least not with a pair of bulky high heels inside it. I got up from my seat and sat on the case. I bounced up and down, but it would hardly close, let alone shut. Tears of rage and self-pity were welling up in my eyes now.

'It's not goin' to shut, is it, lover!' ventured the tweedy woman next to me. She cackled in a friendly manner. 'Reckon you've got too much in there, you see!'

'Certainly looks like it, doesn't it,' I mumbled back, aware that my voice had a wobble in it.

I had one last bounce, but to no avail. Suddenly I could bear it no longer. With a squeal of rage I grabbed the stilettoes and threw them overboard. They hit the water with a satisfying plop! and then sank slowly down into the murky depths, never to be seen again. With a gleeful little shriek, I jumped on the case and snapped it shut.

I heaved a sigh of relief and grinned around at my neighbours. 'I never liked those shoes anyway!' I said to one and all.

Eight or nine horrified pairs of eyes met mine. Their good, honest, hard-working faces were aghast. No one smiled, no one spoke. They just stared. There was a terrible silence. Yes, in one reckless flick of the wrist I'd succeeded in alienating the good folk of Helford and Manaccan. The very people on whom I'd hoped one day to bestow prizes graciously at the village fête were open-mouthed with horror and disbelief. One by one they turned away, and a whispered muttering rose up around me. I caught the eye of the friendly captain. He looked away. I stared at the floor, hot-blooded shame filling my face.

How could I have been so stupid? Those shoes probably cost, oh, let's see, about as much as it took to feed a family for a week – God, a month even! Most of these people probably thought themselves lucky even to own one pair of shoes; their children probably ran around barefoot. I mean, they did in the country, didn't they?

I stared down miserably, not daring to look up. Eight or nine pairs of shoes met my gaze. That confirmed it. All the shoes looked like museum pieces. They were at least a hundred years old, no doubt handed down from generation to generation, from grandmother to mother to daughter, lovingly cared-for and restored – no, cobbled, that was it – over the years.

As we chugged across the water and then into the quay on the Helford side, I braced myself to look up. It was true, my fears were confirmed. Distrust and suspicion had replaced any kindly interest that might previously have helped me to secure a lift into Helston. Take those labour-ers, for example. Now normally I have a good working relationship with labourers. I saunter past, they whistle, I look coy, they make obscene gestures, I toss my head – everyone's satisfied. But not today, oh no. I tried a timid smile as they got off the ferry, but they instantly looked away, jumping into a waiting Land Rover and speeding off without so much as a, 'Cor, 'ello darlin'!' in my general direction.

As everyone else scattered, I realized I was the only one left standing on the quay. Feeling nice and sorry for myself, I took hold of my case, put my head down, and trudged down the lane in search of a bus. Get real, Polly, a bus? It took me half an hour before I could find any-thing that even remotely resembled a bus stop, and even then I wasn't sure. The little red symbol looked remarka-bly like a cattle truck to me. Oh well, I could hardly walk all the way to Helston. I sat down heavily on my evil case and waited. And waited. And waited.

After what must have been a good half-hour, I decided

to take my life in my hands and hitch a lift. I rummaged around in my handbag and, right at the bottom, my hand closed gratefully on an enormous pearl that was stuck in the lining. I pulled it out. Ah yes, there it was, my giant-sized hat-pin. On the odd occasion when I'm forced to hitch a lift, I like to keep it to hand. Lord knows where I imagine I'm going to stick it: somewhere soft, certainly, but I've never got more specific than that, it just comforts me to know it's there. I stood up and struck a pose at the side of the road. I stuck my thumb out purposefully; it was erect and jaunty.

Twenty minutes later, my thumb was wilting sadly. Alas, word had spread about, above and beyond. The good people of Helford had clearly been forewarned: do not, on any account, pick up an overweight blonde girl dragging a case. She's a profligate hussy with more shoes than sense. Not one car even slowed down, let alone stopped.

Eventually though, a little old lady came waddling towards me with an empty basket. Now she must be going into town, I thought, and surely someone of her age and stature – she was wider than she was tall – wouldn't walk all that way, now would they? I watched her approach with mounting excitement. It was like something out of Monty Python. Any minute now I expected a bus to career round the corner, whereupon she'd stick out her foot and trip it up. No such luck. She waddled straight past me.

'Excuse me!' I shouted desperately.

She stopped, turned around, and stared at me with curiosity. 'D'you happen to know if there's a bus into Helston today?'

She cackled with laughter. 'Oh, so that's what you're

waiting for, is it? No, not today, lover. Tuesdays and Thursdays, yes, but not today.'

She cackled a bit more and made as if to walk on. Not so fast, Grandma, I thought. I persisted, somewhat nosily.

'Well, how are you getting into town then?'

'Me? Oh I've got a lift comin', don't you worry about me!'

Her use of the personal pronoun was distressing enough, but just as I was about to disregard it and suggest I shared her transport, sure enough, it appeared around the corner. A milk float. With room enough for one.

'Af'ernoon, Dolly!' hailed the cheery milkman.

''Tis for some!' she cackled back as he heaved her aboard by the arm. She plumped herself down beside him and, with a cheery backward wave, they rattled off into the distance.

Well, that did it. That really did it. Without any more ado, I put my head in my hands and sobbed. And not just the whining, snuffling nonsense that I'd been doing for the last couple of hours, oh no, this was a good, honest-to-goodness sob.

I worked my way through a repertoire of gasping, spluttering, moaning and case-kicking, and was just building up to a nice shoulder-shaking crescendo, when I became aware of a car engine purring away in front of me.

Pausing for a moment from my gasps and heaves, I peered through the deluge and made out an orange Golf convertible, fully converted. It had stopped right in front of me and was humming away quietly. An electric window slid silently down.

'I thought it was you!' A familiar voice foghorned out. 'What on earth are you doing sitting there in the road?'

As the mist and rain clouding my vision cleared slightly, I made out the shadowy figure of Hetty Penhalligan at the wheel. I banged on my Ray-Bans and sprang to my feet, relief and alarm alternating within me. She might at least take me into Helston, but what on earth was I going to say to her by way of explanation?

'Are you trying to get to Helston?' she asked.

'Yes!' I yelped joyfully.

'Well, that's where I'm going. Hop in, and throw your case in the boot.'

I had the suitcase in the boot and my seatbelt clunk-clicked before she'd even blinked.

'Are you all right, my dear?' She peered anxiously over my glasses. 'Only you look absolutely terrible. Why on earth were you sitting by the side of the road like a little gnome?'

'I was trying to get to Helston and I thought there might be a bus, you see. I didn't realize they only ran about once a year down here.'

'D'you mean to say you've walked all this way with that heavy case? How perfectly ghastly!'

She crunched into first gear and we shot off, achieving nought to sixty in about ten seconds. I caught my breath, recovering from what felt like whiplash in my neck, and hung on for dear life as we hurtled round the lanes at a spectacular speed.

'Why on earth didn't Nick bring you?' she shouted above the roar of the engine.

'It was an emergency and Nick wasn't at the house!' I shouted back.

'Oh? Where is he?'

'He's um – he's gone to market!' Wasn't that where farmers went?

'Market? Today? How extraordinary,' she mused. 'It's usually on a Monday.'

'Er, yes, that's right, so he said, but apparently they changed the day because, um, a lot of the farmers couldn't make it last Monday.'

She looked at me as if I had two heads. 'What on earth do you mean, couldn't make it?'

Yes, what on earth did I mean? I struggled to make sense of myself. 'Well, you see a lot of them were away last Monday, on holiday – well, long weekends. You know, because of the good weather and all that. They took an extra day. So the people who organize the market, the, the er, market organizers, decided that since so many of them had missed it, they'd have it today instead!'

Hetty threw her head back and roared with laughter. 'Is that what he told you! Good Lord, that's a good one. Long weekends, eh? Ha ha! Polly, I'm afraid you've been had; he's obviously up to no good. Farmers don't even have weekends, let alone long ones!'

'Oh, really? Yes, well I must say I thought it was a bit odd, I expect it was a little white lie then – ha ha!' It made a nice change to blame my lies on someone else, I don't know why I hadn't thought of it before.

'So what's the emergency?' she yelled, as we took another bend at death-defying speed. I hung on to the door handle and shut my eyes hoping to God it was locked.

'What?' I yelled back, playing for time.

'The emergency, why are you rushing back?'

'Oh! Oh well, I've just heard that my mother's ill.'

'Oh dear, I'm so sorry, what's wrong with her?'

I gripped the dashboard as we shot over a humpbacked bridge, taking off from all four wheels and landing with a smack on the tarmac. Hetty obviously thought we were in Monaco rather than Manaccan. She also had an unnerving habit of leaning over to one side as she took her corners, as if she were on a motorbike. For some reason I felt myself leaning with her. It was quite hard to concentrate on my poor mother when I'd become the indispensable second half of a bobsleigh team.

'What's wrong with her?' she shrieked again.

'Malaria!' I shrieked back wildly.

Suddenly a traffic light loomed. It was red. I shut my eyes and offered my soul to the Almighty, plus anything else he considered worth taking. We screeched to a halt.

Hetty peered at me, full of concern. 'Malaria? How perfectly dreadful, has she been abroad lately?'

'Er, no, I don't think so, why?'

'Well, because one doesn't usually catch it in England.'

'Oh, abroad! Sorry, I wasn't quite with you. Yes, yes, she has been abroad. She went to, let me see – yes, France! She was in France last week, only you see she goes so often I sort of forget that it's abroad really. We've got a house out there, so it's rather like a second home.'

Hetty raised her eyebrows. 'She caught malaria in France? How frightfully unlucky. Especially in April.' She looked doubtful. 'Surely not mosquitoes?'

Damn. Of course, how stupid of me. Malaria was one of those nasty tropical diseases, wasn't it? You could only pick it up if you were spearing crocodiles in the Congo, or going native down the Nile. Why hadn't I picked something average, something close to home, something you could pick up in your local supermarket if you felt like it? Flu, for example, that would have done very nicely. Why did I have to be so ambitious?

'Er, no, you're right, it wasn't mosquitoes. The doctor thought perhaps it was something in the water. She was, after all, very deep in the deep South of France.'

I lowered my voice dramatically in an effort to suggest that my intrepid mother had ventured where perhaps no white man had gone before; certainly no white, middle-aged housewife.

'I mean,' I went on desperately, 'to be honest, we're talking Spain really.'

Happily, this struck a chord with Hetty, who obviously thought anything south of Paris was third world.

'Ah well, that explains it. Spain. Yes, of course. Never trust the Spics.' She shook her head violently. 'Never! The sneaky bastards, I wouldn't put it past them at all!'

I leaned back with relief as we sped off from the lights. At least we'd sorted that one out, but I was none the less confused. Was Hetty suggesting that these untrustworthy Spics had actually put something in my mother's water? I'd always imagined the water just became contaminated naturally, from the archaic water system, or the sewers perhaps. I had no idea that the locals actually went around slipping evil potions into glasses of *aqua con gas* which were then served up to unsuspecting tourists. How appalling! Someone should be told! I shuddered, and it was with some relief that I realized that my mother was not, in fact, lying prostrate in a hospital bed, but was safely at home in Esher, and probably even now absent-mindedly putting

Pedigree Chum into the shepherd's pie and giving half a pound of minced beef to the dog.

We hurtled around another hairpin bend, and I once more adopted the obligatory Barry Sheen position. A lorry swung away from us in alarm as we occupied far more of our share of the road than was strictly fair, and the driver shook his fist at us as we passed. Hetty waved back cheerily. Another bend and yet another lorry loomed, this time with two tons of hay on its back. My knuckles were white with fear as they gripped the dashboard, and my foot pumped away at an imaginary brake.

'Look out!' I screeched, as it missed us by inches.

Hetty looked at me in surprise. 'Am I making you nervous, my dear?'

'No, no, not at all!' I lied, as we roared dangerously into a village and slithered to a halt at another welcome set of lights. My heart was pounding wildly. 'I'm just not used to these twisty little lanes, that's all.'

'Oh don't worry, I know them like the back of my hand. You're quite safe.' She patted my rather sweaty hand.

I smiled but doubted it. In fact I was convinced I was going to die in this car. But on the other hand, I thought brightly, as I looked around at the little village we'd stopped in, if I was so concerned about dying, I must feel I had something to live for, right? Otherwise it wouldn't bother me, right? Right. But what?

I stared dreamily out of the window at the row of cottages we'd pulled up next to. They were all thatched, but each one was different and achingly pretty in its own way. Their pink, blue and white faces basked peacefully in the afternoon sun, their leaded windows sparkling as they caught the light. They were heaven. Crawling with honey-suckle and early roses which were already trying to bud, they had tiny cottage gardens at the front, and were flanked at the back by long stretches of lawn which swept up the hill beyond. The gardens backed on to fields where clusters of little creamy lambs danced and played, butting their patient mothers and snatching at the bright spring grass. I sighed. How beautiful it all was, and how unfortunate for me that I'd not only fallen in love with Nick, but also with Cornwall.

I bit my lip as the eyes welled. That way madness lies, I told myself fiercely, don't even think about it. Instead I stared out of the window fixedly, and concentrated like billy-o on a green Volvo that had just drawn up in front of one of the cottages. I studied the hub caps fiercely. Don't think about Nick and don't think about Cornwall, or you'll flood the car, and then what will Hetty say? I suppose I could have blamed the sudden emotion on my mother's malaria, but I didn't really want to get embroiled in that little malarkey again.

I blinked hard and concentrated on the Volvo. The door was opening and a cloth cap was emerging. It belonged to a young man who was getting out of the driving seat. He slammed the door behind him, not bothering to lock it. Well, why should he? We weren't in thieving Fulham now, were we? I sighed despondently as I realized that I very soon would be. The young man strode up the path towards the pink cottage, taking a key out of his hip pocket as he went. What an idyllic place to live, I thought, as he put the key in the door. I bet it was full of quarry tiles and oak beams.

The lights began to change. Hetty, keen as mustard for a Le Mans start, slammed into first and revved up the engine. The young man opened his front door and made to go in. Funnily enough, although I hadn't seen his face, he struck me as being rather familiar. He had a certain gait which reminded me of someone . . . Yes, it was definitely the way he walked, and, yes, something about those broad shoulders, that hair sticking out from under his cap . . . that . . . red hair.

My hand flew to my mouth. 'Oh my God!' I shrieked from the open-topped car.

He swung around instantly. Our eyes met. I ducked down, and at that moment Hetty saw green and roared off, but it was too late.

'What?' she yelled at me over the engine. 'Oh my God, what?'

'It's him!' I wailed, wringing my hands. 'It's bloody him again, isn't it!'

Chapter Twenty-six

I swivelled round in my seat. Adam was standing stock-still, half-way up the garden path, staring after us. We hadn't fooled him at all, he was still here! Not in Manna-can, of course – having an iota of intelligence, he'd probably realized we'd check that out – no, he'd simply switched villages. How stupid of us to be so sure of our-selves, so arrogant, so complacent! I swung back into my seat again, panic rising within me.

Think, Polly, think. I thought. I gripped the upholstery. Oh my God, if he had any sense he'd act fast! Let's face it, he didn't have much choice now that he knew I'd seen him. In fact, at this very moment he was probably sprinting down the path to his car, revving it up and speeding off to Trewarren to snatch Jamie back before I raised the alarm. Then he'd whisk him off to the nearest port and from there, back to America. I imagined little Jamie, wide-eyed and trusting, bundled up in his blue blanket, hurried on to boats, planes, through customs. My heart lurched. Oh, poor little baby! I bit my lip. It was no good. I couldn't possibly go to London now. There was only one thing to do.

'Stop the car!' I yelled at the top of my voice.

Even though we were at that precise moment negotiat-ing an immensely tricky hairpin bend, Hetty accepted the challenge. She shot me a quick sideways glance, just to ascertain that I was serious, and, having satisfied herself, slammed on the brakes and executed a surprisingly immaculate emergency stop.

'Quick, quick! Turn around!' I urged.

'But why?' she began, 'Why have we –'

'Never mind, never mind, I'll explain in a minute, but please hurry, we must be quick!'

Wide-eyed but unprotesting, she acquiesced, throwing herself into this impromptu driving test with gusto. With a great deal of revving up and sheep-frightening, we performed a five- or six-point turn in the middle of the snake-like lane. Hetty was enjoying herself now. She was keen to please. She leaned forward, gripping the wheel, looking up at me expectantly, eagerly awaiting her next instruction. What she really wanted to hear was, 'Follow that tractor!' or some such other *Miami Vice*-like instruction, suitably adapted to our rural surroundings.

'Quick, quick!' I squeaked. 'Back to Trewarren!'

Crouched over the wheel like a bird of prey and with her mouth set in a determined line, she rose gleefully to the occasion. I had the distinct impression she'd been waiting for this moment for years. With a little whoop of pleasure, she let out the clutch and we shot off in the direction of Trewarren.

My mind was in overdrive now. Of course he hadn't believed us, what fools we'd been to think he would! As we hurtled back past the row of pretty cottages in the other direction, I noticed that the green Volvo had gone. He hadn't wasted any time, but if we hurried, we might just catch up with him.

'Hurry, hurry,' I muttered softly under my breath, but not softly enough for Hetty's keen ears. Her eyes widened and glinted with pleasure as she caught the magic words and the accelerator hit the floor. I gripped the dashboard and prayed hard as an amber light greeted us around the next bend. We screeched through on red, a cloud of dust shimmering in our wake.

Only now, as we zipped along a fairly open stretch of road, did Hetty allow herself to question the abrupt curtailment of her weekly shopping trip to Helston.

'Why the hell are we going to Trewarren?' she yelled above the roar of the engine.

'Because of the baby!' I shrieked back, forgetting for a moment that she didn't know the full story.

'The baby?' she looked at me quizzically.

She was one of those drivers who has to look at you while she's talking to you, unnerving for any passenger, but especially a nervous one travelling at the speed of light. I had to think quickly. The Rachel/Jamie/Adam story was much too long and complicated to go into right now, and Hetty would feel obliged to look at me throughout, which was not conducive to staying alive. I rooted around for a suitable lie.

Hetty helped me out. 'You mean we're going back for the baby?'

'Yes, that's it!' I agreed, grateful to her for providing me with such a marvellous explanation, and so simple a one too. 'I've forgotten the baby!'

'Oh!' Hetty's eyes were off the road and on my face in an instant.

'Yes, you see you were quite right. He is my baby, after all, I was just a bit embarrassed about it when you asked me before. I thought you'd disapprove, you know, unmarried mothers and all that – but he really is mine and the awful thing is, I've forgotten to bring him with me! I only realized, just back there, that he's probably still lying in his cot in Trewarren. I completely forgot about him, can you believe it!'

Hetty obviously couldn't, and was staring at me in a rather horrified manner. We were also slowing down quite dramatically. I licked my lips and realized – too late – that this story wasn't as simple as I'd hoped, and I had quite a lot of explaining to do. Hetty looked scatty enough, and was no doubt capable of leaving all sorts of things lying around – her purse, her car keys, her glasses – but a baby? Who forgets a baby? The speedometer was dropping by the second. Forty, thirty, twenty – she wasn't happy. I struggled to defend myself.

'It's – it's this damn post-natal depression, you see!'

'Ah!'

Was that a look of sympathy? Had I struck a chord?

'Yes,' I went on. 'I went into a complete decline after he was born: couldn't eat, couldn't sleep, and couldn't really believe I'd had a baby at all! I kept thinking he must be someone else's. And – and the terrible thing is that, even though I'm much better now, I still forget occasionally that I'm a mother, and I leave him lying around in the most awful places!'

'My poor child!' She put her hand on my arm in consternation.

Buoyed up by her concern, I warmed to my subject. 'Yes, I left him in Peter Jones once.'

Hetty shook her head and tutted sympathetically. 'Easily done,' she muttered. 'China and glassware?'

''Fraid so. Oh, and once I left him outside the post office, and in the greengrocer's, and the cinema –'

'You take him to the cinema?' Hetty looked alarmed.

Oh Christ, didn't babies go to the cinema? Probably not – wouldn't it have been easier to go into the Adam and Rachel saga? Too late. I struggled valiantly on.

'Oh well, it helps him go to sleep, you see, and I don't take him to see anything sexy or violent, just love stories and that sort of thing, or nature films, you know, anything soporific.'

'Oh, right.' Hetty still looked dubious. 'Was it a terrible birth then?'

'Oooh shocking, shocking! Went on for weeks!'

'Weeks!' Hetty gaped at me and we almost came to a standstill, she was rooting in the glove compartment for a cigarette.

Oh, hell! If only I knew more about birth. What a pity Rachel hadn't been more forthcoming, but surely I'd heard that some women were in labour for ages?

'Er – well, no, not weeks, it just felt like weeks, but certainly days, about, um four or five anyway.'

Hetty looked horrified. 'You poor thing!'

'I know, it was ghastly, all the doctors said it was quite the most appalling birth they'd ever come across. It took five of them to deliver me: they needed forceps, ropes, pulleys, all sorts of things. I made medical history, there's a bit in a textbook about it now. It crops up in exams, and someone even wrote a thesis on it. Anyway, that's why I get so depressed and, well, you know, forget about him occasionally.'

'Well of course, of course.' Hetty shook her head.

'Goodness me, we must get you some help,' she muttered, looking grave.

Happily though, she seemed satisfied with my bizarre explanation, and the speedometer climbed again. I watched it like a hawk. Within seconds we were well into the fifties. It occurred to me that Hetty might consider popping me into the local police station for some routine questioning on child abuse, or stopping at a telephone box to report me to the NSPCC or the Esther Rantzen Childline, but no. Thankfully she was obviously of the opinion that a child's place was with its mother, no matter how hopelessly deranged that mother happened to be.

No more was said, and eventually we rounded the bend that led to Trewarren. We swung through the gates, fairly flew over the cattle grid and, with a spray of gravel, came to an abrupt halt in front of the house.

I was out of that car and leaping up the stone steps to the front door in a trice. Knowing what superhuman strength it took to force the door open, I ran at it, ramming it with my shoulder. Unfortunately it was already deceptively ajar, so I burst in a little faster than I'd anticipated. I careered across the hall like an unguided missile, and cannoned into Nick who was coming out of the drawing room.

'Hey! Whoa, steady on!' he said, grabbing my shoulders as I headbutted him in the chest. 'Ooof! Polly, it's you!'

He obviously recognized me by my entrance. I thought he looked slightly relieved, if a little winded. However, if it was relief, it was very momentary, and it very soon turned to anger.

'Where the bloody hell have you been? I've been looking everywhere for you, why did you just take off like that?'

He spotted Hetty behind me. 'Mum! What are you doing here?'

Hetty was still glowing from the after-effects of having just broken the land-speed record. She fanned her rather flushed face.

'Hello darling, isn't this a surprise? I simply must have a large drinky. I'm absolutely pooped! We've just had the most terrifically exciting car journey, and Polly's been simply fascinating company. Honestly, the things she's been through, you just wouldn't believe it. First the baby, and now her poor mother . . .' She collapsed on a chair in the hall. 'Darling, hurry up with that gin, I'll expire in a minute.'

Nick jerked his head towards the drawing room. 'Help yourself, Mum, would you? Usual place.'

Hetty got up, and thankfully disappeared in the direction of the drinks cupboard before she had time to elucidate further on my fascinating career.

Nick still had my shoulders in a vice-like grip. 'Polly, just what the hell is going on here?'

'Where are Rachel and Jamie?' I blurted out.

'As far as I know, Rachel's reading in the garden, and I think Jamie's asleep upstairs. Why?'

I wriggled out of his hands, pushed past him, and leaped up the stairs two at a time. As I reached the landing, I heard Rachel's voice coming up from the hall below. I glanced down quickly. She was wandering in from the kitchen, book in hand. No Jamie.

She frowned. 'What's going on?' she asked, as she watched me scramble up the stairs like a neurotic mountain goat.

Nick shrugged and leaped up the stairs after me. 'Search me. Polly, what are you up to?'

'Jamie,' I muttered as I flew down the corridor to his bedroom.

The door was open. I raced over to the cot and looked down. A much-sucked teddy bear looked back at me with beady black eyes. The pale blue blanket was pushed back to reveal a white sheet sprinkled with yellow buttercups. A little blue rabbit was half squashed through the bars. Other than that the cot was empty. Somehow, although I'd been expecting it, I wasn't prepared for the reality.

My hand flew to my mouth. 'Oh Nick, he's gone!'

Nick raced in behind me. 'Oh well, hang on a minute, I may be wrong. He may have been in the garden with Rachel, or –'

Rachel was in the room in an instant. She rushed, white-faced, to the cot and looked down. Then she screamed. She gripped the side of the cot and just screamed and screamed as if she would never stop. It wasn't a sound I'd ever heard a human being make before: it sounded more like the shriek of a snared animal, an eerie, primeval sound that tore at the heart and froze the blood.

'He's gone! My baby's gone! He's taken my baby – oh my GOD!' She covered her face with her hands and screamed again.

Then she turned on me, her face drained and bloodless. 'Where is he? Where is he! You saw him, didn't you, you saw him! Tell me where he is!'

She ran at me, beating me with her fists, shaking my shoulders, her white, distorted face inches from mine.

'This is all your fault!' she shrieked. 'Tell me where he is!'

I was terrified. Nick was over in an instant, pulling her off. She gave a moan and collapsed on to him. He held her tightly as she shook violently in his arms.

'It's Adam!' I gasped, shaking quite a bit myself. 'I saw him coming out of that little row of cottages in New Town, he didn't go to London at all – and he knew I'd seen him, so he obviously rushed over here and – and just took him while he still had the chance!'

Rachel moaned again and put her head in her hands.

'Shit!' hissed Nick through clenched teeth. He sat Rachel down on a chair and knelt beside her. She was sobbing and shaking uncontrollably. He took her hands.

'Now listen to me Rachel. It's OK, it's going to be all right. We'll get him back in no time, don't you worry, he can't be far away – minutes at the most. Everything's going to be fine.' He straightened up and shot me a look. 'Look after her,' he muttered, as he rushed from the room.

'Where are you going?' I ran after him.

'To ring the police.'

I bounded downstairs behind him. By the time I'd got to the bottom he was already dialling the number.

'Green Volvo!' I breathed.

'Good. Anything else? Registration?'

'Didn't see, but it was a big one, an estate.'

He got hold of the local police and briefed them in a controlled and lucid manner. A baby had been snatched from its mother at Trewarren. A tall, red-headed American, about thirty, driving a green Volvo. Could well be making for the London road, or possibly a port. Hurry.

'Wearing a cap!' I prompted.

Nick gave me a withering look and refrained from

imparting this vital piece of evidence. Then he slammed the receiver down and made for the door, grabbing his car keys from the hall table.

'Where are you going now?' I cried, running after him.

'He can't be far away, I'm going to look for him.'

'I'm coming with you!'

'No, stay with Rachel,' he ordered.

'Not likely,' I muttered, throwing myself down the front steps after him.

He jumped into the Land Rover. 'For God's sake, who's going to look after her?' he growled as I jumped in beside him.

'Your mother,' I said, slamming the door, 'she's brilliant with distraught young mothers, I know that from experience. Now come on!'

We reversed, and the tyres spun on the gravel drive as we took off. Nick swung the Land Rover around the side of the house, and we sped off down the back drive, bouncing all over the place on the un-made-up, rock-strewn road.

'Where are we going?' I gasped, steadying myself on the window as we roller-coasted down towards the back gate.

'We'll head for the London road,' said Nick. 'We'll just have to take a chance on him going that way. He obviously didn't go back towards Helston or you'd have seen him. I know a short-cut to the main road so we might be able to cut him off.'

'If he's smart he'll ditch the car, he knows I've seen it.'

'What, and charge about on foot? Come on, Polly, a redheaded man carrying a baby for miles is pretty conspicuous, and it would take him for ever to get to the main road and hitch a lift.'

'He might get a train.'

'The police will be on the look-out at Helston station, and that's the only main line around here.'

We paused for a second at the bottom of the drive, before swinging round left into the lane. He flashed me a look. 'What the hell were you doing in New Town anyway?'

I stared out of the window. 'Going back to London.'

'Idiot,' he muttered, but made no further comment, as we tore off down the road.

We raced around a sharp bend, taking half the hedge with us, and I hastily withdrew my elbow from the open window. Nick had obviously learned to drive at his mother's knee, I recognized the style. If I wasn't very much mistaken, this was a former pupil of the Hetty Penhalligan Kamikaze School of Motoring. At least I'd been on a trial run once already today, so I knew the ropes. I planted my feet firmly on the dashboard to act as shock absorbers, and gripped the upholstery with my nails. The tyres screeched around on the tarmac, reminding me abruptly of Rachel's screams. I shivered.

'D'you think we'll find him?'

'I just don't know.'

'How far away d'you think he is by now?'

Nick, thankfully, didn't have his mother's penchant for eyeball contact. He stared straight ahead. 'Hard to say, a mile maybe, perhaps two if he's really motoring.'

He obviously wasn't feeling chatty so I kept quiet. Well, at least for a couple of seconds, anyway.

'What are we going to do if we do see him?' I ventured timidly.

'Follow him of course.'

We lurched sideways as we swerved to avoid an old man on a quivering bicycle.

'Yes, but then what?'

In my mind's eye, I saw us drawing up alongside the Volvo and gesturing for Adam to pull in, whereupon he'd shoot us a villainous sideways glance, snarl, and go even faster – but he'd be no match for us. We'd be right by his side, tearing along through the twisty-turny lanes, neck and neck, until eventually we'd ram him and force him into a ditch. Nick would leap out, drag him from the car, and spreadeagle him over the bonnet in a half-nelson, and I'd be right beside him, frisking him and reading him his rights: 'You have the right to remain silent, but anything you do say . . .'

'Use the car phone to telephone the police and give them his exact position. They'll have a squad of cars after him in no time,' answered Nick calmly.

'Oh. Oh yes, of course, good idea.' I was rather disappointed.

As we rounded the next bend, we nearly went straight up the back of a little red post office van which was tootling along at a leisurely thirty miles per hour. Nick sat on the horn, but the van stood its ground, which happened to be most of the road.

'Oh, come on, you berk! Move over!' I cried, banging the dashboard in frustration and willing Postman Pat into the nearest ditch. He was damned if he was moving over, but eventually the lane widened slightly, albeit on a horrifically blind corner, and Nick shunted down a gear and roared up beside him, forcing him into the hedge. As we shot past I caught a glimpse of a little purple-faced man, waving his fist and shouting obscenities. Blood pressure was clearly a problem, and a heart attack looked imminent, but I had no sympathy. He'd cost us vital seconds.

The next thing I knew, we'd hung a sharp left into a ploughed field and were bouncing along down the side of it. All four wheels seemed to be leaving the ground at regular intervals. Thank goodness I hadn't managed to make much headway with the fish pie, I thought, as my bottom left the seat and my tummy shot into my oesophagus. I gritted my teeth and clutched my bosoms as we took off from a particularly deep rivet. God, I was getting some exercise on this holiday.

At last the dark furrows came to an end, and we swerved into another field, this time, thankfully, of the green and pleasant variety. My organs slipped back into their rightful slots and I managed to speak, or squeak, 'Where the hell are we going?'

'Short-cut!'

'But won't the farmer mind?' I asked, as hordes of terrified sheep scattered in all directions.

'I am the farmer.'

He slammed on the brakes and we screeched to a halt in front of a huge fence. Oh no! What now? Through it? Over it?

'Open it!' he barked.

Oh Christ, it was a gate! I hurriedly scrambled out and fell flat on my face in some very dubious business.

'Oh God, yucky poo! Sheep shit, all up my nose!' I wailed in disgust as I got slowly to my feet.

'Get on with it!' bellowed Nick, banging the steering wheel.

Nausea was rising within me, but I hurriedly wiped my nose and addressed myself to the gate. It had one of those really complicated catches, with bits of wire and binder-twine all over it – the sort of thing you need a degree from Cirencester to open. My fingers were like sausages as I fumbled nervously around.

'I can't do it!' I wailed pathetically.

'Jesus!' a voice hissed in my ear. Nick was beside me. He swept my inept fingers away and muttered something under his breath, but I couldn't quite catch what he said, except it sounded like 'hopeless', 'fucking' and 'prat', but I probably misheard.

He had it open in an instant, then he ran back to the car, revved up, and shot through.

'Now shut it!' he barked from the driving seat.

It was bloody heavy, but I prayed to God and luckily He provided me with some superhuman strength. I rammed it shut.

As I ran back to the car, I suddenly glimpsed a long flash of green through the hedge on the opposite side of the field. The green streak was travelling at speed down the lane at right angles to ours.

'There he is!' I shrieked, 'that's him!' and almost before I was back in my seat, Nick was after him.

We roared up to the crossroads, swung left without stopping to see what was coming, and raced up the lane.

There was no sign of the Volvo now, but at least we knew we were on the right road.

'After him! After him!' I squealed, bouncing up and down in my seat with excitement.

'Put your seatbelt on!' ordered Nick as I bounced a bit too hard and nearly cracked my head on the roof. I dragged it across and snapped it into place.

An uncharacteristically long stretch of road opened before us and, right at the very end, just as it was about to disappear over the brow of the hill, we saw the green Volvo.

Nick opened up the throttle and we fairly flew along, all thoughts of ringing the police forgotten in the chase. As we reached the same brow, the road twisted suddenly – then again – and again – and again. Each time we rounded a bend, I saw a tantalizing flash of green appear and disappear, all in the space of a millisecond.

'Quick, quick! Faster, faster!'

Nick didn't utter, but his mouth was set in a grim line and his knuckles were white on the steering wheel. We were definitely gaining on him. Nick had the advantage of knowing the lanes backwards, so he anticipated every bend and cornered expertly. I tried the motorbike lean so favoured by his mother, but obviously went a touch too far when I ended up with my nose in his lap.

'For God's sake sit still, will you!' he yelled, and I scrambled dutifully back into my corner, hanging on to the strap above the door as the speedometer approached eighty m.p.h. I'd always wondered what that strap was for, and now I knew. Life-threatening situations. They don't mention that in the glossy brochures, though, do they? Added extra – one handy strap for hanging on to when you're looking death in the face.

'D'you think he knows we're behind him?' I yelled above the roar of the engine.

'Doubt it, I shouldn't think he's looked behind him once, he's just driving like a maniac to get the hell out of here!'

We seemed to be gaining on him all the time, but then so, unbeknown to us, was a tractor. Only the tractor was travelling in the opposite direction. It had recently emerged from some fields a mile or two hence, and was trundling back to the farm that bordered on Nick's, just over the hill. It was a large, red, uncompromising vehicle, the old-fashioned variety with huge protruding wheels at the front and a trailer at the back. It was making slow but steady progress down the lane, just as Adam was making fast and unsteady progress up it.

We were far enough behind not to witness the inevitable meeting, but the sickening crunch of metal was unmistakable.

I shrieked and covered my face with my hands. Nick hit the brakes. Within seconds we were skidding around a corner, and then another, before coming to a precarious halt, inches away from a horrifically concertina-ed Volvo.

Its back end was jutting out at right angles to the road. The front was almost totally embedded in the tractor. I couldn't see Adam or the tractor driver.

Nick was out and running before I'd even come to my senses. I stumbled out and raced after him, but as I approached I stopped dead in my tracks and shrank back in horror. Adam's twisted body was draped upside down over the front of the tractor. He'd obviously gone straight through the windscreen and somersaulted down on to his back. Blood was gushing down on to his face, over his eyes, and into his open mouth. His head was slumped forward at a peculiar angle to his crumpled body, and I couldn't see his legs at all. They seemed to be embedded somewhere in the tractor.

Vomit rose up in my throat and I turned away. I threw up on the verge several times. By the time I looked up, which was a good minute or so later, I could see that Nick was crawling precariously over the tangled heap, slowly inching his way towards Adam's immobile body.

'Oh God, he's dead! He's dead, isn't he?' I shrieked.

By now Nick had reached him. 'No he's not, he's still alive – just!' He yelled back. 'For Christ's sake, get Jamie out!'

'Jamie! Oh my God!'

I ran like stink to the back of the car and peered in, bracing myself for what I might find. At first I couldn't see him at all, there was nothing on the back seat. Then I saw him. The carry-cot was on the floor in the back, wedged in between the front and back seats. Jamie's big blue eyes stared up at me. His little mouth was open and getting wider by the minute. The eyes disappeared as they screwed up tight; he took a deep breath.

'WHHAAAAaaaaaa!'

Thank goodness! That sounded healthy. I yanked the door open and dragged the carry-cot out. It was the old-fashioned sturdy sort with rigid sides, and it was completely unharmed; and so, as far as my totally inexpert eye could see, was Jamie. He was bloody cross though. He bellowed in indignation as I grabbed him roughly and held him close, stroking his little back and feeling his warm, comforting weight, heavy against my shoulder.

'Whaaaa . . . wah, whah! Hu, hu, hu . . . whaaa, whaaa, whaaaahhh . . . !'

'Sshhh, shush Jamie, you're all right now, I've got you, you're all right.'

His cries gradually subsided, and after a while he made little snuffling sounds as he snuggled happily into my neck, grabbing at my hair and shoving it into his mouth, suddenly oblivious to the drama surrounding him. I was shaking like a wet puppy, but he didn't seem to mind.

I turned back to the mangled car. Nick was perched precariously on the bonnet, crouching down over Adam.

'He's all right!' I yelled, 'Jamie's perfectly all right, not hurt at all!'

'Thank God. Adam's in a pretty bad way, though. Quick, Polly, ring for an ambulance on my car phone.'

'Right!'

I grabbed the carry-cot from the car and, clutching Jamie, raced back to the Land Rover. I put him in his carry-cot on the back seat, then I jumped into the front.

'Car phone, car phone . . .' I muttered as I scrambled around looking for something with familiar dials or buttons on it. I don't even own a portable phone, let alone a car phone, so I was a bit out of my depth here. Where do people keep these things – on the dashboard? Under the seat?

'Oh please let me find it, please . . .' I muttered desperately as I feverishly rooted around in the glove compartment. 'Please, don't let me be a complete and utter moron!'

I emptied every compartment I could find and threw

everything on the floor; torches, maps, barley sugars, but no telephone – where the hell was it! I dived down on to the floor and thrust my hand under the seat. Was this where it was kept? Under here?

'Oh where is it, Jamie, help me!'

The door flew open and Nick was behind me.

'I can't find it!' I wailed, wringing my hands from my cringing position on the floor.

'Christ, Polly, you're just the person to rely on in an emergency, aren't you?'

I thought this was a bit rich considering all I'd been through, but I kept mum as he leaned over and wrenched open a catch by the handbrake, pulling out a handpiece with buttons on it. He punched out 999.

'I thought that was part of the handbrake!' I whispered.

Without bothering to answer, he barked out instructions to the ambulance service.

I looked in the back seat. Jamie's eyelids were getting heavy. I watched as they closed, his little mouth opened, and his clenched fist unfurled. A second later he was fast asleep. I tiptoed away. Retching violently, I forced myself to go back towards Adam. I crept down the lane with my hand to my mouth. As I tentatively inched closer to the wreckage, I thought I saw his eyelids flicker.

'Adam?' I whispered, from a good ten yards away.

This time the mouth twitched too. I inched a mite closer.

'Adam?'

'What the bloody hell happened?' said a voice out of nowhere.

I jumped about a foot in the air and swung round to see

the tractor driver staggering around in the road holding his head. Oh Christ! We'd forgotten about him. He was about seven foot tall and built like an all-in wrestler, a great bear of a man. He looked as if he was pretty much intact, but he was swaying violently, like a tree in a gale, as if he'd completely lost his sense of balance. I ran to steady him.

'Sit down, sit down!' I cried, lugging him towards the grass verge. As I lugged, I realized he had the most spectacular BO. I wondered whether it was due to fear, or whether he was always so highly perfumed.

He sat obediently. I sat down next to him, then inched away as the odour shot straight up my nostrils. 'What happened?' he muttered.

'There was a crash, you're obviously in shock,' I informed him at arm's length.

He looked at me with bleary eyes. 'And who the hell are you, Florence Nightingale?'

I ignored this smart remark, and peered into his face which was florid and jowly. He had a little cut above his right eye, and a terrific bruise appearing on his chin, but other than that there wasn't a scratch. The tractor was completely open to the elements, so he'd obviously been thrown clear without the added complication of going through a windscreen.

'You don't look too bad,' I ventured. 'Are you all right?'

'No, I'm not sodding all right. I feel bloody awful! I've got a sodding great lump on my head and a pain in my back and my leg's killing me. Who the fuck was that idiot in the Volvo? What the bloody hell was he up to, he must have been doing about ninety miles an hour – ooh, my bloody head!' He swooned a bit.

'Put it between your knees,' I ordered, grabbing hold of the back of his bull-like neck and shoving his face downwards.

'Geddoff, will you?' he protested, pushing away my hand and making as if to scramble to his feet. I couldn't cope with a lumbering man-mountain on the loose.

'Just shut up and sit still,' I ordered. 'I'm a nurse.'

This seemed to do the trick. He looked doubtful for a moment, then lowered his head obediently until his nose was about two inches from the tarmac.

We sat in silence. I looked across at the tangled heap of machinery in front of us. Nick had climbed back to be with Adam again. Adam looked larger than ever, his huge bulk plastered over the front of the tractor like an enormous insect splattered flat by the impact. Blood was pouring out of his head and his shirt was scarlet now as it trickled down his neck to his collar. He was totally motionless. Nick reached out and took his hand. I shivered, hugging my knees to my chest and resting my head on them.

'Oh, please God,' I whispered, 'let Adam be all right. Let him live. I know I haven't prayed for ages, but this isn't for me, it's for Adam and Jamie. I mean, he only wanted his baby, didn't he? Please don't let him die for it.'

I prayed on and on, mumbling into my knees for what seemed like an eternity. I couldn't look at the wreck any more. A great stillness seemed to descend on the scene. After a while I heard voices in the background. Other cars had evidently accumulated behind us: car doors were slamming, people were whispering hoarsely to one another, 'What happened?' 'Is he dead?' Still I didn't look up.

Eventually I heard the distant wail of a siren. I lifted my head from my knees. Flashing lights were appearing around the corner.

A small crowd of concerned but goggle-eyed motorists had gathered, and the police, who had arrived simultaneously, had to organize them all out of the way before the ambulance could even begin to nose its way through. It seemed to take for ever. At last they managed to clear a path. The ambulance pushed its way through, the back door swung open, and a stretcher appeared. A couple of ambulance men inched their way gingerly over the stunted Volvo towards Adam's twisted body. With Nick's help they managed to prise him from the wreckage and lift him on to the stretcher. They covered him in a red blanket and tucked it in around him. At least he looks more comfortable now, I thought, as he was loaded into the ambulance. The tractor driver was also ushered in, grumbling and blaspheming, and the doors slammed behind him.

Nick approached the driver. 'We'd like to follow, if that's all right.'

'You know him?'

'Yes, and we've got his baby here with us. He was in the car. He seems fine, but he should be checked over at the hospital.'

The driver nodded. 'OK.'

In silence we got back into the car, and for the third time that day I sped off down the lanes. We trailed the solid white ambulance with its siren blaring and lights flashing for about a mile and a half and then, suddenly, without warning, it slowed right down, indicated left, and came to an abrupt halt in a lay-by. The siren and the flashing light stopped. We drew in behind it.

The driver opened his door and jumped down. Nick wound down his window. With head bowed the driver walked back to us and crouched down at the open window. He took his cap off and scratched his head.

'I'm sorry, sir, I thought I ought to stop and tell you. His injuries were just too severe and he'd lost too much blood. There was nothing we could do. I'm afraid he's dead.'

Chapter Twenty-seven

There were forms to be filled in at the hospital and questions to be answered for the police who arrived to grill us, but eventually, after a gruelling hour and a half, we were allowed to go home. I'd telephoned Rachel from the hospital to let her know Jamie was safe and well. I didn't mention Adam and she didn't ask.

We drove home in silence and, as we rounded the corner to Trewarren and swept up the drive, I saw a little hunched figure in a grey cardigan sitting on the top of the steps by the front door. She stood up as we scrunched to a halt and ran down to meet us.

I was holding Jamie in the back seat. Rachel opened the door and I passed him to her. She buried her face in his tiny body, tears streaming down her cheeks.

'He's OK,' I said wearily. 'They checked him over at the hospital. Luckily his carry-cot was wedged on the floor in the back of the car and that saved him.'

She nodded, but couldn't speak. I put my arm around her shoulders, but she shook it off violently and turned on her heel.

I sighed and slowly climbed up the steps behind her into the house. She disappeared into the kitchen. I made for the drawing room, helped myself to a stiff gin, and flopped down into the nearest armchair. There was no sign of Hetty; perhaps she'd gone home, or resumed her shopping trip in Helston.

I was exhausted. I felt as if I'd aged dramatically in the last few hours. But then death did have that effect on one, didn't it? It was rather a sobering experience, watching someone die; made you grow up a bit. And Adam was definitely dead. I still couldn't quite get used to that fact, but he was.

Nick appeared and sank down on the sofa opposite me. He rubbed his eyes vigorously with the heels of his hands as only men do, girls being too aware of smudgeable mascara, and yawned widely. I wondered if I looked as tired as he did. His face was drawn and haggard.

There was something I had to ask him. I leaned forward. 'Nick, you don't think,' I began timidly, 'you don't think we chased him into that tractor, do you? It's just I'd hate to think that we somehow caused him to speed up or –'

Nick shook his head. 'Polly, don't even think about it. As I said to you at the time, he probably wasn't even aware that there was someone on his tail. He had to go at that speed because he must have known the first thing we'd do would be to alert the police. He had to put his foot down whether he knew we were there or not. No, it wasn't our fault, although God knows, that doesn't make it any better.' He rubbed his weary eyes again. 'I just wish there was something we could have done to save him. I felt so helpless, I just didn't know what to do apart from be with him, hold his hand, talk to him. I was so terrified of moving him . . .'

'You did all you could,' I said soothingly. 'God, I was

hopeless, I couldn't get within inches of him. You did plenty.'

'Well, it wasn't enough, was it?'

He slumped forward and stared miserably at the carpet. I wanted to reach out and touch him, in fact my hand ventured forth in his direction for a moment, then I remembered Serena and I snatched it back.

It occurred to me briefly that there was no sign of the lovely Serena. In fact, now I came to think about it more than briefly, she hadn't been around when I'd arrived back with Hetty. Probably down in Helston choosing curtain material for the dining room, I thought bitterly. I didn't like to ask. For once, my own problems seemed somewhat eclipsed by recent events. I'd never experienced death before and it made me feel mighty peculiar. I shivered.

Nick noticed. He leaned forward. 'Are you OK, Polly?' he asked gently.

'Yes, fine,' I said, 'just a bit cold.'

'It's probably the shock — here, have this.' He whipped off his jumper and threw it over to me. I put it on and snuggled into its woolly warmth. It smelled delicious. I wondered if he'd notice if I stole it.

Rachel appeared from the kitchen with a bottle in one hand and Jamie astride her hip. She sat down on the rug in front of the fire and propped him up on her knee. She offered him the teat and he latched on to it enthusiastically, sucking greedily. We sat in silence, watching him drink, his eyes half shut, his podgy little hands clutching the bottle eagerly as he gulped away. So small and vulnerable, thank goodness he was all right. He drained the bottle in minutes. Rachel sat him up and rubbed his back to wind him. He let rip with the most enormous belch. We all laughed, breaking the silence.

Then Nick got up and stood by the fire next to Rachel. He licked his lips. 'Rachel?'

It seemed as if she'd never be able to tear her eyes from her baby, but eventually she looked up at him.

'Yes?'

'Adam died in the car crash.'

She stared at him for a second, then a ghost of a smile flickered on her lips. I felt sick.

'Yes,' she said, 'I thought as much.' She quickly looked down at Jamie again.

Nick was taken aback. 'I'd, um – I'd like to be able to tell you he didn't suffer much, but I'm not too sure about that . . . I'm pretty sure he was unconscious most of the time though . . .'

Rachel didn't even look up.

Nick soldiered on, braving her stony silence. 'Look, I was thinking, we'll have to contact his parents . . .'

Rachel raised her head. 'I'll deal with that,' she said coolly.

There was a silence. I stared at her. On the one hand I rather admired her lack of hypocrisy – at least she wasn't pretending to be upset – but, none the less, her cold-blooded attitude unnerved me. She had, after all, been in love with the guy at one time – about to marry him, in fact – and he was also Jamie's father.

I suddenly felt an urge to speak up for Adam. 'Don't you feel anything at all, Rachel?' I blurted out.

She slowly lifted her head and looked at me. Her eyes narrowed. 'Why should I?'

'Oh, er, well I don't know really,' I faltered, backtracking like mad; Rachel rather frightened me these days. 'It's just that, well I can't help thinking –'

'What can't you help thinking?'

'I don't know . . . I can't help thinking you're being very calm about all this, that's all.'

'Really?' she sneered. 'And what did you expect, tears? Hysterics?'

I had a feeling I was well out of my depth here, but I dug deep for courage and ploughed on regardless. 'No, of course not, but – I mean, you were going to marry him at one time and, after all, he was Jamie's father and all he really wanted –'

'Was he?' she cut in, silencing me.

I frowned, puzzled. 'Was he what?'

'Jamie's father?' she said in a cold, flat voice.

'Well – well, yes, of course he was, well, wasn't he?' I blustered.

She looked me straight in the eye and her thin little mouth all but disappeared. 'No, he wasn't,' she said shortly.

I gasped. Nick and I exchanged shell-shocked looks.

'Well, for Christ's sake!' blustered Nick. 'What's this all been about then? Why was he so obsessed with taking Jamie? Why have we been chasing him all over Cornwall? What the hell are you talking about, Rachel?'

Rachel tied a bib around Jamie's neck and took a jar of baby food out of a bag. She unscrewed it and, without a word, calmly began feeding him as if Nick hadn't even uttered. Nick wasn't having that. He crouched down on the rug next to her and took her chin in his hand, jerking her head towards him, forcing her to look at him.

'Rachel, a man has died today. Come to that, Polly and I damn nearly died trying to get your baby back. Now what's going on here? If Adam isn't the father, who the hell is?'

Rachel stared at Nick for a second, her face inches from his, then she brushed his hand away contemptuously. She drew herself up and took a deep breath as if she were about to make a speech.

'If you must know,' she said briskly, 'and to be honest I can't see that it's any of your business, Jamie's father is a man called David Saunders.' She turned to me, 'You'd probably remember him better as Mr Saunders.'

I stared at her. I hadn't the vaguest idea what she was talking about.

'Mr Saunders?' I echoed dumbly.

'From school.'

From school. My God. It came to me. It hit me like a flying grand piano. My jaw dropped, my eyes boggled, I spat the dummy. Jesus Christ, Mr Saunders the music teacher!

'Mr Saunders the music teacher?' I gasped in disbelief.

'That's right,' she affirmed calmly.

Then I remembered. Of course. Mrs Compton had mentioned him when I'd telephoned the school; said Rachel had got on particularly well with him. I'd thought nothing of it, why should I? Jesus. Mr Saunders. Mr Saunders with the . . . ginger hair. I looked at Jamie's red tufts, which had previously made him so obviously Adam's son. But Adam didn't have the monopoly on carrots, and Rachel clearly just had a penchant for it. Well, would you believe it: Rachel Marsden, the brilliant music student with her mind on more than treble clefs. Base clefts, more like. But of all people, Mr Saunders . . . Nausea rose within me. It wasn't the fact that he was a teacher that stunned me – although that in itself was pretty breathtaking – it was more the physical attributes of the teacher in question that had me reaching for the sick bag. We're talking yuck-a-roony here. I gagged quietly.

'Now just hang on a minute,' said Nick. 'This chap Saunders is Jamie's father? Not Adam? Did Adam know that?'

Rachel sighed. 'I tried to tell him, but he wouldn't believe me. Look, Nick, if you don't mind, I really don't want to go into all this right now. It's personal, I'm very tired, and it's a long story.'

She tucked Jamie under her arm, got to her feet, and made as if to go. Nick grabbed her arm and pulled her down on the floor. I've seen him look pretty furious in my time, but nothing like as incensed as this.

'Tell it, Rachel,' he hissed grimly. 'Tell the story in all its sordid personal details because, believe me, we need to know. Polly and I really need to know.'

Even Rachel looked taken aback. She looked warily at Nick's grim, determined face and bit her lip. She sat down again.

'Well, all right, if you must know, I'll tell you,' she said sullenly. 'It's just hard to know where to begin.'

'The beginning will do nicely,' said Nick, still staring grimly at her, 'try starting there.'

Rachel sighed. 'All right,' she said at length. She held Jamie in one arm and twiddled her hair with her other hand. 'David was a teacher at our school. You remember him, don't you, Polly?'

I cast my mind back a few years. Sure. I remembered him all right. Mr Saunders. I could see him now, with his thin white face, his wispy ginger hair, his John Lennon glasses and his goaty little beard which he'd twiddle round his finger whenever he was nervous, which was most of the time. He was totally unsuited to teaching, and had no idea how to control a class full of bored sixteen-year-olds, whose minds were always on boys and pop music and never on Debussy.

I could hear him now. 'Girls! Girls, settle down please!' he'd plead in his thin reedy voice, visibly palpitating behind his glasses. 'Let's have a little hush, shall we?'

This pathetic appeal would only serve to augment the noise, and more desk-banging, rubber-throwing and shrieking would ensue, whereupon, in desperation, he'd put Beethoven's Fifth on at full volume in an attempt to drown the noise and to make it appear to any casual passing teacher that he was in full control. Then he'd slump down at his desk in a deep depression, miserably aware he was an unmitigated disaster.

His shoulders were constantly hunched: weighed down, no doubt, by his sense of failure; but also, I suspected, by the constant avalanche of dandruff which landed in drifts on his musty tweed jacket. Little white flakes would float down, gather, and be brushed off surreptitiously, only for more to land not a moment later. As a bored-out-of-my-skull teenager, it made fascinating viewing.

But dandruff was the least of Mr Saunders' personal problems. The biggest cross this unfortunate man had to bear was undoubtedly his dampness. His nose and forehead were permanently wet and, try as he would to wipe the beads of sweat away with a variety of spotted hankies, the drips would automatically reappear. His hands were obviously in the same state, as he was constantly wiping them on his trousers, and his little horn-rimmed glasses steamed up on a regular basis. Again, it made compulsive viewing, and we girls did a lot of sniggering and mock puking behind his back as we speculated on the probable state of his armpits. In fact, 'snuggling up to Saunders' gushing pits', was one of our 'Fates Worse Than Death', alongside licking Matron's corns and squeezing Dorothy McAlistair's spots. We would dream up these revolting forfeits in the dorm at night, and then stuff our duvets in our mouths and squeal with horror at the thought of executing them. And to think Rachel had done more than snuggle . . . I drifted out of my reverie and stared at her in disbelief.

'Yes – yes, I remember him,' I whispered.

Rachel laughed. 'You probably fancied him yourself, didn't you, Polly!'

I stared at her in horror, choking down the bile. I shook my head dumbly. 'Er, no, not as such, no.'

'Oh come on, we all fancied at least one of the male teachers. Who did you have your eye on then?'

Now this was perfectly true. It has to be said that most of us girls had formidable crushes on the very few men who flitted in and out of our sheltered lives at school. Monsieur Ferout, French master and ultra-smooth froggy dude, had reputedly received no less than fifty-two Valentine cards one year, and I'm ashamed to say mine was amongst them. Clive, the gardener, was constantly finding bunches of half-dead wild flowers placed lovingly in his potting shed, and even Billy, the odd-job boy, had apparently been propositioned behind the guinea-pig hutches by a desperate fifth-former, but never, *never* Mr Saunders.

I licked my lips and stared at her glassy-eyed. How could she?

'Oh well, you know, er, no one in particular. I kept an open mind.'

'I bet you did! Kept your options open, eh?' she smiled nastily.

I was about to rise furiously to the bait, when Nick interrupted sarcastically. 'Fascinating though this tale of unrequited schoolgirl passion is, can we get back to the point? You had an affair with this Saunders chappie, then?' he asked Rachel.

'David and I were in love,' she said simply.

I had a bit of trouble taking this concept on board, but somehow managed to turn an incredulous guffaw into a hacking cough. She looked at me suspiciously as I snorted into a hankie.

'How long had it been going on for?' asked Nick.

Rachel stared into the fire. 'About three months, I suppose. It all started when he organized a trip to a concert at the Festival Hall. He put a notice up on the board in the common room, and I was the only one to put my name down. It was all strictly above board, of course, in fact he even press-ganged another girl into coming too, but she didn't turn up. Anyway, because it was just the two of us, we went for something to eat afterwards. Nothing happened then, of course, but we talked for hours and hours, we got on so well. I felt as if he was the first person in my life who'd ever understood me.'

The flames lit up her face as she remembered. For a moment she looked quite pretty, quite transformed. She smiled. 'We just couldn't find out enough about each other, in fact I remember now we very nearly missed the last train back, we were so absorbed. I think we both knew then that this was the start of something. That there was no going back.'

She turned away from the fire and back to us. The soft, dreamy look suddenly disappeared. 'Anyway, that's how it all started. After that, we'd meet in the town whenever I could slip out of school. Our so-called affair was really just an endless and frustrating stream of cups of coffee or walks in the park; all pretty tame, really.'

'But how did you manage to keep it so quiet?' I felt a certain grudging admiration. If I so much as put a toe out of bounds, I was invariably hauled back by the scruff of the neck and severely punished. The idea of conducting a clandestine affair, tame or otherwise, with a member of staff, filled me with horror.

'We were very careful. It meant a hell of a lot to both of us, and we were determined not to be found out. Occasionally we'd get daring and go to an evening concert or a play together, but that was about it. Until of course – well, until we just couldn't bear it any longer, couldn't control it.' She smiled wryly. 'And naturally, that was the one time we were discovered.'

'What – you mean . . . Where were you?' I faltered.

'In bed, of course. Well, not literally, but certainly figuratively.'

I gasped. 'Good grief, you mean you were actually – you know, doing it – when someone . . . Who found you?'

Rachel gave a wry smile. 'Miss Fisher.'

'Miss Fisher!' I gagged on my tonsils. It couldn't have been worse. Miss Fisher, the deputy head, of the razor-sharp tongue, the biting wit and the fine line in sneering sarcasm. Even now, years later, I cringed at the thought of her.

Nick grinned. 'So where were you when she found you, his place or your dorm?'

'Actually, we were in a deserted boat-house by the river,' she turned to me. 'Remember that funny old place by the broken bridge?'

I gulped again and nodded; by now grudging admiration had developed into unreserved hero-worship. The boat-house had been so totally and categorically out of bounds, it was considered dangerous to come within feet of it unless you had an overwhelming desire to be expelled. It was a beautiful old weather-boarded place, surrounded by reeds and bulrushes and flanked by an enormous old weeping willow which wept all over the roof. It was apparently falling down, and its collapse was always said by the staff to be imminent, but countless girls had dreamed of a romantic tryst in there; it was the perfect setting. It was permanently locked, but I imagined 'David' would have had access to a key. I tried to imagine Miss Fisher's face at finding them there.

'Was she furious?'

Rachel grinned. 'Speechless, literally. She appeared in the doorway, a vision in red flannel and rollers, flashing a torch around. We were lying on a pile of rugs in the corner without a stitch on. We just looked at her and she kept opening and shutting her mouth and nothing came out.'

I gaped. 'God, I wish I'd been a fly on the wall. What did she do?'

'Well, of course it was the middle of the night, and anyone with any sense would have left it until the morning, but oh no, she insisted on marching us back to the school and parading us in front of Miss Harper there and then. She telephoned Harpie, and we sat in the study for ages waiting for her to come down, whilst Miss Fisher breathed fire and paced up and down. Eventually, poor old Harpie appeared in her dressing gown looking bleary-eyed and pissed off, and told us to go back to bed, saying she'd deal with it in the morning.'

I grinned. I could imagine our laid-back headmistress being more than a little irritated at being woken up in the middle of the night.

'Anyway, the next morning I filed back in to see her, and after a brief discussion was unceremoniously expelled. Daddy was summoned to take me away.'

I nodded. 'I remember that. Everyone thought he was dragging you out of school for no good reason. We thought it was terribly bad form just before your A-levels.'

'That was the story that was put around to keep you lot off the scent.'

I had to hand it to old Rachel. There was I, thinking I was a real Jack the Lass for organizing the occasional cider knees-up in the dorm, and discussing what 'doing it' might be like with my virginal comrades, and grilling Rebecca Crocker over and over again because she'd come close to 'doing it' on a skiing holiday, and all the time Rachel, the quiet, mousy scholar was shagging the life out of one of the teachers in the strictly out-of-bounds boat house. Impressed? I was prostrate at her feet in awe and wonder.

'So what happened to David?' asked Nick.

Rachel looked sad. 'I never saw him again. He wrote to me from a school in Kent where he'd managed to get a position. Evidently Miss Harper had told him that if he left without a fuss his family wouldn't be told.'

'Family?'

'He had a wife and two children,' said Rachel calmly. 'Apparently he told his wife he'd been dismissed due to musical differences with Miss Harper. Ridiculous really. Harpie wouldn't know F sharp from B flat, but anyway, she swallowed the story and off they went to Kent.'

'But why was it all kept so quiet?' asked Nick. 'Surely he should have been hauled over the coals by the board of governors and all that sort of thing, made an example of?'

'Very probably, but you see my father was one of the governors and he had a lot of sway. In his position as a judge he just didn't want the publicity – I mean, you can just see the tabloids, can't you: "Teacher in Love Nest with High Court Judge's Daughter".' Rachel smiled wryly. 'Oh yes, Daddy made sure it was all hushed up.'

'So then what, he packed you off to America?' I asked.

'Yep, Daddy arranged it all. He was terrified I might try to get in touch with David, which of course I would have done, so he arranged for me to go and stay with friends of his in Boston. I didn't know at the time that I was pregnant, had no idea. For what it's worth, David and I had only slept together that one time, so I really didn't even consider it. Anyway, by the time I'd missed two periods,

Adam was well on the scene, both as a shoulder to cry on and – well, as a lover, to take my mind off things. I was just so miserable. I knew I didn't love him, but I allowed myself to go along with it, hoping a steamy affair would cure me of David. Of course it didn't. Anyway, by the time I was obviously pregnant, everyone naturally assumed it was Adam's, including Adam.'

'But couldn't it have been his after all?' asked Nick.

Rachel shook her head. 'Definitely not. I know that for a fact, because my dates worked out exactly to that one night with David. I'm glad too.' Rachel held Jamie close. 'I wanted his child. I wouldn't have wanted Adam's.'

'So as far as everyone else was concerned, Jamie was just a bit earlier than expected?' said Nick.

'Exactly. Jamie arrived a month early and I pretended to be as surprised as anyone.'

'And they all believed you?'

'Why shouldn't they? No one knew about David.'

'Except your father,' I said.

'Yes, except Daddy, and I dare say he had his suspicions when he found out I was pregnant; but of course when Jamie arrived with red hair, he promptly breathed a sigh of relief. He'd never met David, so he wasn't to know there was another source.'

Nick straightened up from where he'd been crouching beside her and looked down at her thoughtfully. 'OK fine, that all makes sense, but just tell me one thing, Rachel. When you realized you didn't love Adam, and you wanted to get away and bring Jamie to England, why in heaven's name didn't you tell him he wasn't the father? I know it's brutal, but you could have avoided all this aggro.'

Rachel smiled up at him and shook her head sadly. 'D'you think I didn't try? Of course I did. I told him the day before I got on that plane. We had a fearful row, but he just wouldn't believe me. Then when I got to England I wrote to him, spelling it all out, telling him the whole story about me and David. He still didn't believe it, and he categorically refused to have a blood test, saying it was ridiculous to have to go to such lengths to prove Jamie was his son when it was so palpably obvious. You see, he didn't want to believe it. Yet there must have been a smidgen of doubt in his mind, don't you think? Otherwise, why not do the test?'

'So he just decided to come over here and snatch him back,' said Nick.

Rachel nodded. 'Exactly. He obviously decided not to try to gain access through the courts because he'd have to do a blood test to prove he was the father, so he just planned to grab him. And I knew how single-minded he'd be about it, too. He'd stop at nothing. I'd have spent my whole life looking over my shoulder, always running and hiding and shielding Jamie, never knowing whether he was trailing us or watching us, waiting to snatch him away.'

She stroked Jamie's downy red head, smoothing down his wispy curls. She turned to me. 'You asked me if I felt anything about Adam's death. Well, I do. I feel relief. I feel as if an enormous great boulder has been lifted off my shoulders, because now Jamie and I can relax and try to have a normal life.' She looked at me earnestly. 'You can understand that, can't you? I mean, in my position, you'd feel the same way, wouldn't you?'

It was almost a plea, an entreaty, the first time she'd ever shown a truly vulnerable side, a need to be understood and vindicated – liked, even. I looked at Jamie, asleep in her arms now, traces of milk still on his little pink lips, his head thrown back, one pudgy hand still wrapped around her finger. Yes, I understood. I could never like her, but I understood.

I nodded. 'Yes.'

Rachel gave the tiniest of grateful smiles.

A silence enveloped us all. I looked outside. The window was full of inky black night now. One or two stars were winking away up there. I shivered and turned back to the fire which crackled away in the grate. I stared into the embers.

At length, Rachel spoke. She looked down at her baby. 'Bedtime for you, little boy,' she whispered. 'You've had rather a busy day, one way and another.'

She gathered him up in her arms and slowly got to her feet. Nick picked up his favourite blue blanket, which was lying on the sofa, and draped it over him.

'Sleep well, Jamie,' he said, stroking his hand. 'At least you haven't got the faintest idea what's been going on here.'

Rachel turned to go but, before she got to the door, she stopped and turned back to us. 'Oh, I almost forgot,' she said sheepishly. 'I meant to say thank you. Thanks for getting him back, that is.'

Nick nodded and gave a half-smile. 'I'd like to say, "It was nothing", but that wouldn't be quite true.'

She smiled briefly and nodded. 'I'll be going back to London first thing in the morning and I won't be troubling any of you ever again. Say goodbye to Tim for me, would you?' With that, she disappeared upstairs.

Chapter Twenty-eight

I sank back on the sofa and shut my eyes, more than a little tired. So it was all over. Adam was dead, and he hadn't even been the father. Perhaps he'd known all along, as Rachel had said. It hadn't stopped him loving Jamie, though, had it? It hadn't stopped him wanting him. And what of Jamie? I wondered which parent he would have been better off with. I wondered what sort of a mother Rachel would turn out to be. How would all this affect the way she brought Jamie up? What would she say to him when he was old enough to ask about his father? Would she tell him the truth, I wondered? Somehow I doubted it.

I opened my eyes and gave myself a little inward shake. What business was it of mine what she told him? It was about time I stopped interfering in other people's lives. The only reason I'd got involved at all in the first place was because I couldn't mind my own business. Well, it was time I learned.

Goodness, what was this, a smidgen of wisdom creeping into my soul? It was more like weariness, actually. And a growing awareness that there were some things that just couldn't be changed, and it was foolish and time-consuming even to try. All I could do was live my own life and forget about everyone else's.

I looked up and saw Nick, in a by now familiar position, standing with his back to me, looking out of the window. My heart, from its already sunken position somewhere in my nether regions, plummeted even further down into my boots. The trouble with living my own life, I reflected, was that it categorically refused to go according to plan. Here, for example, was the man who held the key to my future happiness. The man on whom my hopes depended and my dreams pivoted. And what was he doing? He was counting his sheep.

I sighed and got to my feet. Of course. It was time I left. Silly of me to have stayed so long. For a moment I'd almost forgotten I didn't belong here. Another minute more and I'd have been swinging my legs over the arm of the chair, picking up the telly guide, sinking my teeth into an apple, and asking my boyfriend if he could possibly throw an omelette together because I was too knackered to get supper tonight. Wasn't it lucky I remembered my boyfriend was actually engaged to be married to someone else? He was clearly waiting for me to leave, and politely turning his back in order to let me slip away in a seemly fashion. No fuss, Polly, no hysterics, his back seemed to say. What a gent. Well, leave I would. I got up and crept towards the door. Nick swung round as a floorboard creaked.

'Where are you going?'

I froze in mid-creep, like a child playing grandmother's footsteps. 'Oh, er, well, home again, actually,' I faltered guiltily. 'You know, because I was actually on my way when all this – when all this happened.'

He stared at me. Then at length he said, 'Polly, you really do amaze me. After all we've just been through – Adam's death, this whole ghastly business – it's had absolutely no effect on you whatsoever, has it? You just carry on as normal, don't you? Pick up where you left off before you were so rudely interrupted by a snatched baby, a distraught mother, a car chase and a dead man. That's about it, isn't it?'

'No, of course not! I'm absolutely shattered by what's happened, but I've still got to go, haven't I? I mean, it doesn't change anything!'

'So what were you going to do – sneak off without saying goodbye again?' He shook his head wearily. 'Go on then, off you go. Back to Harry, no doubt.'

I gaped at him in amazement. At length I found my voice. 'Back to Harry? Don't be ridiculous, of course not!'

He didn't answer, but he gave me a strange, penetrating look before turning back to the window. I stared at his back. For a moment I felt chastened. Guilt-ridden even. Then I bridled. Why? Why should I feel guilty? How dare he? How dare he talk to me like that! I was only going to make things easier for him! Suddenly all guilt and humility left me and I felt my colour rising. I rounded on him, pink with indignation. 'You've got a sodding nerve!' I blurted out.

He turned back, raising his eyebrows. 'Oh? And why's that? For pointing out your propensity to bugger off when the going gets a little tough?'

'A little tough? *A little tough?* You call what happened this morning a little tough?' I squeaked.

'Look, if you're talking about Serena pitching up here, as I said at the time, I'm sorry, but there was nothing I could do about it, I had no idea she was coming. I also said everything would be all right if you could just be patient, but patience isn't in your repertoire, is it, Polly?

You like everything to be tickety-boo instantly and if it isn't, if there are one or two slight complications, then you really can't cope, can you? You just wait until my back is turned and sneak off like – like some sort of criminal.'

'How dare you!' I exploded. I marched over to him and prodded him in the chest with my finger. 'How dare you speak to me like that! *You're* the one who goes limping off across the fields to see your sheep the moment your girlfriend arrives on the scene, leaving me at the mercy of her unfortunate personality disorder! *You're* the one who refuses to acknowledge me in her presence and lets her prattle on to me about living here as lady muck of the manor!'

'Now just a minute!' Nick grabbed my finger as I prodded away, but I shook him off, well and truly unstoppable now.

'LET ME FINISH!' I bellowed, punctuating each word with more piercing prods to his chest. 'And *you're* the one who led me to believe you even vaguely fancied me, so that against my better judgement – and totally out of character for me, I might say – I allowed myself to submit to some *very* amateur love-making on your part! And all the time – yes, all the time that shameful act was taking place, *you* were thinking how safe you were because of course the *real* love of your life, girl of your dreams, bitch in a million, call her what you will, was waiting patiently for you in London!'

'Polly, wait –'

'Oh yes, you thought it was quite all right to give good old Polly a quick bonk, didn't think there was any question of being found out, did you? Thought knobbing the secretary was an acceptable perk of the job! But you got a bit rattled when the wife-to-be arrived on the scene, didn't you? That was a little inconvenient, wasn't it? And yes, that's what *really* bugs me, if you must know, the fact that you didn't even have the *guts* to tell me you were engaged! And now you have the – the *nerve* to tell me – to tell me-ee . . .'

I ground to a shuddering halt as I realized my head was in danger of wobbling off my neck. My shoulders were being shaken really quite hard.

'Polly, will you shut up a minute!' Nick was yelling into my face. 'For Christ's sake, shut up!'

I shut, panting with the exertion of stringing so many words together in one go.

Nick stared at me. 'What are you talking about? Wife? Engaged? What the hell are you banging on about, for Christ's sake?'

'Oh, don't try and pretend!' I spat with renewed vigour, now I'd shaken off his hands and reclaimed my neck and head. 'Don't come the innocent with me. I know all about it, even down to the dear little boat you proposed in. I was even lucky enough to have the dear little ring stuffed up my nose – or down my throat – as she outlined her wedding plans to me, which will of course be carried out just as soon as you've both compared Filofaxes and found a gap in your oh-so-busy schedules.'

Nick stared at me incredulously. His mouth was open but he didn't utter. I stood panting up at him, face flushed, hands clenched, well fired up now and ready to embark on any number of new accusations at a moment's notice. Just let him try and defend himself, just let him try!

At length he ran his hands through his hair and

groaned. 'Oh Christ. God, I had no idea!' He shook his head despairingly. 'But I suppose I should have known.'

He turned away and sat down slowly on the arm of the sofa. He looked shattered. All of a sudden I felt as if I were floundering around in the dark again, a feeling I really should have been getting used to, as it was not uncommon these days. This wasn't quite the reaction I'd had in mind.

'What? Known what?'

He looked up at me. 'What she was capable of.' He stood up and took my shoulders again. 'Polly, listen to me. The whole thing is a fabrication.'

I felt more than a little confused. 'A fabri – A what?' For some extraordinary reason a roll of chintzy curtain material sprang to my fuddled mind.

He gave my shoulders a little shake. 'A lie, a load of rubbish, a figment of her imagination. Crap, if you will. I've never asked Serena to marry me, never did, never would, never shall.'

I stared at him in disbelief. 'Are you sure?'

'What d'you mean, am I sure – of course I'm sure! Proposing marriage is not the sort of thing you forget about in a hurry, is it! It's not the sort of thing you run around doing every day!' He sighed and shook his head. 'I suppose I should have guessed she might do something like this . . .'

'So – so what's going on? She's still your girlfriend, but you're not getting married? Or – or she thinks you're getting married, but you're not sure, or – or what?' Any number of alarming permutations ran through my crazed mind.

Nick sighed. 'Oh God, what an idiot I've been.'

I was inclined to agree, but I let it pass, if he would just tell me what was going on. 'Nick, please . . .'

He shook his head. 'She really is quite unbelievable. Quite unbelievable. Sit down, Polly. I think I'd better tell you a little bit about Serena.'

He motioned me into the sofa and I sat, dumbly. Nick perched on the arm. He licked his lips thoughtfully and stared into space somewhere above my head.

'When I first met Serena,' he said slowly, 'I don't mind telling you I was absolutely knocked out by her. I thought she was the most stunningly attractive girl I'd ever seen.' He paused and looked down at me. 'Well, you've got to admit, she's bloody pretty.'

I ground my teeth, grimaced, and admitted it. 'Bloody pretty,' I muttered. The first word was easier than the second.

Nick looked back over my head towards the fire. He narrowed his eyes. 'I remember I was at this ghastly drinks party, hiding in the kitchen nursing a glass of warm champagne and wondering when I could conceivably escape, when she came in to get a drink. She asked me if there was any orange juice because she was driving, and I remember, I could hardly answer. I just gaped and stuttered something about there possibly being some in the fridge, I was so floored by her. Anyway, she found the orange juice and wandered off again, but later on, I was in the bedroom rooting around for my coat, and she came in for hers. We laughed, and whispered something about it being an awful party and how we couldn't wait to leave, and we got chatting. We talked in the bedroom for a bit, and then of course we both walked downstairs together and out into the street. I was about to say goodbye and walk off when I thought better of it. I found myself asking her what she was doing, if she wanted to get something to eat. I couldn't believe it when she said she'd love to.'

'Fast work for a country boy,' I said drily.

'Well, why not? I didn't have much to lose. If she'd blown me out, it would have hurt my pride, but that would have been about it. Anyway, we went out for dinner, and over the next few weeks I took her out quite a lot, feeling pretty pleased with myself, I might tell you. We'd walk into one restaurant after another, and a million heads would turn and I'd feel about ten feet tall. Pathetic really, but totally intoxicating.'

I could imagine how good they'd look together. I tried not to, but I could imagine.

'I was mad about her,' he went on, 'absolutely infatuated. The whole film-star bit, the looks – everything. I freely admit I fell for the glamour. Anyway, she seemed to feel the same way about me, and before I knew where I was, she'd moved in with me.'

'Really? Just like that? How long had you known her?'

'A couple of months, I suppose.'

'Wow. Not long.'

'No, I know, but I really thought this was it. I actually remember thinking this would be for ever.'

My insides knotted a bit at this. 'Go on.' (Quickly, please.) I was anxious to pass over this lovey-dovey phase and move smartly on to the bit where hopefully it all went wrong.

He sighed. 'Anyway, that's when it all started to go wrong.'

Ah, good.

'At first it was fine, we were still in the first flush of – well, call it what you will – love, passion, I don't know. But then, everything calmed down a bit and we got down to the business of living together. You know – give and take, and who squeezes the toothpaste where and who does the washing up and all that sort of thing. It was a complete disaster. It was quite obvious that Serena had never had to think about anybody but herself in her entire life. She'd been spoilt rotten by everyone up to now – her parents, her boyfriends, her friends; she'd never had to do anything for herself or consider anybody else's feelings. Life had just fallen into her lap; she'd got by solely on her good looks and superficial charm. And that's what she was, superficial. Shallow, even.'

He turned his eyes away from the fire and back on to me. 'I'm sorry if this sounds cruel, Polly, but I want to try and explain exactly what she's like.'

'Noo, nooo, not cruel at all!' I shook my head vigorously, lapping it up. The more cruelty the better, as far as I was concerned.

'Well, to begin with I suppose I let her wipe the floor with me. Honestly, I ran around after her like a bloody servant: cooking meals, tidying up after her, taking her clothes to the cleaners, picking her up from rehearsals, dropping her off at the hairdresser's or the beauty salon – it was ridiculous. Then one day I just stopped. Said I was busy and I couldn't take her shopping at Harrods because

I had to work. She was absolutely furious. I don't think anyone had ever crossed her before in her entire life. Well, that was the beginning of the end, really. We had a major row and that set the scene for the next few months. We began to argue quite a bit, like every other day, and to be honest, after a few solid weeks of her petulant, spoilt behaviour, I got to the end of my rope. I seriously began to – sounds awful I know – well, to dislike her.'

'Not awful at all,' I murmured. 'Go on.'

'I'd stay at work later and later, partly because I had to, but partly because I couldn't bear the thought of going home. Then when I did get home, she'd go absolutely berserk. She'd usually downed a couple of bottles of wine by then, and she'd fly at me as I came through the door, ranting and raving about how I avoided her and demanding that I spent more time with her.'

'She sounds like the archetypal bored housewife.'

Nick shrugged. 'Perhaps that's it, perhaps she just didn't have enough to do. Actresses spend a hell of a lot of time "resting", as they call it. Anyway, she'd fly into the most incredible rages, throwing things round the room, cutting my clothes up, chucking the crockery out of the window, and then she'd throw herself on the bed sobbing violently, so I'd have to comfort her and tell her everything was all right, although I was pretty damn certain everything wasn't all right at all. I tell you, it was really getting me down.'

I was surprised. This didn't fit in with my image of the icy-cool, controlled Serena. I frowned. 'But she's so – so cool when you meet her.'

'I know, but remember she's an actress, she can be whoever she wants to be. In reality she's completely mixed up. You saw her at lunch today: she just suddenly snaps and goes bananas.'

'She sounds like a bit of a head-case.'

Nick sighed and shook his head. 'Either that or just incredibly theatrical, I was never really sure. She's so tenacious, too; gets her teeth into something and just won't let go. It was when she started ringing me all day at the agency – you wouldn't have noticed because she had my private number – that's when I knew I had to do something. If I told her I was in a meeting, which I usually was, she'd just ring again two minutes later. It was incredibly embarrassing with clients sitting there listening. Then she started turning up out of the blue to drag me out to lunch.'

'I remember that, Pippa and I were amazed when you turned down a famous film star, a convertible Mercedes and lunch at Bibendum, all in the space of one lunch hour.'

'Well, now you know why.'

'Why didn't you just finish it? Tell her it was over?'

Nick groaned. 'I tried, I tried to end it loads of times, but she just wouldn't listen and she categorically refused to leave the flat. I hadn't the heart to physically throw her out and change the locks, although I had the feeling it would probably come to that one day. The thing is, Polly, she knew it was over months ago but she just couldn't face it. I'm not even convinced she was in love with me, I think she just couldn't bear being dropped.'

I was amazed. 'You mean she just wouldn't go? Even though you said it was over?'

'She just refused. In the end I told her I was going to

Cornwall, and I expected her to be gone by the time I got back.'

'That was just before you came down here with me.'

'That's right, the day before. I have to say I didn't think even Serena would have the gall to follow me, and when she turned up I was absolutely flabbergasted. I wanted to keep her from finding out about you and me, because for one thing I didn't want to rub her nose in it, and I also had a shrewd suspicion she'd tear your hair out. It would seem to her as if I'd jumped straight from her bed to yours in the space of a few days, even though, if the truth be told, Serena and I were washed up a long time ago and I'd felt strongly about you for . . . Well, that's another story.'

He broke off here and pulled at a thread in his jumper. I gulped hard and somehow overcame a burning desire to say – oh please, *please* let's get on to the other story! Much as I was enjoying this one, I had an inkling the other one, with me as the heroine, was going to be even better. I was jolly glad he'd asked me to sit down now: my knees were shaking so much from ill-concealed excitement that I doubted if they'd have supported me. I was also dying for a cigarette, but I had an idea that this perhaps wasn't the moment for ashtray breath.

He abandoned his jumper and looked down at me. 'She obviously spun the phantom engagement story when I was out with Larry.'

'Yes, that's right, you were seeing to the sheep. Oh, but hang on,' I thought back, 'what about the ring?'

'What ring?'

'The little green one.'

'Oh that! Yes I did give her that, about two weeks after

I'd met her, at the height of my infatuation. It was an impulse buy, I saw it in an antique shop. It reminded me of her eyes.'

'That's what she said,' I said slowly, as everything began to fall into place. 'So – so where is she now?' I looked around nervously, half expecting her to pop up from behind the sofa, machete in hand.

'She's gone. When I found out you'd disappeared, I was livid. I couldn't continue the charade of pretending you meant nothing to me, and I couldn't bear to have her in the house any more. I went berserk. No more softly-softly, let's tiptoe round Serena's feelings. I let her have it. Should have done it ages ago, it was bloody effective, the only language she understands. And, would you believe it, just as I was getting to the well-worn bit about never wanting to see her again as long as I lived, she gave me a resounding slap round the face, spat in my eye, told me I was a complete and utter jerk and she didn't know what she'd seen in me in the first place. Then she jumped into her Mercedes and roared back off to London. Off to snare some other poor bastard, no doubt.'

Relief flooded over me. She'd gone. Thank Christ for that. I leaned back in the cushions. Bliss. Utter bliss. He wasn't going to marry her, he didn't even love her, by all accounts he didn't even like her. And surely, surely he'd more or less hinted that – well, that he liked me quite a lot, hadn't he?

I was suddenly very aware of his presence. He was perched on the arm of the sofa, his leg warm against my arm, close to me. I could feel his eyes upon me, melting over my face. I leaned my head back, half closed my eyes, and parted my lips very slightly. This was surely our moment. The most monumental touchy-feely moment of all time. I could feel the excitement tingling all over me, right down to my toenails. I waited in an ecstasy of antici-pation. I waited for what seemed like an inordinate length of time. Nothing seemed to be happening. Eventually I couldn't keep the half-closed eyes bit going any longer, my eyelashes were beginning to bat maniacally. I opened them.

He was watching me. 'Polly?'

Jesus. He wasn't looking remotely touchy-feely. 'Er, yes?'

'What about Harry?'

I jumped. 'What about him?'

'Well . . .' He hesitated. 'I need to know how you feel about him. I mean, you were pretty hung up on him in London and – well, I'm almost sure he got in touch with you down here.'

I sat bolt upright. 'How did you know that? Did you hear me on the phone to him?'

He looked uncomfortable. 'No, no, I, er, I heard Serena on the phone to him.'

'Serena?'

'Yes, she knows him, you know.'

'Yes, I know, but why on earth would she be ringing him from down here?'

Nick shifted about a bit on the arm of the sofa. 'Well, she asked him to give you a ring.'

'SHE WHAT!'

'She asked him to – well, to lure you back to London. Said you were in her way down here – I heard it all, I was in the bathroom and she was using the phone in my bedroom. He seemed pretty flattered that she'd called him – most people are, of course. From what I could gather, he said he'd do what he could. I'm sorry, Polly, I wouldn't have told you, only I need to know if that's why you went.'

'Nick, what are you saying! Do you mean to tell me Serena actually *asked* Harry to ring up and pretend he was missing me and that he still loved me and all that crap about being the only girl he'd ever – *bloody hell*! Is that what you're saying?'

'I know, I know it's a little hard to believe, but you see she's quite capable –'

'Hard to believe! Hard to believe! It's bloody monstrous! Bloody hell! I mean, who does she think she is? Did she really think she'd get away with it? I mean, did she really think I'd go panting off back to London to see him! Christ!'

I was seething. Seething with fury at her audacity and seething also with hurt pride. So it had all been a ruse, a hoax to get me out of the way! Thank God I hadn't fallen for it.

'So you didn't,' said Nick.

'Didn't what?'

'Go panting off back to London to see him.'

I stared at him, incredulous. 'No, of course not! I told him to get stuffed, if you must know.'

Nick looked relieved. 'Oh! Oh good. Sorry, I had to ask. You see, I knew you'd dashed off out of the blue, and I was pretty sure it was because of Serena, but on the other hand I knew Harry had probably spoken to you, and I wasn't sure – well, to be honest, Polly, I wasn't entirely sure that you weren't still in love with him. And if you were, I wasn't sure that I could handle it.' He looked at me anxiously. 'You're not still in love with him, are you? I hate to be pushy, but I just sort of need to know.'

I looked up at his kind, honest face, his brown eyes searching mine, looking for clues. I smiled. All my anger drifted away. What did it matter? What did Harry matter, what did Serena matter? They were the losers, after all. The winners were sitting right here. My smile seemed to be spreading all over my body, I was positively wreathed in smiles. I felt unbelievably happy. I wanted him to kiss me quite badly now, but at the same time I felt something even more overwhelming than desire sweeping over me.

'No, I'm not in love with him,' I said softly. The feeling seemed to be getting stronger and stronger, surging from my heart, through my body, until eventually it found its way to my lips. 'Actually, I'm in love with you.'

His anxious look disappeared, his face seemed to clear, and he smiled gently. He leaned down, and the kiss that I'd been longing for dropped onto my mouth at last, soft and full.

'I'm surprised,' he murmured at length.

'Why?' I felt alarmed. Oh horrors, what had I done now? Scared him off already?

He slid off the arm of the sofa and knelt down in front of me, his arms around me felt huge and warm and strong. My heart thumped madly as he kissed me on the neck, working his way slowly and beautifully round to my ear. 'Because you don't strike me as the sort of girl who would fall for an amateur love-maker.'

I gasped and sat bolt upright, gripping his shoulders

hard. 'Oh no, you don't understand!' I pleaded earnestly into his face. 'I just said that to make you angry! I didn't mean it, I – I just said it to get my own back! I didn't think you were amateur at all, in fact I thought – I still think – you're, you're a true professional! Oh no! I mean, not in any awful sense of having been around, but you know, you know what to do and – oh God, I just think you're wonderful!'

He threw back his head and roared with laughter, holding me tightly against him. 'Oh God,' he gasped at length, 'I must say I think you're pretty wonderful too, Polly, but I've never known anyone with quite the propensity to get themselves in such a comprehensive mess!'

I grinned ruefully. 'Well, this is one comprehensive mess I don't mind in the least.'

'I agree,' he said softly. 'In fact, I don't mind it at all, because I believe I'm in love with you too.'

I gasped, which was lucky really, because it meant I took in a great lungful of air which kept me going as he kissed the breath out of me. When we surfaced, moments later, we clung to each other, and I could hear our hearts racing away in tandem. His breath was coming in fast and furious bursts, and I could almost see his ear flapping in the breeze as I hurricaned into it. Love, lust, excitement, and God knows what else, were all contriving to get the better of our breathing apparatuses.

'Now, where were we,' he whispered, as he manœuvred me skilfully down on to the Persian rug, deftly immobilizing me beneath him, 'before we were so rudely interrupted some time earlier this morning?'

My tummy, furious at having missed at least three meals

by now, rumbled ominously as I lay back on the rug. We giggled. I reached up and took his face in my hands, drawing it down towards me.

'You were making toast,' I murmured.

'I've got other plans now,' he murmured back.

Catching up with
Catherine

We donned our wellies and trudged
through the mud to meet Catherine
for a catch-up on writing, reading,
and life in the country . . .

Catching up with Catherine

How and where do you write?

In the garden in the summer, and on a sofa by the fire
in the winter, literally with the nearest pen,
which as a result often runs out.

Any tips for alleviating writer's block?

I'd probably go for a long walk with the dogs but also
never call it writer's block. It's just a day to do
something else; tomorrow will be different.
With luck and everything crossed, the muse
might perch on one's shoulder again.

You live in the countryside in a village not too dissimilar from those you write about. How does country life in your books compare to real life?

There are some remarkable similarities, but obviously
names have been changed to protect the innocent . . .

What do you like to do when you're not writing?

I ride my horses and, recently, wander round poultry
farms. I'm trying to decide which ducks to get for
my new pond: Indian Runners are terribly comical,
Aylesburys would be more geographically
appropriate, yet I'm strangely drawn to good
old Mallards, too. Decisions . . .

If you had to live the life within a classic novel and star as a literary heroine, who would you be and why?

Possibly Jane Austen's Emma Woodhouse,
who lived something of a charmed life,
even if she didn't realize until
it was almost too late.

What's your favourite place to escape to?

Over the hills and far away. The valley behind my
house is actually not very far at all and the Downs
start there so it's very peaceful. Devon is,
of course, heaven, but a little further.

What's the best way to survive a day in the British countryside?

In an ideal world I probably wouldn't take my
own very badly behaved dogs; I would take
someone else's – that way I wouldn't be chasing
them all day shrieking unattractively.

Catherine's top tips
for the perfect countryside break

The same rules apply for children as for dogs (see before), depending on age and reliability of your children – husbands, too.

Never picnic (as in the romantic ideal of rug, hamper, chicken drumsticks à la Delia). Pubs tend to be far more successful, although I am nostalgically drawn to beach picnics. Sand in sandwiches is surely part of any child's education and there's nothing funnier than the man of the family getting to grips with a windbreak in a force-eight gale. Particularly if his own childhood holidays were spent in Tuscany.

Don't be deceived by the English countryside. It looks pretty but can turn on you in an instant.

Leave the horses to the professionals – that doesn't include me. A horse that decides to nap (go home) in the middle of a village which also happens to be something of a tourist magnet is embarrassing for all concerned, particularly the red-faced, middle-aged woman on top.

Again on the subject of horses, 'not a novice ride' means bucks like fury, while 'a fun ride' means carts you into the next county. Male horse-dealers are fond of both expressions, but never forget they are stronger than we are. The men and the horses.

When you answer the door in your coat in winter to a surprised friend who asks if you're just going out, don't be afraid to let them stay an hour or two until they put their coats on too.

If invited to a dinner party in London in January, don't forget there will be women in little dresses who have proper central heating. In the car en route, turn the heater up full blast and try to shed at least three of your layers. Don't forget the Ugg boots. If you stay in the vest and the cashmere roll-neck, you will be in a critical state by pudding, particularly if you're approaching fifty.

If anyone offers you the use of a flat in town in winter, bite their hand off.

Catherine's top ten countryside reads:

The Pursuit of Love
Nancy Mitford

Untold Stories
Alan Bennett

The Irish R. M.
Somerville and Ross

High Fidelity
Nick Hornby

Persuasion
Jane Austen

Pomp and Circumstance
Noël Coward

84 Charing Cross Road
Helene Hanff

The Woman in White
Wilkie Collins

Franny and Zooey
J. D. Salinger

Atonement
Ian McEwan

'If I'm being totally honest I had fantasized about Phil dying.'

When Poppy Shilling's bike-besotted, Lycra-clad husband is killed
in a freak accident, she can't help feeling a guilty sense of relief.
For at long last she's released from a controlling and loveless marriage.

Throwing herself wholeheartedly into village life, she's determined
to start over. And sure enough, everyone from Luke the sexy
church-organist to Bob the resident oddball, is taking note.
Yet the one man Poppy can't take her eyes off seems tantalizingly
out of reach – why won't he let go of his glamorous ex-wife?

But just as she's ready to dip her toes in the water, the discovery
of a dark secret about her late husband shatters Poppy's confidence.
Does she really have the courage to risk her heart again?
Because Poppy wants a lot more than just a rural affair . . .

THE NO. 1 BESTSELLER

Catherine Alliott
One
Day in May

'I was blown away. My favourite
of Alliott's books'
Daily Mail

May is the month for falling in love . . .

Hattie Carrington's first love was as unusual as it was out of reach –
Dominic Forbes was a married MP, and she was his assistant.
She has never told anyone about it. And never really got over it.

But years later with a flourishing antiques business
and enjoying a fling with a sexy, younger man, she thinks her
past is finally well and truly behind her.

Until work takes her to Little Crandon, home of Dominic's widow
and his gorgeous younger brother, Hal. There, Hattie's world is turned
upside down. She learns that if she's to truly fall in love again she
needs to stop hiding from the truth. Can she ever admit what
really happened back then?

And, if so, is she ready
for the consequences?

'A fun, fast-paced page-turner' *OK!*

**Evie Hamilton has a secret –
one she doesn't even know about. Yet . . .**

Evie's an Oxfordshire wife and mum whose biggest worry in life is
whether or not she can fit in a manicure on her way to fetch her
daughter from clarinet lessons. But she's blissfully unaware that her
charmed and happy life is about to be turned upside down.

For one sunny morning a letter lands on Evie's immaculate doormat.
It's a bombshell, knocking her carefully arranged world
completely askew and threatening to sabotage all she holds dear.

What will be left and what will change for ever?
Is Evie strong enough to fight for what she loves?
Can her entire world really be as fragile as her best china?

'We defy you not to get caught up in
Alliott's life-changing tale' *Heat*

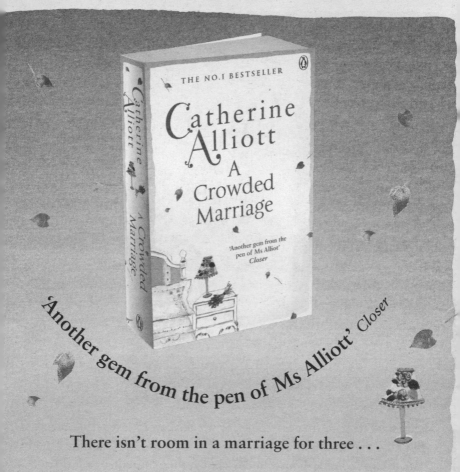

THE NO.1 BESTSELLER

Catherine Alliott

A Crowded Marriage

'Another gem from the pen of Ms Alliott'
Closer

'Another gem from the pen of Ms Alliott' *Closer*

There isn't room in a marriage for three . . .

Painter Imogen is happily married to Alex, and together they have a son.
But when their finances hit rock bottom, they're forced to accept Eleanor
Latimer's offer of a rent-free cottage on her large country estate. If it was
anyone else, Imogen would be beaming with gratitude. Unfortunately,
Eleanor just happens to be Alex's beautiful, rich and flirtatious ex.

From the moment she steps inside Shepherd's Cottage, Imogen's life
is in chaos. In between coping with rude locals, murderous chickens,
a maddening (if handsome) headmaster, mountains of manure
and visits from the infuriating vet, she has to face Eleanor,
now a fixture at Alex's side.

Is Imogen losing Alex? Will her precious family be torn apart?
And whose fault is it really – Eleanor's, Alex's or Imogen's?

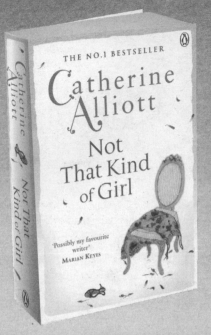

THE NO.1 BESTSELLER

Catherine Alliott

Not That Kind of Girl

'Possibly my favourite writer'
MARIAN KEYES

**A girl can get into all kinds of trouble
just by going back to work . . .**

Henrietta Tate gave up everything for her husband Marcus and their kids.
But now that the children are away at school and she's rattling around
their large country house all day she's feeling more than a little lost.

So when a friend puts her in touch with Laurie, a historian in need of a PA,
Henrietta heads for London. Quickly, she throws herself into the job.
Marcus is – of course – jealous of her spending so much time with
her charming new boss. And soon enough her absence causes cracks
in their marriage that just can't be papered over.

Then Rupert, a very old flame, reappears and Henrietta suddenly finds
herself torn between three men. How did this happen?
She's not that kind of girl . . . is she?

'Compulsively readable' *Daily Mail*

**Annie O'Harran is getting married . . .
all over again.**

A divorced, single mum, Annie is about to tie the knot with David.
But there's a long summer to get through first. A summer where
she's retreating to a lonely house in Cornwall, where she's going to
finish her book, spend time with her teenage daughter Flora and
make any last-minute wedding plans.

She should be so lucky.

For almost as soon as Annie arrives her competitive sister and her wild
brood fetch up. Meanwhile Annie's louche ex-husband and his latest
squeeze are holidaying nearby and insist on dropping in. Plus there's the
surprise American houseguest who can't help sharing his heartbreak.

Suddenly Annie's big day seems a long, long way off –
and if she's not careful it might never happen . . .

'Alliott at her best' *Daily Telegraph*

'What could be nicer than living in the country?'

Lucy Fellowes is in a bind. She's a widow living in a pokey London flat with two small boys and an erratic income. But, when her mother-in-law offers her a converted barn on the family's estate, she knows it's a brilliant opportunity for her and the kids.

But there's a problem.

The estate is a shrine to Lucy's dead husband, Ned. The whole family has been unable to get over his death. If she's honest, the whole family is far from normal. And if Lucy is to accept this offer she'll be putting herself completely in their incapable hands.

Which leads to Lucy's other problem. Charlie – the only man since Ned who she's had any feelings for – lives nearby. The problem? He's already married . . .

'Hilarious and full of surprises' *Daily Telegraph*

'I don't care what colour you paint the sodding hall. I'm leaving.'

When her husband Johnny suddenly walks out on ten years of marriage, their ten-year-old daughter and the crumbling house they're up to their eyeballs renovating, Olivia is, at first, totally devastated. How could he? How could she not have noticed his unhappiness?

But she's not one to weep for long.

Not when she's got three builders camped in her back garden, a neighbour with a never-ending supply of cast-off men she thinks Olivia would be drawn to and a daughter with her own firm views on . . . well, just about everything.

Will Johnny ever come back? And if he doesn't, will Olivia's luck ever change for the better?

'The writing is both intelligent and sparkling'
Marian Keyes

'Alliott's joie de vivre is irresistible' *Daily Mail*

'Tell me, Alice,
how does a girl go about
getting a divorce these days?'

Three years ago Rosie walked blindly into marriage with Harry.
They have precisely nothing in common except perhaps their little boy, Ivo.
Not that Harry pays him much attention, preferring to spend his time
with his braying upper-class friends.

But the night that Harry drunkenly does something unspeakable,
Rosie decides he's got to go. In between fantasizing how she might
bump him off, she takes the much more practical step of divorcing
this blight on her and Ivo's lives.

However, when reality catches up with her darkest fantasies,
Rosie realizes, at long last, that it is time she took charge of her life.
There'll be no more regrets – and time, perhaps, for a little love.

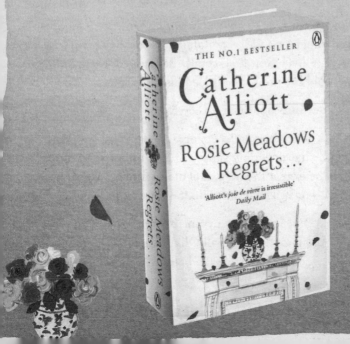

THE NO.1 BESTSELLER

Catherine Alliott

Rosie Meadows Regrets...

'Alliott's joie de vivre is irresistible'
Daily Mail

**Every girl's got one – that old boyfriend
they never quite fell out of love with . . .**

Tessa Hamilton's thirty, with a lovely husband and home, two adorable
kids, and not a care in the world. Sure her husband ogles the nanny more
than she should allow. And keeping up with the Joneses is a full-time
occupation. But she's settled and happy. No seven-year itch for Tessa.

Except at the back of her mind is Patrick Cameron. Gorgeous, moody,
rebellious, he's the boy she met when she was seventeen. The boy her
vicar-father told her she couldn't see and who left to go to Italy to paint.
The boy she's not heard from in twelve long years.

And now he's back.

Questioning every choice, every decision she's made since Patrick left,
Tessa is about to risk her family and everything she has become to find
out whether she did the right thing first time round . . .

'You're in for a treat' *Daily Express*

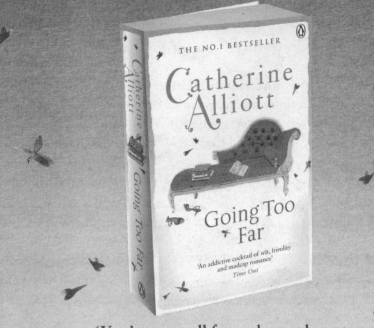

THE NO.1 BESTSELLER

Catherine Alliott

Going Too Far

'An addictive cocktail of wit, frivolity and madcap romance'
Time Out

'You've gone all fat and complacent because you've got your man, haven't you?'

Polly Penhalligan is outraged at the suggestion that, since getting married to Nick and settling into their beautiful manor farmhouse in Cornwall, she has let herself go. But watching a lot of telly, gorging on biscuits, not getting dressed until lunchtime and waiting for pregnancy to strike are not the signs of someone living an active and fulfilled life.

So Polly does something rash.

She allows her home to be used as a location for a TV advert. Having a glamorous film crew around will certainly put a bomb under the idyllic, rural life. Only perhaps she should have consulted Nick first.

Because before the cameras have even started to roll – and complete chaos descends on the farm – Polly's marriage has been turned upside down. This time she really has gone too far . . .

'An addictive cocktail of wit, frivolity and madcap romance' *Time Out*

THE NO.1 BESTSELLER

Catherine Alliott

The Old-Girl Network

'Alliott's joie de vivre
is irresistible'
Daily Mail

**Finding true love's a piece of cake – as long as
you're looking for someone else's true love . . .**

Polly McLaren is young, scatty and impossibly romantic. She works for
an arrogant and demanding boss, and has a gorgeous-if-never-there-when-
you-need-him boyfriend. But, the day a handsome stranger recognizes her
old school scarf, her life is knocked completely off kilter.

Adam is American, new to the country and begs Polly's help in finding
his missing fiancé. Over dinner at the Savoy she agrees – the girls of
St Gertrude's look out for one another. However, the old-girl network
turns out to be a spider's web of complications and deceit in which
everyone and everything Polly cares about is soon hopelessly entangled.

The course of true love never did run smooth.
But no one said anything about ruining your life over it.
And it's not even Polly's true love . . .

'Possibly my favourite writer' Marian Keyes

Step into *Alliott Country*

at www.catherinealliott.com

WIN wonderful WELLIES

by joules

WE'RE GIVING AWAY

10 PAIRS of JOULES WELLIES
MADE TO MAKE A SPLASH WHATEVER THE WEATHER!

To be in with a chance of winning this welly good prize visit www.catherinealliott.com/winwellies

Joules are also giving readers **15% OFF** *plus* **FREE P&P.**
Simply visit www.joules.com and enter offer code **WELLY12** at the checkout.

Competition closing date **31ST AUGUST 2012**
For full terms and conditions and details of how to enter visit www.catherinealliott.com/winwellies